MORE
THAN THE
Game

Happy Reading

MORE
THAN THE
Game

BECOMING AN EVANS
BOOK ONE

JENNI BARA

Point Publishing

More Than the Game
Becoming an Evans Book One

Editing by Elayne Morgan of Serenity Editing
Cover by Kari March Designs
Interior formatting by Alt 19 Creative

Publisher's Cataloging-In-Publication Data
(Prepared by The Donohue Group, Inc.)

Names: Bara, Jenni, author.
Title: More than the game / Jenni Bara.
Description: [Mahwah, New Jersey] : Point Publishing, [2021] | Series: Becoming an Evans ; book 1
Identifiers: ISBN 9781737560012 (paperback) | ISBN 9781737560005 (ebook)
Subjects: LCSH: Man-woman relationships--Fiction. | Women Olympic athletes--Fiction. | Baseball players--Fiction. | Social media--Fiction. | LCGFT: Romance fiction.
Classification: LCC PS3602.A737 M67 2021 (print) | LCC PS3602.A737 (ebook) | DDC 813/.6--dc23

ISBN: 978-1-7375600-0-5 (ebook)
ISBN: 978-1-7375600-1-2 (paperback)

Jennibara.com

To Grammy who taught me to love a story and
Poppy who taught me to love a book.
We all miss you all the time.

1

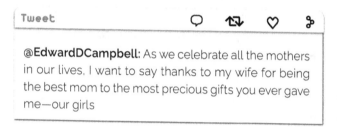

SOMEONE CALLING BETH'S dad a liar on Twitter was nothing new. However, any of the Evans brothers doing it was the type of drama she always tried to avoid.

Her phone buzzed on the counter, the group text with her late husband's brothers blowing up over a screenshot of a tweet her dad didn't even personally write. Beth rolled her eyes at the second screenshot, which highlighted how many likes the tweet had. Then she fired off a message telling the Evans brothers she didn't care if her father got a few hundred thousand likes, they still could not retweet him and call him out for being an awful father.

Beth didn't use Twitter, but she got updates from the Evans siblings group chat. Her famous father, however, tweeted regularly. He was already tweeting about Mother's Day, which was two days away, and her mother's Instagram page was popping with new pictures daily. But she stayed away from all social media platforms like a person with a severe tree nut allergy would avoid a cashew.

Before she got a reply to her message, her three-year-old daughter, Mandy, pushed the jumper seat like a swing, sending the toddler she was babysitting flying back and forth in it.

"Mandy, please stop," Beth yelled over her shoulder, grabbing the seat in one hand and stopping her nephew from spilling his cup of juice with the other. She glanced back at the dishwasher as it beeped, and saw that it was flashing *ERR*.

A broken dishwasher was the last thing she needed today, but life had a way of always handing her precisely what she didn't want.

"Snake in the grass," she mumbled under her breath—the closest she ever got to cursing—when the dishwasher refused to restart. It just sat there, silently mocking her.

As a single mother of two and currently a babysitter of five, the dirty dishes piled up fast. And she *hated* doing dishes.

Dishes used to be Bob's job. The light flickered off the gold band on her right thumb, and she spun it twice. Right before her late husband had headed into surgery, he'd slipped his wedding band onto her thumb and twisted it a few times.

"Don't worry, babe. Everything is going to work out. It always does," Bob assured her.

It had taken a while for her to believe that statement.

It'd been four years since she buried him; four years since she had been able to hide behind the man who protected her. He'd been everything her younger self needed. It was more comfortable, more normal, being Bob's wife—Beth Evans—than it was to be her father's infamous daughter, Elizabeth Campbell.

But she was stronger than she had been as a teenager, and over the years, she'd figured out life without him.

Like, for example, don't call any of Bob's many brothers about the broken dishwasher. While not a sister by blood, they all considered her one of the Evans siblings. If any of them knew about an issue, they'd be over in a heartbeat to "help"—and although they thought they were good at everything, they'd flood her kitchen or crack her granite countertop pulling the machine out. She didn't have time for that, and cash for a new dishwasher wasn't in this month's budget.

Moments like these she could almost regret giving away the share of the Campbell estate that she'd inherited when her grandparents died. One word from her father was all it took to remind her why she didn't want the Campbell money. He had never let her forget how she'd practically ruined the family's good name, and staying out of his way—and out of his debt—were close to the top of her list of priorities.

"Mommy, where me magic purple cup?" Mandy demanded, stomping her foot.

The answer was: in the dishwasher, which she couldn't even get to unlock.

"*My* magic purple cup," Beth corrected absently as she pulled uselessly on the dishwasher door.

Mandy glared. "No, it's me cup, not you's."

"Not *me* cup, *my* cup."

"No!" Mandy stomped away. Beth took a slow breath and prayed for patience.

Luckily for her, she had an ally at the appliance repair shop in the small, seaside South Jersey town where she grew up. The charity organization Beth worked with, Helping Hands, had an arrangement with Demoda Repairs, and she knew they would help if they could. Mr. Demoda was away from the office after a heart attack, but hopefully someone could come out.

She grabbed her phone to make the call before things got too crazy.

"Do you have a project for Helping Hands, Ms. Evans?" asked Glory, Frank Demoda's daughter. Even over the phone, she heard the hesitation in the young woman's voice. With her father out, the shop probably didn't have time for the types of projects Helping Hands tended to need.

"Actually, it's for me—my dishwasher. It stopped mid-cycle and locked. Any chance you could get someone out here this morning to look at it?"

"We're pretty short-staffed, but maybe one-thirty?"

Beth sighed. "I can't do this afternoon." The thunder of two sets of feet echoed around her causing both her dogs to bark. "Go to the playroom if you're going to act like lunatics!" She took a breath before continuing. "Sorry, this afternoon isn't good, the kids have—Mandy, shh, I can't hear a thing."

Glory clucked. "Sounds like chaos over there."

"Does that mean no?" Beth winced as she heard another crash. "Please?"

Glory sucked in a breath before saying to Beth's relief, "I'll see what I can do."

MARC DEMODA PULLED into the gated driveway in front of an average-looking house. It was nothing flashy, as he'd expected after seeing the high security gate. The work order on the passenger seat listed an address and last name; Evans. Even though it was a small town, he knew little about the family. His sister had only said, "She's a widowed single mom," but the amusement in Glory's tone had prompted him to say no, even when she promised it was a quick job. Less than a minute later, though, his dad had called, insisting that Marc help his VIP client. So, like the pitch you'd throw a batter with a full count, he planned on going in and getting out. *Fast.*

Standing outside the gray colonial, he heard the barking of two dogs and the racket of at least a dozen kids. This "quick" job was going to be a massive headache.

He was a baseball player, not a repairman. He needed to remember that.

Well, he *had* been a baseball player. He wasn't currently. But he'd be back in the game soon—he hoped.

The heavy black wooden door opened, seemingly by itself, and a small yapping mutt shot out and grabbed onto his leg as a little girl with dark blonde curls appeared. This tiny ray of sunshine was adorable, and he couldn't help but smile at her. Her gray-blue eyes glared at Marc, silently accusing him of not being the person she wanted to see, and then the door slammed in his face.

He laughed. That wasn't the usual reaction Marc got when he smiled at people. When was the last time he had really laughed? He couldn't remember.

"Amanda Evans," a woman scolded from beyond the door, "how many times have I told you not to open the door for strangers?"

As the door reopened, a woman with the same dark blond curls appeared. But these waves weren't cute; on her, they were striking, especially with her enormous emerald-green eyes and pink lips, which were pursed at the little girl. She wasn't by any stretch of the imagination the leggy, big-breasted type of woman that typically caught his attention, but something about her stole his breath. She was fresh-faced, completely unmade-up, a bit frazzled, but somehow sexy.

He stopped that train of thought in its tracks. He was here to do a job.

Another dog slipped out the door, to join the first one barking at his feet. The woman gestured him inside.

"Come in," she said—to both Marc and the dogs—before turning her attention back to the little girl and lecturing her about stranger danger.

Inside, the place vaguely reminded him of some of his childhood friends' houses. The floor was cluttered with toys and framed photos hung on all the walls, giving it a homey, lived-in feel. He would bet she put coloring-book pictures on her fridge—and maybe report cards, too, if those still existed.

"Only grownups open the door alone, Mandy, so wait for me."

"I'm big, and he gonna save *my* cup." Out of this tiny girl's mouth, it sounded like an accusation.

The woman sighed and tapped Mandy lightly on the nose. "You might be big, but I'm the mommy, and *I* say only grownups can open the front door to strangers. Sorry."

When she bent down to speak calmly to Mandy, who was suddenly cranky, he caught an inch of skin peeking out between the woman's orange shirt and the back of her jeans. He knew he should be professional and look away but his eyes to drifted out of pure reflex before he could stop himself.

Mandy glanced back up at him like she was asking his opinion.

"Your mom's right." Marc sent her a smile.

The little girl glared at them before stomping away, but the woman didn't seem fazed. She simply said, "Thanks for coming. The dishwasher is this way," and headed into the family room.

She stepped over piles of Mega Bloks and around the couch pillows piled in the shape of a play fort. She placed the little rat-looking dog on the floor and scooped a baby out of some contraption hanging in the doorway before grabbing a Nerf sword with her free hand, stopping a little boy from hitting another girl in the head.

"We only hit the couch and pillows, not our sister, remember?" The woman put the sword on the top of the fridge then took something out of another kid's hands before he got it to his mouth. "No pops before lunch."

"Aww, man," the boy whined.

And all of this happened before Marc had taken two steps. She moved quickly through the open-concept family room and kitchen, stepping over the clutter without noticing it was a disaster zone and stopping problems as if she possessed the ability to predict the future. She seemed to see everything, everything but him. She didn't bother to tell him her name or even seem to notice a professional baseball player was in her house and about to fix her dishwasher.

Does nothing faze this woman?

She placed the baby into a different contraption as another kid ran through the kitchen. Seeing the chaos made the need for the gated yard clear. People shouldn't lose their children, and one person surely couldn't keep track of this many, could they?

No one who knew him would call him a "kid person." He'd never spent enough time around kids to have a real sense of how he felt about them. Most of the time, they just looked at him with stars in their eyes as they handed him a sticky baseball card or a ball, and he'd smile and sign it.

Clearly, his sister had purposely avoided saying anything about this circus-like chaos, although he didn't blame her. If Glory had mentioned any of this, he probably wouldn't have agreed to come look at the dishwasher, even if it meant further annoying his father.

No, that wasn't true. If Marc were being honest, he would have come anyway, out of boredom or obligation. Or both the two blended. Ever since last summer's car accident had crushed his shoulder and ended his pitching career, every day was the same mess.

For thirty-three years, baseball had been his life—his *entire* life. From March through October, he'd either stood on the mound pitching or worked to get back on the mound again.

Marc loved the challenge of the game, the fierce competition that came from attempting to be—and stay—the best. Every opponent was a new hill to conquer. It didn't matter who came before or after. You could live in the moment of the contest between batter, pitcher, and catcher. The worst moment of his life had been when he'd opened his eyes after surgery the night of the crash, and the doctor had told him he'd never pitch again.

Now he spent most of his days either in a drunken haze or with a pounding hangover. The last twelve months had been a string of poor decisions, and for a while, he'd struggled to give a shit about anything.

However, as soon as he finished this favor for his dad, Marc was getting back into the game he loved. He knew he would never play, but he could still be part of it as a coach. He'd always been a teaching player, working with the young pitching talent. Marc possessed a sixth sense about who had the "stuff" and who didn't. He wanted to do that again, which meant fixing his ruined reputation with the Major League teams.

He forced himself back to reality as the woman stood over the dishwasher playing with the buttons, talking a mile a minute. He listened until he'd heard enough, then let himself be distracted by the angle of her neck and her great skin... soft, smooth—like she could be in an ad for face lotion. He cleared his throat.

"So can you fix it?" she asked, turning her attention to him, but the baby screamed, and she moved to scoop her up.

"It's all shut off, right?" he asked.

"I switched off the breaker, hoping it would unlock the thing, but it didn't."

"Then, let's see."

He'd been on enough calls with his dad while he'd worked his way through high school and college to know what he was doing, and it didn't take him even two minutes to get the door open. Mandy shrieked with glee over what looked like a plastic cup. The seals were tight, and the racks looked almost new. After another ten minutes, while the woman made lunch and wrangled all the kids to the table, he determined the issue. She didn't need a new machine, just a new motor.

The yappy little black dog perched next to him, looking up suspiciously like he didn't trust Marc.

"You want to unscrew it?" he asked the mutt. "Be my guest."

The kids were eating lunch at the table as he worked so the room was chaos. He tried to hide a smirk when he heard a girl yell out a knock-knock joke that wasn't funny—the tenth joke told in the last two minutes—but the kids laughed at it anyway. Two girls, two boys, one baby. Lots of damn kids.

Since they were busy eating, Marc decided to get the motor out today for a quick install tomorrow. As he leaned into the small opening, the other damn dog jumped onto his back. He sighed.

With the "help" of his new canine friends, he loosened the bolts then turned to the hoses. At the first twist, ice-cold water shot straight up his nose, burning his eyes and filling his mouth. Both mutts yapped and clawed like cats afraid of getting wet. He jerked his head back reflexively and slammed it straight into the top of the dishwasher.

"Fuck," Marc blurted, rubbing his head, coughing. He couldn't move away from the spray because the hose was shooting water all over the kitchen. He reached back in and, with one great yank, tightened the valve that stopped the flow.

He met the gaze of the beautiful green eyes across the room, and glared.

BETH WATCHED IN horror. Because of her connection to the company, she'd known the former Metros all-star pitcher was filling in for his father. But Beth had been leery of him coming. Marc was the type of super-celebrity who filled the gossip pages; even the daily news often covered his tweets. None of that pointed to him being able to fix a dishwasher, and Beth's flooded kitchen disproved Glory's assurance that Marc knew what he was doing.

"When you said the water's off, I guess you meant the sink?" Marc snapped at her.

Beth had meant the dishwasher *power* was off. How was she supposed to know the difference?

"I—no, I thought you meant the power," she stammered.

His eyes were slits of frustration as water dripped off his face, his annoyance clear as day as he stood to his feet. Beth headed toward him with a clean dish towel, but her foot slid in the giant puddle of water and she wobbled. He reached out to stop her as the dogs shot at his legs, tripping him. He and Beth both fell, landing on the wet floor with a thud and a chorus of barking dogs.

"Fuck!" She heard him curse again as her head smacked into his solid chest. Her arms tangled with his, and one of her legs rested between two powerful thighs. His hands were in the air, clearly unsure where to touch.

"You said a bad word two times," Mandy accused while Beth tried to apologize.

"Not now, Mandy," Beth said, mortified. This couldn't possibly get worse. She tried to move off the substantial male body below her, but he tensed and grabbed her, holding her in place.

"Your knee is uncomfortably close to something I deem very important," he said tightly. She pushed up carefully to see her knee less than an inch from his crotch, but before she could move, her daughter reappeared.

"Soap to qween the potty mouf," Mandy lisped as she dumped blue liquid all over him. Beth's head snapped around as her hand suddenly became slick with the soap running off of Marc.

"Amanda!" she yelled. She reached for her daughter, but she slid and fell again. Teeth clenched, Beth pushed up using Marc's chest, but he grabbed her leg as her knee brushed against him, propelling her forward. Her body pressed into him, and Beth's stomach fluttered as she got a whiff of his cologne. She looked his way again; *too good-looking for his own good* came to mind as he brushed his thick brown hair off his forehead. His irritated chocolate eyes, taut lips, and even the locked jaw with the scruff of day-old stubble were sexy. When you added the warm complexion he'd inherited from his Colombian mother, it wasn't surprising he was on some magazine cover at the grocery store being toted as "Sexiest Man Alive."

"Jesus," he snapped. She swallowed the sudden awareness of his proximity.

She shifted, but he jerked when her leg got too close. Before she could attempt to move again, his muscular arms pinned her against his body. He flipped them both, so she was flat on the floor, and he was glaring down at her.

"Stop wiggling around before I end up with permanent damage," he demanded. His eyes sparked, and she blushed. She started to speak, but he cut her off.

"I know—you're sorry. It's fine."

He pulled himself to his feet before helping her up. She skidded like a child learning to ice skate, and Marc reached out to steady her. Unfortunately, soap is worse than ice, and his feet slipped right out from under him. Back down in a heap, they both went.

The kids at the lunch table shrieked with laughter. That sent her dogs into another frenzy—jumping on Marc and barking like crazed animals. Marc pushed and slid across the floor, away from her and the dogs.

"Now I get why no one will look at your damn dishwasher," he snapped.

Then Beth looked on with wide-eyed horror as her dog did the unthinkable.

"No!" she yelled, but it was too late. The dog had already lifted his leg and peed straight onto Marc. And ten minutes ago she'd thought it couldn't get any worse.

Why is life always like this?

2

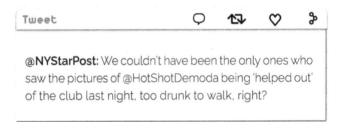

THE MUSIC FROM the stage drifted across to Poison's back booth, where Marc sat across from his friend and agent, Austin Jensen. He swirled his beer in his bottle before bringing it to his lips and taking a deep pull. With the afternoon he'd had, Marc needed it. The whole thing was either a record for inappropriate behavior or the repair call from hell. Maybe both. He shook his head and chuckled.

"Are you *laughing*?" Austin asked, shocked.

Marc shrugged.

He shouldn't be laughing, he knew, since the call had ended with him cursing to high hell and storming out the door. He didn't clean up or say anything about what was wrong with the machine; he just left. At this point, the company owed her a free motor, as his sister had explained once she stopped laughing after he recounted the mess to her, but Glory assured him Beth was a regular client and wouldn't bad mouth the business.

That should have been the end, but for some inexplicable reason, he couldn't stop thinking about the day. And Beth.

He looked across the room at a table of women; one of them, a hot blonde, took a selfie with her friend. He'd always liked blondes. At any moment this woman would post the picture she'd just taken and tag the bar. If he searched for #Poison, he could find the photo in seconds, like it, and she'd be at his table before he ordered his next beer. He knew how it worked. Twitter, Instagram—media in general had been his best friend through the years.

His eyes moved from the stiletto she balanced on her toe, and up her crossed legs to her black skirt, but Beth's short denim-clad legs popped into his mind. The way she'd felt lying on top of him was something he couldn't get out of his head. He'd met lots of gorgeous women in his life, and he couldn't think of another one that had stuck in his head like this. Like a bad pop song. It was ridiculous—

"Are you hearing a word I'm saying?" Austin asked, interrupting his thoughts.

"What?" Marc stared blankly. He hadn't realized his friend was talking.

"While you were glaring at the woman across the room, I told you your image is making you unhirable. So, let's try not to look like more of an ass. Those pictures last night hit a record for likes, yes, but that's not helping your career."

"Anyone who was there knows I wasn't drunk." Marc shrugged, not seeing the big deal.

"I get that, but nobody's tweeting about 'Security slips MD to safety when Boston fans start brawling'. The New York media's painted you as the favorite bad-boy turned irresponsible drunken playboy. None of the teams, not even the desperate ones, want to hire you and run the risk of corrupting their young talent."

Marc's grip on his beer tightened. "I need *something*. Especially since I doubt I'll be keeping my current job after today," Marc said. He chuckled again.

It wasn't a permanent job anyway. Two months ago, his father had a heart attack, and Marc had been forced into helping his sister run the business while their dad recovered. His mother thought it would teach Marc about life outside of baseball, but all Marc had learned was what he already knew. Any existence away from the mound sucked. Ten more days and his father would be back. With that obligation over, Marc could focus on baseball again.

"Why? What happened?" Austin demanded.

"This is a drink with a friend, not a lecture." Austin had lectured him plenty in the last few weeks. Marc thought he'd been behaving better, but seeing how he was trending on Twitter, that didn't matter.

"If you don't want lectures, don't mix business and friendship. You need to change your image. It's a fact, not an opinion. Why not play the 'helping your father in his time of need' card?"

"No," Marc snapped. His asshole father wasn't setting foot in the media.

Austin sighed. "How about some charity work?"

"Write a check. For your charity, the one I always donate to. Uh, Holding Hearts?"

"You get closer with every try. Helping *Hands*." The annoyance in Austin's voice said Marc should know that by now. Unlike Marc, Austin had interests outside of work, which was why he'd founded the charity several years ago with some other donors and clients. "But I meant hands-on work, the kind that comes with photo ops. Helping Hands' carnival is coming up in a few weeks. I'd love it if you showed up."

"Not really my thing." Marc spun his beer on the table again. What was he going to do there? Walk around and spend money? He didn't even have anyone to take with him.

"Then you need to cut out the clubbing, drinking, and random women. Or at least find one you can keep around for a while—preferably one we can claim changed you."

Marc sighed. "I'm not interested in that."

"But it's what you need, babe." Sydney, Poison's owner and Marc's only female friend, plopped down in the booth next to him with another round of drinks.

It wasn't his choice that he and Sydney were friends, he avoided unnecessary attachments, but he'd hung out here since he was a teenager when her parents still ran the bar. Over the years, Sid had wormed her way into Marc's life. She had hooked him up with her now-husband, Austin, and his all-in-one management firm. He'd handled Marc's contracts, his publicity, and his money for the last eight years.

"Anytime you're ready to leave your husband, I'm ready for commitment." Marc smiled at Sid who rolled her eyes.

Austin shook his head as Marc put his arm around his wife. "The last thing you need right now is an affair with a married woman, Marc. Talk about the final nail in your coffin. Even if we both know she's the most amazing woman on the planet," Austin added, winking at Sydney. She took his hand in hers, giving it a little squeeze.

Really, for all his joking, Marc knew she would never leave Austin. They enjoyed one of the best marriages he'd ever seen. There was none of the bitterness he was used to, and they both genuinely seemed happier when the other was around. Sid and Austin were lucky—and rare.

"Marc, there has to be someone who could hold your interest. All he's asking you to do is to stick with someone for a month or two," Sid said, looking annoyed.

"What's going on? You've been distracted by something all night." Austin's bright blue eyes skewered him, waiting for an explanation.

"I'm not interested in having another discussion about my life." Marc looked around the bar again for a way out of this conversation.

He loved *Poison* because although it had become a New York hot spot—mostly since he and his teammates were always here—it wasn't trendy. The bar had been in Sid's family for generations, and it still had the old New York feel. Mahogany wood, exposed brick, and sofas, along with booths, made you feel you were in a bar version of the coffee shop from *Friends*. His eyes scanned to the message on the mirror behind the bar. Sid always put up a *quote of the day* and then let everyone add to it. Today it said, *Tell me something unforgettable.*

He automatically thought of Beth's orange t-shirt which, once wet, had clung in places that made his mouth dry. He scowled.

Damn it, what was the *matter* with him?

"Seems like more than you not wanting to talk about your life choices," Austin said. "It's rare that beautiful women piss you off."

"They don't," Marc argued.

"So why are you glaring at all of them?" Austin asked, his black eyebrows raised.

"Maybe he's irritated because he's thinking of one he can't have," Sid said smugly. "Who is she, Marc? Anyone we know?"

And because Sid had hit the nail on the head, Marc said, "I have no fucking idea what you're talking about."

She frowned; even working in a bar she still wasn't a big fan of the 'f' bomb when said directly to her. That made him think about the soap. And that cute little girl. And—

"Look, Marc, don't get testy. Whoever she is, she could be just what you need."

Although he was right about Beth's potential help in fixing his image problems, it made him feel like an asshole.

"So ask her out," Austin continued. "Most of your baseball groupies would kill for some of your time—and the media's attention." Austin shrugged.

"She's not that type of girl," he snapped without thinking. Then he realized he had just admitted that Sid was right. She and Austin were looking at him expectantly. "Fuck this; I'm going home."

He wasn't in the mood to stay and talk about how to use Beth for his own benefit. Hell, he shouldn't be thinking about her at all. Now, not only was he thinking about her, but they were suggesting *dating* her—and that was something he'd never do.

3

DRIVING TO BETH'S house, Marc wondered what he was doing, but he honestly didn't know. Beth's motor had come in this afternoon, and his sister said she was sending one of the guys over to fix it. He'd told Glory there was absolutely no way the new guy was going. The guy had only worked for the company a couple of months, and he couldn't handle the job.

That was complete bullshit, but it didn't stop Marc from insisting on going himself. He kept replaying Austin's words in his head.

Find one that you can keep around for a while.

Marc didn't want that.

If it hadn't been for the car accident, none of this would matter. When he was pitching, no one cared about anything beyond how he threw the ball. He would have been at the stadium right now with the Metros; instead, Corey Matthews, second in the rotation, was sitting in his spot on the team.

Agitated, he got his stuff and walked to the front door, calming himself down. After a day full of speculation about phantom anger issues, he didn't need Ms. Evans posting something on social media. He hadn't seen anything about his last trip here though; maybe she was too busy to bother gossiping about him or maybe she didn't realize who he was. She hadn't treated him like most people who recognized him as a professional ball player did.

He took a deep breath and pushed the doorbell. A dark-haired boy—a kid he hadn't seen yesterday—opened it. How many kids did this woman have running through her house? This one let Marc in and without a word moved back to the couch where he was playing *Mario Kart* with another green-eyed boy Marc had never seen before. Two more made seven. *Seven* damn kids. She was definitely too busy for gossip.

"I'm in the kitchen; give me five minutes to finish these green beans. I'm finally winning this battle," Beth called.

Moving toward her voice, Marc reached the kitchen area in time to see Beth give the baby a mouthful of some gross green mush. The baby spat it back onto the tray.

"Almost winning," Beth corrected.

"I'm here to fix the dishwasher," Marc prompted. *Had she forgotten about him completely?*

"Oh, the office said you were coming later," Beth said, standing up. "But I think we should probably wait until your dad is back. I don't mind doing dishes by hand." Marc could tell it was a lie as it left her mouth.

"So you think I'm incompetent?" Marc asked, crossing his arms. Now he needed to fix it; there was no other option.

Beth paused. "Uh…"

"Yesterday was my first dishwasher call in a few years, but I could replace one by my senior year in high school. I know what I'm doing," Marc assured her, "And frankly, I'd rather not have to explain yesterday to my father."

She grimaced before she sighed, like she could understand his desire not to tell his father.

"Okay. Sorry," she said, apologizing for the tenth time since he'd met her. She moved over to the sink. "This time, when I say the water's off, I mean all the water is off." She waved her hands in the general area of the sink and dishwasher.

"Yeah," came a voice from behind him. "Uttle Will came here and sut it off."

Marc turned, to see the crazy curls and fierce gray eyes of the little girl who had thrown soap the day before. She stood staring at him, her hand was on her hip, and a scowl was on her face. She was adorable.

"And I toll him about your potty mouf, and he said you were a bad sample."

"Mandy." Beth sighed, but Marc's irritation vanished.

He bent down to make amends. "Can I say sorry? Yesterday was a bad day for me. I promise to be better. No soap needed."

Mandy paused for a moment. "Otay." She put her finger up, "But tish is you fidal warding."

She nodded firmly, letting him know she was serious.

Marc bit his cheek and nodded back. When Mandy walked away, he chuckled.

"How do you not laugh at her?" he asked Beth.

Beth smiled. "Trust me, she's a character. Go ahead. I'm going to have to make dinner around you, I planned for no water so I won't be too much in your way."

"It's fine," Marc assured her. Beth sat down to finish the jar of green gunk that she was giving the baby. Another boy ran in and put a blue baseball hat on her head, and she adjusted it sideways.

"How does it look?" she asked.

"You look silly."

"*Silly?*" Beth jumped out of the chair and caught the boy, tickling him as they both fell to the floor. The little boy crackled with laugher, and Beth laughed right along with him.

Marc wanted to smile or laugh, but his stomach stuck painfully in his throat. *Silly* wasn't the word he would have used to describe Beth at this moment; maybe radiant would be better. Was he high? This woman was a mess—but even covered in green goop, she enthralled him. Why? Bored, he reminded himself; he was just bored. This woman just wasn't his type; she was interestingly different, and once he figured her out, she'd lose her appeal.

The doorbell rang and Beth swept out of the room. His eyes followed the sway of her hips below the yellow shirt the entire way. He reached out to the counter to steady himself. She was *not* his type.

A nervous woman with big brown eyes collected the baby and one of the bigger boys while Marc prepared to install the new part. Beth ignored him as he worked. It wasn't until they bumped elbows at the sink—as she went to grab the squash while he drained the motor—that they spoke.

"Sorry," she mumbled.

He rolled his eyes: apology number eleven. "What are you making?" he asked, eyeing the many vegetables on the counter.

"Seasoned steak, grilled veggies, and rice."

"Kids will eat that?"

"Why wouldn't they?" she said. She chopped the squash with maddening speed. One of the boys came running through the kitchen and she sent him a look that silently said *Stop*.

He shrugged. "I thought they preferred Micky D's or something."

"That stuff is gut rot," she said.

Hearing him chuckle, she glanced his way. Her bright green eyes sparkled.

"My gut is used to paying for my inability to cook. I don't know when my last home-cooked meal was." He avoided his parents' house. Although his mom could be a bit of a nag, it was his father who kept him away. His father, the guy who was well-liked by everyone except his own family. To the world, Frank was the charming, good-looking repairman. To his family, he was an asshole. And since, unlike some celebrities, Marc wasn't uppity enough to employ a chef, he ate out. So even though it was May, his last home-cooked meal might have been Thanksgiving.

She paused, cocking her head. "Seriously?"

"What you eat then?" Mandy asked, having come back into the room at the sounds of conversation.

He shrugged. "I like Burger King."

Mandy scowled. "That make your body sick, and you can't be big and tong, wite, Mommy?"

Beth's eyes flitted shut like she was bracing herself for something, but Marc didn't have any idea what. Mandy's hands went back to her hips, and she stomped her little foot.

"Wite, Mommy?" she asked again.

"Yes," Beth finally agreed.

"You eat wif us," Mandy confirmed with a head nod.

"Uh—" Marc's eyes shot to Beth. Now he understood her unease.

Mandy's gray eyes quickly got big and wet. "We want him to be big and tong wite Mommy, so he eat wif us?"

"Well..." Beth looked like a trapped animal. "I guess." She swallowed. "Yeah, you can stay for dinner, if you don't mind the crazy." As soon as she said the words, she looked like she wanted to wish them back into her mouth. He could see it on her face. If he'd been a complete jerk, he could have refused and made the little girl cry, but he couldn't bring himself to do it.

"How can a man say no to a home-cooked meal?"

Marc moved back to the floor, but not before he flashed Beth a charming smile, trying to ease her discomfort. But she sucked in a breath and froze before she swallowed, glancing away.

MANDY ALWAYS HAD the worst timing—first the soap and now this. If she'd just stayed in the playroom for five more minutes, Marc Demoda wouldn't be eating dinner at her house. Beth should have been quicker on her feet, explaining to Mandy why he couldn't stay.

She looked his way again. Today he was smiling, frequently. And the dimpled smile *was* cute. No one his age should have such a boyish charm. Not to mention that in the skintight black shirt, it was easy to see his broad shoulders, the corded muscles of his forearms, the flat stomach above the belted cargo pants that sat low on narrow hips. A hard-tight body, but there was a gracefulness to his movement that softened him. A strange combination of hard and soft that was very—

Beth swallowed.

She was immune, she reminded herself. She didn't get involved with people with larger-than-life reputations anymore. The hard lesson she'd learned as a teenager had taught her to keep her personal life far away from anything involving the media, and that included the paparazzi's favorite bad boy.

Most people dreamed of the intense, all-encompassing lose-your-head kind of passion. Beth didn't. She'd done that as a teenager and crashed and burned. Now she wanted the comforting partnership of someone being there through the hard times, not just riding high on the fun. She wanted *normal*; she was even okay with boring as long as it was comfortable. So she went back to her vegetables and ignored the well-known playboy in her kitchen who was everything she was looking to avoid.

"Mom, you promised to throw with me today." Steve, her eight-year-old, came in tossing his baseball. Beth snapped her hand out, grabbing the ball before it could hit his mitt.

"No baseball inside."

The guilt flashed in her son's eyes before he turned it on her.

"Please, Mom, you never have enough time. I need to throw every night if I'm going to be any good." The constant guilt of being a single parent struck her again. She never had enough time.

"We will," she promised. "I just need to finish dinner and get the girls in bed first."

"It's going to be dark by then," he exaggerated.

Marc cleared his throat getting her son's attention. "I'm almost finished up here. If I'm still invited to stay for dinner, I could toss the ball around."

Beth shot suspicious eyes at Marc. Why would he offer?

"Can he, since you throw like a girl?" Steve asked.

"I do not," she retorted. That statement must have come out of one of his uncle's mouths.

"Uncle Danny says you do." Steve shrugged, proving Beth right.

"Ask Uncle Will instead," Beth suggested, but her son looked exasperated.

"He's prejudiced. You broke his nose with a football. I can ask Uncle Clayton tomorrow, but he'll probably side with you too since you're his favorite person on the planet."

Well, not right now. Beth and nineteen-year-old Clayton were currently arguing about why he couldn't waste half his inheritance on an overpriced car. But since Bob had died, she got the final say on spending his money until Clayton graduated college or turned twenty-five

Although she had known the Evans family her entire life, she and her late husband had begun dating when she was eighteen and Bob was twenty-five. His youngest brother, Clayton, hadn't even been nine. After the boys' parents died, Beth and Bob raised him, and she was more of a mom than a sister to Clayton in a lot of ways.

"I have a ton of uncles, and most of them think Mom throws like a girl," Steve told Marc. Beth frowned again.

"Well, since none of those uncles are here, I'll have to do," Marc said. "Let me put this stuff away, and then I'll be right out."

"Awesome!" Steve said. He went flying out the back door, tossing the ball up in the air and catching it again.

Marc turned to walk out of the kitchen, but Beth caught him by the arm. Her pale skin stood out against his tan complexion. Their bodies were close, and she could feel the heat vibrating off of him. He glanced above her head, not looking at her. Did Marc regret the offer, as much as she regretted the dinner invitation?

"You don't have to play with him." Beth waited until Marc's warm brown eyes finally met hers.

For a minute, everything else in the world disappeared. The air buzzed between them, and her stomach flipped. Marc stepped toward her, so that her chest brushed lightly against him, and she couldn't breathe. He reached out like he was going to touch her.

Beep! The oven timer blared and they jumped apart.

Beth quickly shook her head, and Marc cleared his throat.

"I know I don't have to, just like you didn't have to offer to feed me. But I'm currently not busy, while you seem to have a lot on your plate," Marc said, a small smile creeping across his lips as the timer beeped again. "Plus, it seems like he needs someone besides you to tell him not to use 'throw like a girl' or any of the other sexist phrases that so many men throw around."

Beth stood in stunned silence as Marc grabbed his hat off the counter, pulling it down over his eyes before he walked out. The media made Marc out to be the exact type of guy who'd use a sexist phrase without a thought—not one who'd correct it.

She shook her head again.

Anything Marc said would become Steve's gospel. Steve loved the former Metros pitcher; he had two Metros posters and Marc's signed jersey hanging on his bedroom wall. He had known Marc was coming, and Beth had warned him to leave Marc alone. They'd discussed the concepts of privacy and respect; thankfully, having grown up with her father's fame as a normal part of his life, Steve grasped them. Still, she knew Steve was excited about Marc's offer to throw with him.

A few minutes later as she stood on the back deck shutting the grill lid, she turned to Steve and Marc in the yard. Instead of throwing the ball back and forth, Marc was squatting next to Steve; they each held a ball in their hands and Marc was teaching him how to grip it correctly. Her son was drinking in every word.

Marc stood back up and demonstrated the windup. Steve mimicked the motions a few times before throwing his ball at the pitchback, hitting it straight in the center of the red square. Beth could tell that Steve was about to explode under Marc's praise and encouragement. She frowned and spun the ring on her thumb. She needed to finish dinner and straighten up, not worry about a pitching lesson.

Beth was cutting steak for one of the five kids when the back door opened.

"Shoes off," she called to Steve as he tried to skip that vital step.

"Sorry." It was Marc who answered, and he toed-off both sneakers. Before Beth could tell him he didn't have to, Steve made that impossible.

"Mom's real strict about muddy shoes; she loses it if you track in mud," Steve told Marc as if they were best buddies. They moved to her sink to wash up together. Seeing the sparkle in her son's eyes, she couldn't regret letting Marc eat with them. There wasn't much Beth wouldn't do to keep that sparkle there, and if it meant letting Marc hang out for the evening, it was worth it. "Rule one, shoes off. Rule two, hands washed."

"Place looks different," Marc commented, glancing around.

Yeah, because while they were playing, she had disarmed the bomb that went off in her house multiple times a day. Now Marc could see things—like the floor.

"Rule three, clean up before quiet time and dinner," Steve said softly, and Marc chuckled.

"You must need to stay organized with—what, two sets of twins?" Marc let the question hang as he moved to sit at the opposite end of the table.

Before Beth could correct him, her nephew Travis spoke up. "Only me and Trevor are twins," he explained. "Ava's our sister and Mandy is our cousin. *Two* sisters would kill me." Beth tried not to laugh, but Marc did.

"Aunt Beth watches us while Mommy and Daddy work all the time," added Ava. "She and Mommy are sisters."

"Yeah, Dad says Aunt Beth needs the cash because she squatted her money away," Trevor chimed in helpfully.

Beth frowned. That was far from what had happened. It was true that she no longer controlled the money she'd inherited from her father's family. Donating it to start Helping Hands hadn't been irresponsible, but her family never saw it that way. Letting go of the money from her father had been more an act of self-preservation, a way to separate herself further from the parents who had never wanted her but for public opinion couldn't disown her completely. Playing the part of a family man to the outside world had always been her father's priority.

She cleared her throat.

"You mean squandered, or wasted. Squatted means 'bent down.'" She corrected the verb, but not the idea.

"Oh, yeah," Trevor agreed, his mouth so full that a bit of rice fell out as he spoke.

"Swallow before you talk," Beth reminded.

"Rule number four," Steve mumbled to Marc. "And Mom didn't waste her money. She gave it to people who needed it more."

Most eight-year-olds wouldn't have known this, but her family regularly reminded her how they felt about her 'wasting' her money, and she couldn't let her kids believe that helping those less fortunate could ever be a waste.

Marc's eyes jumped to Beth's. "I get the impression she's a bit too responsible to waste anything."

Beth wasn't sure whether it was the dimpled smile he sent her way that made her blush or the inaccurate compliment, but the uncertainty didn't stop the blood from heating her cheeks. She swallowed hard.

"Use your fork, please, Mandy," Beth said, distracting herself by stopping her daughter from grabbing steak with her fingers.

Mandy's gray eyes glared back at her accusingly. "You mate my life so hart."

Marc coughed, and Beth glanced up to see him hiding a smile behind a napkin. It was going to be a long dinner.

The evening was made even longer because the boys insisted that Marc follow the household rule of girls cook and boys do dishes. Beth thought Marc would bow out and try to run for the door, but he simply smiled and washed dishes with six little helping hands.

DINNER AND CLEANUP were so entertaining that Marc almost hated to go. Beth kept things organized even in the funny-as-hell kid chaos, and her smile was infectious. So it was a pleasant shock when he got an excuse to stay.

When Steve, Travis, and Trevor suggested an after-dinner baseball game, he didn't think Beth would agree. But when she came down after putting the girls to bed, not only did she agree to play, but she also consented to the unfairly unbalanced teams: Steve and Marc vs. her and the twins.

"Mom can never say no when you make it a challenge," Steve explained. "It's the athlete in her."

Marc doubted she had any real athletic ability; kids often made their parents greater than they were. She'd probably played tennis in high school.

"What does the winner get: control of the remote for the day or their choice for dinner tomorrow?" Beth asked the boys.

"Remote," all three shouted at the same time.

"Remote?" Marc asked. He expected them to say dinner so they could have pizza.

"You must live alone." Steve shook his head in a gesture that seemed to age him ten years. "When you live with other people, you realize how important it is to hold control of the television."

Beth chuckled, and the sound twisted weirdly in Marc's chest. This woman possessed a laugh that did all kinds of things to him.

Steve looked up, his eyes serious. "Let's win, okay? I can only handle so much *Paw Patrol*."

Unfortunately for Steve, it wasn't Marc's night. They started in the field, which meant Beth helped the boy's bat. She bent at the waist, enthralling him with the way her hip jutted out, and made her ass wiggle with each swing of the bat. When it was her turn to the plate, she took a stance that pushed out her chest and ass, drawing his eye helplessly. When Marc told her not to stand like that, Steve looked at him like he was ridiculous and knew nothing about baseball.

When Steve single-handedly got the three outs, and it was Marc's turn to bat, he couldn't hit the ball because she bounced when she threw it. Her form wasn't bad, but the scoop of her yellow shirt dipped, and two perfectly round breasts jiggled with every pitch, and his eyes stayed glued to her chest as the ball soared past him.

Every. Single. Time.

He'd been playing baseball for thirty years and never had he been so unable to concentrate on the game he loved. They ended up losing by two runs—which said something about how good Steve was. Marc had done nothing but try not to drool.

"Next time I get Mom. You're as bad as Uncle Corey," Steve mumbled, slamming his mitt on the ground while the other two jumped up and down, celebrating. Until this moment, the frequent mentions of these many uncles had annoyed him. But Marc suddenly felt sorry for Uncle Corey. Playing against this insanely attractive woman was a version of sweet torture.

What was he going to do about his attraction to Beth?

MARC STOOD, HANDS on hips, lecturing the three boys on being a good sport, something none of their uncles encouraged. They all went by the adage that 'Winning isn't everything; it's the only thing.' The brothers made rubbing it in look like an art form. She tried not to laugh when Travis asked what the point of winning was if you can't be excited about it? Marc started his lecture over.

Part of her didn't want to like the man. It was bad enough he exuded masculinity and sex like it was a cologne he wore. But watching him teach the boys something important was even sexier than his dimples.

Once she was sure he'd finished his lecture, she called out, "All right, head upstairs, teeth and PJs. Say thank you to Marc."

After a few fist bumps and head pats, the three boys took off with cries of "Last one to the bathroom is a stinky toadfoot!"

Marc chuckled as they ran off.

"Thanks for that." Beth smiled.

"The game?"

"Well, that too," she said as she walked him to the door. "But I meant the lecture. Most of the men in their lives promote that kind of poor sportsmanship."

"Even if it makes me old and no fun?" The corner of his mouth twitched like he was trying not to smile as he repeated her nephew's words.

"Well, now that you mention it…" Beth smiled and cocked her head to the side playfully.

"Are you saying I'm old or no fun?" Marc demanded as his brow furrowed, and his hands slammed onto his hips, much the same stance he'd used to lecture the boys. Was he about to scold her? Beth shrugged as she turned and led Marc out the front door.

"We're pretty much the same age. I wouldn't call you old," she said once they were on the porch. Her teeth dug into her bottom lip. His brown eyes turned dangerously dark as she met his gaze.

"I know how to have fun," he said, his voice dropping to a husky whisper, sending a shiver down her spine.

He stepped closer and stared into her eyes. His chocolate irises flooded with a desire that pounded into her system. Her tongue snaked out and wet her lower lip as she stared, hypnotized by him. One more step and they were close enough that she could feel his breath on her face. Slowly his hand came up, and the warm, callused skin pressed against her cheek. His eyes dropped to her mouth, causing her stomach to tighten. She swallowed back the lump in her throat as Marc dropped his forehead to hers.

"These uncles, they anyone I should worry about?" he asked, and his breath danced across her lips.

"I have a big family, but they're not that bad," she said.

He smiled. "Does anyone babysit?" he asked. "You know, so you can have one night off for some grown-up time?"

Was he serious? Get a babysitter for a one-night stand? She suddenly remembered what a playboy this man was, and it was like a bucket of ice-cold water doused any heat she felt.

"Never going to happen." She turned back to the house, and slammed the door behind her.

4

MARC WALKED DOWN the ramp over the dunes in front of his house with his water bottle, cooling off after his evening workout. He took a selfie and sent it to Austin, telling him to post it with a comment about keeping in shape. For fuck's sake, he wouldn't let anyone think he was getting fat. He pulled his shirt back on and leaned against the railing overlooking the Jersey coastline.

Who knew getting good media was so hard? When he'd been pitching, even bad press wasn't that bad. He'd been patient with being called a drunk, a drug addict, a hothead, even a whorish disease-infested sleaze bag, but he drew the line at fat.

His eyes scanned the beach while he sucked in a breath of salt air. He sank into one of the two chairs he'd placed on the wooden planks, watching the runners who dotted the sand this time of night. Nothing caught his eye until he landed on slender, toned legs in a pair of tight Sideline shorts. The woman reached down to tie her shoelace, allowing him to catch a glimpse of her heart-shaped ass.

He swallowed, feeling relieved. For days he'd tried to drudge up interest in the women he met in bars and clubs, but he couldn't. It had been years since he spent so many consecutive nights alone.

Seeing this woman, watching her bend down, Marc found himself interested. He smiled as he brought the water bottle up to his lips, but it stopped halfway to his mouth when the woman turned around, and he realized it was Beth. *Shit.* How had he not known this was the same woman he'd spent days uselessly trying to forget? He shook his head in frustration.

Ever since that night, when he'd been close to placing his lips on Beth's, he'd spent most of his waking hours thinking about her. He couldn't believe how badly he'd messed up by asking her to go out with him. He winced.

But he'd have to think about what that meant later if he wanted to catch up with her now. Marc left the bottle sitting on the chair's arm and took off down the ramp towards the water.

"Beth," Marc called, but she didn't hear him. When he got closer and she still didn't answer, it became clear she was ignoring him. No one ever ignored him–especially not women. Marc picked up his pace, putting himself in her path, forcing Beth to acknowledge him. Her eyes tracked over him, and his stomach tightened before she glanced away.

"Marc," she replied coolly. Her tone clearly showed her annoyance. He'd have to try harder.

"It's beautiful this time of night," he said awkwardly.

That was the best he could do?

He shook his head as he moved in step beside her, slowing his long legs to match her shorter strides.

"I usually enjoy it alone." Her eyes took in anything and everything apart from him.

"Lucky you; now you don't have to," he joked sending her a smile—knowing full well by her body language that she didn't see it as lucky.

She didn't even crack a grin back.

"I realize I owe you an apology." Her glare turned softer as, at last, she snuck a glance at him, so he continued. "Beautiful women make men nervous and we say stupid things."

"It's been two weeks, and that's the best you got?" She shook her head and tried to speed up, but he easily matched her pace.

"I was trying to ask you out for a drink or dinner or something, and it came across like I was trying to get you into bed. That's not what I meant." Those words felt strange coming out of his mouth. They were true *now*, but for most of his life that statement would have been a lie.

"You think I don't know Marc Demoda's reputation?" Beth rolled her eyes, but Marc almost missed his footing.

"You know who I am?" He made a poor attempt to keep the shock out of his voice.

"Of course." Beth stopped suddenly and turned in the opposite direction. "This is where I head back. Enjoy the rest of your run."

Marc stood frozen after her apparent dismissal.

In hindsight, it was obvious she knew who he was. His father had called her a VIP client, and his sister spoke about Beth as if Glory knew her. On top of that, repeatedly Beth called him Marc without him having to introduce himself. But he'd assumed as soon as she discovered who he was, she would be falling over him like every other woman he met. She was so different.

"Beth," he called, taking off down the beach after her. She seemed not to hear him, or maybe she was ignoring him again, but that didn't stop him. "Did Steve know too?" He slowed down and matched her stride again.

"Yes."

"He didn't care either?" Damn, kids were always impressed with him. She shot him a look that said, *Are you kidding me?*

"You're definitely not going to be his pick for a teammate anytime soon."

"I had an off night." He couldn't even blame it on his bad arm; it was *her* fault. "Normally I'm more impressive."

"Marc, you flooded my kitchen and played bad baseball. That's the extent of my *impressive* experience with you."

"Then give me a chance to do better."

"I've told you I'm not interested," Beth sighed.

Couldn't she spend some time getting to know him before she decided he wasn't worth her time?

"Well, I am," he huffed. *Wow,* that was his comeback? Maybe even given a chance, he wouldn't impress her.

"Why, Marc?" Beth stopped running and looked at him.

It was a good question, and one that he damn well wished he could answer, but he didn't know. Well, that wasn't exactly true. His eyes slid over her sweatshirt and then lingered on her hips. He reached for curl that had fallen out of her ponytail and tucked it behind her ear.

"I can think of a few reasons," he said, his voice low and throaty. Without consciously deciding to, he'd fallen back into seduction mode.

Instead of backing away, Beth let her hand run down his arm before grabbing his wrist and pulling him closer, so almost no space existed between them. She stood up on her toes and let her mouth move to within a centimeter of his ear. His gut clenched as a jolt shot down his body and he licked his lips in anticipation of what she'd do. He finally had her.

"Sorry, hotshot. I make it a point not to sleep with anyone I read about in a magazine," she whispered before backing up and leaving him. *Again.*

God, she was maddening. Her satisfied smile as she jogged away said she knew what she was doing. Feisty—he always liked feisty. He stared after her, trying to figure out how to get her to see him again. Then he had a flash of inspiration.

Thank you, Steve. I owe you one.

"Want to race back?" Marc asked when he caught up with her again. "You make the rules, and the winner will choose dinner tomorrow night."

A crack of a laugh broke through Beth's lips.

"I didn't agree to go out with you." Instead of sounding annoyed, this time, Beth smiled as she replied.

"Exactly. If you win, you eat alone—but if I win, you eat with me. Unless you don't think you're up for the challenge."

Her eyes flashed with the sparkle that had drawn him from the start. She looked down the beach toward his house before turning back.

"I pick the rules, right?" Beth eyes shone like trouble danced in their green depths.

"Sure." He expected her to give herself a considerable head start.

Her reply was almost immediate. "My only rule is you run backward, and no turning or glancing around. If you look towards the finish line, you forfeit. I run facing forward. We stop where I always do, two blocks after the end of the boardwalk." Beth stopped running and waited for his answer.

She couldn't know running backward was his warm-up, but that was something he wasn't about to share.

"You're on," Marc said instead.

He turned around and lined up right next to her. He didn't understand why she looked so cocky, but it was written all over her face along with a touch of excitement. That he could relate to—the adrenaline rush of competition. He liked a woman who could handle his sense of sport, and Beth could. Marc doubted most women he hung out with would take him on in a foot race, much less think they could win.

But before he could analyze it, she took off down the beach, and he had to go. He caught her quickly, but Beth kept pace, staying a bit behind him so he could see her without breaking his looking forward rule. Halfway back, he increased his lead. But she didn't look tired. Beth watched him expectantly, almost like she was waiting for something.

Suddenly his foot missed the ground behind him. Moving as fast as he was, his other foot lost the ground a second later, and he couldn't stop himself from falling backward, landing half in and half out of a hole in the sand. The wind was knocked out of his lungs and it took a second to get his bearings. Once he did, he heard Beth laughing. He turned to glare at her before realizing she had moved and he was breaking her rule.

"Looks like I win, hotshot." Beth smiled that same cocky smile.

"You didn't think you should mention the hole?"

Beth's eyes sparkled with the trouble he'd seen before. It was in that second it clicked. She'd seen the hole before she agreed to the race. She had purposely let him fall flat on his back.

Beth knew she couldn't beat him in a flat-out race, so she'd outwitted him because she wasn't about to lose. Impressive.

"And if I'd gotten hurt?" he asked.

"Other than your pride, you're fine," Beth assured him, laughing again before extending a hand to help him up.

Payback's a bitch.

He got to his feet, holding her arm, and then grabbed her waist. He tossed her over his shoulder. He turned and headed straight into the water as she shrieked. She was kicking and squirming, but Marc had secured a firm hold behind her knees, and she wasn't getting away. He walked until the water hit his shorts, then tossed her straight into the oncoming wave before he backed up out of its way. He laughed as the wave crashed directly over her head. Damn, she was fun.

"You snake in the grass," she shrieked as she righted herself. She stood glaring at him, looking a bit like a drowned rat—but a cute one.

"I'm a *what*?" Had she called him a snake? Unlike him, she didn't look amused; she looked thoroughly pissed.

"My phone was in my pocket!" Beth's voice sounded shrill, but Marc was laughing.

One minute she was marching toward him, and suddenly a hard sweeping kick knocked straight into the back of his knees. Both gave out from under him, and he was flat on his back again this time with a wave crashing over him. His head whacked the sand, and he wasn't sure which way was up or down as he spun in the surf. He got a few delightful mouthfuls of saltwater before someone pulled him toward the beach. It didn't occur to him it might be anyone other than Beth getting him back onto the sand. But two powerful arms that weren't female dumped him on the ground, just out of the water.

"What's going on?" a male voice asked, sounding somewhat amused.

"Is Will having you watch me while I run now?" Beth demanded, in full-on feisty mode. "Because, as you can see, I handled this."

"Seeing as it's my *job* to watch this part of the beach, you can't blame my brother." The man laughed and Marc saw that he was wearing a red swimsuit and white windbreaker labeled *Lifeguard*.

He was tall, built like a linebacker, but with bright blue eyes that Marc could see from where he was sitting.

"Drowning a person is a crap idea, and don't tell me you didn't know you caught him completely off guard. Most people don't know that such a small person can be so much trouble." The man's hand came up and waved off a second lifeguard headed their way.

Neither of them seemed worried about him sitting in the sand, coughing up water. Didn't anyone realize he was not a person to be ignored? Marc's ego took another bruising as he realized that this guy, like Beth, didn't care who he was. His attention was all on the beautiful, drowned rat.

Marc tried to follow the conversation, but his ears were ringing from hitting the ground twice. The man handed Beth his lifeguard jacket, and she took off her sweatshirt, handing it over to him. The flash of her skin took over Marc's thoughts.

"I'll bring it back over later," the man said.

"Whenever," Beth answered.

They had plans?

Beth's gaze finally fell on Marc, but he didn't see sympathy or humor in those green eyes. He'd pissed her off—again. Usually, he was good with women, although, he really never tried; being there and being himself was enough. If he'd always had to work at it, would he ever have had any luck with women? He wasn't one of those naturally lovable guys like the muscular lifeguard standing in front of him.

The man murmured something at Beth, and she rolled her eyes before she turned and stalked away.

"You doing okay, Mr. Demoda?" the man asked him. Given the situation, Marc wasn't thrilled this guy recognized him.

"I'm fine. Call me Marc," he said. He stood up, embarrassed.

"I'm Danny. Don't feel bad. She's tougher than she looks. Beth could take me down too." Was that supposed to make him feel better? "And she wouldn't have let you drown even if I hadn't been here," Danny said, watching Beth as she headed off the beach.

"I'm not sure about that."

Danny laughed.

"You don't know her. But you did put her in a nice little tiff, which is shocking. These days she rarely lets herself get good and mad."

Marc didn't believe that for a second. Since he'd met Beth, he had pissed her off plenty.

But he couldn't blame her. He'd flooded her kitchen, yelled at her, implied she was the type of woman interested in one-night stands, thrown her in the ocean, and ruined her phone. He was acting like a ten-year-old pulling a girl's hair to get her attention. As opposed to the man standing in front of him, who had come to help Beth, given her his jacket, and handled her wet crap.

"Seems like *you* do," Marc said. Danny was probably as interested in Beth as he was, and *he* had secured an invite to hang with her tonight. Something Marc hadn't.

"Nah, I usually just amuse her."

"I meant you know her," Marc corrected, trying futilely to brush the sand off his wet clothes. But there was no dignity at this moment, so he gave up.

"Well enough to know that her run is her alone time and not the best time to mess with her. Although now you know that too." Danny chuckled again.

"Few chances to get away from the rugrats, I guess."

Danny's face hardened for the first time.

"They're good kids," Danny said as his eyes narrowed, and Marc recognized the protectiveness there.

"Are you in love with her or just hooking up with her?" Marc asked. Danny was a bit young, but if he and Beth were together, Marc would back off.

"Neither," Danny said with a hint of a smile touching his lips. "She's my sister."

"Shit," Marc mumbled and then ran his hands over his eyes.

"Your bad reputation proceeds you dude."

"No, I'm sorry, really." Marc shook his head. "It's…" He paused, looking for a way to explain that what he wanted with Beth differed from his usual MO. But how could he describe it? "Beth's—" He couldn't find the right word. "—great," he finished lamely, then looked up to see Danny smirking.

Danny crossed his arms over his chest as his smile grew.

"She *is* great," he agreed. Marc could have sworn he saw a touch of friendship in the guy's face now, but he knew he must be misinterpreting it. "If you were to ask Beth, you and I aren't that different. A smart man knows who you can fuck with and who you can't. You don't fuck with Beth. She isn't that type of girl."

Marc nodded.

"You aren't a quitter Marc Demoda, so I know you won't give up easy. Just don't say no one warned you." Danny smiled like they were old friends.

It made Marc wonder about Beth's brothers, especially when a younger version of Danny headed their way. Another blonde-haired blue-eyed linebacker; this one though had a face that belonged in Disney's fairytales. Marc groaned as he remembered what Beth had said; there were five more of these guys somewhere.

5

BETH WOULDN'T USUALLY describe her kitchen as small, but the men in it currently dwarfed the room. Sometimes she felt like Snow White, but instead of seven dwarfs to take care of, she had seven giants. Her late husband's brothers weren't only big in size but in voice and personality as well, so their presence wasn't something you could ignore.

She was grateful their sexual conquests over the last few weeks was taking up most of the conversation, and no one was talking about her run on the beach. Not that they had forgotten she was in the room; they'd just stopped censoring themselves around her long ago.

Clayton, the youngest, returned home from college, so there was plenty of catching up to do. The siblings sat at her table drinking beer while she stood at the counter, setting up tomorrow morning's coffee. Missing from the gathering were the guys who didn't live in town but if they'd been nearby, they would have been there too. Her table was where the boys met to drink, BS, and swap stories.

All the brothers were close to each other, and to Beth and her kids. When she and the boys were together, it was hard to break into their little clique. Beth had dated a few guys since Bob's death, but her brothers always scared them off quickly. Only one person had successfully broken through the gates and become part of the family: Corey Matthews, the man currently opening her front door.

"Look what the cat dragged in," Danny said sarcastically as all six foot three inches of the New York Metros' new starting pitcher ducked through the front door.

"Don't start," Corey snapped, his chiseled face sporting a scowl. He headed straight to the fridge for a beer.

Corey'd had years with the guys to get into their good graces. Beth and Corey had dated when she was in high school, bringing Corey into the Evans fold. And after all the two had gone through, they remained friends even after she married Bob at nineteen.

"Nice game," said Will, Corey's best friend, giving him a smirk from across the room. Will, the oldest of the local Evanses, was Beth's age. And most of the time, she felt like he was the only other adult in the room with her. When she needed help to shut off the water or watch the kids, that was Will's job. Giving her a hard time—Danny and Clayton covered that.

Corey flipped Will off, and his two-tone brown eyes glared at the three guys sitting at her table.

"If you say one word about how I'm trending, I will beat you," Corey warned. He was known for his inconsistency on the pitching mound, and the harsh New York baseball fans and media regularly killed him for it on social media.

Beth rolled her eyes at his drama before clearing her throat. Corey's gaze followed the line of her pointed finger to a pile of cell phones on the counter. Hers was missing, of course, since Danny had predictably forgotten to bring it. She invoked the 'cell phones on the counter' rule as soon as any of Corey's games were heading into the toilet. This way, there was no talk about what the world was saying.

"Thanks, baby." Corey sent her a weak smile and headed to the table, dropping into a chair next to Will.

"We don't need our phones to know you stunk," Danny teased cheerfully.

Corey's teeth clenched before he blew out a breath and slumped further into the chair. Nothing he said would stop the good-natured rib-fest. "At least I know no one's going to be waiting outside this house and hounding me for a comment in the morning."

Corey and Beth's friendship was something they kept from the media so no one would ever look for him here. Back in the day, they had flaunted where they were because they loved the attention their relationship garnered, but neither of them was the same person anymore.

"No joke though, you sucked ass today, bro," Clayton said, drawing glares from all the guys for breaking the no-cursing rule. "Sorry, just got back. But nine runs in five innings? That's garbage."

"It's great you're home to add to the insults," Corey said.

"I wasn't insulting you; I was *describing* you." A burst of laughter flew around the table. "If they're going to pay you the big bucks and give you the top spot in the rotation, you can't blow multiple games in a row. You're lucky Marc Demoda's shoulder is shot; otherwise, he'd have his top spot back." Clayton laughed and pulled Beth onto his lap. The baby of the bunch, pushed everyone's buttons simply because he could. "Speaking of Marc Demoda…"

Danny, his constant partner in crime, chuckled with Clayton this time.

Beth's glare tore through Clayton. "No, we weren't."

"I never said *you* were." Clayton's blue eyes sparkled as he smiled evilly, which played weird on his storybook prince face.

"I ran into the frogger last night, and he's in a real mood. Left the bar alone, and by choice." Corey shook his head.

"Hear that? Marc went home alone last night." Danny waggled his eyebrows, ignoring Beth's reprimanding look. A wiser man would have shut up, but wisdom wasn't something the twenty-four-year-old possessed.

"Why does Beth care?" Corey asked, finishing his beer before opening one from the middle of the table. "You can't have suddenly joined the many women in the world who lick the shoes he walks in, can you?"

"She's not licking his shoes; like his mouth," Clayton said, earning a slap on his head.

"How is it that *you* know what this is all about, and I'm in the dark? I live here. You just got home," Corey complained, looking from Clayton to Beth.

"Yeah, and she normally likes to gossip like an old lady." Will smirked, scratching his nose with a particular finger. "I thought you told me nothing was going on between the two of you?"

Will had shut the water off after that embarrassing first day. The heat crept up her cheeks thinking about it.

"I dropped by the beach this evening and Danny was walking one Marc Demoda home after our girl tried to drown him. Marc seems to think …" Clayton and Danny both started laughing, but silence settled over the other men at the table.

"I'm not drunk enough for this," Corey said, guzzling his beer before adding. "You can't seriously be interested in him?"

She wasn't. At least she didn't want to be. But once she'd gotten home and dried off, she wasn't so annoyed about Marc hijacking her run. In fact, she could almost say it had been— fun? But she wasn't admitting that to anyone in this room.

"He fixed my dishwasher, and he played baseball with the boys, and he interrupted my run today. That's it."

Will, ever the adult, asked pointedly,

"But you tried to drown him?"

"He made some stupid bet he could race me back to his house. I let him fall in a hole so I'd win, and he tossed me in the ocean as payback. I had to lay him out after that," Beth mumbled. The boys all hooted and hollered, and she couldn't help but smile. Yeah, overall, it'd been fun. "My father will flip, so no mention of it tomorrow."

"I love that you took him down." Corey smiled.

"That's because *you* can't get out of his sexy Hispanic shadow," Danny said, doing a little cha-cha shoulder shake. "Me, I can appreciate his talent on *and* off the field—right?" He wiggled an eyebrow at Beth again as she sighed.

"You know you guys are my brothers, you could act like it," Beth said, to another round of laughter.

"Does he know who you are?" Will asked, too responsible to miss the obvious.

"Doubt it." Beth sighed. "I keep telling him I'm not interested, but he won't back off."

"Maybe you're giving him some mixed signals?" Danny raised his eyebrow at Beth. That was a fair point, but not one she would concede.

"And I told him both when he was here for dinner and when—"

"Wait, he was here for dinner too?" Corey interrupted, and Beth wished she could call the words back.

"Mandy invited him."

"So you invited him over for dinner, played baseball with him, and let him run with you, but you don't understand why he isn't giving up. If I were him, I'd take that as a green light every time." Danny raised his beer to point it at her.

"Snake in the grass! I told him multiple times I wasn't interested. He's not listening."

"Beth? What's the deal here?" Will asked, reaching over and tugging on one of her curls. "You know if you're dating, we want to meet him. We need to give him the 'we will castrate you' speech."

"I gave him a warning tonight, very brotherly," Danny assured Will, who didn't look convinced. Danny was Will's opposite and much better at BS than warnings.

"One favor, Beth?" Corey looked pleadingly at her, sitting perched on Clayton's lap.

"What?" she asked suspiciously.

"I get to be the one to tell him you were mine first." Corey laughed.

Beth snorted. "Jerk."

"Welcome back, Elizabeth Campbell. We missed you the last few years," Danny chuckled.

"Life is about to get a heck of a lot more interesting boys," Clayton added.

"You guys stink," Beth mumbled.

"You know you love us, doll. And if you say the word, we'll get him to back off," Danny said, laughing with the rest of them. But they meant it. If Beth wanted them to, they would get rid of her Marc problem for her. All she needed to do was ask.

So why wasn't she asking?

6

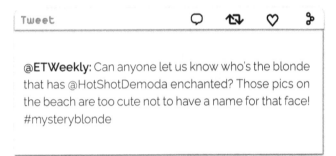

BETH'S CRAPPY MORNING started with a sharp kick in the face courtesy of her daughter. Since some of the guys stayed over and stole her bed, she'd fallen into Mandy's bed around three and it wasn't even seven yet, but it was time to start her day. She took a quick shower before throwing on a tank top and sweats.

Five kids needed breakfast, and they all needed to get ready for church. Her parents were coming from DC to meet her and her sister, who had returned home from LA last night. After the service, her brothers, a few friends, and her family were coming over to celebrate Mandy's third birthday. That meant she had to get the kids ready for church and get the kitchen cleaned up from last night.

When the doorbell rang at eight, both the disturbance and the fact that Clayton didn't shut the gate when she kicked him out a half-hour ago irritated her. He stayed over last night but he was definitely going to go back and get ready for church like the rest of them. If she had to suffer through extra time with her father, so did they.

"Steve, can you get the door? Everyone else to the table. We need to get breakfast." Beth headed for the kitchen for another cup of coffee. "What do we want to eat?"

"Bagels," Steve called across the room.

"Steve, I don't have time." But the words died on her lips as Marc walked into the house.

"I brought breakfast," he announced, handing Steve a brown paper bag. "There's a dozen. I wasn't sure how many kids would be here since they multiply every time I come."

The kids seated at the table cheered as Steve brought the bag over. Each quickly dug in, fighting to get their bagel, none of them the least bit bothered by Marc's unexpected appearance. They were used to their uncles showing up uninvited. So was Beth, but Marc wasn't family.

His dimples flashed as he stepped toward her. Beth's eyes were bloodshot from too much beer and not enough sleep. She didn't have a drop of makeup on, was wearing sweats, and hadn't bothered to brush her hair. And Marc was standing there in khakis and a polo shirt, looking bright-eyed and perfect. She suppressed a groan; she wasn't even wearing a bra.

"What are you doing here?"

"It's good to see you too," Marc said with a chuckle, but when she rolled her eyes, he added, "I thought we should talk, and I brought you this." He passed over a bag, and she eyed him suspiciously. "I felt bad about your phone." He shrugged like it was no big deal.

Inside the bag was a box with a picture of the latest iPhone. Beth hadn't thought about her phone this morning, except to be grateful it wasn't beeping with a new text message every minute.

"I brought your old one with me last night when I got this. Since I'm me, one autograph convinced the guy to switch the old crap phone for the new one on your plan and set up your phone. It's good to go." Again, this didn't seem like a big deal to him.

"How did you have my phone?" Beth set the bag on the counter and rubbed her forehead a few times with her fingers.

"Danny let me take it last night when I told him I wanted to replace it."

"Uh, thanks," Beth said, not sure what to make of this. He was openly admitting to stealing her phone and hacking her account.

"I didn't notice Twitter on your phone or Instagram?" Marc said hesitantly. Apparently, he didn't have issues with being nosey either.

"I don't do social media. The idea of trending is my worst nightmare," Beth said a bit too sharply, and Marc swallowed hard. Snapping wasn't fair. "I appreciate you did this." And she did; nosiness aside, it was nice of him to take care of it for her. "I wouldn't have thought you'd bother." Everything she knew about Marc told her he was so self-absorbed that he wouldn't have remembered that he ruined her phone, let alone spent the time and effort to replace it.

Marc stared at her before leaning his muscular forearms onto the counter, bringing his offended eyes down to her level.

"Exactly how did I give you such a poor opinion about me? Was it fixing your dishwasher, cleaning up the dishes after dinner the other night, or playing baseball with the kids? I know I wasn't at my best when I asked you out, but I apologized."

He laid the guilt on heavy. And really, this Marc didn't jibe with the guy the media made him out to be.

"I'm sorry," Beth said. "I know it isn't fair to believe everything you hear about someone." She'd grown up knowing that.

"No, it's not. I can't control all the tweets about me," Marc agreed. Then he walked over to the breakfast table.

She watched as he joined the kids' laughter and helped break her niece's bagel in half. Steve told Marc about his game the other night and his improved fastball; Marc praised him and said maybe they could work on it again sometime. Who exactly was this man?

"Marc?" Beth called. He looked over at her from where he was squatting next to her nephew, scraping some cream cheese off his bagel. "You want some coffee?"

"That would be nice." His dimpled smile implied forgiveness. He finished the bagel before coming back to her. She handed him the coffee and pulled the creamer out for him, but he shook his head. "Black is good." He took a sip.

"Thank you. For the bagels *and* the phone. It was more than you needed to do." Beth smiled at him, and he looked at her over the top of his coffee cup.

"Why do I feel a 'but' coming on?" he asked.

"Because right now I'm not in a good place to have a high-profile relationship." For a split-second, guilt flashed across Marc's face, but he recovered.

"I'm not looking for that. We can keep this to ourselves— more like a casual thing." He smiled at her like it was that easy.

"Marc, you're a paparazzi favorite. You are the definition of high-profile. Nothing about you could be on the QT," Beth sighed in exasperation, and Marc glanced away, not meeting her eyes. She didn't want to feel guilty for disliking his fame, which at this point, he might not even be able to control. Fame took on a life of its own quickly. "When was the last time you had a casual quiet fling?" Beth asked, giving him a chance to prove her wrong.

"Define fling." Marc's mouth twisted into something that was almost a smile.

"Same woman for a couple of weeks."

Marc took another sip of his coffee. "Never. But I've never wanted that either."

Beth narrowed her eyes. "What is it exactly you want from me?"

He muttered something—it might have been, "damned if I know," but she wasn't sure. Marc set his coffee mug back on the counter.

"My best guess," he said finally, "is that you make me work for everything. No one else ever has. I have to work to get your attention, and when I finally do, I feel like I earned it and I like that. Honestly, I keep figuring you're going to start falling all over me, and then I'll move on, but you don't, and neither do I."

Beth laughed.

"You don't have the competition of the game anymore, so you're looking for a challenge somewhere else?"

At least he had the decency to look embarrassed by her question.

"Thank you for coming over and for replacing my stuff, but Marc, you'll never be able to hide who you're dating." She knew that firsthand. Marc met her eyes, then glanced away again. "I'm sure there's another woman out there who isn't interested in you—why don't you make it your mission to find her? I have to get the kids dressed, teeth brushed, hair done, and shoes on to meet my parents, and now I only have about an hour to do it."

"I'm here, and I can tie a tie and a shoe. Let me help." Marc flashed his dimples at her again and Beth sighed. "I heard you loud and clear: I'm the last thing you need. But it looks to me that maybe a second set of hands is something you could use. Let me help you get the rugrats ready, and then I'll go."

She wasn't sure why he wanted to stay. She almost thought he might be buttering her up for something, but Beth couldn't imagine what, so she gave in. He cleaned the table, then wiped hands and faces so they were no longer white with cream cheese while she brushed the kids' teeth. She helped everyone get dressed; Marc tied the three boys' ties, helped them with their belts, and everyone with their shoes. She did the girls' hair in braids, and he did the boys' hair. They were finished, and it wasn't even nine o'clock.

Man, it was nice to have another set of hands around.

"We make a pretty good team," Marc said as she walked him out the door.

"We do," Beth said as she shut the door behind her, leaving the kids inside. She leaned against the side of the house as she spoke to him. "But Marc, I don't think you're hearing me. I'm flattered by the attention, but..."

His hand came up and rested next to her head as he leaned in closer, blowing her train of thought. A mix of soap and warm-blooded male filled her nose as he invaded her personal space.

"But?" Marc encouraged, and put his other hand on her shoulder. He let his fingers rub her tense muscles, and her heart pumped faster. God, did those warm hands feel good. *Million-dollar hands*, she reminded herself.

"I'm not interested in anything starting between us." She sounded a little breathless as his thumb moved up her neck to find her pulse, which was now racing. A warm tingle filled her belly as she savored another breath of him.

"So you've said." Marc leaned closer as his hand moved behind her neck. "I'm just not sure I believe you."

She tried not to moan as he softly kissed her neck. Little electric pulses danced across her skin anywhere his lips touched. She knew she shouldn't move to give him better access, but when he nudged her head back, she did. His jaw was smooth like he'd just shaved, and it glided against her neck as his warm lips moved to find her pulse once more. She swallowed another moan. This needed to stop. Now.

"Marc, wait," she murmured breathlessly.

"Wait, what?" he asked, pulling back slightly and resting both hands on the wall on either side of her face.

"I know I'm sending mixed signals, but I mean it when I say this can't happen." Beth didn't want to have to tell him who she was. And dating him would cause a media frenzy she was desperate to avoid.

"Why?" He was so close. His breath danced on her lips as he spoke.

"Does it matter?" Beth asked warily.

"Probably not." A smirk touched the corners of his mouth. "Please."

His brown eyes burned into her, making her feel like she wanted to squirm.

"Kiss me, and I'll leave," he said finally.

"What?"

"I want your mouth. I want to feel it on mine, and after that, if you want me to go, I'll go." He raised his eyebrows, sending her a look full of challenge. Did he think if she kissed him, she'd melt, and tell him she would see him again? She could kiss him and then tell him to go. Maybe a good kiss would get him out of her system.

He waited, putting the ball in her court. She lifted a hand, cupping his smooth cheek before reaching behind his neck, pulling his face towards hers. That was all the encouragement he needed. He took possession of her mouth with his. His palm slid to her hips, angling his body closer as his lips moved softly against hers, coaxing her to open for him.

The second her lips parted, and her tongue touched his, he opened his mouth with a groan, and his tongue moved in search of hers. The kiss quickly went from soft to hot and wet. With sweeping motions, his tongue teased her, driving up her heart rate. Beth's breathing became rough. His hand moved down to find her breast, possessing it like it was his, like he had every right. His thumb moved slowly back and forth over her breast through the thin cotton of her shirt and the throbbing beat deep inside her. She dropped her head back and couldn't help the moan that escaped. He quickly took advantage of her exposed neck, moving his lips down before nipping on her shoulder.

"God, Beth, I want you. It's not about the challenge. You're amazing," Marc said into her neck before he moved back to her mouth. He deepened the kiss, devouring her like he was starving.

His touch ignited a fire in Beth. It had been so long since she'd felt this way about someone. Desire swept hot through her, making her forget where they were. She yanked his shirt from his waist and pressed against the stiff muscles of his abs, which she had been imagining ever since he'd tossed her over his shoulder last night. His warm skin was made rough only by a small line of hair leading down to his belt. He shuddered under her hands, then pushed her hard against the side of the house, grinding his hips into her pelvis. The level of passion and desire coursing between them was unlike anything she had experienced before, and she let herself ride its wave.

"Elizabeth!" A familiar voice called her name, the snapping of cameras echoing behind it.

She pulled back, but Marc planted his hands firmly on her waist and twisted, blocking her from the people and cameras coming up the driveway. He moved smoothly, with an expertise that said he'd done this before. Beth hadn't heard any of the three cars pull into the driveway. She'd been utterly oblivious.

She rested her head against Marc's chest and groaned. How had she let this happen? What was she thinking? Right—she wasn't. His lips had touched hers and thought went right out the window.

"Please play along until we get inside." Beth heard the desperation in her own voice. Marc looked down with half-lidded eyes and nodded before wiping his lips with a fist. "I'm sorry," she mumbled before pushing him away and turning to the group in front of her.

"Daddy!" Beth said. She walked down and threw her arms around her father, the current secretary of state.

"Marc," Beth said softly. On the off chance her father hadn't instantly recognized Marc, he'd be able to drop his name for the reporters behind him.

"Marc, my boy, good to see you. I was so glad when Elizabeth told me you would join us this morning." Her father smacked Marc's back in a friendly gesture that suggested the two men knew each other well.

No one would have guessed that the secretary of state was about to rip into his daughter as soon as they got through the door.

7

THE DOOR SLAMMED shut, leaving most of the secretary of state's staff outside with the media he'd brought with him. Marc stood in Beth's family room with both of her parents glaring, surprisingly, not at him but at her.

"Golden doughnuts!" her father said, and by the tone Marc gathered it was a curse. "What were you thinking?"

"You said you were meeting us at church," Little Miss Feisty yelled right back. She was hot when she got worked up, especially now—standing there looking all rumpled, her lips swollen from his kisses.

Focus.

"That was before you blew up on social media, sweetheart." Even though he was calling her 'sweetheart,' the secretary's tone suggested he wasn't feeling a lot of love toward his youngest daughter.

"What?" Beth asked, her face white as snow.

"Your picture started floating around last night," her father snapped as he flashed his phone at her.

Marc knew about the photos trending on social media. He'd seen them even before Austin had called asking about the 'mystery woman' on the beach hanging onto Marc. The photos looked a lot flirtier than reality: Marc running so close almost no space existed between them; her face snuggled against Marc's ear; him carrying Beth over his shoulder. But social media did that. Marc had come over this morning to tell her about it, but had hesitated to bring it up after learning that it was a nightmare for her.

Beth shot him an accusatory glare.

Her father continued. "Last night it was 'who is this girl,' but this morning, someone realized you're my daughter." The tone of his voice indicated that at the moment, he wished she wasn't.

Marc didn't know they had identified her in the photos. He checked his pocket for his phone before remembering he'd left it charging in the car. Austin was probably blowing it up.

"And now the speculation about you two has taken on a life of its own."

Marc was trying to keep up, but since his blood supply was only slowly moving back to his brain, he found it difficult to process. It was like he had suddenly lost forty IQ points. Beth was a *Campbell*. The Campbells were one of the wealthiest, most well-connected families in the country. Not to mention that Edward Campbell was the secretary of state.

Holy shit.

On top of that, Campbell was the person most likely to be the Republican vice-presidential candidate in this coming election. Everyone knew what going to country fairs meant.

No wonder she'd said he was the last thing she needed. Politicians like her father didn't need scandal, and Marc's life had been full of it lately. Now, between the pictures of them from last night and whatever the press got outside…

"Fuck," he groaned.

"Fudge or fig, please; this is a cuss-free zone. You could also go with 'snake in the grass' or Edward's favorite, 'golden doughnuts,'" Beth's mom whispered. She smiled at Marc; clearly years in politics had taught her never to let her feathers get ruffled. "Elizabeth is a real stickler about it. I'm Mary Campbell." She held out her hand, smiling. It might have been the perfect blond bob or maybe the flattering skirt suit she was wearing, with big pearls around her neck, but something made him think she was too perfect to get upset.

"Marc Demoda," he mumbled, watching the father and daughter as he shook the woman's hand.

The secretary and Beth didn't seem to have taken the same *never let your feathers get ruffled* course. He wanted to step in and shield Beth from her father, but he didn't feel it was his place.

"We met two years ago when you won the World Series," Mary said politely, as if they were making small talk at a cocktail party instead of her having walked up on Marc humping her daughter against a wall. The thought made him groan inwardly.

"I'm sorry about this; maybe I should say something to…"

Who should he say something to?

Damned if he knew.

"No. Edward's people—Paul, particularly—are spinning the story as we speak. But you'll probably want to call your publicist." She said this as if it were no big deal. She'd already moved on to spin mode while he was still in *oh my fucking God* mode.

Beth's father was the secretary of state.

Holy shit.

There was no way this could be a quiet thing like he'd wanted. Austin was going to kill him.

"What is it with you, baseball players, and political campaigns?" Beth's father yelled, and her entire body suddenly seemed to shrink. "Do you *need* to embarrass me?"

"No." But her voice was so quiet he barely heard.

Just when he thought his world couldn't get any stranger, someone stomped down the stairs.

"What's all the yelling? Do you people know it's not even nine o'clock?" The voice sounded vaguely familiar but with his brain haze, Marc couldn't place it.

"It would figure you'd be here, since Elizabeth's showing the world how much she loves to sleep with idiots," Secretary Campbell said, not even looking at the man.

Marc felt like he'd had the wind knocked out of him when he saw Corey fucking Matthews standing in his boxers in Beth's living room. Corey Matthews, the man currently in Marc's spot in the Metros' rotation. The guy who'd been nipping at his heels for years. The guy who, a year ago, got into one car while Marc got into the other and ruined his life.

"I'm the one who slept in her bed, and I assure you, Ed, I'm not an idiot," Corey said, with no respect in his voice at all.

"Butt out," Beth said, not looking glad to see him.

"Wow, someone's got her panties in a knot. Did I not let you get enough sleep last night?" Corey wrapped his arm around Beth's shoulder, which made Marc's stomach curl with disgust. Beth had said she wasn't in a place where she could date—she hadn't mentioned this fucking guy.

"Sugary game yesterday." The secretary smirked at Corey, who sighed like he'd heard it before—and considering his performance lately, he probably had. Marc had watched enough of Corey's last few games to know two things: Corey had release point problems; and he didn't know the root of his bad pitching or how to fix it. "Stay away from the windows. The media's outside; I don't need you on top of this mess. And I would prefer you to keep your sleeping arrangements with *my daughter* to yourself."

"Little faith, Ed. I don't want to expose my hideout. Where's Mrs. C?" Corey turned to find her, and stopped in mid-spin. "Demoda," he sneered before turning back to Beth. "I need coffee."

"And I told you to butt out," Beth said, but there was no fire behind the comment.

Corey's face softened, then he reached out, looking at her with an expression that said a thousand things. But Marc didn't know what they were. Beth shut her eyes, and Corey pulled her into his arms.

Secretary Campbell started to say something, but Corey cut him off.

"Back off," he snapped, putting himself between Beth and her father. Marc felt a surprising stab of jealousy. He couldn't understand why he wanted to be in the middle of whatever this mess was. Even more surprising was the fact that her father said nothing else. Marc wanted to know what the hell was going on, and he was about to ask when he got another punch to the gut.

"Uncle Corey!" Steve bounded out of the kitchen, straight into Corey's arms.

This was Uncle Corey? Marc had heard Steve say the name before; he should've realized it as soon as Corey had walked down the stairs, but it hadn't clicked. His focus was on the fact that Corey had slept with Beth last night, so he'd missed the obvious.

She'd slept with Corey last night, then kissed him this morning while Corey was in her bed. What kind of woman does that?

"Hey, Slugger," Corey said with Steve in one arm and Beth in the other, the picture of a perfect fucking family. It made Marc want to slam his fist through a wall.

"I knew you'd be here! I wanted to wait up last night, but Mom said I had to go to bed after they pulled you," Steve said.

"Why don't you take Uncle Corey into the playroom to see Mandy?" Beth said, taking a deep breath and signaling Corey to go with Steve. He nodded and let go of her, then headed into the playroom. Steve shut the door behind them.

There was more than sex going on between her and Corey. Watching the two of them, that was clear. And it pissed him off that she'd never mentioned it. He didn't take other people's women.

"I should go." Marc turned to leave.

"Oh no you don't," Secretary Campbell demanded in a voice that made it sound like a law. "You're staying. We'll find a way to make this work for you."

"Please, he doesn't have to stay," Beth huffed. All the sass had disappeared, and Marc stood looking at a sad, tired woman.

One who had lost too many fights with the man standing next to her, a guy who pretended online to be a family man, but cared little about his daughter.

"Go upstairs and get dressed," her father demanded, and Beth spun on her heel and bounded up the stairs. "Something conservative!" he yelled, shaking his head.

"She's getting better," Mrs. Campbell said, walking toward her husband.

"If she wasn't so damn impulsive. She has the right to date, but I thought she was past this," he grumbled, looking up the stairs. Then he turned to Marc. "How long have you been sleeping with my daughter?"

Marc narrowed his gaze. Beth had just told him they weren't sleeping together. Did he listen to anything his own daughter said? Did he even care?

"And don't bother giving me the whole *you love her* routine. You let me chew into her, and you had nothing to say about another man sleeping in her bed."

"I'm not sleeping with her, but with all due respect, even if I were, it's not anyone's business but hers and mine." He paused before begrudgingly adding, "And I suppose Corey's."

"Corey's?" The secretary looked blankly at Marc. Did this man not understand the concept of another man's woman? For fuck's sake, he was a married man.

"If my girl was f—sleeping with someone else," Marc stumbled, "I would want to know. But I don't take other guys' girls. If she had mentioned being involved with Corey, I would have backed off. Now that I know, I'm gone."

"Oh no you're not," Corey said from the doorway. "You won't do this to her again. She won't be that girl, because she's *not* that girl."

"You don't know—" Secretary Campbell began, but Corey cut him off again.

"I have a lot better idea than you do," Corey snapped. "I know the entire story and not Twitter's version." Corey shook his phone before turning to glare at Marc. "Demoda, she told you plenty of times to back off. Instead, you flaunted her on Twitter. So man up. Go to church, come back here, smile for all the pictures at Mandy's party. And Ed, don't bother saying there won't be coverage of your granddaughter's party. You've been promising all twenty million of your followers pictures of it all week. I'll stay out of the way. I've had years of practice."

Years? He couldn't have been dating Beth for years. Corey might be discreet about his love life, but Marc knew there were women. If he'd been with Beth for years, then he was cheating on her. And that pissed Marc off. But before he could speak, Corey continued.

"Demoda, you can't handle more scandal right now. Nothing better than Mr. Screw Anything Female and the secretary of state's daughter getting hot and heavy for the camera." Corey ran a hand roughly through his hair and glared. "She deserves better, Demoda, even from you. But the fact of the matter is that you need to change your image, which is probably the whole reason you're here. Right?"

Edward Campbell turned to Marc with a raised eyebrow, looking more hopeful than upset.

"Well, yes, I do, but—" He wanted to explain that he hadn't even known who Beth was until about fifteen minutes ago, and he certainly had no intention of using her for anything, but a new voice cut him off.

"Okay, that's settled."

Marc turned to see a short, stocky guy putting away a cell phone and looking pleased with himself. *What the—who is this guy, and when did he get here?*

Before he could ask, the man said, "You were right, Corey. It looks like Elizabeth will help Mr. Demoda with his image problem. We'll have to work out something with the reporters outside, but it shouldn't be too hard. We have all their cameras and cell phones already. We'll let them have family shots this afternoon and answer some questions." He was talking too fast for Marc to get a word in. "We'll get our story out. We'll need a lot of confidentiality agreements. We can work out the paperwork for—"

"Who the hell are you?" Marc finally blurted.

"Paul," he said, like that explained everything. "You two will be in an exclusive relationship as far as the public's concerned. What goes on behind closed doors—well, none of that should reach the media. Two months should give the public enough time to have forgotten when the relationship started. If Secretary Campbell gets the VP nod, we can always reevaluate." Paul's eyes cut back to Beth's dad. "And having an in with the Latino vote would put you over the top."

This tool had to be fucking kidding. "I'm sorry, *what?*"

"Welcome to politics, Demoda," Corey said smugly. "You're now a commodity. Make sure that what you provide is worth more than what you cost."

"Don't be ridiculous." Beth's dad turned to him with a fake smile. "Marc, I'm sure this arrangement will meet both our needs."

Marc wasn't sure what he was more surprised by: that no one cared what Beth thought about pretending to date him, or that Corey didn't seem bothered by the idea. Marc was dead sure that *he* wouldn't have the nerve to speak for any woman in his life without asking her opinion, nor did he have any delusion that if he were dating someone, there would be a third fucking person in the relationship.

"What makes you think Beth would agree to any of this?" Marc demanded. He could give two fucks about Corey, but he cared about whether Beth was okay with what these idiots had come up with. He could see the value in it for himself, but he couldn't imagine why Beth would do it.

"Elizabeth won't have a choice," Secretary Campbell answered, not making Marc feel any better about their plan.

"You and I need to talk, Demoda," Corey said, heading for the stairs as if he expected Marc to follow. "I also need pants, and I'll loan you a shirt for church."

Finally, they could have it out. But Corey said nothing as they walked up the stairs. He knocked on a closed door and whispered, "Beth?"

"You better be getting your pants," she answered.

Corey opened the door and motioned for Marc to follow. Marc got three steps into the room before he stopped short. Beth had her back to the door, and was wearing two off-white thigh highs while she flipped through her closet. The scrap of cream-colored lace that was supposed to be panties didn't nearly cover her perfect heart-shaped ass. The lace rested nicely along the tops of both cheeks, contrasting with her pale skin. He'd always been a lingerie guy; nothing was hotter than a great body in a few pieces of lace. And Beth was just that, but she didn't know he was there. He should leave, but his feet seemed bolted to the floor, and he couldn't take his eyes off the woman standing across the room.

"Which dress—green or blue?" Beth asked.

"Pissed, huh?" Corey replied, barely looking at Beth before grabbing his pants off the top of her dresser and sliding his legs into them. He didn't bother to mention that Marc was in the room.

"You know I'm pissed. It would have been nice if my father had called," Beth snapped, but she didn't turn around. "Which dress?"

"Green." Corey grabbed his watch off the nightstand and clipped it on. "So turns out I'm not the one trending this morning, huh?"

"Don't make me invoke the counter rule," she replied.

Beth stretched up on her toes, her leg muscles tightening as she reached for a dress hanging on the top bar of her closet. He swallowed his groan seeing a sexy little mole on her left cheek. Not only did she have beautiful legs and a perfect ass, but the curve of her back was sexy, and he loved how her neck looked when her hair was up. Right now it was in a French twist, which was supposed to be classy. But dressed like she currently was, it was more erotic. All he could think about was pulling the pins out and letting her shake all that hair loose, preferably while she straddled him, back arched, head thrown back—

Stop it. She's Corey's.

But he couldn't figure out why Corey would invite him up here. Marc's life hadn't included a girlfriend since early college, but he still knew he damn sure wouldn't parade his girl around in her panties for another guy.

"Want to tell me what happened this morning, or do you want me blindly on your side?" Corey asked, now scrolling through his phone.

"Blindly supporting me is good," Beth said, finally pulling the dress down. Then she spun around.

Two minutes ago, Marc would have said the view couldn't get any better, but seeing Beth from the front, he knew that would have been wrong. His gaze took in the lacy bra holding two round breasts and trailed to the V of her thighs before heading back up again.

"Cor!" Beth shrieked, pulling the dress in front of her and heading to the bathroom. "You snake in the grass!"

"What?" Corey said innocently, but he smiled. "Come out when you've got the dress on and I'll zip you."

"You're ridiculous. I swear, sometimes I hate you," Beth called from the bathroom. Corey continued to laugh silently.

"When Paul asks what color, make sure you tell him cream," Corey said.

"Paul?" Marc asked, rubbing his eyes as he sat down on the bed. This morning sucked. If someone had asked him last night if getting his hands on Beth's breast and seeing her in lingerie would qualify as sucky, he would have laughed at them. But last night, he would have assumed that if those two things were going to happen, he would be fucking her, not sitting on her bed with her boyfriend.

"The guy who works for her father," Corey replied. "When she walks into the room, he's going to be looking at her like he can see through her clothes, and then he'll ask what color."

"You tell him what she's wearing under her dress?" Marc hissed. Why should some random douche know anything about Beth's panties? He'd always thought of Corey as a sensitive guy, but it turned out he was one shitty boyfriend. Corey should punch that fucker in the nose, not tell him about his girlfriend's panties.

"Corey, what did you want to talk to me about?" Marc sighed.

"Nothing. I just wanted you to see what she was wearing under her dress." Corey chuckled. Marc would have lost his shit right there, except Beth came back into the room.

"Corey, you're not funny. Now zip," Beth demanded as she turned to open the armoire. Marc got another small peek at that great back while she reached for what looked like pearl earrings. Corey zipped her dress and then pulled out her pearls, stringing them around her neck. They moved in sync, as if they'd done this before.

But something was missing between the two of them. When they spoke, it was like a brother and sister bickering. But Marc had a sister too, and *he* didn't come into the room and help her dress, that was for sure.

"It's not like he hasn't seen more than that," Corey said, and Beth spun on him.

"Why doesn't anyone believe that I'm not sleeping with him!" she all but shouted at Corey, who simply raised his eyebrows. And then she said quietly, "Oh, of course."

What were they talking about? He wondered if everyone in this damn house spoke in code to annoy him or if that was just a side benefit.

"I'm going down to see if I can charm the pants off that redhead on your father's staff while you guys are at church, so change the sheets this afternoon." Corey laughed as he left the room, and Beth rolled her eyes again. What the hell did she see in him?

A loaded silence filled the air as Beth slipped on her shoes, carefully not looking at him. She straightened to a stand and fiddled with a ring on her thumb. Half of him felt like throttling her, and half of him wanted to just unzip the damn dress and get her onto the bed. He vaguely remembered feeling this way last night, too. The woman was maddening. And even after all he had learned in the previous half-hour, she still twisted his gut.

"Did you know about the beach pictures?" Beth asked, unable to meet his eye.

Shit.

"Yes, but I didn't plan on leaving without talking to you about it."

She frowned.

"So, the low-profile casual fling talk was... what?" Beth asked, finally looking up to glare at him.

Marc sighed before running his hands through his hair in frustration. He should have mentioned the photos then, but he had been trying to talk her into seeing him again, and that information was the opposite of helpful. He hadn't been lying; he knew he'd have to be more careful, and he was willing to be. But none of it mattered now—because she was dating Corey fucking Matthews.

"What I want and what I can have don't always line up. But at least I was honest—unlike you," Marc accused.

Beth sighed.

"I'm sorry I didn't tell you who my father was. I thought you might like the idea of dating a Campbell or the secretary's daughter. You know—*attention.*"

That wasn't why he was mad. Especially after seeing how the 'family man' treated his daughter. He was familiar with the idea of a parent who presented a nice-guy image to the world, which didn't match what dear old dad was like at home. She had not, however, apologized for not telling him about Corey.

"That's not my issue," Marc said, staring hard.

"Huh?" Beth's confused eyes met his own.

"Were you not planning on telling me about you and Corey?" And then she had the nerve to laugh.

"Listen, I know you don't know me from Adam, but I don't make it a habit to kiss another man's woman, so I'm feeling like a... a... nothing I can say in this house," Marc said, stopping himself from cursing.

"Marc," Beth said, holding her hands up. "Corey and I aren't dating."

If she was about to give him some line about fuck-buddies or something, he'd call her a liar.

"He slept in your bed. Don't tell me you two aren't something."

Beth moved to the bed, sitting next to him. "Corey is *family,* but we aren't together. I slept with Mandy last night, and Corey slept here. Normally when Corey stays, he sleeps in one of the guest beds, but my nephews and niece were here."

"You let him in the room when you were wearing..." Marc trailed off, becoming tongue-tied in thoughts of what she had on under the dress. That image was burned into his mind: Beth stretched up on her toes, leg muscles tight, her back arch, a sexy little mole on her ass. There was something familiar about that mole, but he couldn't figure it out. He would have remembered if he had seen Beth naked before.

Beth was talking again, and he shook his head to clear it.

"Corey and I dated for a while; he believes he can take liberties because of that. I've tried to stop him, but he doesn't care what I think and really hardly looks at me, so I ignore it." Beth chuckled.

However, Marc found it very unfunny—what's more, it was something he would need to put a stop to. But it made sense. Corey showed no possessiveness toward Beth, and he happily flaunted her. But it was a 'look what I've got that you want' flaunt—something Marc had done to Corey plenty of times from the top spot in the Metros' rotation.

"So, Corey has nothing to do with why you keep insisting you're not interested?" Marc asked. "It's just your father?"

"Pretty much." She moved on quickly, leading Mark to believe there was more to it. "The thing is, no one knows that Corey and I are friends, or that he's here. We want it to stay that way," Beth pleaded.

Marc nodded in agreement. "You and Corey dated as teenagers? Steve's eight... you're twenty-eight, twenty-nine?"

"Yes. Our fathers knew each other, so we grew up together. I was sixteen when we started dating."

"I'm surprised your father let you two date after what happened with that gymnast Corey was dating," Marc said, looking at Beth. Her gaze fell to the floor. "Have you heard about those pictures of him having sex with his girlfriend— what was her name?"

"Elizabeth Campbell," Beth added helpfully, but didn't look at him.

And Marc got his fifth gut punch of the morning. He now knew where he had seen the mole before.

8

Newsweek Cover—March 2012:

Republican Presidential frontrunner Ed Campbell's campaign got into hot water this week when his daughter, Olympic gold medalist Elizabeth Campbell, released intimate photos from a photoshoot with her on-again off-again boyfriend. This killer blow came just in time to ruin the family-values candidate's chances for delegates on Super Tuesday.

Starz Cover April—2012:

Intervention: Campbell's parents beg her to stop the partying after she quits gymnastics cold turkey! Inside the gold medalist's fall from grace: alcohol, drugs, and random sex tapes.

Entertainment Weekly—April 2012:

Corey Matthews says he is not the victim, admits to consenting to release of sexy photos with Elizabeth Campbell Plus: Elizabeth disappears into rehab

IT STUNNED MARC silent, and Beth couldn't look at him. Corey always took flak in the locker room about the photos, and she knew all his teammates had seen them. They were easy to Google, as was every awful untrue article written about her. But Beth hadn't fully realized Marc had seen the photos until Corey's comment about Marc having seen her less than dressed. She fiddled with her ring. She hated being Elizabeth Campbell.

"Could you please say something?" Beth demanded. She should be used to this; it had happened ten years ago. It shouldn't wig her out when someone realized it was her, but it did. Most people didn't associate Beth Evans, widowed single mom, with Olympic gymnast Elizabeth Campbell—and clearly, Marc hadn't either.

"Ah," he stumbled, and his hand rubbed gently on her upper back. "I'm not sure of the right response. I can't lie and say I've never seen them. But I know how spin works, so why don't you tell me what actually happened?"

"Corey must have told you," Beth said quickly.

"Well, until today, the most Corey and I have ever said to each other was pretty much 'fu—fudge off.'" Marc glanced down and scratched the back of his neck.

"Yeah, he doesn't like you."

"Teammates are usually like family, but Corey and I never quite got there," he admitted, but avoided her gaze.

Corey hadn't said anything good about Marc since his trade to the Metros three years ago, but he never would explain why. And in the last year, Corey's dislike of Marc had grown—which was strange, since they didn't see each other anymore.

"Even not knowing you all that well, you don't seem like the type of person who would let someone photograph you during sex," Marc ventured before she could question him further.

"I *never* would allow that," Beth sighed.

"So… Corey didn't tell you?"

"No; he wouldn't do something like that, either."

His face said he didn't believe her. The press's story at the time had been completely inaccurate, but her father banned her from speaking up so it wasn't surprising Marc had doubts.

"Corey and I started dating before we both went to the Olympics. I won the gold for the gymnastic all-around and became America's golden girl. Especially considering the story behind my coach. She died of cancer the month before the Olympics." He looked blank, which told her he hadn't known. "I lived with her for years before she got sick. She was more of a mom to me than my mother ever was. My dad used to tout how hard it was to be away from me all the time to the media, but he would play the 'I'm letting her live her dream' card." Marc nodded, and she continued. "Corey pitched the gold medal-winning game for America's baseball team, which—along with having baseball star Orlando Matthews as a father—made Corey America's golden *boy*. The media went crazy when they realized we were dating. At first, it was cool, but that was short-lived, and soon cameras took over my life. And I had more important things to worry about than my media presence."

"Like your sponsors and appearing on Disney television?" Marc asked, smiling.

If those had been her most significant problems, she would have felt lucky. But she didn't have time right now to explain the details of all the drama of her life.

"We were in Corey's dorm room; it wasn't like our first time or anything. Oh—you've seen the pictures…" Her cheeks turned red and her stomach sank. She hated this. She dropped her face into her hands. Marc's comforting arm came around and pulled her into his warm embrace. She leaned right into the steady strength, grateful for it.

"Look, I'm not one to judge. You have some unconsented photos out there, but I think if you ask anyone who has the shadier rep, I win hands down. I'm known for making an ass of myself *and* sleeping with anything with boobs," Marc said quietly into her hair.

"Big boobs," Beth corrected with a smile.

"I don't discriminate by cup size." Marc chuckled. "Which again makes my point. So, finish the story. I figure this is why you aren't interested in getting to know me."

Something, maybe how he was listening or the feeling of his arm around her, prompted her to continue. He wasn't judging, and it *was* the reason she didn't want to get to know him.

"Tabloids pay a lot of money for dirt on big names, and nineteen-year-olds need money. Corey never imaged his room-mate would set up a hidden camera. We didn't know until the pictures came out. His roommate made a hundred thousand dollars, but got quietly kicked out of Penn State. My father was in the Senate at that point, but trying to get the nomination for president. And he would have, but the photos came out in time to ruin it. My dad's always been 'the family-values guy.'"

Marc looked skeptical, but she continued.

"So the photos killed his presidential bid, but Corey and I had to deal with the fallout. Dad wouldn't let me comment, even when the story snowballed, and when Corey tried to comment, it got spun wrong and made everything worse. He and I didn't last much longer; we talked less, then not at all for a while."

"Did you blame him?" Marc asked.

She shook her head. "There's a huge double standard in the media, especially for women. So it whitewashed his role in the story because everyone knew he was going to be a great pitcher."

"Baseball royalty," Marc said, quoting half the stories ever written about Corey.

"And politicians' families are easy targets because both sides are always willing to beat on each other any chance they get. So, because of my dad, everything became front-page news. I'm surprised you don't remember."

"I would have been knee-deep in baseball at that point, trying to make it from the minor leagues to the pros. I didn't care about anything else."

"To protect his career, my father needed the stories to make me seem uncontrollable and him sympathetic. So for months the media claimed I had a drinking and drug problem. I apparently went to rehab." Beth rolled her eyes. She'd never so much as smoked pot, but that didn't stop the stories. Marc became tense next to her, and his hand stopped its motion on her back. "None of it was true. But it took a year before they could claim I'd calmed down. By that time, I had a different name and a different life. Corey has never escaped it, though."

"I hear about it more than I'd like." Corey stood at the door, stone-faced.

"Sorry. Hard to talk about it and leave you out," Beth said, looking at him and sliding away from Marc. His hand now felt hot and heavy on her thigh.

"Not a big deal."

That was a lie. That time in her life wasn't something Beth talked about, Corey knew, and the fact that she would talk about it to Marc spoke volumes.

"Here's one of my shirts for church." Corey tossed Marc a button-down.

"Pink?" Marc raised his eyebrows.

"Beggars can't be choosers," Corey said. "Sorry to break up the love fest, but Ed wants you downstairs."

"Cor, nothing is going on with us." Beth shook her head, tired of pointlessly repeating herself.

"Guess you didn't tell her the game plan," Corey said curtly. "Come on. We'll give him some privacy to change." Corey reached for Beth.

"I don't need privacy," Marc said quickly and slapped Corey's hand away before he could grab hold of Beth. Corey glared at Marc, and then they were standing toe to toe, each glaring at the other.

"Stop. I will not become the new pissing contest," Beth declared, claiming both men's attention. "You don't like each other; neither one of you wants to explain it. Fine. But you only have to be together for five more minutes, so deal."

Corey looked pointedly at Marc before saying, "Enjoy the *loan*. I better get it back in one piece." Then, spinning on his heel, he left the room.

Beth's eyes flitted shut as Corey stormed out. He had told her last night, all joking aside, to be careful where Marc was concerned. He didn't want to explain; Beth was supposed to just trust him. Corey thought she wasn't taking his advice.

"I can't believe he thinks you'd do something as childish as ruin his shirt." She opened her eyes to see Marc, pulling his polo shirt over his head before slipping his arms into the sleeves of Corey's pink button-down.

Marc shook his head. "That wasn't about a shirt."

"Then what *was* it about?" Beth was confused. Corey hadn't loaned Marc anything else that she knew of.

"Never mind," Marc said. "And before you ask, I'm going with you to church."

"You don't have to."

"Your father already said I was," he answered as he buttoned the shirt and jammed it into his pants without undoing them. "I didn't get the impression we had a choice. Was I wrong?"

They both knew he wasn't.

Beth walked downstairs behind Marc, who headed straight over to Paul. She couldn't hear what they were talking about, but from the look on Marc's face, he wasn't happy.

"What was that about?" Beth asked when Marc returned to her.

He shrugged like it was no big deal. "The end of his obsession with colors," he said, as if that answered her question instead of confusing her more.

But before Beth could ask what he meant, her father walked into the room carrying her niece in his arms.

"The limo's out front."

"I don't ride in limos." Marc crossed his arms in front of his chest and stood up straight, highlighting just how intimidating every one of his six-foot-three-inches could be.

"You do today," her father shot back. He might be short, but he didn't let anyone intimidate him.

"No. I either take my car, or I don't go, Secretary."

"Why?" Beth asked, but Marc ignored her.

"You need to ride with Elizabeth," her father demanded as Mary entered the room with the other kids.

"I don't do limos," Marc repeated. "Beth can ride with me."

"Can I ride with you too, Mom?" Steve asked, looking up at Marc. Beth wished she could tell him he could, to save him from the lecture her father would deliver on the way to church. She met Marc's eye, and he answered.

"Sorry, only two seats. Next time I'll bring one of my other cars, and you can ride with me then." Marc patted Steve on the head. The boy looked disappointed, and Beth couldn't blame him. Then she realized what Marc said.

"Next time?" Beth asked, looking from Marc to her father. "What do you mean?"

"If you two are dating, you're going to have to do things together," her father said, as if this was an undeniable fact.

"You're dating Marc?" Steve asked, confused.

"He's a friend," she assured him. "Mother, can you take the kids out to the limo, please?" Beth waited until they were out the door. "I've explained to you, Marc and I aren't dating. I know you said he was going to church with us, and he's nice enough to come, but—"

"It has nothing to do with 'nice,' Elizabeth; don't be naïve. Besides, between the speculation circulating everywhere and what I've announced, there's nothing left to discuss. It's done. Now let's go before we're late. I don't need another scene this morning." Her father stalked out, leaving her standing with Marc.

Beth fumed. She didn't want to date Marc. And now the choice was out of her hands. She was sure it had already been mentioned on her father's website, tweeted, and posted on Instagram. The entire world knew whatever story he'd announced. She glared at Marc.

"You knew, and you okayed it?"

"He didn't ask, just told me the plan," Marc said. His gaze bounced around, unwilling to look at her, and then he swallowed.

Her eyes flitted shut. It was the story of 2012 all over again—Dad didn't ask. Her father didn't ask her if she wanted to be stuck with Marc, and he didn't ask Marc if he wanted to be stuck with *Elizabeth Campbell.*

"We can make sure this doesn't turn into a shit show," Marc said.

"Don't curse in my house."

The car was quiet as they snaked through the side streets of the small town. Marc didn't look happy, and his eyes cut to her occasionally as if he might say something, but he didn't. It was only a ten-minute drive, but the silence was grating on her before they even got halfway to the church.

"So, you don't ride in limos, or did you catch the allergy people develop to my dad?" She tried to make her voice light, hoping to cut the tension in the car.

Marc was quiet for a moment before saying,

"Last year I was a passenger in a car accident that ruined my life. Since then, I drive. I won't crash; I don't trust anyone else not to."

Beth paused. She knew little about his accident, just that it was severe, ending his baseball career. There had been casualties, she knew, but she couldn't remember if they'd been the people in the car with him or in the other vehicle.

Beth waited for him to say more, but he didn't. And her mind flicked back to the question she needed to ask.

"Marc?"

"Hmm?"

"What did my father say to get you to do this? Did he offer you something?"

She waited. He was silent for so long that she started to think he wouldn't respond—until, finally, he said, "I think arguing with him would have only caused you problems, Beth."

The statement caused a warm flutter in her stomach; he was thinking of her?

9

Tweet   💬   🔁   ♡   ⸮

> **@USWeekly:** Well ladies sorry to break so many hearts but we're getting more confirmation that Marc Demoda is off the market. Although many of you might be holding out hope he's still single until @HotShotDemoda confirms it himself

"DON'T GET OUT of the car until I come around," Marc demanded, pulling the keys from the ignition. He glanced down at his phone as another tweet came up. His cell had been vibrating for the entire drive, and each buzz made Marc's guilt grow. The screen showed twenty-seven missed calls from Austin, but Paul was supposedly reaching out to set up a meeting, so Marc ignored his agent.

Hearing Beth talk about her past had made it clear he should have been more careful, but he hadn't realized that fame was bad. There had been times things had been blown out of proportion for him, but not the same way the media had chewed into her. And even now, when the baseball teams were calling him too crazy to hire, no one was forcing him to go to rehab. Not like they'd done with Beth.

It might be possible to get her out of this, to claim they were just friends—except for the porch pictures. His brain was spinning, trying to figure out a workaround for that.

The parking lot was a circus. It reminded him of the outside of the stadium after a playoff game. The secretary was big news, and representatives of every media outlet were apparently willing to stand around hoping for a comment from the man himself.

Marc opened the door for Beth and she quickly moved ahead into the cameras, ignoring the questions they were throwing at her left and right. She was robotic—so different from the woman he knew. Marc caught up with her and placed his hand on the small of her back, propelling her through the jackals. She was a ball of tension. Once again, he wanted to protect her. He just wasn't sure how.

To make matters worse, Marc had withheld another piece of information Beth should know about. He hadn't lied: He was standing in this parking lot because he felt like he shouldn't leave the woman standing next to him. Especially knowing that ten years ago, both her father and Corey had left her to flounder in the media's harsh glare alone.

But that didn't change the fact that Marc *was* going to get something out of this arrangement. Social media would blow up with pictures of him and the secretary of state's daughter heading into her church, and that wouldn't be a bad thing. It would give him some stability, maybe. However, it was something Beth didn't want. And he didn't know how to balance those two things.

He never would have thought he'd be grateful to see three large, angry guys eyeing him like he was a son of a bitch, but when he saw Beth's brothers standing by the steps, Marc was relieved. Mostly because he knew her brothers would help her.

Once inside, Beth introduced them.

"This is Will. He runs Flip, the gym in town," Beth said, pointing to the shortest of the three giants. "You already met Danny and Clayton," she added. Then Mandy called for her, and Beth joined her daughter, leaving Marc with her brothers.

Marc looked at the men, who didn't move. They all had a few things in common. First, they were all huge—tall and well-built. Second, they were all extremely good-looking. Marc preferred ladies, but he was comfortable enough with himself to acknowledge when another guy was attractive. And third, they were glaring like all of this was his fault.

"I told you not to fuck with her." Danny seemed completely comfortable cursing in church. "This," Danny continued, shaking his phone at Marc, Twitter visible on the screen, "is fucking with her." He spun on his heel and walked away.

"She hates this." Clayton shook his head. "I don't know what happened between last night and this morning, but it has *you* written all over it." The younger guy also walked away, giving Marc a look of disgust. Boy, wasn't Marc Mr. Popular.

Will's brown eyes glared, and he said, "You'll explain what your intentions are toward my sister when we get home." Marc didn't get the impression that it was optional.

The question would be, what *were* his intentions? He didn't know. According to the secretary, Marc and Beth would spend the next few weeks dating. As in, a relationship with responsibility. His whole being rebelled against that idea. But he had to admit: This *was* an excellent opportunity to improve his image. If she agreed.

Marc followed Will into the church's sanctuary, thinking that the Evanses were finally acting like Beth's brothers. The fact that there were four more of them was slightly intimidating, and he hoped they wouldn't be at her place when he and Beth got home.

So when he pulled into Beth's driveway later that afternoon, Marc was less than thrilled about finding two *different* giants standing on her front porch. He knew instantly that these were new Evans men. Instead of suits and ties, these guys wore jeans and t-shirts, and the blond one was wearing cowboy boots—but that didn't make them less intimidating.

Marc grabbed the bag from Ambera, the bookstore where they had stopped on the way home so he could buy Mandy a birthday present. Beth had chosen the book. It was Pink-a-something, but she assured him Mandy would like it.

Beth hopped out of the car and ran into the arms of the blond giant. The masculine arms and hands that had looked so menacing a moment ago now seemed soft and careful as they wrapped around the woman, pulling her tight to his chest.

She practically screamed in the man's ear, "Luke! I didn't know you were coming!"

"I wouldn't miss my niece's birthday party. I took an early flight. Grant picked me up in Philly on his way from the farm. You're stuck with me until Tuesday." He kissed her on the cheek. 'Stuck' seemed inaccurate, as it was easy to see Beth was glad to have him here.

Beth released Luke, then hugged the other man as he kissed her gently on the forehead.

Luke tipped his chin toward Marc. "This must be the acorn."

"Be nice," Beth sighed. But Marc doubted these men were going to be any nicer than the others.

"You got a house full of people and papers to read in there, girlie. Better get moving," the other man said to Beth as he released her.

"This is Marc." Beth flung her hand in his direction. "Marc, this is Luke and Grant. And don't worry, my other two brothers aren't coming."

With that, she went inside, leaving him with the boys. Again. Marc was feeling a bit pissed that she kept stranding him with them; she had to realize they didn't like him. Was it too much to ask that she ease the tension?

"You don't do my sister against the side of a house in broad daylight. And if a picture of her less than fully clothed ends up anywhere, I will kill you." Luke slammed his finger into Marc's chest, then stormed into the house after Beth.

Wow, that's a low expectation, Marc thought. Although he had to admit the pictures from this morning didn't make him look good. And in truth, neither did his reputation.

Marc turned to Grant. "Do you have something you'd like to say? Because your brothers have all had their pound of flesh."

"They covered it," Grant said coolly. He turned and went into the house, leaving Marc alone on the front porch.

He might not understand a lot of things about the day, but one thing was clear. All the Evans brothers were very protective of their sister. And although they were technically the brothers of Beth's late husband, he didn't miss that they all left out the 'in-law' part when they referred to each other.

"Marc," a voice called, and he finally felt like he was on solid ground. "What is going on?"

"Sydney, what are you doing here?" Marc asked, spinning around.

"Well, it's my goddaughter's birthday party. But turns out, I had to be here early because Austin's going over paperwork—regarding you." Sydney's look said 'Explain—now.'

"Mandy's your goddaughter?" It all clicked together. Finally. "Which would mean Beth is Austin's friend, the one who's on the board of his charity."

This kept getting worse.

"I know we've been telling you to find a nice girl, but I wish you had asked me about her."

"I didn't know you knew Beth."

"Where to start with that?" Sid shook her head like she was trying to decide. "Austin talks to you about Helping Hands all the time; how did you not know about Beth?"

"Golden doughnuts, Sydney," Marc said, almost shouting, and she raised her eyebrows. Yeah, that sounded dumb; it wouldn't be a curse word replacement he'd use again. "You can't cuss here," Marc explained.

"I know the rule. I didn't realize you would *follow* it. You know I hate it when you curse, yet you do it around me all the time."

He sighed. "She asked me not to."

Sydney looked at his face, searching it, and Marc was beginning to feel uncomfortable before she finally said, "You genuinely like her, don't you?"

Did he? He hardly knew her to know if he liked her or not. He kicked the front porch with his toe.

"Every time I'm with her, I feel like I have no idea what's coming next, and half the time, I think I might want to strangle her." He cracked a laugh, but then paused. "But it's been fun. Even this morning—all we did was get the kids dressed, and yet I enjoyed it. Sid, I never have *fun* anymore." He didn't like the desperate tone in his voice, and was grateful that Sid ignored it.

"I saw the pictures, and you two did more than dress the kids. But maybe spending time with her would be good for you." Sid's look said, 'You're going to fall for her.'

Marc had to pull her back. "Hopefully it'll help me get a job."

She frowned, but he held the door open for her and then followed her into the house. The second he was inside, he heard them laughing.

"So basically, I'm peeing my pants, and I call Beth." Luke shook his head as the other two guys laughed. "She says, 'Well, maybe you should call her?' Yeah, that's a conversation I want to have! And Beth, being ever so helpful, adds, 'Isn't it better than morning sickness and afterbirth?'"

"I'm surprised she didn't give—" Corey stopped talking as soon as he saw Marc, and the other two men turned to follow his gaze.

Marc felt about as welcome with these guys as a discussion about afterbirth. It added to his already bruised ego; usually, men liked him on sight. To these guys, his being Marc Demoda meant nothing. That was new ground for him. He'd spent the last ten years coasting by on his good looks and ability to pitch a baseball. Like Beth, none of the Evanses cared about those things.

Marc headed for the kitchen where his friend was waiting for him. Although today, Austin wasn't his friend but his agent–an agent who also represented other people in this house and couldn't blindly take Marc's side. Not the way Corey and

Beth's brothers would do for her. And for the first time, he realized his life might lack something, although it was something he'd never wanted.

Beth was sitting at the table with Austin. She'd changed into jeans and a yellow top. She looked almost as good as she had in the dress, and he couldn't pull his eyes away. Austin was talking and pointing out a few things on the papers in front of them, but Beth's big green eyes glanced up. Marc braced himself for her anger.

"When I asked you what you wanted from me, or what my father said, you could have mentioned that he offered to help improve your image." She didn't sound mad. She made the statement as if mentioning she needed milk from the grocery store.

"You weren't open and honest either," Marc said, then cringed. His tone had a defensiveness that hers had lacked.

Beth simply nodded and looked back at the papers, not at all surprised when he didn't explain. She had to be mad, though; she'd asked him directly, and he had mentioned none of this. And she didn't know that he didn't want this, either.

He'd spent the entire time at church trying to work out a way to explain the front porch pictures without saying they were a couple, without forcing her back into the spotlight she called a nightmare. The problem was that the only other explanation opened the door to the media going after her for simply hooking up with him.

Marc slumped down at the table across from Beth. Austin pointed to different parts of the contract, and she nodded a few more times before picking up a pen. She was going to do this. Even though Beth was probably mad at him, even though she'd been telling him no ever since he'd met her, she was going to agree to 'date' him for the next two months.

Why? Her father had said she would, but why would she? He'd felt her tension in front of the camera; he knew it wasn't something she liked. Yet she was going to put herself in the spotlight—for him?

"Why are you agreeing to do this, Beth?"

She looked at Austin before turning to Marc. "There isn't another option." Her voice lacked any discernible emotion.

He scoffed. He knew he was acting like a real ass, but he didn't want her help. He wanted her to remember that this was the last thing she wanted, that she hated the media that turned her into an emotionless robot. He didn't want her to agree. He wasn't going to fake a relationship just to get good press. He'd find another way.

"I'll buy the pictures back, say everyone's wrong, and we're friends," he said. But it was a crap idea that wouldn't work. Both her parents had confirmed the "relationship" on Twitter and Instagram. Marc was reasonably sure her sister had liked their parents' posts.

"Honestly, Marc, I didn't want this, and I tried to tell you. I know I'm not your type."

"How do you know my type?" he interrupted, finally getting a glare from her.

"You parade yourself around with one brainless blond Barbie after another, and I'm not that. So you can stop insulting my intelligence by trying to convince me otherwise," she snapped, and slammed both hands on the table as she stood up.

He glared at her. She was wrong. His ideal woman wouldn't be brainless, although Barbie didn't sound so bad. But at the moment, 'Barbie' was petite, with curly blonde hair and big green eyes.

"Look, neither of us was straight with the other from the start. But at least tell the truth *now,* because we're stuck in this. So there's no reason for *you,* who wanted it from the beginning, to act like a jerk, because I will call you on that." By the end of her tirade, the calm coldness she had been tossing his way had disappeared, and the feisty woman he recognized was yelling at him.

Finally!

"Elizabeth, let's not get this off on the wrong foot," Paul said, quickly attempting to rein her in and bring back robo-girl. "Don't make a scene and ruin things."

What did it matter if she made a scene? She sure as shit had the right, Marc thought. It wouldn't even be much of a scene: No one was in the room other than people who worked for her and for Marc.

"You need to sit down and stop this; you two have a photoshoot in a few minutes. We don't want you angry because it'll show." Paul put his hand on Beth's shoulder.

Marc's fist slammed on the table, shocking everyone but Paul, who quickly stepped away from Beth.

Marc had been clear with the asshole earlier. When he had come down from Beth's room, the first thing he'd done was explain to this little fucker how it was going to be: If Paul spoke to, touched, or looked at Beth wrong, Marc would happily take him apart.

Marc continued to glare at Paul until he finally left the room. Austin cleared his throat, but his eyes said, *'What the fuck, Marc.'*

"This is a pretty simple contract: two months dating in public. You support each other; neither of you brings up past bad press. Behind closed doors, I think we need to pull back to a platonic thing. You have two months together in public, maybe longer. Anything more than friendship will clearly become messy."

It was hard to argue. There were three women in Marc's life: his mother, his sister, and Sydney. That was it. No one else lasted through an entire night. He didn't want to deal with the morning after, let alone weeks, so he purposely picked the type of woman who wanted that same thing: a one-night fling, where no one got hurt, nothing got complicated, and there were no expectations aside from a night of mutual satisfaction. He had known from the start that Beth wasn't that type, which was why he'd tried to move on from her. Even this morning, he hadn't come here looking for a serious relationship. And he still didn't want that. So what if they had some chemistry? It wasn't like he'd be unable to control himself around her. He could agree to a friendship with her like the one he had with Sydney.

"Fine." Marc grabbed three of the pieces of paper sitting on the table and started reading. He'd gotten through two paragraphs before he stopped, hearing the kids in the other room. Beth pushed back from the table and headed into the family room.

Marc put the papers down. "Can you figure out some way out of this that I missed?"

Austin frowned. "Marc, you aren't leaving her—"

"That's not what I meant," he snapped. "I'm not asking how to fix it for *me*. I'm asking if there's a way that gets *her* out of it—cleanly."

Austin's blue eyes blinked twice. "You're worried about her?"

Not exactly.

"I don't want to get stuck in a relationship, real or pretend. I told you this repeatedly. We need to walk away, her cleanly and me—well, I'll deal with whatever sh… sugar I have to," Marc said.

Sitting next to her husband, Sydney lit up like a firefly. "I was right. You're crushing hard." She smirked.

Marc huffed. "Sid, I'm not a total as—" *Fuck this cursing rule.* "Jerk. Had I known Beth's backstory, I would have…" Marc paused, trying to find the truth. "I would have done things differently. But don't get ahead of yourself. I'm trying to be decent while I run away."

"If that's all it is, then how come you're working so hard at the no-cursing rule?" Sid asked, cocking her head to the side with a smile.

"Because," he said, not understanding it himself.

"Could it be because her opinion is important to you since you care more than you're ready to admit?" Sydney asked pointedly.

"*Do* you?" Austin cut in, unable to hide his surprise.

"I don't know. But even if I walked away right now, I don't think I'd forget her. And I can't even remember the name of the last woman I slept with."

Austin frowned, but nodded. Sydney smiled as if Marc had agreed with her.

"But Beth and I already went through the 'Is there any other way out of this' stuff. And the answer is a hard no," Austin said. Marc raked a hand through his hair. He'd known that was the case. So he turned back to the contract.

"One other thing," Austin said before Marc could put pen to paper. "While you're with her, there won't be anyone on the side. If we want to fix your image, we can't have women coming out saying that you're sleeping with them. So realize you're taking an abstinence pledge. Because, even more importantly than rehabbing your image, you won't do that to *her.*"

Austin was right. This was a commitment, a two-month commitment, and he would see it through. Marc had never condoned cheating of any kind, and wouldn't start now. They were "in a relationship," so he wouldn't be sleeping with anyone else. Two months would be nothing. And Beth was right about not being his type. She was beautiful, but it wasn't like she was irresistible.

10

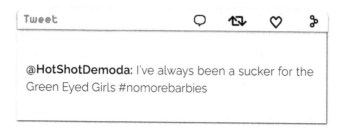

THE AFTERNOON WENT by quickly as she and Marc played the happy couple, posed for pictures, and answered questions about how long they'd been dating. Their answer was three weeks, since it had been three weeks ago that Marc had slept with another woman. He didn't know who she was, just some random girl. It bothered Beth that he couldn't even remember the woman's name, but it proved that not everything the media said about him was a lie.

This whole situation was a mockery of what she wanted. The bubble of anonymity she had found in being Beth Evans had popped. And her pretend relationship added one more job to her long list of responsibilities in life. Beth missed having someone she could share the responsibility of the family with. She missed the gentle touches of support, the ease of knowing what the other was thinking, and all the unspoken communication between a couple—the team aspect of a relationship.

For a few minutes this morning, when Marc had helped her get the kids ready, she'd felt that again. And when he'd said he was doing her father's bidding to help her, that swell of 'we're in this together' had enveloped her. But that was all a lie.

"Calming down?" Austin asked as he sat next to her.

"I'm calm," Beth said, picking at the grass as she watched the baseball game that Luke had forbidden her to play, saying it was boys-only. 'Boys-only' included Marc. Her murderous glare hadn't changed Luke's mind; he'd even suggested she play cheerleader. She was watching the game, but not cheering for either side.

Austin watched Beth ripping the grass up, then reached out and touched her hand, stopping her before she put a hole in the lawn.

"Sorry. I guess I'm agitated."

"Agitated is an understatement," Austin said. "You would have kicked him out of your house a couple of hours ago if I hadn't asked you for a favor."

She couldn't deny that. She'd been furious when Austin explained Marc's current image problems and the solution she could provide. Her feelings shouldn't be hurt, but no matter how much she would like to tell herself otherwise, a part of her had thought that maybe he *was* interested in her. And that pissed her off—at herself.

"You did well with the photographers, though. If I didn't know your current mood, I wouldn't have realized it. There were some great pictures."

According to Paul, she and Marc had done great with the media. He said everyone could feel the sparks when they were together, and the press lapped it up. When asked about his playboy ways, Marc cheekily said she'd knocked him off his feet when he first saw her and he hadn't been able to think of another woman since. She'd leaned over to him and murmured, telling him how full of it he was. He laughed and rested his forehead on hers, and the cameras clicked away. Marc had posted that picture on every one of his social media sites with a cutesy comment.

"Did you write that tweet, or was it Sid?" Beth asked.

Austin chuckled. "I take no responsibility for that. That was all Marc. I said women were going to claim sexism, but all we're getting is heart emojis."

"And about me?" Her hesitance was clear in her voice.

Austin frowned. "I promised you that if you did me this favor, if you helped him, then I would spin this to keep any mention of 2012 out of the media. Every connection, every favor I have, will go into that. Only good press for you."

Beth bit down on her lip. "I'm not sure I can fix his image."

"It's more than his image that needs fixing, Beth. I wouldn't have asked you for this if it was just about a job. He's a mess."

"In what way?"

"Marc's entire world revolved around pitching. Once he lost that, he lost himself. Apart from my wife, his friends are all either people involved in his career or baseball players. His family is different," Austin said.

She'd met Marc's parents a few times, although she didn't know them well. His father had always seemed friendly when he worked on projects for Helping Hands.

"My parents are far worse." Beth's eyes flicked to her parents.

"You've always had the Evanses and Corey," Austin said. "Marc has nothing like that, and he needs some real friends."

"So, you're asking my brothers for a favor too," Beth said. She fiddled with her ring on her thumb.

Steve was in mid-windup when Marc yelled for him to stop. He headed straight to Steve, who was holding the ball, and spoke quickly before bending down and showing him a specific spot on the ground. Steve started a windup and hit his foot on the spot Marc pointed out. Marc nodded and went back to first. Steve threw a strike, and Marc called out praise for him. Steve was glowing.

Beth didn't want to like Marc, but something about him pulled at her. Was he the self-centered ass the papers showed him to be, or was he the guy who'd bought her a new iPhone and taught her son to pitch?

"He's not a bad guy, Beth."

She smiled at Austin and stopped fiddling.

"I wish he'd been honest about this whole thing, but then again I wasn't either," she said. "Who knows—maybe after two months, he'll become like another one of my brothers."

Austin laughed beside her.

"What?" she asked.

"The sparks between the two of you could start a fire. Marc's never going to look at you like a sister." Austin shook his head.

"Marc needed something from me and didn't know how to get it other than to seduce me."

That was the part of this that really stank, because as much as she didn't want to be, she *was* attracted to Marc. The sizzle that had come through in those pictures was because he set her skin on fire when he touched her. But she was smart enough to realize she needed to ignore that. Marc was sexy and masculine, and he would have that effect on any woman. In two months, she reminded herself, he would move on to set many other women on fire. She didn't need to be anything more than his friend.

"Yeah, that sounds about right."

The sarcasm was thick in his tone, but she couldn't pull her eyes away from Marc long enough to look at Austin.

11

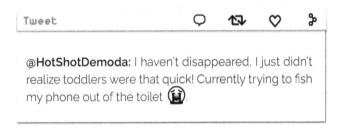

MONDAY NIGHT, MARC was back at Beth's kitchen table. He hadn't planned to spend the evening there; it had just happened.

That night as he'd driven toward his house and seen the jackals camped out waiting for him, he'd kept going. When he stayed at his apartment in the city, the paparazzi followed him a lot, but they rarely bothered him in Jersey. He was a paparazzi favorite, mostly because he was always willing to give them their picture, and it was usually a good one. Marc liked the attention, and what he should have done was wave and smile at the cameras. He should have let them follow him to Beth's so they could see he was spending time with her. He should have posted a few more tweets about how great Beth was. But Marc wasn't doing any of that. For the first time since he could remember, he'd gone twenty-four hours without posting anything.

Before he realized it, he was on his way into Beth's house. His only detour had been to pick up a box of clementines on the way because he'd heard Mandy asking for them the day before. He wasn't sure why, but like athletes, Beth's kids seemed to eat only healthy food.

Although mildly surprised and not altogether thrilled, Beth didn't give him any grief for showing up. Not only did she not bitch about him coming over unannounced, but she handed him a key fob and told him to shut the gate after himself, and said if he lost the fob, he'd replace it. Luke laughed, explaining that she'd already made him replace it twice, which involved rewiring the gate and getting everyone new key fobs.

Her house was as crazy as ever, with all five extra kids there until their parents came to collect them. Even so, the second he was in the door, he relaxed. And the little toddler, Katie, helped solve his social media problem when she took his phone and tossed it in the toilet.

Beth tried to be diplomatic and swallowed her laughter, but Luke cracked up like it was the funniest thing that had ever happened. Marc shrugged with a smile; he couldn't post crap or talk to Austin if he didn't have a phone.

Trish, Katie's mom and Beth's good friend, was the only person who got upset. It took him almost ten minutes to convince her not to replace the phone. This was apparently a recurring problem for little Katie. If anyone had mentioned that before, he might have given her his phone yesterday.

It didn't make sense that it was only Beth's house where he felt like his life wasn't over, that there were things to enjoy—he'd had nothing but disasters here. But this was the only place he'd been able to smile and relax for over a year. He could have analyzed it, but instead, he savored it.

And he wasn't the only one who felt that way, because the Evans brothers soon showed up for dinner. Beth didn't seem at all surprised, but it wasn't like she had invited them either. They'd all come unannounced, exactly like he had. That could be why she'd taken his unexpected arrival so well: She was used to it.

In groups, especially amongst men, Marc usually found himself the center of attention. But not tonight. The brothers only seemed to put up with his presence because Beth allowed it. He got the idea that if she weren't around, they wouldn't want anything to do with him. And that left him feeling empty. Not that he wished for friends—that was the type of thing Marc's father had always warned would get in the way of his baseball dreams.

As they'd done the other night, the boys took care of the dishes while Beth took Mandy up to bed. No one mentioned it; the guys knew what they were doing and fell into step like a well-oiled machine. After the dishes were done, Will got Steve upstairs, and the other boys settled around the table, dropping a few unopened beers in the center. Will returned to the kitchen before Beth did, but he didn't join them. Instead he stood, hooking his hip against the counter.

Beth padded back into the kitchen in sweats. She looked tired, but she made no move to kick anyone out.

"Beth," Will said before she could sit down. "Can we go over a few things with the gym before the beer goes to your head?" He inclined his head toward the folders he'd dumped on the counter when he had come over earlier.

"I'm not drinking, but I'm all for doing it now." Beth motioned for him to follow her into the other room, which he did, but not before grabbing the stack of folders and wrapping his arm around her shoulder. Marc wondered why he needed Beth's help with the gym he owned. He suspected it was more likely that Will wanted to get her alone for a while.

"Don't hog her for too long. I want to talk about my new car," Clayton called over his shoulder, smiling, and Danny chuckled next to him.

"You're not getting an Aston Martin. Pick a different car, and I'll be happy to discuss it with you," Beth yelled back from the other room. Why did she get to choose Clayton's ride?

"Here we go again. Clay, stop giving her a hard time about a car you don't even want. Eventually she's going to get pissed," Luke said. "We all know it."

"No, she won't," Clayton said, tipping his bottle to point at Luke. "'Cause I'm her favorite." But his smile was evil, giving Marc the impression he didn't mean it.

"That's such horse poop. We all know *I'm* her favorite," Danny said, rolling his eyes.

"Both of you are her cross to bear. I'm the favorite," Luke said.

"I don't get it," Marc said, shaking his head.

"What?" Danny said, looking at Marc as if he'd forgotten he was there.

"What's the deal with you guys and Beth? You call her a sister, but you let her boss you like a mom, and you treat her more like a friend," Marc asked. He had a sister, but he didn't feel the need to be her favorite anything.

The men looked at each other and then at Marc. It was Clayton who finally answered, not Luke.

"It's complicated." Clayton glared at Danny when he laughed. "You think it's so funny, you explain it, then."

"Simple: She's the person I don't want to let down or disappoint, and the person I know will be there for me no matter what it costs her," Danny said.

"And the person I'd cut off my left nut for before I let her get hurt," Luke added, looking directly at Marc. The implication was clear. "And there isn't one of us who feels differently about that." Another little warning, similar to Corey's remark yesterday. The one Beth had thought was about a shirt.

"What did she do for you guys?" Marc asked. His sister didn't inspire this type of loyalty.

"When we needed her, Beth was there for us without worrying about what she was giving up," Luke said. "And I know you think it was mostly for you, Clayton, but it was all of us."

Marc looked from one man to the other. They were all looking down at their beers, not saying any more. This shit hit too close to home. He needed to know what had happened. Unwilling to beg like a gossipy girl, he sat back and crossed his arms. He looked directly at Clayton, a question in his eyes, until the man finally looked up at him.

"She helped Bob raise me and our brother Joey after our mom died."

"She was seventeen!" Marc said, looking at Luke. He'd done a little googling when he'd gotten home last night and found out all about the teenager Elizabeth Campbell had been. Her coach—the one who'd died—was the Evans boys' mother. Beth had apparently lived with the family for a few years before Lynn Evans' death, although Marc wasn't certain why. But everything he'd read said the Evans family was close with the Campbells.

"Will and I were the same age as Beth when our mom died." Luke's voice carried a defensive tone Marc hadn't expected. "Our other brother Nick was already a Navy SEAL; Grant lived in Pennsylvania, running the farm; and Bob was twenty-four and hadn't lived at home for almost six years. Beth was there for the days before Mom died and through the funeral. But then she went to train with the women's gymnastics team. NBC flew us out to see her win the gold medal because it made a great story, but we left a few days later. She got back more than a month after we did. As soon as her plane landed in New York she came here, and boy, was she *pissed* that they had been lying to her. She talked to Will and me several times, and we assured her everything at home was fine."

"But they lied," Danny said. "Dad took Mom's death hard." He let that hang for a minute. "He kept up with the basics, but barely. No one smiled, no one laughed, and we stopped talking much. Bob was a cop, and he worked crazy shifts. He couldn't be around enough. So things sucked."

Danny had to stop to clear his throat, and Luke took over.

"When Beth came home, she could have looked at the misery that we had become and left us high and dry, but she didn't. She stayed and started helping Bob with everything."

"What she really did was remind us to laugh, ask about our days, make us smile, or hug us. I remember I made her a macaroni necklace, and she wore it for a week straight." Clayton smiled. "She gave up gymnastics to be there for us."

Marc remembered Beth saying she'd had a lot going on in her life when she got back; he had joked about television shows and ad campaigns. He'd never imagined she meant this. And if he had the timeline right—

"And this was when the media was saying she had drug problems and was in rehab?" he asked.

"Don't get me started on that," Danny said. The men's faces all hardened.

"But, uh, not that long after that, she and Bob got married. He fell hard for the light that is our sister," Luke said, then looked at his brothers with a pang of guilt that even Marc could see. "Dad died a couple of years later, and Beth and Bob became full-time parents for Clayton, Danny, and Joey."

"So although she's more like my sister, she was also the person at almost every 'mom event' in my life," Clayton said.

"And I always had the hottest mom at the firefighter Mother's Day brunch," Danny added.

Luke glared at them both. "What these idiots are saying is that Beth was there for us when we needed her, and we're there for her—always."

"That's what family is for," Beth said, walking in the room and settling herself right into Clayton's lap.

Will sat back down in his chair. He and Luke exchanged a long look, and Will seemed to understand what had taken place.

"You never wished you hadn't quit gymnastics?" Marc asked. He knew what it was like to be the best at something. He'd pitched multiple World Series games, winning them for the Metros. The most memorable moments of his life had been the times he'd headed down the Canyon of Heroes during the ticker-tape parades, millions of people there cheering for him.

"No. Lynn treated me like a daughter when she didn't have to, and I wanted to make sure that everything she taught me got passed on to her boys," Beth said, smiling at them. "And she'd be so proud of all of you. Well, most of the time, anyway. Sometimes you're idiots." She laughed.

"What made you stay?" Marc asked, trying not to feel guilty for prying into her life—which was something he didn't want her doing to him.

"Oh." She looked questioningly at Clayton, and he shrugged. "When I came back and walked into the house, Clayton was sitting on the sofa. He'd been crying, and I asked him what was wrong. He said, 'There's no one's lap to sit on anymore.'"

Beth wrapped her arm around Clayton's shoulders, and he pulled her up tight against him. It wasn't a sexual gesture. It was more profound than that; it was reassurance and love, something you would do if you had a scared child on your lap. All the touchy-feeliness of this family was just that: reassurance and love.

"She asked me if she was chopped liver," Clayton added. "And then sat down so I could climb on her lap."

"I think Clayton was fourteen—definitely bigger than Beth—when Bob finally said 'Enough; you're squishing her.'" Danny laughed again.

It had been a simple gesture, but to Clayton, it had apparently been much-needed stability. And she'd given it to him without question, like everything else she'd done.

They moved on to other topics of conversation, but Marc was thinking about his own family.

Marc's mom had been in the United States on a student visa when she began dating his dad, who'd been a minor league ballplayer. She was getting ready to go back to Colombia when she found out she was pregnant. Frank, Marc's father, always said he'd married her so that Marc could grow up in the US instead of Colombia—he claimed he'd done Marc a favor. But, unable to support his family on the uncertainty of a minor league baseball career, Frank quit. He gave up his dream and took a job fixing appliances until he eventually took over the business. And he resented it.

So although it was the last thing Marc wanted, when Frank had needed someone to help Glory with that same business for a few months, Marc had stepped up. And he'd hated every minute. In the last few months, Marc had come to understand his father's resentment better than he ever had before.

But Beth didn't seem to harbor any resentment toward any of these guys.

She deserved none of the bad press she'd gotten years before. From what he could tell, almost nothing that had been reported was true. And now, because Marc had done stupid-ass things for a year, he was dragging her back into the media to fix his image. None of it was fair.

"I need to go," he said, putting his nearly-full beer back on the table.

"What?" Beth asked. They all looked surprised.

"I need to go," he repeated, then got up from the table and headed out of the house. And when Beth tried to stop him and find out what was wrong, he snapped at her, then left her standing on the front porch.

He was such an ass, but he couldn't help it—even if he'd ruined any goodwill left between them.

IT WAS OUT of character, but Marc left his waterlogged phone sitting in the cup holder of his car instead of trying to dry it out or get a new one. But he didn't feel like dealing with it—or with people. Austin had called his landline, and Marc told him to post something cute about the phone going for a swim. Because he didn't want to be *Marc fucking Demoda* today.

Usually, if he wanted to shoot the shit with someone who didn't care who he was, he would text his former teammates. But during the season, they were busy playing baseball—which he didn't do anymore.

The real reason his teammates hadn't come around since Marc's injury was that he was a living reminder that they were all one twist of fate away from not playing anymore. Baseball wasn't like other sports, where you went into every game knowing it could be your last. Pitchers could play well into their forties. To see Marc, dried up at thirty-three, was a painful reminder of their own futures. Consequently, he wouldn't see the guys next off-season either. But he was sure that would be different if he were coaching.

He was stewing in front of his television, watching the Metros game, when his doorbell rang. Clayton burst through the door with pizza before Marc had even opened it all the way, and Will followed carrying beer. Neither of them had said hello or waited for an invitation.

"Nice," Will called from the open concept living area. "I wasn't sure if you would have the game on."

"Come on in, guys," Marc muttered sarcastically to the empty front porch.

"Danny'll be here in a minute," Clayton yelled. "If you leave the door unlocked, we won't have to get up."

Marc walked through his large foyer into the living room and saw that the brothers were already making themselves right at home. Both had opened a beer, and Clayton had kicked his shoes off to rest his feet on Marc's stone coffee table. Three pizza boxes sat on the table, along with a case of beer.

"Don't worry," Clayton said, making himself comfortable on the leather sectional—in Marc's spot. "He'll be good with the game too."

"What the hell?" Marc asked. These guys were unbelievable. He'd never known anyone in his life ballsy enough to barge into his house uninvited.

"The ump needs fucking glasses," Clayton said, shaking his head.

"No, I mean what the hell are you *doing here*?" Marc demanded. He looked from Clayton, in his corner of the sectional, to Will in the other.

"Watching the game. We brought shit," Will said, as if that made it okay to barge in.

Somewhere in his brain Marc realized he had done that to Beth lately, but that was different. She didn't mind; he did.

"And if Daily pitches as good as last week," Will continued, "it should be a win. Although the bats have sucked lately."

"I think they need a new batting coach," Clayton added, taking a drink of his beer. Marc agreed, but kept silent about it—acknowledging it might give them the wrong idea.

"Did Beth refuse to let you come over?" Marc asked, not sitting down. Not that he knew where to sit; the two best seats were already taken. He never invited people here.

"Nah, we can always come over. She loves to have the house full. And she's got a killer TV; you could upgrade, dude." Clayton pointed his beer at Marc's sixty-inch flat-screen on the mantel of the stone fireplace, then continued without giving Marc a chance to defend his TV. "She always loved that her house was full of my friends hanging out. If she didn't have so many rules, I'd still live there."

"I have rules, too, asshole," Will said, looking pointedly at his brother.

"He wants me to move out of his house," Clayton said, laughing. Will glared, and Marc got the idea that Will didn't want Clayton to leave yet.

"You cramp my style, bro."

"Oh, please. I understand your needs and stay at Beth's whenever you ask me to," Clayton shot back. "Though it's not like you return the favor."

"You're practically a *teenager!*" Will said, sounding like an exasperated parent.

Marc cut in with, "So why aren't you at her house tonight?" These guys got off-topic quickly. He wondered if it was on purpose, or if ADHD ran in the family. "Is she planning a Kardashians marathon or something?"

"No, she has a soccer mom meeting," Clayton said.

"Who plays soccer?" Marc thought Steve only played baseball.

"No one. Isn't that what you call it when moms go to school and talk about shit?" Clayton asked Will.

Will snorted. "She has a PTA meeting, but the babysitter is a sucker for this idiot." He tipped his chin at Clayton. "She'd let him watch whatever he wanted."

Clayton rolled his eyes. "She's jailbait, *and* the last time I saw her, she said she had a boyfriend."

"Probably hoping to make you jealous," Will teased, laughing. "See the green-eyed monster yet?"

"Oh, yeah." Clayton's voice was thick with sarcasm.

"You're here to run away from the babysitter?" Marc asked.

"Nah, he's an attention whore," Will said, and Clayton smiled unapologetically and shrugged. Marc, exasperated with their non-answers, sighed. Then Will said, "Beth said you couldn't come over. Apparently you upset her."

He winced; he'd said something about her not being the Queen of England as he stormed out. But he hadn't meant it. Were they here to yell at him?

"Yeah, so sometimes it's best to give her a break. We make her nuts," Clayton said, with another shrug. "What the fuck are you swinging at?" he yelled at the TV.

"Assholes stranded two again. I think that's about twelve in the series," Will huffed.

"So you're at my house because…?"

"I talked to Austin earlier. *Sports Illustrated* wants to do a story since I might go into the NFL draft a year early," Clayton said.

"You're not," Will corrected.

Clayton rolled his eyes. "Yeah, yeah, finish college, blah blah blah."

"Is this relevant to why you're here?" Marc asked. Trying to keep them focused on a topic was like herding cats.

"Fuck, you're uptight. Austin said you wanted to stay home," Clayton said, finally turning to look at him. "Would you rather have come to our house? 'Cause you know, we have a bigger TV too. We're slumming for your crap-ass company."

Marc stared at them blankly. What did these guys want from him? Not food, not beer, not attention; they didn't even need his damn TV.

"Are you going to lecture me about being an asshole?"

"To who?" Will asked, seeming genuinely surprised by the question.

"…Beth?"

"Were you?" Will looked blank.

Yes. He was. But apparently she hadn't told them.

"Why are you *here*?" Marc snapped at them.

"Do you want us to leave?" Clayton asked, not looking like he was getting ready to move.

"I get the feeling that you wouldn't even if I said yes." Marc sat down and grabbed a beer. He didn't know what they wanted, but they were staying, welcome or not.

Will smiled. "You're smarter than you look, dumbass."

"I'm not a charity case," Marc mumbled. Beth must have

sent them over, he figured, though he didn't know why she would. Did she think he was lonely? Because he wasn't.

"Hell to the yeah, one time you're providing the pizza and beer. We take turns, and you're fucking rich, so don't be a leech," Clayton said.

Marc gave up. It was impossible to argue with these guys. Suddenly he understood why Beth let them take over her house whenever they came by. It wasn't like herding cats, it was like herding *flies*. They went off in any and every direction; no way you could get them all out.

And they multiplied. Danny arrived before the game was in the sixth. Marc had gotten his seat back from Clayton, and the Metros had a small lead.

"I don't get what's so exciting about a game where nothing happens," Clayton complained, annoyed by the lack of action in the shutout. "At the very least, they should be able to hit each other with the balls."

"No one said you needed to watch it." Marc rolled his eyes. It was a lot harder to pitch a shutout than it looked, and Mr. 'I'm Going To Play In The NFL' should know that.

Will's phone rang. Marc assumed it was Beth checking in, but as soon as he heard Will's tone, he knew he was wrong.

"You *what*?" Will said. "You're shitting me... Fuck." He laughed. "No, you would've liked it... You should... I'd leave that part out; otherwise, you're in for one hell of a lecture." He laughed again and ended the call.

"Luke finally home?" Clayton smirked. "Texted me earlier to say he was sitting on the tarmac. He didn't seem to mind." He raised his eyebrows at Will.

"Yeah," Will said, answering the silent question.

Danny seemed to know the code too. "Are you fucking serious?" he asked.

Will shrugged. "It's a good thing he's in Colorado; otherwise, she'd slap him on the back of the head, especially since he wasn't exactly prepared."

"You know, you guys all pounded that shit into our heads," Clayton said. "But it's completely *'do as we say, not as we do.'*"

"*'It isn't just about respecting yourself; it's about being respectful to the girl you're with.'*" Danny parroted someone, using air quotes.

"Damn right it is," Will said, sounding like the parent again.

"Somebody forgot to tell Luke," Clayton said, shaking his head in frustration.

"Beth tries," Will said. "And if he tells her about today, his ears are going to *bleed.*"

"So, Luke didn't glove up when he hit up a girl in the airplane head because he didn't have a condom on him?" Marc took a sip of his beer, hoping he'd understood the back-and-forth correctly. "I make it a habit to always keep a condom in my wallet, and all of you should too. Beth's right about it being disrespectful not to use one, not to mention you don't want a bunch of kids running around."

"Damn, Marc, you fit right in, you know that?"

Marc couldn't believe how Clayton's words affected him. He shouldn't care whether or not he fit in with this band of idiots. But hearing Clayton say that made him feel like a part of something for the first time in a long while.

"But sure as shit, I always have one."

"Me fucking too," Danny agreed.

They all looked at Will.

"My girl's in DC," he said simply.

"Secretary Campbell helped her get a job. They're doing the long-distance thing," Danny explained, but judging by his expression, he didn't seem to like the girl.

"Believe nothing they tell you about her," Will said gruffly, giving his brothers a look that dared them to say anything.

"Well, if that's true, she's a peach," Clayton said in a perky voice that made everyone laugh. Then the conversation died away in favor of watching the game.

Marc kicked the boys out at midnight. He had to admit he'd enjoyed himself; honest to God, the boys were hard not to like.

The next night followed much the same pattern. They even invited him to poker night on Saturday at Danny's. They said he could take Corey's spot since the Metros were playing a doubleheader. He accepted with a smile, knowing how Corey would feel about that.

Marc didn't want to admit it, but having people around who wanted nothing but his company was... well, it wasn't a burden. And Marc liked it, even if he didn't plan on telling Beth that.

12

@**EdwardDCampbell**: So proud to be there to cheer on our girl today. After three years of hard work, finally the ribbons are being cut on the new NIC wing of @oceanregionalmed. Join us at noon! Pictures to follow

BETH REACHED FOR one handle of the oversized scissors while Austin took the other, fake smiling for the cameras as they officially opened the NICU at Ocean Regional Medical Center. Helping Hands had provided the funds for the much-needed addition to the hospital, which could now handle babies born as early as twenty-eight weeks.

Beth had anonymously donated most of the initial funds to get Helping Hands off the ground, but she never did things like this. Right from the start, she'd told Austin she didn't want to be the face of the charity. Beth never knew when her past might blow up, and she didn't want the work they did to be cast in a poor light because of her. Austin respected her decision and let her stay in the background—usually. But given Marc's need for positive publicity, Austin suggested she, as the Helping Hands board member who had driven the hospital addition project, come to the event. He kept assuring her that the best way to keep the press saying good things was to give them plenty to talk about.

Her father helped make that work, because now that she was getting useful attention, he praised her on Twitter every chance he got. And when he'd found out she was coming to the grand opening, he had decided to show up too.

Her parents moved in for a group photo next. "Ms. Evans, could we get pictures of you and Mr. Demoda?" a photographer called out. She hadn't seen Marc in days. Not since he'd flown out of her house like his hair was on fire, telling her he couldn't stand another minute of everyone treating her like the Queen of England. If he hadn't looked so lonely and miserable, she might have gotten mad.

Her eyes cut to him, standing off to the side and watching. Marc flashed her a damn dimple, and her heart picked up a couple of beats. He was wearing a charcoal suit—probably Armani—with a light gray button-down. The dark colors should have been depressing, but with Marc's complexion and stylish hair, he looked like he belonged on the cover of *GQ* magazine.

Standing next to her, Marc placed his hand low on Beth's back, tucking her against his warm chest. Her nose was suddenly full of the spicy, clean scent that was Mark Demoda. She swallowed hard as her body broke out in goosebumps. Marc noticed, and rubbed her arms lightly with his large calloused hand—which did nothing but intensify the problem. She shivered.

"They always keep hospitals cold; you should have worn a suit like your mother and sister. There's nothing to this dress," Marc commented softly in her ear so that no one else would hear. At least he didn't realize the effect he had on her.

"I knew I could count on you for a compliment," Beth sassed back, knowing her stylish dress was correctly business casual.

"I didn't say you didn't look good," Marc said. "I was questioning your judgment."

"You and my father both." Beth smiled and pinched his arm—the one that was out of view of the camera—but Marc laughed.

"Mr. Demoda, can you give us your thoughts on the project?"

Austin had prepped him well. Marc sounded informed as he smiled down proudly at Beth. She wanted to roll her eyes; he was pissed, about having to come here today as well as about her brothers' recent takeover of his house. He'd given her crap for a good ten minutes when he'd first arrived.

Tuesday, for the Metros game, the boys had gone over at her insistence. She was trying to work the favor for Austin, but the guys all had fun. Marc was all they'd talked about for the last few days. She wasn't responsible for the rest of the nights, or that they were dragging Marc out to Poison in the city tonight. Beth wondered if he knew about tonight's plans yet. She doubted it: Planning wasn't her brothers' thing.

Marc moved back toward Austin, and Beth finished answering questions, adding a mention of Helping Hand's carnival next week. She threw out a few of the big names who would be there, and said she hoped they would get a good turnout.

"We know Marc rarely does that kind of thing; will he be there next Saturday?" a reporter asked. She confirmed, having no idea if it was true. But it seemed like the right answer. After all, she was here because of him.

Finally the questions died down, and the press slowly left. Marc came up behind Beth and took his jacket off, placing it around her shoulders.

"No sense freezing to death."

The jacket was huge, enveloping her in his warmth. He pulled her tight against the wall of his chest, so that her entire back rested against his heat. The tension built in her stomach as his steady hand slid up to rub her shoulders. She melted deeper into him.

"Elizabeth." Her father walked toward them looking unhappy, and she straightened herself up. "We all need to get back to work. Not everyone has the entire afternoon to fritter away. This already took far too long for a simple photo op."

Beth didn't have the afternoon free either.

"I'll take her home, Secretary Campbell," Marc said formally. *Kiss-up.*

"Good. And please don't make a scene," her father said, looking only at her. "We don't need another mess to clean up for you."

"Of course." She forced a smile and turned to Marc. "We better go."

"Sure," he agreed, but questions lingered in his eyes until Paul cleared his throat.

"Remember to have your people reach out about next week's rally," Paul said.

Marc frowned, but gave him a clipped nod.

Marc waited until they were alone outside the hospital before he asked, "Why do you let your father talk to you like that, Beth?"

"What do you mean?"

"Like you can't get anything right." Marc shook his head.

"You mean how he questions my judgment? Like my dress?" Beth pointedly reminded Marc.

Marc's eyes automatically moved to her dress and down her legs, which his jacket now covered to her knees. "And don't forget the shoes."

"There is nothing wrong with my shoes!" Beth eyed her well-loved light blue heels. "I like to have heels on when I stand next to Austin. I look tiny compared to him otherwise."

"You are tiny, even in those sexy little heels." His voice was thick as he stared at her legs, and her insides throbbed. But then he frowned. "Everything about you is tiny."

And that reminded Beth of where they stood. That wasn't a compliment; it was a reminder that she was not the leggy, big-boobed type of woman he preferred.

"It's funny how you surround yourself with big men," Marc went on. "It makes you seem smaller. My jacket swallows you."

"Yeah, I'm tiny," Beth snapped and sped up. Marc mumbled something, and she practically shouted at him as she whirled around. "What?"

"Nothing." Smiling, he placed his hand on her back and edged her toward where he had parked the car.

"You said something," she hissed once they were inside.

"I love it when you get all feisty," Marc said as he started the car. "Sometimes when a girl gets all riled up, it's bitchy, but with you, sweetheart, it's sexy."

"I'm not riled up," she said, glaring.

"Ooooh yes you are." He laughed.

He glanced at her legs more than once as he drove; finally, steaming, she said, "They're not gonna get any longer."

"Huh?" Marc looked at her out of the corner of his eye.

"My legs. They're short no matter how many times you look at them wishing they would grow."

Marc had the nerve to smile. "You're right. How about your boobs? Should I watch 'em just in case?"

"Well, I went to see the surgeon yesterday, but even though I explained it was an emergency, he said he couldn't fit me in for implants till September, so I wouldn't bother." Beth smiled sweetly at him.

"Now, that's a shame," Marc said, but his smile grew.

"On a positive note, he said that he would happily squeeze you in for an ego-ectomy tomorrow," Beth said flippantly. "He knows your neck must be tired carrying that big head. Apparently he's a fan of yours, hotshot."

Marc threw his head back and laughed. When he finally stopped, he said, "I'll have to call and cancel. After a few more weeks, you'll have cut me down to size."

"What's that supposed to mean?" Beth asked.

"Sweetheart, when I'm with you, no one gives me the time of day. You are the complete and total center of attention in any room. It doesn't matter if it's your brothers, your parents, or the press. Half the time I think people forget I'm there."

"I don't do it on purpose; it just happens," Beth mumbled.

"I know you can't help it." Marc looked over at her again. "That makes it all the more deflating. You're not trying for attention; you just naturally command it."

"Too bad I'm not better at it." Beth turned to look out the window; that was honesty she hadn't meant to release.

"Better at what?"

"At *being* the center of attention. It's why my father talks to me like I'm a child. I make scenes without meaning to. I've done it my entire life. It embarrasses both my parents."

"What?" Marc looked genuinely shocked.

"I embarrass them. And unless it's on Twitter, they don't have many good things to say about me. When I was ten, they went to Washington, and I stayed back out of their hair. Originally my parents thought they would leave me with a nanny, but Lynn Evans wouldn't hear of it so I moved in with her. I became the daughter Lynn always wanted. I lived with them whenever my parents weren't in Jersey, which was most of the time."

"What could you do at ten that would embarrass them?" Marc asked, looking sideways at her.

Beth looked away. "I talked too much, couldn't sit still, put runs in my tights, spilled on my dress. People always noticed."

"That doesn't seem like a reason to send a child away."

"Maybe not to you, but dumping red wine on President Clinton didn't go over well, and neither did my game of hide-and-seek with the Secret Service."

Marc laughed. "Jesus, you were always feisty, huh?"

"I tried hard not to be, but I told you—I can't help it. When I got older and became a dewy-eyed optimist, Dad wanted to strangle me because I would say the darndest things. For a while, after I won the gold medal, I was his golden girl. But we all know what happened next."

"You quit to be with your brothers," Marc said.

She turned to look at him. "No. I took my clothes off for Corey Matthews—and, as it turned out, the rest of the world." Marc said nothing. "These days I prefer to stay out of my father's way."

"As long as you stay out of the media, you can't screw up again?"

"Oh, I screw up plenty. But I do it quietly." Beth looked out the window again as they neared her house.

"It doesn't seem like you screw up, ever."

"How about last Sunday?" Marc didn't reply, so Beth assumed he agreed.

Neither of them spoke for a while, until Marc finally broke the silence. "Beth?"

"Yeah?"

"You know we need to… to go out together. Like on an actual date?" She couldn't tell if the hesitancy was because he knew she wouldn't want to, or because he didn't want to either.

"I know." It didn't thrill her, but he was right. If they didn't go out, the press would start hounding them for pictures. And if there wasn't a story about them to print, the rags would make one up.

"Can I take you out to dinner tomorrow night? We'll eat at Slush. The jackals love to swarm there, so they'll get plenty of pictures," Marc said, then added, "I promise not to care if you spill on Hollywood's hunk of the moment or the 'It' girl in the next booth."

Beth laughed. "So long as you know what you're getting into."

"I don't think I have any idea, Beth." Marc sounded worried.

"The good news is that if you don't embarrass easily, most people find me fun," Beth said with a shrug, trying not to make a big deal out of her insecurities with the media.

"Oh, sweetheart, you're definitely fun." Marc laughed, but she could see the disappointment in his face but she didn't know why it was there.

13

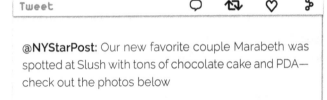
BETH TRIED ON three different dresses before finally deciding on pants. She slid her feet into her highest heels before taking a last look in the mirror. The tight black pants, paired with the emerald green top, balanced the line of trendy and sexy while still appropriate and classy. At least she wouldn't be on any worst-dressed list. That's what she told herself while she continued to put too much effort into getting ready. It had nothing to do with Marc. Definitely not.

"Wow, Ms. Evans," her babysitter said as she walked into the kitchen.

"I was going for casual-chic. What do you think?"

"It's perfect. I'd never know you spent an hour getting ready." The teenager smiled.

"An hour, huh?"

Beth winced as Marc's voice called out from the playroom.

"Mr. Demoda got here about five minutes ago," the sitter

murmured. "He's in there playing ponies with Mandy. It's almost as funny as when Clayton does it."

"I'm sure," Beth said, heading for the playroom door.

Marc sat on the floor with about six My Little Ponies standing on his gray wool-clad legs while Mandy sat between them. Sitting in the middle of a rainbow of little girls' toys should have made him look ridiculous, but it didn't. His cologne lingered in the air, and the musk left her uneasy. Her eyes ran over his shoulders to his neck. His blue button-down was open, so the hint of a silver chain showed before it tucked into his shirt. She followed his arms down to his graceful hands and long fingers. He was the dictionary definition of handsome, and there was something very sexy about a man who was willing to play ponies.

"Having fun?" Beth asked, leaning her shoulder against the door frame.

Marc turned in her direction, and her skin prickled as his eyes ran over her body before slowly drifting back to her face. He cleared his throat.

"So you're one of those women who spends hours getting ready, huh?" he asked indifferently before turning back to his pony.

Beth's heart lodged in her throat, and it took a moment before she could swallow it down.

"Not normally, since I usually avoid the type of attention we're trying to get tonight," Beth said, blinking back the sting in her eyes. She didn't care what he thought; she looked good.

"Don't worry, Ms. Evans; I'd kill to look as good as you do right now," the sitter assured her. The seventeen-year-old was smarter than the stupid man in the playroom.

"You look like you always do," Marc pointed out as he came into the kitchen, followed by Mandy. Her eyes flitted shut. She took a breath and tried not to let herself get upset that he couldn't even manage a compliment.

Beth kissed Steve's head, hugged Mandy, then grabbed her black bag off the counter and followed Marc out the door.

As soon as they were in the car, Beth turned the music on. He'd hurt her feelings, but she wouldn't let him realize it.

"Not an Eagles fan?" Marc asked as she flicked the station quickly.

"No." She hated all classic rock. It made her think of limos and lectures. She wanted rap. She finally sat back and let "Get Buck in Here" fill the air. Marc reached over and snapped it off, then glared as she reached over and turned it back on.

"You can't *possibly* like that crap."

Beth smiled and turned the volume up. Marc watched her on and off as they drove to the city, but she simply played radio DJ, ignoring him completely. It turned out he didn't like pop any better than rap.

Marc shut the music off as they pulled into a parking garage almost an hour later. Neither of them had said another word the entire car ride, and now the silence was awkward. He parked his car in a numbered space before turning to give Beth his full attention.

"I'm a jerk," he said with an earnest look on his face.

"I won't disagree on principle, but what in particular are we talking about this time?"

The corner of Marc's mouth twitched as he tried not to smile. "You look gorgeous tonight, and I'm a jerk for not saying you completely took my breath away the second I saw you."

Beth blinked. She realized her mouth was hanging open and she slammed it shut, but was still at a loss for words.

"I'm not sure how this whole 'friend' thing works. But as we were driving here, I realized that if Sid had been standing at the door looking like you do, I would have made some teasing comment about stealing her away from Austin. I know any of your brothers would have told you how good you looked, too. And the fact that you're always gorgeous isn't an excuse not to tell you. So I should have. You look beautiful; every one of those sixty minutes was worth it." His eyes bore into hers. He meant every word he'd said.

Beth cleared the lump in her throat. "Thanks." The flush of embarrassment heated her cheeks, and she fiddled with the ring on her thumb. His compliment held way too much weight in her mind. She didn't want to care that he thought she looked good, but she did.

"And I promise that next time you take my breath away, I won't make you wait to hear it," Marc said. He climbed out, then reappeared at her window, opening the door. "Just for the record, you said you would tell me when I'm acting like a jerk, not turn on that robotic cold shoulder you have."

"I don't do a cold shoulder," Beth said as he took her hand and helped her out of the car.

Marc laughed. "You've perfected politely robotic, and I hate it. I much prefer it when you yell at me."

"Yeah, right." Beth chuckled.

"I know you've spent a lifetime hearing people tell you to calm down, but I like to know where I stand, so if you're pissed, tell me."

"If you want me to," Beth said.

Marc grabbed her wrist and spun her to face him. "Beth, I mean it. I like it when you're *you*, not when you're trying to be good. I want to know how you feel, whether we're in front of ten cameras or alone in a room."

"Okay."

No one had ever told her that before. It was strange having someone say, "I want you to make a scene," but it was freeing in some ways too.

"On that note, you ready to show the world how much we love each other?" Marc asked, smiling at the contradiction between reality and his words.

"As far as I'm concerned, for the rest of the night, the sun rises and sets in your eyes," Beth said sarcastically, and Marc laughed as he steered her out of the parking garage.

The sidewalk was crammed with paparazzi who called out to both of them. "Marc! Over here!" "Elizabeth! This way!"

She steeled herself and plastered on a smile.

"Give them their picture," Beth whispered, and Marc stopped walking. He placed his hand on her back, and the two of them smiled while Marc talked to a few of the photographers. She hated it, but she kept her smile on. It was only two months, she reminded herself, and then—hopefully—she could have normal back.

Fifteen minutes later, Beth sat in a half-circle booth beside Marc.

"I've never gone out with someone who gets stopped by more people than I do. How did you get on a first-name basis with the entire defensive line for the Giants?" Marc asked, resting his arm on the booth behind her.

"Helping Hands." Beth cleared her throat and reached down to twirl her ring a few times. She didn't want to lie to Marc.

She'd talked to Bob about Helping Hands stuff, and sometimes even mentioned it to her brothers—but they understood how destructive gossip could be.

"Did you date one of them or something?" Marc asked, frowning as he looked over at the men. She chuckled, and his frown deepened.

"I told you, I don't date people I can read about in magazines," Beth said, rolling her eyes.

"Why are you acting coy?" Marc asked, looking back at the men and at her again. "Unless I read you wrong, you had no problem discussing everything that happened with the Evanses when I asked about it, and you were okay talking about your parents and Corey. Why the sudden shut-down?"

Beth sighed. "I don't mind when you ask about *me*. But I helped one of them with—something, and ever since, the entire defensive line has been great."

"Ah. It's not *your* privacy you're protecting," Marc said, understanding.

"Exactly," Beth confirmed, and Marc let it drop instantly.

Adoptions were private; she couldn't break that confidentiality with someone who might repeat the information. But maybe Marc understood privacy. Again she had trouble relating this man to the one she'd read and heard about everywhere. His life was always out there for anyone to see.

Once the server had their orders dealt with and had brought them each a glass of wine, Marc jumped right back into the conversation.

"Can I delve more into your personal life?" Marc asked and scooted closer so that their legs brushed. His touch radiated through her entire body, as if he'd jump-started her nervous system.

Beth couldn't think of anything she wasn't willing to share with him. "What do you want to know?"

"I'm curious about what happened between when you moved in with the Evanses and now." Marc paused and chuckled. "Which I know is a lot of ground to cover. It sounded like Bob was too busy to be there for his brothers, so I can't imagine you two were on good terms. And yet, a year later, you got married."

"Bob and I were always on good terms. He was around helping with the boys," Beth corrected. She leaned forward, resting her chin on her hand and inadvertently shifting closer.

"So how did you end up together?" he asked.

Beth tensed. "When the world turns on you—even friends, teammates, and family—trust is hard." She frowned, remembering her father telling her it was simpler if they let the story run its course and burn out instead of correcting it. Although he had never helped spread the lies, he'd never stopped them either. Stoically silent. "But my saving grace, through it all, was the Evans family. Yeah, the world was crucifying me, but their lives were falling apart, and they needed me." She smiled, thinking about her late husband. "Bob became my best friend—my shoulder to lean on, someone I could trust without question. At a time when I couldn't even trust my parents, getting that continuous unconditional love all his family gave me was heaven. The quiet life he offered was everything I needed to stay out of my father's way. And that was really the thing that mattered most to me then."

Marc sucked in a breath as he read between her words. It shocked her how easily the truth came out when she was with him.

She nodded slowly. "Yes; with the Evanses, I've always been out of the public eye. I knew Bob was interested in me. We were going to raise the boys together."

The look on his face prompted her to continue.

"I *loved* him." And she had. It was just a soft, undemanding, protective love. "It was a simple transition to go from co-parenting to becoming his wife." She shrugged.

"But then he died?"

She swallowed before nodding. "Second-worst moment of my life." Then she blinked. That was a truth she *never* shared. She always said it was the worst.

"What was the first?"

She looked at him.

"Corey," he said flatly, and she nodded. Marc was quiet for a minute. "You were pregnant when Bob died?"

"Yip." That was a weird question to follow with, she thought. "He died suddenly. The Evanses have a gallbladder deformity that runs in the family, and makes it prone to infection. Bob didn't want to have his taken out unless it became a problem. He got an infection; when they did the surgery, the infection moved to his heart. He never woke up," Beth said. Under the table Marc's other hand came to rest on her thigh, turning them both to face each other.

"And you've dated no one with a media presence since," Marc finished.

Beth looked up. "Until you and my front porch."

His eyes heated immediately as they both remembered that kiss. Beth swallowed, and he leaned closer, his pupils dilated, those brown eyes clouded with desire.

But Beth was acutely aware of where they were and how many people were watching them. With Marc's hand gently massaging her shoulder and his leg pressed against hers, the moment felt private, but she knew they were sitting in a fishbowl. She glanced around again, and her stomach felt sick. She could see the newspaper headlines tomorrow: 'Elizabeth and Marc spotted making out in Slush,' the quotes from the servers about not being able to keep their hands off each other. Her heart pounded in her ears; she couldn't do this. She scooted back from him.

"Beth?" Marc asked, more surprised than irritated.

"Huh?" She took a sip of her wine to calm her nerves and somehow finished her glass.

"You look like you're about to pass out."

She swallowed. "I'm fine."

"No, you're not. I thought we agreed that you were going to tell me what's going on in that beautiful head of yours," he said and scooted closer. Too close. She swallowed again. "Is this about Bob?"

"No. I need space," Beth said, and gently set her hand on his leg, pushing him away.

"What?" She could hear the confusion in his voice.

"I'm not into public displays of affection, and there's a roomful of people watching us," Beth said.

"Sweetheart, you were fine at the hospital, and the other day in your backyard. And I was a lot closer then."

"That was different." She didn't feel this gut-wrenching fear in those situations. Those were more of a job, like she was posing for an ad campaign; this felt intimate.

"Okay, scoot back over, so it doesn't look like you're afraid of me," Marc whispered. Beth moved, but her hesitation was evident. "I'm going to put my arm around you, but I promise it won't look like anything more than me wanting everyone in this restaurant to know you're here with me, okay?"

Beth nodded, even though she wasn't okay.

"Now, take a deep breath because I can see your pulse jumping out the side of your neck."

"I'm sorry," Beth mumbled. Oh man, did she have issues— and she was revealing more about them than she wanted to—but Marc said nothing more.

The server appeared with their food, and by the time they'd finished eating, Beth felt better. The conversation changed to lighter topics, mostly her dating history since Bob. The stories of her dates and her brothers amused Marc, but her brothers' skill at chasing men away was why she had started using babysitters instead of having them watch the kids. With her second glass of wine finished, she relaxed again, and he made no move to overstep the boundaries she had set.

Marc ordered chocolate cake to share, and when it came, he took control of the fork, feeding her a bite.

"Mmm." She shut her eyes in pure bliss. "I love choco-late cake."

"I can tell." He laughed. "The surprise is this orgasmic smile from someone who doesn't keep even a cookie in her house." He put another bite on the fork for her and held it out of her reach. She leaned toward it, and he pulled it back further. "Come get it."

"You're a tease." She reached her hand out to grab his wrist, closing her mouth around the fork.

"It makes me wonder what else I can do to put that satisfied smile on your face," Marc whispered, and she shiv-ered as his breath danced against her neck. She swallowed before opening her eyes, looking straight into Marc's chocolate-brown gaze.

"You've got a little cake on the corner of your mouth," Marc said, leaning closer to her again.

"This side?" She tried to get it with her tongue.

His hand came up to rest on her cheek. "No, let me." Marc leaned closer. His lips touched her mouth—not briefly, but he didn't linger too long, either. "Got it." The words brushed against her lips.

"Uh-huh," Beth said breathlessly. She shook her head. "What did you do that for?"

"To see how firm your lines in the sand were," Marc said, and smiled. "Want me to test you again?"

She wanted to tell him no... or maybe yes—but just then her phone started ringing in her purse. The haze she was in faded, along with the rest of her plans for the evening, when she looked at the caller ID.

14

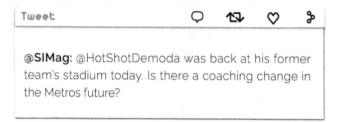

"WHAT IS YOUR PROBLEM?" Beth demanded as Marc slammed the car door shut. He'd been in a mood ever since they'd left the restaurant.

"Maybe it has something to do with the fact that we're supposed to be on a date, but now we're running back home to hold your ex-boyfriend's hand because he had a terrible game," Marc snapped.

"We're not on a date. We're drumming up good press for you. There's a difference. There were plenty of pictures, and I'm sure that by tomorrow morning everyone will know what we ate. Tonight was about *you*."

Marc glanced at her with that familiar look of disappointment, but she continued.

"Second, there is nothing between Corey and me, and hasn't been for ten years. And third, I'm not holding his hand. I'm saving the babysitter from the overload of testosterone that is about to invade my house! My brothers will know Corey stank again, and he's heading there. You think they'll miss the opportunity to tell him?"

"We get to spend the night telling Corey how crappy he is?" Marc mused. He didn't have to sound so cheery about it.

"*They* get to tell Cor. *You* get to sit and enjoy a cold beer." None of her brothers would like it if Marc picked on Corey.

"Oh, shi–sugar," Marc cursed.

"What?" Beth's eyes flew to the road.

"We have to stop and get beer," Marc said, shaking his head.

"Huh?"

"It's my turn."

"What?" she demanded again.

"Apparently I've been freeloading. If your brothers know I'm coming, they'll expect me to bring some."

Beth laughed.

"What's funny?"

"When was the last time anyone accused *you* of freeloading?" she asked, chuckling. Her brothers had taken Marc in like a stray puppy.

"Never, and that's why we're getting some beer," Marc said, but he smiled. "And not Coors Light either. We're getting real beer."

"Yuck."

"What?" Marc eyed her warily.

"What men call 'real beer' tastes like sewer water," Beth complained.

Marc snorted. "Okay, then we'll get a six-pack of Coors for you."

He patted her thigh, and Beth's breath caught in her throat. He meant it as nothing more than a friendly pat, like her brothers gave her all the time. The problem was she couldn't separate herself from this lust she had for Marc, and since the moment he'd kissed her tonight, she still couldn't get over it. For Marc, it had been about the challenge of getting her to kiss him. But that simple brush of his lips against hers had sent her into a tailspin.

"Unless you'd prefer some White Claw," Marc added, oblivious to his effect on her.

"I'll stick with the Coors," Beth said, picking his hand up and moving it off her thigh. She couldn't let it sit there and have a normal conversation.

"Oh. Sorry," he mumbled.

"We don't need to put on a show when we're in the car."

"Yeah, right," he said, and ran his hand through his hair. It was an absentminded gesture that made Beth's stomach knot. She wanted to run her hands through that thick gorgeous hair, and wanted his hands on her—not in the friendly gesture way. "We'll stop when we get by your house."

"Sure," Beth said.

She hated this situation. She hated that she was dumb enough to fall for the seductive smile Marc flashed at any woman who turned her eyes his way. She hated that they had to go out and sit in a fishbowl and be all touchy-feely when it made her stomach sick. And she hated that when they were alone, she *wanted* to be all touchy. Couldn't she be smart enough to stay indifferent to the man? The whole thing plain old sucked.

Beth got rid of the sitter before heading into the kitchen to deal with the boys.

"Holy camoly," Clayton said, and Will choked on his beer.

"What?" Beth said, slamming her hands onto her hips.

Danny shrugged. "You look hot."

"How come you don't get all dressed up like that for us?" Clayton asked.

"She likes me better," Marc said. He carried a few beers to the center of the table, smiling at the guys. "What can I say? I'm her favorite."

"Oh, for Pete's sake. I told Austin this would happen. Just another one of the boys," Beth huffed.

"*What?*" Will asked.

"Less than a week, and he's fallen into the 'hey wait, I need to stop and get the beer' routine." She tried to make her voice sound deep, which made all the men laugh. "And 'oh, I'm her favorite.' I *told* him it would happen, and he laughed at me. *Laughed.*" Beth crossed her arms and stomped her foot, while all the men looked at her as if an alien being had invaded her body.

"Whoa, what's got you so worked up?" Corey strolled into the kitchen, pulling Beth into his arms for a hug. "You look hot, by the way."

"Thanks." Beth sighed. "Ignore me. I'm not making any sense."

"Okay," Corey said before putting his palm on the top of her head, shaking her hair all over her face. She whacked him in the stomach, and he smirked before joining the others at the table.

"Nice game, blowhole. I only caught the beginning, but by the second inning, it wasn't worth watching anymore," Clayton said as Corey sat down across from him. Beth sat on Clayton's lap.

"Fig off, Clay," Corey snapped, then glanced around the table. "Why do you look like you should be on the cover of some men's magazine, Demoda?"

"Beth and I went to Slush for dinner." Marc shrugged as if to say it was no big deal. She shot him a glare, and his mouth twitched.

"Ah, a public outing—hence the mood," Corey said, smiling at Beth before turning to Marc. "You should have gotten chocolate cake. She likes chocolate almost more than sex."

"We got cake," he said tightly as if Corey's comment upset him. Marc's glare moved from Corey to Beth and it softened. She flushed, remembering his comment about making her smile.

"So why are you in such a snit then?" Corey asked.

"Maybe because my kitchen is full of men again," Beth muttered. Not that she minded, really. She was in a snit because Marc was turning into one of her brothers, and she didn't want that. But she would cut her tongue out before she admitted it, even to herself.

"Oh." Understanding rang in Corey's voice. "No one told me. Did anyone bring anything?" Corey asked, looking at Beth's brothers like they were about to provide drugs. They all smiled as Danny picked up a bag from the floor and dumped multiple chocolate candy bars on the table.

"Take your pick," he said, looking at Beth and then the four candy bars on the table.

"I had cake; I don't need candy. I told you to ignore me." Beth shut her eyes.

"It's four games in a row, Cor," Will said, changing the subject and letting her have her moment. They knew her well enough to know when not to beat a dead horse. It wasn't PMS, but she'd let them think it was if it meant not having to explain that it was Marc making her crazy. "Dead arm?"

"No," Corey huffed.

"You're missing your mark with your left foot. It's missing with your release point," Marc said simply, but he gained everyone's attention.

Corey's head snapped around to Marc, and his eyes narrowed. "You serious?"

"Hasn't Ross said anything?" Marc asked, taking a sip of his beer. But Beth could see he was enjoying having the attention of the men in the room.

"Ross says it's my head again," Corey answered.

"Maybe it is." Marc shrugged. "You've always been a headcase, but your left foot's still missing its mark."

"Hey," Danny began, but Beth stuck her hand in the air, cutting him off.

There was no hostility between Corey and Marc this time. These two were feeling each other out. Marc had said something about Corey needing help with his release point as they were leaving the restaurant. She'd gotten the impression that Marc wanted to help him.

"My head's fine," Corey said, his eyes fixed on Marc.

"So fix the other problem." Marc met Corey's gaze, waiting for him to ask for help.

"I can't," Corey said, frustrated, but not willing to make the first move.

"That's a shame." Marc smiled and took another pull of his beer, unwilling to offer his help unless Corey asked. Silence fell over the kitchen.

"Ridiculous," Beth said. These two were more stubborn than anyone she had ever met. Marc was dying to help Corey, and Corey wanted Marc's help, but neither would admit it.

"What?" Clayton said, rubbing her back.

"Men are stupid," Beth said, shaking her head. Someone objected, but she simply ignored them and continued. "Marc, if you want to hang out here anymore, go outside and help Corey. Corey, if you're planning on spending the night, then you better go out there and figure out what the problem is because I'm tired of your moods."

Both men pretended to protest but ended up going outside.

"That was stupid," Beth complained.

"It's like asking for directions," Will said. "You know you're lost, but it's hard to admit it out loud."

"The question is, who's lost?" Beth asked.

"Both of them," Will answered. "But hopefully they can figure it out, because I refuse to pick a side, and they don't seem to hate each other as much as they both claim."

"SHE'S BOSSY," MARC said as he walked into the backyard.

"Darn right, but if she weren't, those guys would have walked all over her years ago."

"Who are you kidding? She has every one of them wrapped around her finger," Marc scoffed.

"Most people don't realize that." Corey chuckled. "So are we going to stay out here until she thinks we've worked the problem out? Because I can't throw tonight."

"No, I'll help you. I'll meet you at the stadium tomorrow. You still do afternoons, right?" Marc waited for Corey to confirm, although pitchers were all about routine. "But I want some answers, which is why we're out here," Marc said.

"What do you want to know?"

"What made you throw her under the bus ten years ago?"

Marc had to ask; he'd read the articles, yet he couldn't find a reason for Corey to have said anything that came out in those interviews.

Corey's teeth locked, and he glared. "Of all people, I would think you'd know you can't believe what you read."

Marc raised his eyebrows; he also knew a direct quote was just that.

"My full statement was 'I'm not a victim here, Elizabeth is. I keep getting slapped on the back while you cut her off at the knees.'" Corey sighed. "The first half of my quote played over, and over, and over. *I'm not a victim.*" Corey's jaw clenched. "Not once did the full statement come out, and every media outlet used the first bit to say we took the photos willingly." His hands fisted at his sides. "After that, I didn't trust myself to talk about it, and Beth wouldn't talk to me at all, and her father was furious."

Marc was seeing the full picture: two young kids floundering, neither with any media savvy or much help.

"So you lost her for good," Marc said.

"Yip," Corey agreed, popping his lips on the *p*, like Beth did. "Nothing will ever happen with us again. Too much there. I'm not your competition, if that's what this is about; still, there's not much I wouldn't do for that girl," Corey said. Both men's gazes flicked to the window, where Beth was whacking Clayton on the back of the head.

"If she needs anything, you'd have to get in line."

Corey smirked. "Nah, we're family. We share well. We'll take turns throwing the punches at your pretty face."

There was too much pleasure in that statement for Marc to want to rise to the bait. "She has some media issues?" he asked instead.

Beth's reaction earlier in the night had shown him that much. What surprised him was that it didn't put him off. He wanted to understand, to help her move past it.

Corey flinched.

"Can you explain?" he asked, hopeful that Corey would give some insight.

He shrugged. "We don't talk about it." Corey had that same stone-faced look he'd had last week when he walked in on Marc and Beth's discussion.

"What?" Marc had watched Beth and Corey together; they were close. How could they not talk about something that had affected them both so profoundly?

"Demoda, she's not over any of it. I know that, but I can't help you because we don't talk about it," Corey snapped. "*You've* talked about it more with her than I ever have. Don't you realize that's why we broke up, why nothing will ever happen with us again? Why she immediately ran away and married someone the opposite of me in every way?" He fisted his hands. "Now, are you done with the inquisition?"

Beth wasn't the only one with issues, and Marc realized he shouldn't push Corey. They weren't even friends. But, pressing his luck, he said, "One more."

Everyone in Marc's life had assumed the accident had been the start of the downward spiral he'd been in for the last year. Only one person realized it had started *before* that night. Before the injury that ended his career. And he felt like crap about blowing off the only person who had tried to help him. "When you offered to bring me somewhere the... the night of the accident, was it here?"

"Yes. Nobody seemed to notice, but something had been off with you for a while. I thought maybe you needed to talk to someone. In this group, there's usually someone who can listen. Wish you'd come?" Corey asked.

Marc nodded. "Although it wouldn't have changed anything that night."

"Then why do you care?" Corey demanded.

"Because it changes things between us." Marc remembered that night so clearly. How hard Corey had worked to offer Marc an olive branch of friendship.

"What?"

"Corey, you care about these people. This place is more than a hideout. You're closer with these guys than you've ever been to the team. Even though you and I never got along, the idea that you would bring me here—that means something to me."

"You wouldn't have come," Corey said, looking disgusted. "But why? Why were you so determined to throw everything away?" He glared at Marc.

"The girl—"

"Oh please. You didn't give a flying fu—flip about her." Corey threw his hands up and spun around, clearly giving up on Marc. And that was what made Marc admit it: He didn't want anyone in this group giving up on him.

"She was pregnant," Marc said quietly. Corey turned around slowly and his eyes widened. Marc nodded. "My baby."

Corey blinked but said nothing.

"A baby's supposed to be a great thing, but it messed with my head, made me compare myself to my dad. And he's not someone I ever wanted to be." Marc had held those words in for so long, and Corey wasn't who Marc would've thought he would open up to, but he was doing it. The comparison between Marc and his shitty-ass father was so glaringly obvious.

"You're not him, Marc," Corey whispered.

"Yeah, right," he snapped.

"Marc—"

"Corey, you don't know me." Marc kicked the ground.

"How'd you keep it out of the media?"

Marc looked at Corey, but saw only questions in his eyes. No disgust, no anger, no judgment.

"Release enough other crap, tell a story the media can run with, anything to distract. I have a team of people I pay for that," Marc replied. "Same as you."

Corey's mouth opened and then shut, and he glanced down, not looking at Marc anymore. A light in Marc's head switched on: Corey didn't know how to handle the media. That was shocking. Everyone probably expected that Corey, having a famous father and having lived through a considerable scandal, already knew. He wondered if anyone had ever shown him the ropes.

"Maybe there's something else I can help you with while we deal with the release point," Marc said.

Corey's eyes flashed to him in surprise.

"We don't have to keep hating each other."

"I've always wanted to be *friends* with you, Marc." Marc couldn't hide his shock, but Corey didn't slow down. "One reason I forced a trade to the Metros was you. Not only are you one heck of a pitcher, but you're one of the best teachers in the game. I wanted to play with you, learn from you—and you wouldn't give me the time of day. I assumed it was because you didn't think I had the stuff."

"You have the stuff, Corey," Marc said, shaking his head at the irony.

"So why leave me out in the cold? If you see the talent, you hone it, focus it, develop it. You're doing that with Steve—he's only eight, but you can't help it. Everyone around us always knew you didn't think I had it in me to be a great pitcher. Don't you know that?"

Was Marc responsible for the head game Corey had developed since joining the Metros? That stung. Marc hadn't meant to mess with the younger man's head. Maybe some honesty would help Corey.

"The year before you came to the Metros, the media spent the entire season pitting us against each other. Blue-collar ball versus pitching royalty," Marc said. "And that's exactly what we were."

Corey winced.

"You were born to be an All-Star: You're the son of one of the GOATs of pitching, you went to a Big Ten school, wore the Olympic gold before you were twenty—the media nicknamed you Captain America," Marc said. "I worked to pay for what my baseball scholarship didn't cover at Rutgers, then struggled for two years in the minors before I got lucky with the Metros. And I have none of the charm that shoots out your butt when you laugh with reporters. I felt you breathing down my neck from the moment your name went on your locker. *Why help my competition?*"

"Really?" Corey's eyes widened.

"You have the stuff," Marc repeated, then he smiled. "But don't let that go to your head. You also have one heck of a head game and, right now, problems with your release point."

"Better than dead arm?" Corey suggested.

"Only if you can fix it."

"I'm kind of hoping you'll help me with that," Corey finally admitted.

"I've been itching to fix the problem. You've got too much talent to play like garbage every six days," Marc conceded with a teasing smile that Corey returned.

Neither said anything else for a minute, and Corey paced the yard. "Hey Marc," he said when he finally stopped.

"Not done with the girly stuff yet?" Marc asked.

"Just don't hurt her, okay? Be who you are, not who you think you are." Corey's voice was grave.

Marc shook his head. "She doesn't like me enough for you to worry about that. She's just holding up her end of the deal."

Beth had knocked Marc completely off his feet early in the night. By the time her phone rang while they were sitting in that booth, she had become a girl he wanted to spend time with—even time outside the bedroom. That wasn't something he *ever* wanted. But Beth had quickly reminded him that it wasn't to be. Nope, he couldn't hurt her at all, and that was exactly how it should be.

Marc could never be the kind of guy her late husband was. He couldn't be what she needed. And he couldn't change that.

15

IT WAS A yearly tradition: Marc rented a house in the Keys
for his parents' anniversary, and Glory, his sister, came down
to spend time with them. Since he had to come to Miami to
help Ed "get out the vote," Marc had decided to spend a few
days with his family. What a fucking mistake.

Now he sat by the pool, sunglasses on, trying his best to
feign sleep. It didn't work; they all knew he was awake.

"If you're so serious about this girl, why did you not invite
her along?" Since Marc had stepped foot in the house, his
mother had spent the entire time nagging.

"Mom, stop freaking out. It's only been a couple of weeks;
Twitter is making everyone crazy," Glory said.

How many times had they had this conversation in the last
few days? In the morning, at lunch, at dinner; in English, in
Spanish. It was ridiculous. His sister was sick of it too.

"The boy knows better than to tie himself to one woman," his father said simply.

Marc didn't explain what was going on; he had decided to let the media story be the truth. He didn't want to have to get into all the details.

"Yeah, three weeks is your record, right?" Glory said mockingly.

"Something like that," Marc mumbled.

"When do *we* meet her?" his mother, Luciana, asked for the hundredth time. The reply *Never* jumped to his mind every time. It was ridiculous: Luciana was acting as if she had never met Beth in her life, but that wasn't true. They had met several times through Helping Hands.

Were all families this annoying? The Evans family—they didn't annoy each other. Well, to some extent they did, but they enjoyed the banter. Beth's brothers had enjoyed giving her a good ribbing on Saturday afternoon when a blue jay flew into her window. Beth was worried about the injured jay, and insisted that someone help her check on it since she hated birds. Marc had ended up going outside in the rain with her to find the damn thing, and she had been relieved to know the crash had simply stunned it.

"Well?" Lucina asked, pointedly reminding Marc that she had asked him a question.

"Ma, you already know Beth."

"Yes, well, I don't know her as my son's girlfriend." Her accent got stronger, a sure sign she was working herself into a tiff, and Marc sighed.

"I promise she's the same person, and if I marry her, I'll introduce you before the big day."

Frank choked.

Even if Marc were to develop a sudden interest in marriage, he knew Beth wouldn't marry him. He suspected he was like the stunned bird that she didn't *want* to help, but felt compelled to go out in the rain after. That was depressing the hell out of him.

"We've gone out a few times, nothing more to it." He'd lost count of how many times he had given the same reassurance.

The vacation was for a week, but Marc had flown down late. He, Beth, and the kids had gone to the Metros game on Sunday to watch Corey pitch his first good game in weeks. Marc was also leaving early because of the Helping Hands carnival on Saturday. Still, he felt like it was the longest five days of his life. Having experienced the Evans family together made it more apparent how awful his family was. There was no way he was bringing any of the Evanses to meet his parents.

Two hours later, Frank got him alone and started the conversation Marc had known was coming.

"Marc, we need to talk about this girl."

Marc didn't like how his father referred to Beth, as if she wasn't good enough to have a name. "Dad, it's not a big deal. *Beth* and I are less involved than Twitter makes it seem."

As if to prove his point, his phone chimed: Austin posting a picture of Marc and Beth to Marc's Instagram and Twitter. Marc stared at the photo. He wasn't sure when Austin had taken the candid shot. Marc's hand was tucking a blonde curl behind Beth's ear, and there was a hint of a smile on her face. God, she was gorgeous. He glanced at his own face—he looked like an enthralled puppy. It took him a second to realize his face bore the same expression right this moment. He shook his head and glanced back at his father.

"Everyone's noticed that you're spending all your time around the house." His father's implication was clear: Marc hadn't been picking up random women at local bars. Even the idea of that left a knot in his stomach.

"What?" Marc hedged, unsure what to say, and not understanding anything he was feeling.

"Marc, you and I have always had what one might call a 'don't ask, don't tell' agreement about your sex life."

Marc couldn't help comparing his words with the open and honest dialogue Beth and her brothers shared about everything.

"Your mother and I know you're sleeping in your bed every night while we're here. It's not your normal routine, and you even mentioned *marriage* earlier." Frank said it like it was a curse word Marc couldn't use. "Don't tell me this girl isn't different."

"I like her enough that I won't fuck around on her, Dad," Marc said flatly, trying to keep all the emotions he didn't understand out of his voice.

"That makes her different."

"No. I don't cheat. Never have. That's not anything different."

His father frowned.

Dear old dad wasn't faithful, and Marc had seen how it hurt his mother even as she turned a blind eye. He had resolved to never do that to another person, neither as the cheater nor as the other man. Marc had always promised himself he wouldn't make his father's mistakes—any of them. Including pretending to be a family man.

"The question I have is, when was the last time someone mattered enough to you that seeing another woman became 'cheating?'" Frank asked expectantly.

Instead of admitting he had a point, Marc ignored it. "Just say what you want to say."

"You and I are the same. We're cut from the same cloth. You don't need to be chained to someone else's family, so don't get attached and ruin your whole damn life."

Marc sighed. This wasn't a new conversation. But now it wasn't only an *idea* that he shouldn't get attached to; today, it was real people.

"I know Beth—great lady. I can understand her appeal." Marc frowned at Frank. Realistically a man would have to be dead not to see Beth, but there was something inherently wrong with his father noticing his girlfriend. "She has strong ties to the community, not to mention two kids. A lot of responsibility. She won't pick up and move because you got a job as the pitching coach for the Arizona Diamondbacks." Frank observed Marc closely for his reaction.

Marc's gut reaction was to tell him to go to hell. His father didn't know what Beth would do or say. Still, he was probably right.

"Dad—"

Frank interrupted him.

"Marc, you're thinking with the wrong head. Pussy isn't something to give up your life to get. You can get it anywhere. It's all the same. Don't hang around here with your mother—go out."

If Marc wanted some random fuck, he could get it. Been there, done that. But he didn't want to explain it to his father. Instead, he took the easy way out and agreed to go out with Glory that night.

"Marc, are you babysitting tonight?" Glory asked him after twenty minutes at the bar.

"Nope," he said, too sharply.

"Then why are you here? Because you don't want to be," she said. "You've never come out with me before."

The pang of guilt told him his sister was right. He couldn't remember any other time in his life that he'd gone out with her. They'd worked together for months, but he'd never offered to take her to lunch. He couldn't remember a birthday dinner, and he was pretty sure he'd had a game the night Glory graduated from high school. What kind of brother did that make him? Even if he wasn't close with his dad, it made him suddenly sad to realize that he'd formed no relationship with his sister—and perhaps not even with his mother.

Marc said nothing. He let his eyes scan the room, looking at the crowd.

"You know it's okay to like someone enough that no one else matters. I mean, speaking as a girl," Glory stumbled over her words, "I would love to find a man who could sit in a bar full of women looking at him like he was a three-course meal, and be completely distracted because he only wanted to be with me."

Marc wanted it to be that easy, but it wasn't. It wasn't a love story causing his current unease; it was stress, disappointment in himself, annoyance with his parents, and lack of a sex life. He had no intention of telling his sister any of that, but she needed to understand that men shouldn't cheat. At twenty-one she was old enough to know that already, but having grown up in their house, it would be easy for her to assume that it was acceptable behavior.

"I'm not going home tonight. I'm getting a hotel room. I'll be there alone. The *only* reason I'm not going home is that Ma and Dad are driving me insane."

This was a conversation that, a few weeks ago, he wouldn't have had with Glory. He wouldn't have wanted to have any type of talk with her, because he'd never wanted a close relationship with her. But now he felt like not having one was missing out on something. Beth had, in the few short weeks he'd known her, changed him more than any other person he'd ever known.

"Good men don't cheat, Glory, even if you aren't having sex with them. They won't go looking for it elsewhere."

Glory snorted.

"I mean it," Marc said.

"You're telling me if Beth wasn't... you know... you wouldn't?"

Marc could have lied, but he didn't. "Beth and I aren't having sex, and I'm not looking for it anywhere else. And trust me, it wouldn't be hard to find."

"*What?*" Her shock overwhelmed Marc.

He had never been a good brother, and he needed to fix it as best he could. Things were going to change between him and Glory from now on.

"I've been a shitty brother, Glory, and a terrible example. I'm sorry. Women are more than sex. Anyone worth your time should know that. I'm not saying men aren't obsessed with sex; even men who like to spend time with you, they still want you," Marc admitted, and tried not to cringe. This was harder than the Evanses made it look. "But the right guy will realize it's worth the wait—*you're* worth the wait—and will be respectful enough to have a condom." He choked out the words, but he was determined to say them: "Because not using one is disrespectful to you."

"Mom's right; you're different. Beth's special, isn't she?" Glory asked, turning the conversation back on him.

"I was talking about you and men. Not Beth and me," Marc said, and got up. "Come on, we'll order some room service and watch a movie. That way we both get a break from Ma and Dad."

He couldn't leave her at the bar, but he couldn't handle any more of this serious talk. He hoped he had opened a door tonight—and he needed to make sure that, from now on, it stayed open.

16

BETH JUMPED UP, arching her back and kicking her feet out behind her, making a C-shape with her body before landing her toes on the ten centimeters of leather below her feet. She made it look effortless. On the other end of the balance beam, a ten-year-old—face pursed in concentration—jumped up and fell.

"So close." Beth smiled.

"One day I'm going to beat you, Ms. Evans." The young girl frowned.

"I bet you will." Beth smiled for a picture with the girl, then turned back to the crowd. She'd been doing this for about three hours; usually she enjoyed it more. Today, her problem was that she kept looking out into the crowd for Marc, which frustrated her every time. But as she scanned the crowd she saw the woman who was replacing her heading their way. "Okay last one before I turn over the beam—who gets the last attempt to beat me?"

"Me." Marc stepped forward, and Beth's heart skipped a beat.

She hadn't seen him since the Sunday afternoon Metros game. He'd spent most of it trying to convince Beth that PDA wasn't the end of the world. Her worry about embarrassing them both had become a game to him, and she didn't like how easy it was to suck her in.

In the last week, she'd had a lot of time to think without him around, using his Marc-mojo to mess with her mind. She felt stupid to admit it, but she'd missed him during his time away and was nervous about seeing him again.

He, on the other hand, looked completely at ease in his cargo shorts, black Sideline shirt, and sneakers, even though he was volunteering to jump on something that was narrower than his foot.

"Only if you're ready to get beat by a girl, hotshot," Beth teased, trying to sound lighthearted.

"In your dreams, sweetheart." Marc chuckled as he kicked off his sneakers and removed his socks. He moved to the beam and ungracefully hoisted himself, then stood with his hands on his hips, waiting for her as if he wasn't in the least bit worried about jumping up and down on the four-foot-high wooden bar.

Beth walked over, placed her hands on the beam, and slowly lifted herself into a handstand before making a quarter-turn and letting her feet down one at a time.

"Got some serious abs, Evans." His eyes lingered on her black Sideline crop shirt before drifting down to the fitted black Sideline short-shorts.

"Don't bother sweet-talking me. I won't go easy on you," Beth replied, and he laughed. "I pick the first five moves, and you copy them. If you get through those, you pick the next five. First to hit the mat loses."

"Are we playing for dinner or control of the remote?" Marc asked. Beth raised her eyebrows. "You're right, the remote all the way." Beth resisted the urge to roll her eyes. Marc had his own remote; he didn't need control of hers.

She walked to the center of the beam, did a half-turn on her toes, and walked back to the edge, looking at him expectantly. He copied her walk first without issue, then nailed the leg kick, and finally mimicked her tuck jump without falling off. She hadn't expected him to last that long. Her fourth move was a full turn on her toe, and she accomplished it without a balance check, then turned her eyes back to Marc.

A devilish smile crossed his lips as he moved to closer to her side of the beam. He put one foot in front of the other, like he would try to spin, but reached out and caught her wrist, pulling her toward him.

Taken by surprise, Beth lost her balance. Marc took advantage of that, pushing her down toward the mat and falling right along with her. She landed with an "Oof," and he landed on top of her, his arms bracing his weight.

"You okay? I think you slipped," Marc said, his eyes silently laughing at her.

"Oh yeah, *I* slipped." Beth rolled her eyes and pushed him off so she could stand up, but he was quicker and pulled her up into his arms for a hug.

"I missed you," he whispered, wholly unashamed. Their eyes met for a pregnant moment, and she just *knew* that everyone around them could feel the heavy tension.

Marc looked toward the crowd. "Don't worry, she's okay. She just doesn't like to lose."

"*Lose?!*" Her head snapped up.

"You hit the mat first," Marc said, his eyes crinkling with laughter. "Everyone saw you." Most of the crowd nodded or voiced their agreement, some more vocal than others.

"Unbelievable," Beth muttered.

"You should be clear about the rules," he whispered. His breath danced against her neck, sending the butterflies straight to her stomach, and she barely resisted the urge to shiver.

Marc put on a show for the crowd, kissing her lightly on the cheek. He let his lips linger—a slight turn of her head, and they would be on hers. Her breath caught.

"I hereby add a new rule." The remark from Beth's replacement saved her from having to answer. "Anyone who tackles me off the beam loses, and there will be no autograph or photo."

"I second that rule, but I think you're okay. Marc's the only cheater I've had today," Beth said as Marc chuckled beside her.

"Is that—?" Marc asked, trying to remember the name of the girl about to hop onto the beam.

"Yeah, Simone," Beth agreed as the Olympic gold medalist did a tuck on the beam, showing off for the crowd. "Simone's amazing. I don't do those skills anymore."

"You look better in your Sidelines, though." Marc's eyes trailed down her body.

Beth swallowed before responding. "Flattery will get you nowhere," she warned.

"Payback for a certain hole incident. If you can't win fairly, bend the rules, right?" Marc smiled knowingly. And Beth couldn't disagree; she'd done it to him.

She pulled on her white zip-up hoodie, then playfully whacked him in the stomach. Her hand felt like it had hit a rock, and it lingered a little too long before she finally pulled it back. Marc cleared his throat.

"Since you're done, can I buy you a drink?" Marc asked. "Austin didn't give me the game plan, and this isn't what I expected."

"Everything's under control. You only need to be here for the press. What *did* you expect?" Beth asked, tipping her chin toward the food truck at the edge of the parking lot. There wasn't a line at the moment but all the tables were full of people enjoying their food. Beth led them that way.

"I don't know," Marc admitted as they walked.

MARC LOOKED AROUND again. He hadn't expected it to take over the Meadowlands parking lots. Two of the lots were for parking, but the rest were strictly for fundraising booths, games, and food trucks. On the practice field and in several of the lots, professional and Olympic athletes ran activities for all ages. And sprinkled throughout, Hollywood's elite signed autographs and raised money.

"Honestly, I don't know much about Helping Hands."

Beth didn't look all that surprised by his revelation. "You always refused anytime we tried to get you involved, apart from donations."

"They're supposed to be anonymous," Marc mumbled, embarrassed. If he had wanted people to know he could give money away like it was candy, they'd know.

"They are," Beth assured him. "Your secret's safe with me."

Marc moved up to the counter, and was surprised to realize he knew the woman who turned to take his order.

"Marc! I didn't expect to see you here," said his housekeeper. Marie looked as genuinely shocked to see Marc as he was to see her. She glanced past Marc to see Beth standing behind him. "Beth—of course; I should have realized he would be here with you. I heard about you two. I couldn't think of two people better suited."

Beth's puzzled expression almost made him laugh—he couldn't see it either—but she continued.

"You and Marc have both been such a blessing to our family. I don't know what we would have done if Helping Hands hadn't found work for Tony and me. And then Marc helping pay for Tori's dancing—"

Marc winced. "Marie." His voice warned her that this was not something he wanted her to share. When Austin had told him their daughter would have to quit dancing because they couldn't afford to keep up with lessons, Marc had offered to pay for it.

"And honestly, the man's house is always perfect," Marie continued. "It's a showroom, and I know he doesn't need me in there every other day. Half the time, he hasn't even been home since I was there last." Marie smiled. He forced a smile back, and didn't dare look over at Beth.

"You're going to make me blush," he said quickly. "Can I get two Diet Cokes, please?"

"Of course! Marc needs two Diet Cokes," Marie called to the woman working with her.

"Marc Demoda?" the woman said, looking up. She was young, maybe in her mid-twenties. "I know you probably don't remember me." He started to worry he had slept with this woman and she was about to point it out. It wouldn't be the first time that had happened. But she said, "I wanted to thank you."

Marc groaned internally. He didn't know what she was going to say, but he didn't think he could stop her.

"My husband is your mechanic," the woman continued, then thanked him for taking care of their son's medical bills the year before.

"Just glad your son's okay," Marc said, and grabbed the sodas before someone else could publicly thank him for things they'd promised not to share with anyone.

"Does everyone from Helping Hands work this carnival?" Marc looked around desperately for anyone else who might know him.

"Unless they have a reason they can't. It's an 'everyone-pitch-in' type of organization, and this is our biggest fundraiser of the year," Beth said. Her voice sounded strange, like she was trying to keep whatever she was feeling in check.

"Then you might as well know that there are about ten more people who are going to make similar comments. Austin hooked me up with all of them, so I have to assume they're all here. We have an agreement that they don't tell people, but for some reason, they don't seem to think you count as 'telling someone,'" Marc said. He turned to look at Beth and frowned. "And don't look at me like that," he added.

Her mouth turned up at the corner, and then she took a sip of her drink. "Like what?" she finally asked.

"Like you suddenly forgot what a jerk I am," Marc said, taking her hand.

"Trust me, the whiplash reminds me of what a jerk you are." Beth smiled up at him again. "I'm surprised you get it."

Her eyes sparkled like they did when she watched her son playing baseball or her daughter singing her ABCs. His stomach tightened: She was proud of him. He frowned again.

"'Pay it forward' is the basis of the entire organization. It's about doing something for someone without wanting or expecting anything. Helping each other because we can. That's what you do," Beth explained.

He needed to clarify this before she started thinking Marc was something he wasn't. "I can't spend the interest I make in a month. These people need money; I need to get rid of it. That's all it is."

"Exactly. You're not doing it expecting attention or praise," she agreed, smiling. "That's what I mean. That's why when Austin approached me with the idea, I signed over my inheritance to get it off the ground."

"Wait—you did what?" Marc asked. He suddenly remembered the conversation about squandering her money. Knowing her parents, he'd bet Beth had invested money in Helping Hands, and they thought it was a waste. "Like, all of it?"

"Well, I invested some in Will's gym and in Grant's farm, but the rest I turned over to Austin." She shrugged.

"You gave away millions of dollars?" he asked.

Beth looked at the ground. "The simplest answer is yes. But, after Bob and I got married, that money was the last link to my father. I was no longer living with them, didn't share their name—not using their money was the next step. It made sense to give it to something that could do some actual good." Beth finally looked up to meet his eyes. "The money gave Helping Hands a solid start, and leaving it behind gave me a fresh one." Beth waved her hand around her. "This means a lot to me." Her eyes twinkled, and her face lit up with contagious energy.

Marc couldn't help but smile. "Everything Helping Hands has done is great, and this carnival is amazing." But it was the woman who stood next to him, blushing, who was truly wonderful.

He didn't want to make her more uncomfortable, so he decided to change the subject. "So, where are the kids?" Marc asked, looking around before realizing how ridiculous it was to think he could spot them in a group this large.

"They're with Danny, over by the trucks bonding with the other firefighters."

"Let's go find them. I'm looking forward to seeing them again." Then Marc froze as his father's words echoed in his head.

"What?" Beth looked up.

You're going to get attached.

He wasn't getting attached. Marc could look forward to seeing Beth and the kids without it meaning he was getting stuck.

"Nothing," he said quickly and then placed his hand on the small of her back. He *liked* Beth and the kids. It was that simple. It was nothing he couldn't walk away from and come back to see periodically, like he did with other people.

Marc and Steve spent the next hour dragging the girls to every game in the parking lot, having more fun than he'd had in years as they moved from one booth or activity to the next. Marc even won a Disney Cinderella doll for Mandy, which put a smile on her face.

The paparazzi and press were everywhere, so he gave Beth plenty of space, keeping her comfortable and spending his time with Mandy on his shoulders. Finally, as the kids prepared to play a water-gun game they could both handle on their own, he decided he was going to get Beth a little closer.

He was using the excuse of helping Beth get over her issues with the press to keep her close. However, his hands had been itching to touch her since he'd seen her in the barely-there Sideline outfit. He might be the spokesman for the brand, but he'd never loved it as much as he did seeing her in it. A natural smile spread over his lips as his arms wrapped around her waist, pulling her soft body tight to his chest. Although she was tense, he liked how she felt in his arms.

"It's okay," he whispered, but kept his hold firm as she tried to wiggle away. "If I don't start touching you, people won't believe we're dating. Everyone knows I'm all about giving the cameras the money shot." He didn't plan on sticking his tongue down her throat as he'd done with women in the past, but he wanted to be able to touch her in public.

"You're supposed to be turning over a new leaf," Beth hissed.

"I am. Instead of hanging all over *lots* of girls, I'm just hanging all over *you*." He kissed her hair. Man, she smelled good. He took another breath, drinking in the scent of her. It was fruity—maybe peaches? The familiar burst of lust that Beth brought out rushed through him.

"Hey, Marc!" someone called, and he turned his head, keeping his arms around Beth's waist. He scanned the crowd for a minute, but didn't recognize anyone. A camera flashed, taking their photo, and people milled about, but no one stood out. It was a familiar occurrence—strangers thinking they knew him because they knew *of* him, having seen him on TV or in the papers. Although it was irritating, he was used to it. He turned back to what mattered.

"Relax," he whispered to a tense Beth.

The kids moved to the next game, a giant ball pit. Beth settled against his chest as they watched. Marc let his finger run along the edge of her hoodie before lightly skimming the satin skin of her waist. Marc hadn't been lying when he'd said she had some nice abs. His fingers danced up along her ribs; she felt like heaven under his hand. Her breath caught again, and he sighed. This 'just friends' thing sucked. But he pulled his hand back, releasing her before he got carried away.

"Mama, Marc, see me," Mandy called out to them, drawing their attention as she launched herself into the air and somersaulted into the pit.

"Good job!" Beth called back.

Beth struck a perfect balance in parenting and it impressed the hell out of Marc. She gave them space to be themselves and try things, but she was there if they needed her. He'd never had that as a kid, so he hoped his parenting style would be like Beth's.

His parenting style? What the hell? He didn't plan on having kids, which hadn't changed, so he wouldn't need a parenting style. He shook his head.

Marc moved to the bench to sit down, and Beth walked over to sit beside him.

"Don't suppose you would sit on my lap?" he teased.

"Marc." She sighed. He took her hand in his, simply to touch her. "I know you see this as a personal challenge because you need some sort of competition in your life, but I'm not a game." She looked down at her shoes. Today she was wearing flip-flops, not those fuck-me heels she'd worn too many times lately. He missed the heels. But at the moment, he needed to focus on what she was saying. This was important.

"I don't think you're a game. We're friends, and I'm trying to help. It's been ten years; you need to let it go," Marc said. She tried to yank her hand away, but he held on. He wanted to understand how she felt, and that meant he had to push her to talk.

"You have no idea."

He was sure there was more to that statement, but he interrupted anyway. "So tell me."

"It would be *easy* if it had been ten years ago and I could move on, but it's not," Beth said, turning to look at him.

"What do you mean?"

"When was the last time you saw the pictures?" she asked, raising a single eyebrow.

Wow, he didn't want to admit that.

"See?" she said pointedly. "Recently."

"I googled you, and they popped up," he admitted sheepishly.

"Embarrass you?" Beth asked, flatly looking toward her kids again.

"It made me mad." Marc left out the other emotions.

"Yeah. It made lots of people mad at me." Beth sighed, and her entire face fell.

"No!" The woman was exasperating. "Not that—not mad *at* you. Mad *for* you."

"What?" The confusion in her face was utterly absurd. Why she thought what had happened was her fault was beyond him.

"It's an invasion of your privacy," Marc snapped, although he was trying not to direct any of his anger at her. He'd like to kill the nineteen-year-old who'd thought it was no big deal to sell photos Beth didn't consent to. More, now that he knew how much it affected her. "Seeing them made me want to hit something."

"It doesn't embarrass you?" Beth asked, looking at him like she didn't believe a word he was saying.

"What do you mean? What would embarrass me?"

She took a minute to play with her ring before she answered. "That you're dating me—well, as far as the world knows,

175

anyway—and anyone can google me and see…" She couldn't finish, and she crumpled into his shoulder. Her compact frame curled into his side as she burrowed her face into his neck; her breath danced on his skin, sending tiny pulses of electricity through him. He swallowed, forcing his attention back onto their conversation.

"No," Marc said honestly. Pissed off, jealous, turned on— any of those worked, but not embarrassed. And then Marc figured it out. "That's what you're afraid of, embarrassing yourself with a picture of us that will bring it all back up."

"Not only me," she mumbled into his shoulder.

"Your family?"

"Them too, I guess."

"Who else?"

Beth shrugged like it didn't matter, but the deep blush of her cheeks told him.

"*Me?*" He spun so he was facing her. "You're worried about embarrassing *me?*" Marc said, looking down at this sweet, stupid woman resting on his shoulder. He smiled above her head and bit back the laughter that was bubbling up, because she was serious. But the idea that she might care sent a surge of happiness through him.

"You want me to help you fix your image, but look at the other people around me. My parents, Corey—I embarrass them." Beth sighed. "And every time we're out together, supposed to be fixing things for you, I'm waiting for whatever ruins it."

Marc bit the inside of his cheek.

"Beth, I don't think you could do anything to embarrass me." He had made an ass of himself regularly for the last year. His image and reputation could only improve with her no matter what happened, but it was so damn sweet that she was worried about it.

"You don't know me that well."

And he laughed. She might not think he knew her, but he did.

"I already told you to yell at me in public. I *want* you to if I piss you off. You've been told you say the wrong things, but you could spout all your opinions and although I disagree with some of what you say, unlike your father, I won't mind standing there next to you smiling while you say it."

Beth frowned at him. Marc smiled. "I already told you I don't care if you trip or dump something on anyone. And I'll include the president in that statement, because I'd have to laugh if that happened."

"What about my outfits? You don't like them."

"What?" This one he couldn't explain.

"You hated that blue dress at the hospital, and earlier, you glared at my Sidelines until I put on my sweatshirt."

"I wasn't glaring." 'Staring' would be the correct word, and inappropriately so—which was why he'd been glad when she put on that white hoodie.

Beth pulled her head up off his shoulder and shot him a look that said she didn't believe him. But the truth was, he couldn't think of anything he'd ever seen her in, including her sweats, that he didn't like way more than he should, considering this whole platonic thing they had going on.

He had to correct this ass-backward idea. "Beth."

"What?"

"Speaking strictly as your *friend*, you have a hot little body, and it looks good in pretty much anything—or nothing." Marc shrugged. "Even if it were you and me in those pictures, I wouldn't be embarrassed. I'd be mad, but honestly, ninety percent of men who see it are thinking what a lucky son-of-a-gun Corey is."

"I doubt that." Beth rolled her eyes.

"I would doubt *that*." Beth might be a smart woman, but she missed things–very obvious things.

"You mean it, don't you?" Beth said, looking up at him with those big emerald eyes that made him want to promise her the moon and the stars.

"Yes, so you don't need to worry about it. And Beth, no matter how many pictures people take of us, they will always be strictly PG; you can trust me on that. I promise I won't ever embarrass you." Marc tilted her chin up with his index finger. She smiled, and he forgot they were just friends. He leaned in and brushed his lips lightly across hers, just as a camera flashed behind them. "Son of a gun," he huffed, but Beth smiled as they both turned.

"Wanna bet that's one of the highest retweets for the next twelve hours?"

"And I'll bet it's very PG," Marc said, but for the first time in his life, he felt like a photographer had invaded his privacy.

17

@NYStarPost: Is it only his eyes that wander? @HotshotDemoda caught with his eyes on the wrong girl. Is he losing interest in the single mom?

@USWeekly: What did Elizabeth Campbell do to cause @HotshotDemoda to lose interest so quickly? As the saying goes, though, once a playboy, always a playboy. Be careful w/ your ♡ Elizabeth!

"WHERE IS HE?" Austin stormed into Beth's living room when she opened the front door. She was alone this morning. The kids had spent the night at Uncle Will's house while she stayed late after the carnival to get it shut down and cleaned up.

"I told you, he's not here," Beth said. "What's the matter?"

"This." He handed her page six of the New York Star Post.

> Is it only his eyes that wander? She loves him, and he loves women. Some things never change.

179

Under the headline were two photos of Beth and Marc from yesterday. The first was cute. They were sitting together on the bench. He had one arm around her back and one finger under her chin as he kissed her. They looked like a blissfully happy couple.

The other photo—not so much.

Marc's arms were around her waist, and she was leaning against him, watching the kids play the water balloon squirt game. It would have been the picture of a happy family outing, if not for the fact that Marc was staring at another woman as he held Beth in his arms.

She was gorgeous, Beth had to give her that: bleached blonde and beautiful, with legs that went on forever. Of course, the high heels and incredibly short skirt could have helped with the illusion. Exactly Marc's type—beautifully trashy.

Beth sighed.

This woman was the type Marc had been photographed with plenty, so why did it feel like she had been punched in the stomach? It forced Beth to admit the truth: She wished their pretend relationship was real.

It was feeling real; too many things didn't seem for show. Whispers no one could hear, touches hidden from view, and conversations like the one they had yesterday. All of it made it seem like a relationship, not just a business deal.

But it wasn't, and she needed to fix that in her mind.

She sank onto the sofa and read the article, which started out saying Marc had gone away alone for a week, then all but accused him of cheating.

"It's everywhere, right?" she asked, clearing the lump in her throat, and Austin nodded. "This isn't good for him."

"Especially not if you're mad about it," Austin said.

"I'm not," Beth assured him, shaking her head as she looked at the pictures again. No, she wasn't mad, and she was trying not to be hurt either. She racked her brain to find a response that wouldn't get her attacked in the press. "I'm going to say they're making a mountain out of a molehill and redirect to the success of the carnival, right?"

"Is that how you want to spin it?" he asked.

"Honestly, whatever will make it go away. I don't want to become a target."

"We won't let that happen, but yeah, laughing it off and redirecting seems to be your best option." Austin shook his head like he was disagreeing with the words coming out of his own mouth. "Go out together to places you'll be seen, hot spots; don't hide out. And let them take more pictures like that one," he said, pointing to the photo of Beth and Marc kissing. "That one looks like a couple in love. We'll post a ton of our own as well."

She wouldn't say she'd fallen for Marc, but why did he have to turn out to be... nice? The self-centered jerk the media portrayed him to be—she could resist that guy. But the guy Marc was turning out to be was a lot harder not to fall for.

Austin's phone rang. "Where are you? ... I'm already here. She's—" He stopped looking at Beth. She gave a half-hearted smile and walked toward the kitchen to get some more coffee.

Austin followed her after a couple of minutes.

"So, how are you going to play this with him?" he asked casually. "He's on his way here and wants to know how you're taking it."

"What do you mean?"

"Are you going to tell him he hurt you or not?"

She plastered on her fake-as-hell smile and lied to her friend. "He didn't. It's nothing. Do you want some coffee?"

"Sure," Austin said, helping himself to a mug out of her cabinet. Finally, after a few moments of silence while he poured his coffee, he admitted, "As his agent, I know you're doing the right thing pretending everything is fine. But as your friend, who saw your face a few minutes ago, I'm having a hard time convincing myself he doesn't need a good knee to the balls." Austin leaned back on his elbow and looked up at her as Marc stormed in.

"You can yell in a minute, Austin," Marc said before coming up beside her and taking one of her hands in his. "Beth, this isn't what it looks like." He slammed the newspaper down on her counter with the other.

"So it's not a publicity nightmare?" Beth asked.

"No. I mean, yes, it is. But we were watching the kids—"

"Marc, you don't need to explain it. I get it." Beth cut him off, laughing lightly. The comment didn't mollify him, though. If anything, he seemed angrier.

"You don't get it. The first time I saw this woman was today in the paper," he said, through clenched teeth.

"Don't lie about it," she snapped, pushing away from him and the counter. "I was there."

"I'm not lying, Beth," he said, reaching out.

"*Stop.* I felt you notice her," she hissed, not wanting to have this conversation with Austin listening. Even though he had walked to the far side of the kitchen, he was still in earshot.

"What do you mean?" Marc demanded.

"I was standing between your legs, Marc," Beth said even more quietly. "It's not a big deal. Can we let this go?"

"No, I can't. It's just—" Marc pinched the bridge of his nose.

Beth understood; he had a strict moral code about cheating, and he felt like this was wrong. "You have no reason to feel guilty. We're not actually dating, and if I'd seen you check her out, I'd have made some comment about how you probably wish she and I could have a body transplant." Beth opened the cabinet and pulled out another coffee mug. "Do you want some coffee while we talk about how we're handling this?"

Marc nodded but glanced away, clearly mulling something over. His eye fell to the counter, and his fist knocked on it twice before he glanced back up to Beth. Then, the frustration clear in his voice, he said, "Just so you're aware, after this, a lot of things are about to change."

18

MARC LOOKED AT the flowers on the seat next to him. They were Sid's idea. Unlike everyone else, she believed him when he said he wasn't checking out other women, despite the picture. Too bad Beth didn't believe it.

After over a week of spotlight dating, Beth had claimed exhaustion last night and begged out of dinner with Sid and Austin. He couldn't blame her. She'd been great, smiling for the reporters, laughing off the photo from the papers. Even when they were alone together, she wasn't cold. She acted like everything was normal, and it was no big deal.

But it was a big deal to him. He'd felt something change between them that day at the carnival, but now that had disappeared. It wasn't anything he could put his finger on, but somehow, she'd pulled away.

Not so much physically. He took her to Beatrice Inn on Tuesday, and she even danced all night with him. Boy, did he love how she felt moving in his arms. Of course, that meant he needed a cold shower when he got home, but it had been fun.

Last night, however, he had not had fun. His one-eighty on dealing with the media not only made Sid think something was different, but it had Austin asking questions that Marc wasn't willing to answer.

Anything with Beth was private. That was the new policy they all needed to work with—which Austin pointed out was ridiculous because she was in the media, making him look good. Marc didn't care. He wasn't so unreasonable he wanted a 'no comment' policy but he wanted to limit what his team told the media and if any outlet printed anything not approved, he wanted to sue for character defamation. If Beth okayed a shot of them, then that was fine; otherwise, it was off fucking limits. And he didn't care how much it cost him.

Austin still said that was completely unreasonable and wouldn't work. Tying up millions of dollars in retainers with lawyers wasn't the answer. One lawsuit might give the media pause, but Marc couldn't go crazy.

The problem was, he *felt* crazy. He'd always let the media into his life, because for him it was never a big deal. But now it was different. Marc hadn't known how the press became a third person in a relationship, causing conflict, adding drama. It was one thing when the media was talking about him; he had thick skin. But it was something else when they went after someone he cared about. He wasn't happy to hear Austin telling him that the most he could do was redirect, give them something else to talk about, and move on.

So he did the only other thing he could: He added security. He couldn't stand the idea of having a shadow always with him, or forcing that on Beth and the kids, but he could have a team to sweep her street, and his. They'd stay in the background, unnoticed but *there*, just in case.

He clicked his key fob and opened her gate, then drove slowly into the driveway. With the two dozen white roses in hand, he headed for the door. The house sounded like a circus, but that didn't worry him anymore. He looked forward to the madness. It kept things interesting.

He rang the bell, shocked when Beth opened the door, not seeming to care that her dogs ran out yapping. She looked awful—she was pale, with dark circles under red-rimmed eyes. She stood there in sweats, Katie on her hip, and just stared at him. He hadn't realized she was this tired. No—something was wrong. The panic that bubbled up inside his gut shocked him even more than Beth's appearance.

"Go away," she said, but there was no force behind the words. She tried to shut the door, but he was quicker. He wasn't leaving until he knew what was going on. He went inside, bringing the barking mutts with him.

"Are you okay?" he asked, reaching out to touch her forehead. "Beth, you're burning up."

"I know." She coughed.

"So why aren't you in bed? You need to be resting, not babysitting."

"Because it's my *job*. I can't stay in bed and leave everyone downstairs alone."

Beth wobbled on her feet, and he grabbed the toddler before she sank onto the floor in a puddle. Even after he got Katie into the contraption that hung from the door frame and set the flowers on the counter, Beth still hadn't moved. She was *sick*.

Marc didn't do sick; he should go. This was one of those responsibility things he didn't want and hadn't signed up to handle. But then she coughed again, a deep rumble in her chest.

He wasn't leaving her alone. Marc squatted down beside her, scooped her into his arms, and headed upstairs.

"What are you doing?" she moaned, but she leaned into him.

"I'm getting you into bed and then calling one of your brothers, which is what you should have done."

"Please don't." She sounded pathetic. A surge of protectiveness washed through him. This woman needed someone looking out for her, helping her, taking fucking care of *her* for once.

"If they knew you were sick, they'd be here. So why didn't you tell them?"

"They'd buzz over me like I'm an invalid. They have issues. I'll be fine."

He could understand that; her brothers tended to be over the top about everything in life. "Beth, you need some sleep," he said, and pulled back the blankets of her unmade bed before setting her in it. "How long have you been sick?"

"Yesterday." Beth shivered, and he pulled the covers up over her.

"Why didn't you tell me last night when you called?"

"You would've told someone."

He thought about shaking some sense into the woman. Of *course* he would have called someone.

"Why do you have extra kids?"

"My sister was out of town last night so I've had her kids since yesterday morning," Beth mumbled. "And Trish knew

I wasn't feeling great, but her situation is complicated and she doesn't have any other options. I couldn't just leave her hanging. And you're not calling my brothers. I forbid it."

She tried to make the threat sound serious, but her voice was comically weak. She shifted into a sitting position, but Marc pushed her back down, pulling the covers over her again. She was the weakling here, yet she held all the power. He would do just about anything to keep her in bed, including dealing with the kids himself.

He didn't understand what was going on with him. This was exactly why he didn't do relationships. But the idea of her getting out of this bed left him ridiculously unsettled.

She had to get better. He needed her to be okay. He didn't know why it mattered so much. But it did.

"I'll watch the kids. Take a nap," Marc said, and relaxed when she eased back against the pillow.

"Okay, a nap, and then you'll go," Beth agreed, and she was asleep before he even got out the door. She needed to think more about herself. A little selfishness wouldn't hurt her.

Hours later at almost nine thirty he'd finally gotten all the kids off with their parents or asleep in their beds. He had spent the day keeping Beth in bed and taking care of everything, but he wasn't anywhere near as organized as she was. Her sister had chuckled at the mess and brushed pizza off his shirt when she picked up her three kids two hours ago, and Beth's friend Trish had rushed her two out the door around five thirty. Steve's bedtime was eight, but Marc hadn't even gotten Mandy into bed until almost eight thirty. She had begged to stay up 'just ten more minutes,' which led to him carrying her up already sound sleep. Steve had been up until ten minutes ago. Unlike Mandy, he hadn't wanted Marc to take him up. Instead, he'd shot him an edgy look and rushed upstairs alone.

Exhausted, Marc headed to Beth's room with a bowl of soup on a tray. The kids had tons of energy, never slowed down, and Mandy—she never shut up. Man, that girl could talk. Even if she was alone in a room, she talked to herself. The day had seemed never-ending.

Marc opened the door quietly when his knock got no response. He had heard the shower turn on about an hour ago, so it was no surprise to see Beth's damp curls lying loosely around her face and bare shoulders as she slept, snuggled into the comforter. Her arm rested against her chest and her hand curled on the pillow under her chin. Against the white pillowcase, her face was still pale, but most of the color had come back; the circles that had been under her eyes that morning had almost disappeared.

He stood there, watching her breathing steadily in and out. Setting the tray on the dresser, he crossed to the bed and tucked a blond curl behind her ear, and she stirred when he pressed the back of his hand against her forehead. Her fever was gone.

She moaned softly and stretched in a very feminine way, sending the scent of peaches into the air. His body reacted instinctively. A beautiful pajama-clad angel squirming always got his hormones raging, and the blood that had been racing through his body moments ago took a beeline south.

His reaction amazed him. The moment Beth opened her emerald-green eyes and smiled weakly at him, all he could think about was climbing into the bed and pressing himself inside her until she was screaming his name.

He frowned. There was something wrong with him. Sick women should not turn him on. But Beth did—although lately she always did, even if she didn't believe it.

"Are the kids in bed?" she asked, interrupting his thoughts. She moved a stray curl off her face, her hair looking rumpled as if she'd spent hours having hot sex instead of a nap. He felt like he could pull that comforter away and push her right back into the pillow.

"Marc?" Beth asked. She was obviously waiting for an answer, but he couldn't remember the question. God damn, he had been like a randy teenager from the moment he'd walked into her bedroom. Suddenly he couldn't form coherent thoughts. "The kids—are they okay? Are they in bed?"

"Kids... Yeah, in bed or at home," he said. Now he was staring at her mouth while she bit that hot little lip between her teeth.

"Thank you so much for today, Marc." Sheer gratitude reflected on her face.

He shrugged, feeling a bit embarrassed. "You hungry, or did you want to sleep some more?" Marc asked, looking at the tray of soup and crackers. The reason he had come into her room.

"I'll eat. I was watching Corey pitch; tell me he didn't blow it. I'm not up for a pep talk." Beth looked from Marc to the television, which was showing a disgusting public service announcement about not smoking. Perfect turn-off.

"No, he's doing fine. Probably done though—bottom of the eighth."

"Want to watch the end with me? I can go downstairs."

"No, don't get up," he blurted. He wouldn't be able to think if he saw the rest of those barely-there PJs.

"Okay, we can watch up here." She scooted to the other side of the bed, making room for him. *That* wasn't what he meant.

The comforter fell away, and front and center on that tank top were two hard, round nipples. Goosebumps covered her arms, indicating the cause of her reaction, but reason be damned. They were like bullseyes, taunting him, saying, *'Come and get me. Don't you want to feel these under your hands? Don't you want a taste?'* Yes, damn it, he did.

Do not get into that bed.

"Uh." He cleared his throat. "Sure," he said, knowing it was a mistake even as he grabbed the food tray and settled next to her on the bed.

Don't think of it as a bed.

"What's the score?" Beth asked, shifting positions again to eat the soup. Now he could see her short pink shorts. Was she *trying* to torture him?

She had some messed-up ideas about how to be friends with a guy. He blamed her brothers for that. Although they treated her like a girl in some ways, they also treated her like an asexual being. She had no idea that lying in bed with a man you weren't fucking wasn't normal. He doubted many men would be able to sit in a bed with her and not think about what else they could be doing.

We're friends. We're not having sex. Get over it.

He grabbed one of the many pillows all over the bed and placed it on his lap to hide the evidence that he didn't want to be just friends. With his arms crossed, he uncomfortably settled in.

"Marc?"

Damn it, what was the question—ah! The score. "Five to three Metros," he said. "As long as they don't blow it, Corey'll finally get a win." Surprisingly, his voice sounded normal, even though he was gritting his teeth.

"He'll be happy, although he'll probably want to die before he admits you were right about his release point. But the proof's in the pudding—three good games in a row. Did you eat?" Beth asked, moving to set her tray on the floor.

Marc was proud of himself for not groaning when he got a glimpse of her ass.

Watch the game. Don't stare at your friend's ass. Because that's what we are. Friends. That's it. That's what she wants.

"Marc?" she asked, looking at him with those big candy green eyes that made him think of green M&Ms. At that moment it was clear how pathetic he had become. Her eyes made his stomach tighten.

"Yeah, we got pizza from Ray's. By the way, you've ruined those kids. They made me get them veggie pizza. What kind of kids ask for veggies on pizza?" Marc said, focusing entirely on the TV as Beth settled herself back against her pillow. His muscles clenched, and he had to cross his arms over his chest again to keep from touching her. He was dying to touch her. He took another breath of peaches and almost groaned.

She didn't realize what she was doing to him. She didn't seem to be aware of how close they were sitting, but he was very aware of her in every respect. The heat radiating off her body, the sexy sound of her voice that echoed into his bones as she talked, the smell of her freshly bathed skin, the way she looked in that skimpy tank top...

Don't groan.

He stared at the TV. She was saying something, but he had no idea what because he was working on the mother of all hard-ons, and she didn't seem to notice or care.

This was a mistake, and it wasn't one he would make again. He should never have agreed to get into bed with her and watch TV. He wanted her. It didn't matter that she'd spent the entire day sick; it didn't matter that they were just friends. Hell, it didn't matter if the house was on fire—he'd happily burn if it meant getting this woman. He wanted her in so many ways, and not all of them involved seeing her naked.

She was still talking about something. So far, she hadn't required a response, which was good because Marc wouldn't have been able to give her one. She squirmed against him, trying to get more comfortable, and he snapped.

"I can't do this," he practically shouted. He jumped off the bed, leaving her toppling over.

"Huh?" She looked up, baffled.

"Beth, I don't want to be your friend. I don't want to lie in a bed with you and watch TV. I don't want you to sit next to me and *chat*, because I can't have a conversation with you."

Beth averted her eyes, looking like he had slapped her, and he felt like an ass.

"I'm sorry," she mumbled, but didn't look at him.

Shit, he'd just made everything ten times worse because she didn't understand.

"Sweetheart, I didn't mean to hurt your feelings. I know we agreed to stay friends, but—"

"It's okay. I'm sure if we spend a few hours a week together in public for the press, that'll be enough." Beth's teeth sank into her lush lip, and he couldn't stop the groan. *He* needed to be the one nipping at her mouth.

"Beth, you're not getting it. I want to spend *more* time together, not less. I wouldn't mind being with you right now, sitting here, if I wasn't consumed with thoughts of getting you out of those skimpy pajamas." She started to say something, but he held his hand up. "If I get back in that bed with you, I'm going to kiss you, and it's going to be the 'ravage your sexy little mouth' kind of kiss."

She looked utterly shocked. She might have looked less stunned if he'd told her he thought he was Santa Claus.

"I didn't think..." She let her sentence trail off and fiddled with the ring on her thumb. "But I have short legs," she finally managed.

She had some weird thing about her legs that he didn't understand. Her legs made his mouth water. Her legs made him picture them wrapped around his hips while he sank into everything she offered.

"I—" He paused, unsure what to do with that. He decided to get back to the point. "I want you more than I've ever wanted any woman in my life."

It was probably a terrible idea to sleep with her, and he didn't care. He'd worry about the consequences tomorrow.

She said nothing, just looked at him with uncertainty. He moved slowly, giving her time to stop him, but she didn't seem like she was going to. His heart rate sped up as he climbed across the bed to her.

"Last chance," he said gruffly and grabbed the back of her neck.

She looked at him and smiled slightly. "If you get sick, it's your fault."

He laughed, really laughed. At this moment he didn't give a flying fuck if he got sick. He placed his lips on hers.

For a moment, she didn't respond to his kiss—just sat there, letting him brush his lips over her mouth. Then she relaxed and wrapped her arms around his neck, pulling him against her. Surrender.

Finally. She's mine.

But of course, since this was Beth's house, the damn phone rang.

"Ignore it," Marc growled. He kissed a sensitive spot on her neck and she drew in a sudden breath. "They'll leave a message if it's important." His lips trailed lightly along her neck and jawline until she melted into him.

"Okay," she said breathlessly, and caught his mouth with hers.

Of course her machine would be in the bedroom. Who doesn't have their answering machine in their bedroom? *Who the fuck still has an answering machine?*

Her brother's voice rang through the air. "It's Clayton. Pick up your phone. I know you're there. Doug's here, and he said he dropped pizza off at your house earlier and Steve told him you're in bed sick. Why didn't you call someone? Pick up, or I'm coming over to check on you!"

Just what he wanted—her brother here, just when he'd finally gotten her in bed. Especially since they were like fruit flies: Once you let one in, they multiplied before you could stop them. And they were all but impossible to get rid of.

"Get it," Marc demanded, and Beth nodded.

"Sorry," she mumbled.

So was he.

"Clayton, I'm in bed," Beth said as she picked up the phone. "No, my cell's downstairs. I was, uh…" Her eyes met Marc's. "Watching the game." He chuckled when she blushed. Guess she didn't want to tell him she was about to have sex.

Probably not a bad idea. The brothers had already interrogated Marc about their relationship. Danny had been the one to ask the question, but the intense stares of the others while they waited for Marc's answer had made it clear that he was speaking for them all. Marc had told them nothing was going on, and Will had informed him that the boys would want to know if that changed. He owed the boys the conversation, and hopefully they'd give them their blessing and not castrate him. He just didn't want to talk about it *now*.

"But I'm fine… I didn't need any help… Well, Marc stopped by… Yes. Why is that surprising? I *didn't* call him. He just came over… You *all* do that." Marc chuckled again. That was true. "No, don't come. I'm okay. Steve and Mandy are asleep; there's no reason—" She looked helplessly at him. "Fine, in the morning then. … Okay, love you too. Bye."

Beth dropped the phone back onto the nightstand. "He's mad."

"I get that." It irritated him too that she hadn't called for help, but he wouldn't bring that up right now. "Now, where were we?" he asked, and rubbed his thumb on her cheek, letting his fingers run through those curls of hers. Her teeth began to gnaw on her bottom lip again. At this point, that should be his job, and he wasn't letting her overthink this.

"I think we were right about here," he said, catching her mouth with his again—just as Mandy screamed. "Oh, for the love of God." He flopped himself back onto the pillows.

"Mama, it's too dark," Mandy screeched from the other room.

"Her closet light must not be on," Beth said with a sigh. She pulled herself out of bed, leaving him alone in her room.

This wasn't working. Too many people needed Beth's attention, and when he finally got her into bed, Marc wanted it all for himself. He sat up and accepted that tonight wouldn't be the night—but it wouldn't be much longer, he promised himself. He'd had his fill of cold showers.

He slammed his feet back into the sneakers he had kicked off not long before and headed into the hall.

Beth walked out of Mandy's room. He looked at that little pink tank top and shorts and his gut clenched, and he almost reconsidered.

Good things come to those who wait.

"Are you leaving?" He couldn't help but be pleased to see a trace of disappointment on her face when he nodded. But he didn't want her to think he had changed his mind.

"Tomorrow night, you're going to get a babysitter. I want you all to myself," he said.

"Tomorrow?" Beth asked, looking up at him with that sparkle in her emerald eyes.

"Yes," Marc said, and settled his mouth on hers for one more taste before he had to leave. He was going to plan a night that had nothing to do with anything but him and Beth.

He was taking her on their first real date.

19

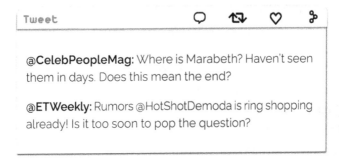

@CelebPeopleMag: Where is Marabeth? Haven't seen them in days. Does this mean the end?

@ETWeekly: Rumors @HotShotDemoda is ring shopping already! Is it too soon to pop the question?

BETH LIFTED HER hand and knocked on the apartment door. Trish answered right away. Not only was Trish Katie and Nate's mom but, she was one of Beth's closest friends.

"Hey, you look great," Trish said as her brown eyes ran over her while Mandy and Steve pushed past her to get inside. Trish's immaculate apartment was about to get torn up by the four kids. Knowing Trish though, she'd have it cleaned up before the kids were in bed for fifteen minutes. The single mom was always on top everything. "I love that white dress on you."

"Thanks," Beth said she wasn't worried about the short white halter dress. Plus, Beth wasn't prepared to admit the change in her relationship with Marc to any of her brothers yet. She didn't understand why, after spending the day helping while she was sick, he had suddenly decided he wanted her, and she'd never be able to explain it.

Sitting in bed with Marc last night had been a weird experience. The second his weight had dropped onto the mattress, her stomach lodged in her throat. She rambled on incessantly, trying to forget about the heat of the attractive man next to her. The column of Marc's throat, the strength of his forearms, the smell of his cologne—it all whispered desire into Beth's ear. And then he'd said he wanted her.

But did he want her for one night? For one date? Was this purely the thrill of the chase?

Her pillows still carried the musky scent of him this morning, and her body shivered when she thought of him—but the questions mattered more. She wanted to know what was going on.

Marc had called her at lunchtime to make sure she'd found a babysitter, and told her he would be there around six thirty. She said she'd meet him at his house instead, since she was dropping the kids off with Trish. He reluctantly agreed.

"Beth?" Trish asked clearly not for the first time. She tucked her brown hair behind her ear as her head cocked to the side, the frown taking over her face.

"Uh—sorry what?" she asked.

Trish chuckled. "I just asked how you were feeling?"

She groaned. "Not you too. I'm fine, it was a cold, but Clayton and Danny hovered all day, Will even wanted to make dinner. They were all up in arms I'm going out with Marc tonight."

"Yet you think they aren't going to know what this sleep over means?" Trish asked with a knowing smirk.

"I'm not telling them about this," she reminded her friend pointedly. Not that Trish would spill the beans, she was the steady silent friend Beth needed in life.

"I know them, and they will find out. But I'm happy to have the kids here," Trish said, turning to watch the kids. Steve and Nate were already well into the LEGOS on the coffee table while the two little girls played with their babies in the corner of the small room.

Trish had been through a lot in her life, but she was one of Beth's most dependable friends.

"Thanks," Beth said.

"Anytime," Trish assured her but her smile almost had Beth groaning again. "And I saw Marc last night, so I'm clear on the fact that anytime might mean this happens more often."

Beth's cheeks heated. "Marc's not the type to look for something that happens often."

"Just the type to be covered in pizza sauce cleaning up after seven kids so you can sleep?" Trish asked. Beth opened her mouth but Trish continued. "Beth, I owe you, you have Nate and Katie every day, I'm happy to have Steve and Mandy as often as you want. And I'm happy that you seem happy."

"Do I seem happy?" Beth asked. Because she felt like a nervous wreck.

"Yeah, you do, so have fun," Trish assured her and then turned.

"No Mandy, don't touch my stuff," Steve snapped.

"Go," Trish said before Beth could intervene and Beth nodded.

She was a ball of nerves driving over. Since she had all day to think about tonight, she worked herself into a hot mess. She couldn't sleep with him tonight without knowing what was going to happen tomorrow. They had to talk first.

"You look gorgeous," Marc said, full of his typical sexy confidence. He glided out the front door to stand next to her on the porch. His hand ran up her bare arm to the crook of her neck. He leaned into her so she could feel his warm breath on her cheek. "Don't overthink this. Just be here with me." Every syllable bounced off her neck and ear, and she shivered as he placed a soft kiss, his lips barely open, on her cheek.

"Okay," she said, feeling slightly off-balance. Marc's eyes ran down her legs to her white platform wedges, and she saw him smile. "You have a thing about shoes, don't you?"

"No." Marc laughed when she gave him a look of disbelief.

"Are you worried I'll wear two different shoes?"

"I can honestly say that's never entered my mind," he assured her. "Come on, we have a seven o'clock reservation."

A reservation was good and bad. Dinner meant they would have time to talk, but the reservation meant a circus would probably be waiting for them at the restaurant. They had worked their way through the crowd once this week already, and she couldn't say she was excited to do it again.

Beth had assumed they were heading to the city for dinner, so she was surprised when Marc didn't take the highway to the tunnel.

"Where are we going?" she asked, turning down the radio—which was currently playing Taylor Swift, much to Marc's displeasure. He never took control of the music, and he had given up commenting anything more than a raised eyebrow at her taste, but she could tell he didn't much care for her choices.

"A little Italian place," he said, and then his brow furrowed. "You like Italian, right? I didn't ask."

"You haven't asked me if I liked *any* place you were taking me."

Marc frowned. Something about him was different tonight.

They pulled into a small parking lot next to what looked like a house except for a sign that said '*Caniro's.*' He got her door, but there were no cameras anywhere. Even as he guided her forward with his hand on the small of her back, she looked for the jackals.

After the rumors of cheating had spread, their relationship had become a bigger deal. Marc's demands for privacy hadn't helped.

"They're not here," he said, realizing precisely what she was searching for.

She didn't understand, but he said nothing more as they walked through the door. Hadn't he said he made a reservation?

They entered a front foyer with rooms on either side. Each contained a few tables of couples or families, but the place wasn't crowded. The hostess greeted them with a flash of recognition, but nothing else.

"I have a reservation—Marc Rojas," he said, flashing his dimples and rolling his 'r' at the girl, who blushed, flustered. Beth might have felt bad for the poor girl if she wasn't so shocked herself. Rojas? He hadn't used his actual name—no wonder no one was here.

"Yes, right this way, Mr. Rojas," she said and led them through the door to the right, into a windowless room closer to the back. She set the menus down on one of the four empty tables before turning back to them.

Marc helped Beth with her chair, then turned and said something she couldn't hear to the hostess. The girl left the room, closing the door behind her.

"Rojas?" Beth asked as he sat down beside her, only the table's corner between them.

"My mother's maiden name." She blinked. "If I had used my actual name, the place would be swarming."

"Yeah, but I thought…" She shook her head, trying to understand. "I thought that was the point."

The server came in with an open bottle of wine, introduced herself, and poured some into Marc's glass. He took a sip and then nodded. After filling both of their glasses with the dark crimson liquid, she retreated, leaving the bottle on the table.

"Thought what was the point?" Marc asked, returning to the conversation.

"That we be seen together." She picked up her glass and took a sip of her wine. The rich, heady flavor lingered in her mouth. She wasn't a wine connoisseur, but knew enough to know it was an '*impress me*' bottle of wine. Why was he suddenly ordering expensive wine?

"Not tonight."

He ran his thumb slowly back and forth over the top of her hand before bringing it up to his mouth. His lips pressed into her palm and then the inside of her wrist before blowing slightly on the damp skin. Desire shot through her like a shock. She shivered as he smiled against her wrist.

"I thought you understood that this was a date. Not even Austin knows where we are, and no one here will call in a tip. I made sure of it. Complete privacy."

Her comment about their dinner at Slush not being a real date flicked through her mind. This was an actual date?

"I thought you liked the attention."

"But *you* don't," Marc said and set her hand back on the table.

Her stomach fluttered; he was thinking of her. "Thank you."

"In the interest of full disclosure, I have to admit that part of it is selfishness." Marc's brown eyes sparkled as he leaned back in the chair.

"Why am I not surprised." Beth rolled her eyes and shook her head. Familiar ground, at least. "What's in it for you?"

"This." His hand reached up to trace her cheek then flowed down her neck. His fingers danced along her collarbone before running down her arm. She swallowed hard when his thumb drifted along her bottom lip, which involuntarily separated from its mate. Awareness ripped through Beth again. It amazed her, his ability to turn her inside out with a simple touch. He leaned in slowly to brush her lips with his, and she sighed. He smiled against her lips before he leaned back. "See?"

"Huh?" Beth's thoughts spun.

"You're relaxed," he said. "I can touch you, kiss you, and you can enjoy yourself." He took her hand in his again.

She paused. "Does that take some fun away for you?" she asked, pulling her hand back. She started fiddling with the gold band on her thumb.

The server interrupted the conversation again to take their orders, which took longer than it should have because Beth hadn't even opened the menu. Marc ordered without looking at his.

When the server left, Marc picked up his wine glass. Keeping his eyes on her, he spun his wine a few times before he answered her question with one of his own. "You think I prefer you to be nervous and uncomfortable with me?"

He took a slow sip, watching her over the top. Beth didn't think he looked *mad*, exactly, but he also didn't look happy with her.

"I don't know." Her eyes fell to the table. "I don't understand your complete change of heart about this, Marc. Is it that it's been too long, and I'm all that's available?"

His eyes flitted shut. He muttered something before finally looking at her. "This is supposed to be a do-over for us."

Beth shook her head. "I don't understand."

He swallowed, and his throat bobbed. "The morning I showed up at your house with a new iPhone? I let you assume I had come wanting to use you to change my image. I let you believe I thought I could get something from you."

"You didn't?"

Marc shook his head, "No. I came to get you to come out with me—to come *here* with me. After I got your phone, I came here for dinner. I wanted to test it out for a quiet, non-public date—with you."

Beth glanced down, feeling her cheeks heat, but his finger forced her gaze up to meet his own.

"I wanted to get to know you, to spend time with you. And nothing about that has changed." His eyes beat into her and the truth spread like a blush across her skin.

He leaned forward so that they were only a whisper apart; with each exhale, his breath brushed against her wet lips. She felt every single puff of air pound deep inside her.

"Beth, give me a chance. Get to know me as more than an obligation or favor," he said, then closed the gap, brushing his lips against hers.

She wanted to give in, but she had questions. She pulled back. "And what happens to the agreement?"

"Nothing. We finish it, but we have a lot more fun doing it." Marc smiled.

She paused at the simplicity of his statement—which wasn't at all simple. "So basically a real relationship but with an expiration date?"

"A clearly delineated, well-understood, temporary relationship—because I don't want to hurt you. I know you're the kind of woman who wants forever, and I'm never going to be the guy who can offer that."

"I realize that, Marc."

"Do you? I don't want you to get the wrong idea," he said seriously. But his face broke into a playful smirk. "I'll give you a month of the best sex of your life, but that's all I can offer."

"You're a little cocky, aren't you?" Beth said, raising her eyebrows as he laughed. She narrowed her eyes. "Do you like to make it harder for yourself?"

"I like that you make me work for things, but I'd still want you if you threw yourself at me. Maybe we should test that theory." His brown eyes sparkled as he teased her.

"In your dreams, hotshot. If you want me that badly, you're going to have to work for it," Beth sassed back. When their eyes met, they both realized the shift that had just occurred.

So he worked for it. All throughout dinner, he seduced her—with lingering touches and soft dimpled smiles, a brush of his leg, a gentle stroke of her arm, the touch of his hand until desire pulsed through every nerve ending in her body. His arm kept her close as they made their way to the car, and his hand crept up her thigh as he drove to his house.

She hadn't been inside his place before, and although it was a typically beautiful Jersey Shore house, it wasn't nearly as big as she had expected it to be. It was smaller than any of her own parents' many homes. But it was the kind of house that you might be afraid to spill something in, or worried you might leave fingerprints. It was perfect, the type of home that didn't fit in her life.

But that didn't matter; Marc had been clear. He liked her, but he wasn't looking for anything more than a friendship that came with some short-term bedroom privileges.

"You have great taste. It's beautiful," Beth said, looking around at the mix of stone, wood, and leather. It wasn't feminine, but there was a warm feel to the furniture.

"I can't take credit, since I paid someone to do it for me." He tossed his keys onto the granite counter, then set her purse on the black wrought-iron stool.

She gazed out the back window. Every few feet, thick chestnut-colored columns held up vine-covered pergolas. Two hot tubs sat high on opposite sides of the pool, situated so waterfalls fell from each into the water below. Bushes, small trees, and a wrought-iron fence surrounded the area, offering privacy but not cutting off the view completely; there was still a fantastic vista of dunes and crashing waves. Although it was dark, the moon reflected brightly off the water, lighting up a picture-perfect view of the Jersey coast.

"I've redone the pool, but the view was the reason I bought the house," Marc said. "Maybe we'll bring the kids over tomorrow to swim."

"They'll love it," Beth said, turning to the front.

An archway opened onto a cathedral-ceiling foyer, and her heels clicked on the tile as she moved into the room, stopping next to the curved double-staircase that led up to the second floor. This room was perfect too.

But the house felt empty. Not that there wasn't enough furniture in it; it was the lived-in feel that was missing. There weren't any photos of friends or family, no small touches that showed someone lived here. There were no books sitting on a table, no newspaper forgotten on the counter, nothing taped to the fridge. Marc had an apartment in the city, too; maybe that was home.

"Do you stay here a lot?" Beth asked, wandering into a dark office to the right, which also lacked any personal touch, and then an empty room to the left.

"Not until recently, but I've been living here for the last five months," Marc said, moving behind her and wrapping his arms around her stomach.

She remembered what he'd said; he didn't want anything to tie himself to one place. A home locked you down. She would bet his apartment in New York was as devoid of anything personal as this house was. She felt a stab of pity for the man. What made him so determined to cut himself off from anything permanent?

He interrupted her thoughts by nuzzling her neck. "I'm supposed to be turning this into a barroom. But much to my designer's dismay, I can't drum up the enthusiasm for it."

"A barroom?" she asked. She tilted her neck to the side as he leaned down, brushing his lips against her. His soft, warm mouth pressed against the pulse along her jaw, and the heat of desire warmed once more inside her.

"Yeah. She wants to turn the room into a bar—with the stools, a mirror, crap like that. I'm not sure what I'd use it for," Marc murmured, but all Beth could think about was his warm, smooth skin brushing across her shoulder, the musky smell of his cologne filling her every breath. The taut muscles of his arms held her close to his chest, every beat of his heart pounding into her.

Standing so close to him she felt unusually flustered and grasped for anything to say.

"I guess you wouldn't want to cartwheel across it." Beth's heart stuttered at the random comment as Marc's breathy laugh blew against her ear.

"I wouldn't mind watching you do that," Marc said, and she turned to meet his eyes. "Although I doubt you could in those shoes."

Beth rolled her eyes. "Please." She *so* could. Four-inch strappy platforms couldn't stop her from being able to cartwheel.

She moved away from Marc to the center of the room while he crossed his arms, leaning on the door frame, shaking his head. She lifted both arms in the air, then kicked over two perfect cartwheels.

She thought she'd see a smile when she glanced at Marc, but the heat in his eyes took her breath away.

"Your shoes and your panties both belong in a strip club." His voice was a deep rumble as he stalked toward her.

"I'm not sure if that's a compliment," Beth said as he reached her. His hands started at her thighs and slowly slipped under the hem of her dress. Her stomach tightened as the tip of a hot finger traced the lace along her leg and hip.

"Okay, how about this: If I'd known these were under this dress, I would've made sure I got to see them sooner," Marc said, and dropped his mouth to hers.

This kiss didn't start slow. He jumped right in and took possession of her mouth with a hot urgency. His hand on the small of her back pressed her tightly against him so she could feel the hard contours of him against her. His teeth tugged on her bottom lip, and she gulped in a breath, light-headed. Suddenly there was only Marc—his lips, his hands, just *him*. She was swimming with desire.

"I want you," his voice whispered against her ear before he trailed his lips down across her jaw. She moaned agreement. "I need to hear you say it, sweetheart." Marc pulled back to look into her eyes.

It wasn't a statement to feed his ego. It was him making sure he wasn't pushing her too far. He was putting her above his desires, and that was sexy as hell.

"I want this too," she whispered. And he claimed her mouth again.

Marc's lips never left hers as his hands skimmed slowly down along her body,reaching her hips, and lifted her from the floor. He pressed her tightly against him, deepening the kiss. His groan came from deep in the back of his throat, and with her in his arms, Marc headed upstairs.

20

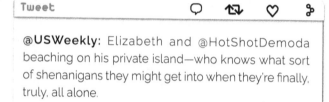

MARC GENTLY LAID her back on the king-size bed, making sure her dress lifted to leave him a view of the white lace panties. His gaze tumbled her stomach. Her breath caught, and he reached for one of her legs.

"I *love* lace, and seeing it on you, I feel like a kid on Christmas about to open the best present ever." His guttural voice pulsed through her.

He lifted her leg straight into the air and let his eyes run from the tip of her shoe back to her panties. Liquid heat shot straight to her center under his intense stare.

"I know you have this thing about your legs," Marc said as he kissed her ankle, his hot lips gliding along her calf while he unhooked the slingback of her shoe. He let it fall with a *thunk* to the floor. "But really, get over it, because they're fantastic."

His mouth pressed against the soft skin behind her knee, and she quivered. His smile was evil when he lowered her right leg and turned his attention to the left.

"And when you put them in shoes like these"—he unhooked her other shoe—"it makes it hard for a man to think about anything but getting them wrapped around him. In the car on the way to the restaurant, all through dinner, on the way home—all I could think about was your bare legs wrapped tight around my hips."

She swallowed a moan as he pressed his lips against her inner thigh, moving teasingly close to the part of her demanding his attention. But instead of pressing into her center, he continued his torture. He let her leg fall gently back to the bed, trailing his hands along her hips. He kissed her lightly under her belly button, and she arched against him.

He looked up and chuckled. "That answers my other question," he said, lifting eyes full of dark desire up to her face.

"What. Other. Question." She forced the words out, and then swallowed. Marc moved so his face was even with hers and his hand rested on her breast. His thumb flicked slowly back and forth over her hard nipple. The wanting built, warming her entire body.

"If there was anything else under this dress." He dropped his head and sucked through the cotton fabric. She arched against him, and he slipped his hand up to untie the strap of her dress. He pulled her to her feet and let the dress fall in a heap to the floor.

She stood there in nothing but her white lace panties, while he was fully dressed, looking entirely too pleased with himself.

Slowly she moved to undo the buttons on his shirt, pushing it off. He tossed it quickly away while she went straight for his belt, ridding him of it. He tried to pull her back into his arms. But she shook her head with a smile and pushed him back onto the bed.

"It's my turn. Keep your hands above your head where I can see them." He obeyed, and she sat, straddling his hips. "I expect you to keep them there, no matter what."

"Do you now?" he asked, but his grin faded as she settled her heat against his.

The moonlight streamed in through the bedroom window, catching the need in his eyes when she met them with hers. The air felt heavy with their matching desire as her fingers trailed lightly through the dark curls that started on his chest and circled around his belly button before heading further down. Her fingertips skimmed the smooth, tight muscles and she leaned forward, kissing the pulse of his neck, his muscular chest, his taut shoulders. His breaths became ragged. When she looked up, his eyes were closed, his lips tight. His pulse beat hard, but he hadn't moved his hands.

She undid the button and zipper of his pants before she moved. She didn't pull them off, but took them down just enough to lean over and slowly kiss him through the white Sideline boxer briefs. He groaned as she let her tongue make a quick circle.

And suddenly, she was no longer on top; she found herself under him, his weight pressing her firmly into the mattress.

"You're done," he croaked, gazing at her through half-lidded eyes clouded by the raw need she had unleashed.

His lips silenced her, and he shifted to give his hand access to her. He ran his fingers softly over the sheer lace of her panties, and the familiar throb of wanting built, burning stronger and more deeply than ever before. The barrier against his fingers was driving her crazy as she pressed against his hand. She thrust her hips, wanting more. Slowly he slid under the lace, teasing her before he pushed them down.

Her thighs fell apart, giving his fingers room to play with the patch of curls before finally touching her where she most wanted him. He knew his way around a woman's body. His hand was magic, and she rocked against it. As he slipped his finger inside her, his thumb continued its circular motion, driving her up. The circles became stronger again and her senses swirled; the pressure inside her was growing, spinning, demanding. She tensed. White-hot bolts of desire shot through her.

She looked up into his eyes.

"Come for me," he whispered.

And with that, she did. Pleasure racked her senses. He didn't stop, continuing to pull every pulse from her until she finally came back to herself.

"I need to be inside you," he groaned.

He shed the rest of his clothes, and opened the nightstand drawer.

"A sign of my respect," Marc said, handing her a condom, and she smiled. She took his fully aroused length in her hand, letting her thumb circle the tip as he hissed in a breath. Her hand ran down the thick cord before giving him a small squeeze, then slowly rolled the condom in place. She lingered on the thick long shaft, and he shuddered. "Careful or it'll be over before it starts," Marc choked, and used his own hands to pull her away.

He nudged her legs apart and moved over her. She pressed her face into his neck at the pressure of his entrance, and then with one hard thrust, he filled her.

"Yes, Marc, more," she moaned.

"Christ." The mixture of the prayer and curse vibrated in her ear. "You feel…" He swallowed. "G-o-d." The word dragged out, his voice humming pleasure. "You're so tight," he panted.

He dropped his head into the crook of her neck and took a deep breath. "This is what heaven must feel like."

He moved slowly at first, letting her body adjust to his size, but need soon took the reins as control slipped. Her name was a whisper in the dark, his name a moan leaving her lips. He moved to thrust himself more deeply, taking care to roll his hips over the sensitive bundle of nerves that would help carry her over the edge again. Her hips rocked in time with his. The frantic rhythm was driving her up again. Too soon, she was flying. This time he found his release along with her, and collapsed on top of her, groaning her name.

He didn't move; neither did she. She liked the feel of his weight as he stayed buried deep inside, listening to the quiet of the night.

She was in trouble. Marc had told her he would give her the best sex of her life. She no longer doubted that, but she did doubt her ability to not end up in over her head by the time the six weeks was over. Never in her life had she tried to separate sex from love, until tonight—and honestly, she had thought it would be easier.

He was everything she wanted to avoid. She craved a quiet life, not one in the fast lane. He loved the fast lane, and even if he had made tonight about them, that wasn't his life. It was just one night. Still, from the moment she'd stood and watched him playing baseball with her son, she had slowly let him chip away at her resistance. And it needed to stop. She could and would enjoy him; sex with Marc was fabulous. But that would be it. She wouldn't let herself fall in love.

Her fingers trailed along the bumps of his spine until finally he rolled off her. He looked down at her with the strangest expression and tucked a lock of hair behind her ear.

"Don't you move." It was an order, but there was tenderness in his voice. He leaned down, kissed her softly, and then headed for the bathroom.

He swaggered out of the room, completely naked and not even a tiny bit embarrassed by it. Although she teased him about his overconfidence, she admired it too. Of course, he had every reason to be confident: He was beautiful. His body was on billboards. The only imperfection was the scar that marred his shoulder, giving him a dangerously sexy look.

Beth pulled a pillow from behind her and hugged it to her chest.

As soon as Marc reappeared, he frowned. "You know I've been waiting weeks for this, and now I want to enjoy the view." He grabbed the pillow and tossed it away.

"I hate to be the one to break it to you, but the world doesn't revolve around what Marc Demoda wants," Beth replied and grabbed another pillow. Marc smirked, and the bed sagged as he lowered himself down.

"And I hate to break it to *you*, especially when you're so cute, but," Marc said, catching her wrist and pulling it over her head as the pillow fell to the side, "there are advantages to being significantly bigger." He pushed her back against the pillows and rested his weight on the arm holding her wrist.

"Cheater," Beth teased, and Marc chuckled. She attempted to wiggle away, but he reached his free hand down to her legs and pinned them in place. With that, she put no more effort into moving.

Marc stared down at her, then lifted his hand from her legs to cup her cheek.

"You did it again," Marc whispered.

"Did what?" She hadn't done anything.

"Took my breath away."

Beth smiled. "I've only just begun."

WITH ONE ARM hooked under his head, Marc lay in bed looking down at the woman asleep on his shoulder. The wild curls he'd had his hands in not so long ago splayed across his chest, along with her hand. His arm had fallen asleep at about the same time Beth had, but he wouldn't move no matter how much the tingling annoyed him. She was right where she should be, finally.

Finally. Marc had been thinking that a lot lately. The first time he'd kissed her; when he got her in bed last night; when she called his name as she came in his hand; when he came inside her. It was like his mind thought he'd been waiting a long time for her. He kept reminding himself it had only been a few weeks, but 'finally' kept echoing through his thoughts.

Usually, instead of getting comfortable, he'd talk the woman back into her clothes. He wouldn't hurt Beth's feelings by sending her home, even though he'd made it clear what this was. The problem was, he didn't *want* Beth out of his arms, or his bed, let alone out of his house. He didn't want to look too closely at the reasons behind it; he just accepted the difference. He had known it was different going in.

There was something else unusual about the night, something he hadn't expected. He didn't want to dwell on how much better sex was with Beth, but he couldn't help himself. In the past he had jumped into bed quickly, and he took it for granted that if he wanted something, he could have it. That wasn't the case with Beth. Not only was he feeling sated sexually, but he also laughed constantly when he was with her.

Marc had thought that after he and Beth finally had sex, the appeal would disappear. But it hadn't. She took control the second time, and teased him for much longer. He'd ended up begging her, and he'd never begged before in his life. He wouldn't have complained about begging her again, either, although he needed some time to recover.

He was looking forward to the morning, when he planned to seduce her all over again, this time with coffee and breakfast in bed. Then maybe they could get the kids and bring them over. Marc knew Beth had meant it when she said the kids would like the pool, and he wanted to see them enjoy it. He didn't plan to make any permanent commitment, but for now, he would enjoy Beth and their kids.

Whoa.

Her kids.

He would enjoy Beth and *her* kids.

He pulled Beth tighter against his side, closed his eyes, and let himself drift off with, for the first time in his life, a woman in his arms. Finally.

21

MARC'S PHONE BUZZED, but he reached for Beth before he opened his eyes. He wanted her warmth tucked against him, but when his hand connected with only the cold sheet, he was instantly wide awake.

The dented pillow was empty, the sheet on her side of the bed tossed back. One glance around the room showed that her stuff was gone too. What the hell? When did she leave? He smacked his hand on the nightstand a few times before finally encountering the phone, which was buzzing once again.

He would have ignored it, but Danny's name was on the caller ID and Marc's blood turned to ice. If Beth's kids had an emergency and she'd left without waking him, he might lose his shit.

"What's wrong?" he demanded.

"Well, let's see, dipshit. I woke up to see my sister doing the walk of shame in front of your place on your *Twitter feed*."

Danny's voice rose at the end of the sentence until he sounded like someone was stabbing him in the eye with a hot fork.

Marc winced as he switched the phone to speaker. He opened Twitter and frowned at the picture, then sighed. Two different gossip sites had tagged him in it, and about seventeen more had retweeted it, not to mention everyone who'd retweeted from there. Clearly the random security sweeps in front of his house weren't cutting it. He'd have to pull back more from the media. *For fuck's sake.* Every time his relationship with Beth took a step forward, Twitter screwed it up.

His fingers were already shooting off a text to his security guys and Austin when Danny added, "What the fuck, Marc?"

He finished the text and rubbed his hands over his face. Marc had no idea what had possessed her to leave his house without waking him. But it sucked. He'd thought for sure she understood that he wanted her here. So either Marc hadn't been clear, or she wasn't on the same page. And now he had to explain it to Danny before he even knew where he stood.

"Fucker, answer me," Danny growled.

He cleared his throat. "I don't know."

"You don't know what?"

"Why she left. I just woke up."

"I can tell you, dumbass. The morning after a hookup is fucking awkward."

"Don't go there."

"Go where?"

"I respect the hell out of your sister, so not only am I not going to diss her by calling her a hookup, I won't let you do it either. I like her a whole fucking lot. I'm actually reeling a bit that she's gone. So give me a minute to get my shit together and figure out where she is." Marc pushed his hands through his hair.

There was a long pause, and Marc held his breath. This would tell him exactly what the brothers thought about him and Beth.

"Steve," Danny finally said.

That answered nothing. "What?"

"Steve has a game at nine, at the Sunset Field behind the middle school." It was begrudging, but it was an olive branch, and Marc would take it and run.

He blew out a breath. "Thanks."

"You need to make it clear to her how you feel, asshole, because I don't want to see any more walks of shame." Marc could actually hear Danny's jaw clench.

"I know," he agreed.

"And you better not hurt her."

"I won't." But even as Marc said it, he was looking on Twitter and seeing the comments, thinking about their arrangement, and wondering if that was a promise he could keep.

"YOU LOOK MUCH better," Will said, sitting next to Beth on the bleachers.

"Yeah, you got some color back," Clayton added. He regarded her carefully for a moment. "You look more than better; you look… happy."

Beth smiled. "What's not to be happy about?" Although she had gotten little sleep last night, she didn't feel tired. She felt wonderful, and she couldn't stop her smile.

When she woke up with Marc sound asleep next to her, she wanted to snuggle into his arms, but this type of situation was new to her. She knew from her brothers that most men didn't like the morning after. She felt strange about waking Marc when she needed to leave for Steve's game anyway, so instead of an awkward *I'll see you later,* she'd slipped out of bed and headed home for a shower before picking up the kids from her sister.

Her cell phone rang before Clayton or Will could comment further.

"Morning," she said to Marc, feeling a smile creep onto her face.

"Yeah, yeah. I'm in the parking lot," Marc said, sounding grumpy.

"What?" she asked, standing up and spinning around to look behind her. Marc was leaning against his Viper, with one arm folded over his chest, looking in her direction. "How did you know I was here?"

"You have five seconds to get your cute little butt down here," he said and snapped his phone off. He put one finger up in the air, counting. She didn't know what he wanted, but she didn't think he was kidding.

"Will, keep an eye on Mandy for me," Beth said, then jumped off the side of the bleachers and headed for Marc. By the time she got there, he had all five fingers in the air. His silver aviator glasses were hiding his eyes, but from his tight-lipped expression, she could see he wasn't happy. Her stomach clenched; he didn't look like he was floating on the same cloud she was.

"Hi?" she said awkwardly. This was precisely what she'd been trying to avoid.

"*Hi?* Is that what you have to say?" he asked, crossing both arms over his chest. "I wake up alone after spending an amazing night together, and all you can say after I track you down is *hi?*"

"You're... upset I didn't wake you?" Beth asked, perplexed.

"I finally let a woman spend the entire night in my bed, and she slips out before she even gives me a good morning kiss. So yes, I am."

"Steve had an early game," she explained.

"Yes, I figured that out with Danny's help," he said wryly.

"Wait," she said as his words hit. "What do you mean, 'finally'?"

"You're the first woman who has ever actually *slept* in my bed, sweetheart, and let me tell you, this is *not* how I imagined our morning going. Honestly, if I'd known they'd slip away without a word, I might not have kicked so many out in the middle of the night," he said, frowning.

She wasn't sure what to make of this. "Oh. I would have gone home last night. I didn't realize you wanted me to."

"If I had wanted you to leave, I would have told you. I *wanted* to wake up, roll over, and kiss you. Preferably followed by another hour in bed. But I would have settled for a quick shower with you before getting Steve for his game. What I *didn't* want was to wake up and find myself alone." Marc glared at her.

"I'm sorry," Beth said, but she was smiling.

She was trying not to make a big deal out of the fact that he'd never wanted a woman to stay over before, but her heart was going pitter-patter all the same. Last night hadn't made Marc want forever, but his admission told her she was different from his other women. *How* different she wasn't sure, but at the moment, different was enough.

"Damn right. Next time you better wake me, even if you have somewhere to go," Marc said, but he was smiling at her now too. "So let's start this morning over."

He reached out and pulled the belt loop of her capris until she was snug against him. He planted a kiss firmly on her lips before stepping back and pulling two cups of coffee from the car. He handed her one and then grabbed her hand, leading her back up towards the bleachers.

Beth smiled as she took a sip of her coffee. Then her smile faded to a puzzled expression as she stared at the cup. "Hey, this has my creamer in it."

"I know how you like your coffee, Beth," he said simply, like it was no big deal—but it was. To her, anyway. And just like that, she lost a little piece of her heart.

"Morning, boys," Marc said as he made his way up the bleachers. "How's the little man doing?" He settled in, and Beth sat on the bench in front of him, leaning back into his thighs. Marc smiled down at her and rubbed her shoulder with his free hand.

"Oh shit," Will said suddenly.

"What?" Clayton asked, and Beth's eyes flew from Mandy playing in the dirt in front of the bleacher to Steve on the mound.

"Are you two sleeping together?" Will demanded.

Beth's eyes closed; she should have known she wouldn't be able to keep the change in their relationship to herself.

"The entire world doesn't need to know, Will," she said.

"You're sleeping with him?" Clayton asked, shocked, looking from Beth to Marc. "I swear, dude, we *had* this conversation."

"What?" Beth asked.

"Danny asked him," Clayton explained. And didn't that

figure. "Marc was looking at you like—like he was starving. And Danny wanted to know what was up."

Beth couldn't believe her brothers. Well, yes, she could. They all believed it was their personal right to know about her sex life, or lack thereof. Now they were going to put Marc on the spot. If they started the whole '*What are your intentions*' speech, she was leaving.

"When did this start?" Will demanded.

"Oh my God. If you must know, it started last night. Now please butt out." Beth sighed. "I didn't realize I needed to ask permission."

"I think it was me who was supposed to ask permission, sweetheart." Marc chuckled. He didn't look embarrassed, and that made her even more annoyed. "So I guess you two are going to have to speak for the group. I like your sister." He smiled down at her even though he was talking to them. "She's pretty great, and I'd like permission to date her—and sleep with her sometimes too, if that's all right."

"Marc!" Beth said. He was ridiculous. She wasn't about to let them decide this. He laughed and squeezed her shoulder again, acting like he knew what he was doing.

"Not if the kids are in the house," Clayton said pointedly. Beth was the one who had established that rule.

"Glove up; be respectful," Will said. Another Beth rule.

"And don't mess around on her," Clayton added.

"We've had this discussion before, guys. As long as I'm sleeping with Beth, I'll *only* be sleeping with her." Marc turned Beth's head so she was looking at him. And although he was talking to the boys, he stared straight into her eyes. "I won't sleep around on her, *ever.*"

Beth swallowed. She'd never heard him use this serious tone. And she believed him.

"We're good then," Clayton said, shocking Beth and breaking the spell of Marc's intense gaze. They were good? That was it? She waited for one of them to add something.

"I should've known you got some last night with that smile you got going on," Will said, laughing. "You can see your afterglow."

"Can you now?" Marc asked, and she heard the smile in his voice.

"Can you what?" Danny said as he appeared and sat in front of Beth.

"See her afterglow from sex with Marc." Clayton chuckled. "We're cool. We talked."

"Yeah, I heard," Danny said, and Beth sent him a questioning look. He shook his phone at her. "You're trending; apparently you two are moving in together. Naturally, I had some questions."

"I should start following you. What's your douche handle—something about being hot, right?" Clayton asked as he unlocked his phone.

Beth sighed, but Marc leaned forward. "Austin's taking care of it, I promise," he assured her.

She trusted Austin, and honestly, she trusted Marc too. She turned to look at him, and the stress was clear in his eyes. She sent him a small *'it's okay'* smile, which he returned with another shoulder squeeze.

"So, I gotta ask," Danny said, smiling at Beth a little too sadistically. "There's been so much talk about both Demoda and Matthews having 'million-dollar hands.' So I thought you, as the resident expert, could settle the debate: Which Metros pitcher has the better hands?"

Everyone, including Marc, looked at Beth.

Oh, great, here they go.

"I am *so* not going there," Beth said, shaking her head, but Marc leaned over to her ear.

"It's okay. I was there last night; I already know." He chuckled as he kissed the top of her head. His never-ending confidence still amazed her, even if—this time—he was right.

The guys all laughed, then turned back to concentrate on the game. It seemed they were all good with Marc.

22

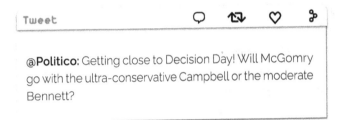

MARC SAT ON Beth's sofa with Mandy and one of the mutts on his lap. Beth was beside him, talking continuously, but Marc was trying hard to tune her out. He looked across the couch at Steve, who met his eyes in silent agreement; neither of them cared about the orange throwback uniforms the players wore that Beth was complaining about nonstop.

"Sweetheart," Marc interrupted. "We can't hear the game."

"Oh, sorry," Beth mumbled.

Life had gotten quieter with beefed-up security in the streets around both their houses and Marc's own policy of not feeding the gossip. Their relationship was good and seemed solid to the world, so it became uninteresting, which also helped.

For the last few weeks, the standard nightly routine was Marc and Steve pitching the ball for a while, and then dinner. While Beth went for a run, he watched the kids, followed by sitting with them watching TV, with Beth or Mandy talking over the television.

Beth had no desire to watch stupid shows. She was okay with baseball, golf, or NASCAR. And although he couldn't hear the announcers over her talking most of the time, it was usually at least somewhat relevant to the game. Nights at Beth's house weren't like nights with his parents, some tacky reality show on the television while his mother bitched at his father. Nights in Beth's home were nice.

Marc's relationship with Will, Clayton, and Danny hadn't changed either. After the stories he'd heard from Beth about them chasing boyfriends away, he had been worried they would try to scare him off. But they hadn't. One night, he'd even begged Will to watch the kids so he could get some time alone with Beth. Unfortunately, that had been almost a week ago, and he hadn't gotten her naked since.

"Mandy needs to go up anyway," Beth said, hopping up off the couch while Mandy gave Marc a goodnight hug.

Once the girls left, Steve looked over nervously at Marc before quickly turning away. This happened a lot. At first, Marc had assumed that Steve would get over whatever it was. But after a month and a half, it was time to talk about it.

"Hey, kiddo," Marc said, drawing Steve's attention away from his uncle's pitching. "It seems like sometimes I make you nervous."

Steve's eyes widened.

"I thought maybe if I knew what I did, I could try to fix it," Marc added, figuring it was better to blame himself. "I've noticed it's when your mom's not around."

Steve mumbled something, looking at the couch cushions.

"Sorry? I didn't catch that," Marc said.

"I don't want to make you mad," Steve whispered.

"When did I get mad?" Steve had never made him mad. Frustrated maybe, but more at himself than at Steve. Helping Beth with the kids was like shooting in the dark, although he was getting better at it. It was like learning a new pitch: You had to work on your rhythm, but things went smoother once you got it down.

"Not you," Steve said.

What? "Not following you here, buddy," Marc said.

Steve was looking more embarrassed by the minute. "Sometimes people are nicer to me when Mom is around, and when she's not, they get mad if I bother them," Steve admitted.

"Who makes you feel like a bother?" Marc asked, but he had a general idea. He could imagine men tried to use Beth's children to get her attention.

"People like Paul," Steve said.

Marc suppressed his frown. The fucker who worked for Beth's father didn't sit well with him. His 'relationship' with Beth only had a few more weeks before it was over, but Marc needed to have a one-way conversation with that asshole and remind him how to treat Beth and her kids.

Steve continued, "I don't like him very much."

"I don't like Paul much either," Marc said.

"You don't? Doesn't everyone like him?" Steve asked.

"Not really. He's a di—a dork." Marc smiled as he caught himself, then hurried on to the critical issue. "But I enjoy it when we hang out, even if your mom's not around."

"Really?" Steve asked, looking up hopefully with those green eyes that reminded Marc so much of Beth's. It had surprised Marc to learn he was a bit of a kid person—at least with good kids. Ones like Steve and Mandy.

"Of course. Why do you think I make time to play baseball?" he asked, rubbing Steve's head.

"What if I didn't like baseball?" Steve asked, glancing away.

"If you'd rather do something other than throw the ball and watch the game, we can. I thought you liked it," Marc said, putting his arm around and Steve tucking him to his side. "We could play Switch or go to a movie, or there's that water park we could try one day. I even have a motorcycle we could take for a ride." Marc tried to pick things he thought Steve might like.

Steve's smile was enormous. "Would Mom and Mandy have to come?"

"Well, sometimes, but not always."

"Mom said you won't be around forever because you're getting a new job. Is that true?" Steve asked.

Marc wondered how much Beth had talked to her son about them.

"I'm probably going to get a job with a baseball team," Marc said honestly. "If I do, I won't be around as much as I am now."

"Like coaching?" Steve asked.

"I hope so."

Steve nodded and turned back to the game, but he leaned against Marc's side, looking entirely at ease.

"So that was surprising," Beth said when Marc came downstairs after putting Steve to bed.

"What?" Marc asked. It was the first time he'd gone into Steve's room, and it had shocked him to see that Steve had Marc's signed jersey. He hadn't known. Marc was sure kids all over the county had his jersey on their wall, but because it was Steve, it left him with one of those gut-clenching feelings. And he didn't know what to do with it.

"He's never asked you to take him up before." Beth now looked worried, the same look Steve had given him not that long ago. He could handle her worry much better than Steve's.

"We talked. Steve thought I was being nice to him to get into your pants," Marc said as he sat next to her. "I told him not to worry; I already did that."

Beth's mouth fell open.

"I'm kidding."

Her mouth snapped shut, and her eyes narrowed. Now she was giving him the stink-face that her daughter used so often. Marc laughed.

"Not funny."

"We talked." Marc reached around Beth, pulling her so she straddled his lap. "Steve asked about me not being around so much in the future."

Beth's head dropped to Marc's shoulder.

"Thank you. I'm worried about them getting attached to you," she breathed.

"I hope we'll see each other sometimes." He went on quickly, not wanting her to think he meant sleeping with her now and again. "You know—beer nights, Steve's games, things like that."

She nodded. They might be about to have a serious conversation that he didn't really want to have. But then she surprised him by turning her head and pressing her lips against his neck, letting her tongue lick his skin. His blood supply went straight south, and he moved his hand to scoot her closer so that she pressed right against his erection. The only thing left between them was his mesh shorts and the thin leggings she had put on after her shower. He ran his hands over her thighs and ass.

"Are you not wearing panties?" Marc asked.

"Nope," Beth admitted devilishly.

"I suppose it's too much to hope you've changed your mind about the kids being home?" he asked.

Beth chuckled, and her breath brushing over his ear made his cock twitch.

"Maybe we can stretch the rules, just a little." She smiled at him.

Damn, he wanted her. "If I didn't know better, I'd say you're as eager as I am," he said, then caught the back of her neck, guiding her mouth to his own.

The ringing of her phone made them both jump, but Beth laughed and moved to get it. Marc wanted to shake her. The boys pulled her in twenty directions, and he would bet his left arm it was one of them. He didn't understand how grown men could be so helpless, but they couldn't do anything without her. It was a reminder, however, for him to keep his distance. Beth was easy to get caught up in.

"I dare you not to answer that," he teased as she reached around him for the phone.

"What if I do?" she asked.

"I wouldn't test me." It was a warning, not meant to be a challenge. But, too late, he saw that wasn't how she would take it.

She answered the phone, of course.

Marc groaned. Now what was he going to do?

"Hey, Grant. No, I'm not busy. How's the farm?" she said, smiling at Marc, her emerald eyes sparkling.

Torture her.

He pressed his hands into her hips, holding her tight as he leaned back against the couch. Slowly he started rocking his hips, moving her heat against him. The first stroke was all it took for Marc to remember precisely the feel of her tight, warm, velvety flesh. The memory, along with the sensation of her rubbing against him, took him from 'playing around' to 'in over his head' quicker than he would have thought possible. It only took about five strokes before her eyes glassed over, and he couldn't help but feel smug.

"What?" She sounded dazed and tightened her legs, trying to stop Marc while shooting him a dirty look that didn't faze him.

She shifted herself slightly, and the angle was perfect. He kept going, speeding up slightly. It was too good, even through two layers of clothes. He could feel the dampness of her leggings as they rubbed against his shorts, stroking him.

Over and over.

It would be easy to get her out of those pants, and he could be inside her, surrounded by flesh. All her wet heat would grip him like a vise. He sucked in raggedly, continuing the motion of his hips against her.

"I don't know, Grant." She sounded drugged. "Just email it or whatever."

Marc should stop, but he didn't—or maybe he couldn't.

"I'll call you tomorrow and let you know," she blurted, not giving him a chance to respond.

She dropped the phone on the couch, and he expected her to yell, but she leaned forward and kissed him. A deep, wet, needy kiss, sucking his tongue into her mouth, bringing him deeper into his haze. Her hips started moving on his lap faster, and he lost control of the situation. Yeah, he'd be done in less than a minute, but she would go first. He could wait that long. He bucked his hips against her as she pushed just as hard into him. The motion was driving him wild even as she pulled her lips away, resting her forehead against his.

"Marc... I'm..." She stumbled over the words between gasps.

"Me too, sweetheart," he said and watched her face as he drove her right off the edge, and fell right along with her.

BETH SLUMPED AGAINST Marc's shoulder. They were both breathing too heavily, and she could feel his arms shaking as they held her. She couldn't believe what had just happened.

Marc cleared his throat. "I'm not sure if I'm embarrassed or impressed," he finally said.

"That makes two of us. That was further than I planned on *stretching* things."

Marc chuckled. "Yeah, but it proves we need more alone time."

"Probably."

"Give me a second," he said, shifting her off of his lap and heading for the bathroom.

Beth wished she could have alone time with him for a few days. But it was hard, with the kids.

"So what did he want?" he asked, pulling her back onto his lap when he returned.

"Huh?"

"Grant." Marc's chuckle brushed against her neck.

"Oh." She had forgotten about him for a second. "Stuff about the farm. He's sending papers over. And he wanted to know if you were coming with the kids and me this weekend."

"You're going to Grant's for your birthday?" Marc asked, surprised.

It seemed none of her brothers had mentioned it to him. She'd wondered if they had since Grant had said, "Will told me to invite Marc this weekend; so is he coming or what?"

"Yeah, we all spend my birthday in Pennsylvania every year. We say it's for the Fourth of July, but since my birthday is the third, they all make sure they're there by the second and then spend the third playing golf." She laughed when Marc made a face. "I don't play. It's boys and kids only. It means I get a day of peace."

"By 'all,' you mean *all* your brothers?" Beth nodded. "Including the two I haven't met?" She nodded again. "Do the boys not want me to come?" Marc asked, forcing her to look at him.

"Uh." She paused. "I don't think they mind; Grant invited you." She couldn't swear to that, since she hadn't talked about it with anyone but Grant. And although he had begrudgingly invited Marc, that phone call couldn't really be called a conversation.

"You haven't brought it up—so you don't want me to come?" He was staring at her with the same look he had given her right after she picked up the phone.

"I wasn't sure how you would feel about it. It's weird having an expiration date," she admitted.

"What do you mean?"

"Well, if we were normal-dating, I would invite you, but our agreement's over in three weeks. And since you don't want me to meet your family, I wasn't sure if coming away with us would be crossing some line." She'd also noticed that he refused to leave anything here—not even his baseball glove. He brought it back and forth, although he and Steve threw every day.

"Do you want me to come?" Marc asked again, cautiously.

Of course she did. Part of her would have loved to spend as much time with him as she could—but then there was the other part, the part that needed to keep some space between them.

"You get along well with the guys," Beth stalled, and dropped her forehead back against his shoulder.

He said nothing for a minute, and neither of them moved.

"Maybe we should get rid of our expiration date."

For half a second, her heart stopped.

"*What?*" Her head shot up as she spoke, and if his arm hadn't been around her, she might have fallen backward off his lap.

"Whoa, careful. You nearly took off my head," he said calmly. "I didn't mean it to sound horrible."

"'Shocking' is more accurate." Every time she thought she understood him, he threw her another curve ball.

"It changes nothing," Marc said.

How could not breaking up at a certain point not change *everything*?

"I don't…. Do you want to come with the guys? Because if you do, you can." She sighed. Beth was happy that Marc got along with her brothers, but she didn't want that to be why he wanted to go.

"No. I like your brothers, but if you weren't going, I'd have no interest. When you said only three weeks, I didn't like it. Why don't we take this like a normal…." He paused, looking like he might swallow his tongue. "You know. See how things go."

She stared at him. How had she ended up in a relationship with a man who couldn't even say the damn word?

"I won't be the guy you grow old with; we've agreed on that. But we're not done yet. After what just happened between us, you can't think anything different. There's no reason we have to walk away just because a piece of paper says so."

"You're saying we just—what, stay together until one of us gets tired of the other?" *Translation: until he gets bored with me and moves on.*

"Or I get a job that takes me somewhere else. Because I'm looking, and with all the interest the colleges are giving me, Austin is sure the minors will be sniffing around soon. I don't want you to forget that I want back into major league baseball. I won't be here forever."

"Yeah," Beth said, but she shook her head again. "I know what's important to you." To be back on a team was what he wanted. It was more than playing baseball; he wanted to go back into the only thing he'd ever felt a part of. "Okay, no expiration date. One day at a time."

It would have been smarter to say no. Because the longer Marc was around, the harder it would be when he wasn't. But when it came to Marc, it didn't seem like she could make the right decisions.

Marc smiled. "So, did you want to ask me something?"

Beth rolled her eyes.

MARC LOADED THE bags into the back of his Jeep, thinking about the morning with his parents. Although he'd tried to see his sister once a week for the past month, he saw his parents as seldom as possible. His father's continued bashing of Beth was part of the reason. Again today, he'd told Marc to leave her. The only time his father hadn't been a complete ass was when Marc had mentioned his second interview with the New England Sports Network for the Boston commentary job. Austin was sure that NESN was going to be sending him an offer soon—which thrilled Frank—but Marc didn't feel excited about it, and he wasn't sure why.

And it had pissed his mother off that he was going away with Beth's family when he hadn't introduced her to his own. She worried Marc was leading Beth on.

He wasn't.

Their conversation on Tuesday night had thrown Beth for a loop. But it had thrown *him* for a loop too.

Thinking back left him as mystified as he had been when he sat holding her in his arms. Even as a teenager, Marc had never got off by dry-humping a girl, but the thought of how she'd felt rubbing against him made him hard.

And after *that*, she looked at him and said they'd only be together for three more weeks?

He wanted more of Beth.

If he was honest, it wasn't just sex that he wanted more of. Everything with Beth was going great, and Marc wanted to be done when he felt done. He had expected her to be happy about his suggestion, but she'd seemed hesitant. For a minute, while she was staring at him, Marc had thought she didn't want to keep seeing him, and he could barely put together a sentence. The words he'd been about to say had died on his lips, and he had to take a second to regroup.

Between the potential job and the idea of his and Beth's relationship, Marc's head was a mess as he walked back into Beth's house after getting the car packed. Her dogs were at Corey's for the weekend, and she was doing a last-minute check to make sure the lights were all off and no water was running.

"Did you guys try to pee?" he asked the kids, and Mandy's mouth dropped.

"You tant say that, it's tintle," Mandy said

"Okay." Marc mentally cringed at using the word. "Did you try to tinkle?"

"Yes," she chirped back, and Steve rolled his eyes but nodded.

"Let's get in the car then," he said, scooping Mandy up and putting her in the car seat Beth had put in his Jeep.

Marc went around and opened the door for Beth before heading back to his side of the car.

"How come you always do that?" Steve asked once Marc was sitting behind the wheel.

"Do what?"

"Open the door for Mom, like she can't do it herself."

Beth's mouth twitched as she turned to him. She was going to let him field this one.

"Well, my mother taught me that when I meet a pretty girl, I should use good manners to impress her," Marc said, trying to sound serious. "Opening the door for your mom is good manners." He hoped they wouldn't have to get into a conversation about why he was hoping to impress their mother.

"Like not burping at the dinner table or wiping your nose on your sleeve?" Steve asked. The mind of an almost nine-year-old boy.

"Exactly," Marc said, and reached across the armrest for Beth's hand as he pulled out of her front gate.

"Just so you know," Steve added, "Mom thinks it's important to wash your hands after you go to the bathroom too."

Marc bit the inside of his cheek. Steve wasn't trying to be funny, and Marc didn't want to hurt his feelings.

"I'll keep that in mind." Marc smiled as he said the words, and Beth squeezed his hand.

He took a deep breath and let go of the jumble in his brain.

23

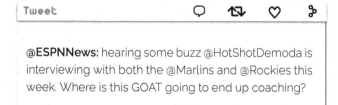

THE FOUR-AND-A-HALF-HOUR TRIP ended up taking almost six, and it was nearing three o'clock when they drove down the main road leading to the farm. Off to the right sat a small store and a big dirt lot with a few cars. Behind the lot was a Christmas tree farm and an apple orchard, and maybe a peach orchard too. There was a field growing a few different crops to the building's right, and behind that were two barn-looking structures and some fences for livestock. People were wandering through the fields and around the rails. A creek and woods ran behind the barns, blocking off the view on the other side.

"Keep going down to the dirt road on the right," Beth said. "This is the public farm."

The property was enormous, much bigger than Marc had expected. Once you got past the forest, the fields seemed to go on as far as the eye could see. Marc wasn't sure what Grant grew, but he had a ton of land.

The main house looked exactly like an old farmhouse should. A large white square against the fields surrounding it. The enormous windows were dark, almost black compared to the white shingles. There was a swing on the porch, which wrapped all the way around the house, and four brick chimneys rose into the sky. The house looked inviting. He could almost smell an apple pie baking and hear kids laughing as he looked at it.

"Big house," Marc said as he drove down the driveway, which was longer than two baseball fields. "I was hoping we might all have to squish." He smiled as Beth rolled her eyes.

"Mandy and I usually stay downstairs in the room Grant's grandparents used. Grant stays upstairs in his father's room. There are also three bunk rooms, three small rooms, and two bathrooms."

"I'll take the next best thing," Marc said, then called over the music into the back, "Steve, you want to bunk above me?"

"Cool!" Steve chirped back happily.

Men began walking out onto the front porch as they got closer, until Marc counted all seven brothers watching their arrival—giants waiting for two kids and one little lady. And him. The dark silhouettes of the men against the white building suddenly made the house look intimidating instead of inviting. It was ridiculous. He knew most of these guys; hell, some of them he would call friends. There was no reason to worry—but driving up to the house with Beth and the kids in the car felt like an audition. And it was one he wanted to go well.

"Uncle Joey and Uncle Nick are already here!" Steve yelled from the back. He was out the door as soon as the car stopped.

Beth reached around the seat and had Mandy unhooked before Marc got around to open the doors for them. Marc lifted

Mandy down out of the Jeep, and quickly became chopped liver as the girls raced away to hug the Evans men. He hung back, watching the exchange. Finally, one man he didn't recognize pulled away from the group and headed Marc's way.

This man seemed to be the oldest, and that meant it was Nick. But he looked nothing like Marc had expected. He knew Nick was a Navy SEAL, so Marc had pictured a clean-cut military man. Instead, Nick's jet-black hair was almost to his jaw, and his beard was a few inches long as well. He was wearing all black. Marc would have pegged him as crazy if not for the intense and intelligent gray-blue hawk eyes that met his own.

"Nick Evans." Nick put his hand out.

"Marc Demoda." Marc shook it as Nick's eyes took him in.

"So you're dating my sister," he said, and it sounded like an accusation.

"Yes," Marc said, and cleared his throat. It seemed stupid to be nervous, but something about Nick put him on edge—most likely the killer instinct that poured off him in spades.

"Hmm," Nick said, leaving Marc wondering what he thought until Beth walked toward them. Nick smiled at her. "I can't believe you're dating a pretty boy. I've heard he's not a wimp, though."

Pretty boy? Through his aviator sunglasses, Marc looked down at his plaid shorts and polo shirt, ending up at his Sperry's, then back up at Nick. Just because he didn't look homeless didn't mean he was a pretty boy.

"Must be why Clayton and Will like him so much," Nick added, and Beth smirked. Marc looked over to the group of men again. The only two not wearing ripped jeans or sweats and t-shirts were Clayton and Will.

"Birds of a feather," Beth said, and took Marc's hand. "Come on, say hi to Luke and Grant." Beth tugged his arm, heading for the group on the porch.

"You think I'm a pretty boy?" Marc asked.

"I think you're pretty." She laughed. "And you're male. And they put your face and body on billboards, hotshot."

It was true, but in this group, he didn't think 'pretty boy' was a compliment.

"I like you, anyway," she added, and he smiled.

The only brother Marc still hadn't met walked down the porch to greet them. Although Joey was as massive as the other guys, the hunch of his shoulders and the way he kept his eyes cast to the ground made him seem smaller. If Marc hadn't known that Clayton was the youngest, he would have assumed this brother was.

"Hi," he said. He didn't offer Marc his hand; it stayed against his thigh, which his thumb repeatedly tapped against.

"Marc, this is Joey," Beth said. "He's not around much because he's about to get his masters in biochemistry from Stanford," Beth bragged, but Joey's jaw tightened like he didn't enjoy the attention. Marc wanted to put him at ease.

"I'm sure you've heard about me from your brothers," Marc said, and Joey's eyes flicked up to him. "Do me a favor and only believe what comes from your sister's mouth."

Beth snorted, and Joey gave a sharp laugh.

"That's fair," he said with a grin, but then he leaned close. "I'll deny it if you repeat this, but the Jersey guys over there"—Joey's eyes cut to Will, Danny, and Clayton—"all have a bit of a man-crush going on."

Now it was Marc's turn to laugh. He and Joey were going to be fine.

Unlike the last time, when Beth had left him to deal with her brothers alone, this time she stayed with Marc as they said their hellos and unloaded the car. Her presence by his side did more than her 'be nice' last time. Luke was as friendly as the other brothers, but Grant was distant.

"Oh," Grant said when they went into the family room and Beth headed for a bedroom off it, "I moved downstairs."

"I'm glad," Beth replied.

Grant rolled his eyes. "It's convenient," he said.

"Yip," Beth said, but she walked over and rubbed his arm in a gesture of comfort.

There seemed to be more to moving downstairs than he understood, but he didn't ask. Beth turned to follow her brother Nick, who had the kids' stuff. Marc could only trail behind. He had both bags, so he opted to put his in the room he would share with Clayton and Steve before taking Beth hers.

She stood in the doorway, looking around the room.

"How long have you been coming here?" Marc asked.

Beth turned and took his hand, pulling him out into the hallway. She walked to one of the framed photos. It was an image of the Evans family from years ago sitting on their front porch.

"We take a group photo every year," Beth said. She pointed out everyone, ending with Clayton as a toddler, sitting on his mother's lap. "So I guess this is the eighteenth year."

They moved down the hallway, and Beth told stories about the different summers and Christmases she had come. Sometimes she laughed, and she was serious for others, but the love was clear in her voice in each story. This family loved each other. He had nothing like that. It was strange to realize he was jealous of something he had never wanted.

"What are you guys doing?" Clayton called down the hall.

"Just showing him the family pictures," Beth said with a smile.

"This one." Clayton pointed, tapping his finger against a frame. "This is my favorite." Beth laughed, like she knew which one he was talking about without seeing it.

Marc walked down to look. It was a recent one; Mandy was a baby in Beth's arms. But right away, it was clear why Clayton liked it. The family was on a picnic table, and Clayton had shoved his brother Nick, who in this picture looked like the clean-cut military man Marc had expected. Nick was in mid-fall, bumping Corey off the bench. Danny and Clayton were both laughing at them instead of looking at the camera.

Marc's eyes moved to another photo, one that included Bob. He looked a lot like Danny and Clayton, the blond-haired and blue-eyed combination that none of the other brothers had. Marc could see the resemblance to Steve too. Bob looked happy as shit with his arm around Beth, pulling her close. Beth's head tilted off-center the way it did when she was truly happy. Marc frowned. It was uncomfortable to be jealous of a dead guy, especially since Marc had never heard anyone say a bad thing about him, but his gut didn't like the idea of Bob's arm wrapped around Beth.

"Who's this?" Trying to distract himself, Marc pointed to a young blond-haired woman sitting with the group.

"A cheating fucking bitch," Clayton sneered.

"Language," Marc corrected Clayton for the millionth time.

"We're not at her house. The rule is no cursing in *her* house," Clayton complained.

"Semantics. Don't curse in front of your sister," Marc reminded him with a slap on the shoulder. Beth snaked her arms around Marc's waist and hugged him. "So who is she?"

"Grant's ex-wife," Beth said, and Marc could hear the distaste in her voice too. It surprised him; Beth rarely disliked people. "She left him."

That made sense. The Evanses stuck together like glue. This woman had hurt Grant, and none of them would forgive her for that.

"Anyway, I was supposed to make sure nothing was going on up here," Clayton said and winked at Marc.

"Ha-ha." Beth rolled her eyes. "We're coming down."

Marc looked at the picture again as Beth and Clayton walked away, thinking about his former teammates. The Metros took team pictures, and much like the Evanses, the guys picked on each other and ruined perfectly good shots. Marc missed the camaraderie with the guys on the team; he wanted that back. He wanted—no, *needed*—to find that again. But for the first time, Marc wondered if finding that trust, that group, didn't have to be through baseball.

24

"WE'RE GOLFING." FROM Nick's tone, Beth didn't think it was up for discussion, although half the group had already said they weren't going. "All of us," Nick added, looking at Danny, the biggest anti-golfer in the bunch.

"Oh?" Clayton, who was also on the anti-golf team, asked. "Who died and made you the boss?"

"Are you kidding? I brought the clubs all the way here." He went on, using his hands in a series of wild gestures. "I checked the clubs in San Diego, flew to Chicago, got them rechecked for my flight to Kennedy. Put them in a cab to Danny's place, then walked them into the subway to the *ferry* because he left his car at Will's. Then I had to walk from the ferry to Will's with them before the drive out here. And I'm going to have to do it all again on the way back. A boat, a plane, a car, and a train." He slapped the back of his hand against his palm to emphasize each word.

"Does that mean you don't like green eggs and ham?" Danny asked. All the guys laughed, except Nick, who frowned. "All right, since you went to all that trouble, I'll go, but I'm not getting up at the asscrack of dawn this time," Danny added.

"Seven o'clock is not the crack of dawn. Try having an actual job where you get up at five every day," Joey scoffed.

"I can't help that I'm smarter about choosing a job with reasonable hours," Danny replied, and he and Clayton fist-bumped. Neither were morning people.

"Danny, you don't *have* a real job. You're a lifeguard," Will pointed out.

Luke laughed. "Burned."

Chaos reigned as the boys talked more smack to each other. Beth shook her head as she listened to the back and forth.

"Beth," Nick finally said and smiled. "Sweetie."

She knew what he wanted. "Yeah, I'll call about a tee time. And I know—not at the crack of dawn, and not so late that it'll impede happy hour." She headed for the phone, and Marc followed her.

She liked the fact that he'd stuck with her since they had arrived. She'd wondered if he wanted to come to be with her or her brothers; his focused attention told her she was his priority.

"I'm not going golfing on your birthday, and neither are the kids. I know the idea is to give you a break, but we want to spend the day with you," he mumbled.

"Afraid to tell them?" she teased.

The only one Marc seemed even slightly afraid of was Nick, which was silly. Although Nick resembled a hermit now, it wasn't his usual look. He'd been in Syria and would go back after this week's leave. Blending in there was easier if he didn't look like a military man.

"More hoping you could get me out of it. I thought the two of us could do something with the kids while they're gone." He wrapped his arms around her waist and pulled her to him.

"What did you have in mind?" Beth asked.

"Since it's your birthday, I'll take care of the plans. You just come." He leaned down and gently kissed her lips.

"And get you out of golf," she teased.

"I thought we already established that." He smiled as he headed back into the room to join the boys.

They were all laughing over their 'five o'clock somewhere' drinks—in Pennsylvania it was only four, but Nick had grabbed a beer a few minutes ago, and they all followed suit.

"Okay, tee time at ten-thirty for the seven of you." She smiled as the men all frowned at her.

"Seven?" Nick asked, and his eyes fell on Marc.

"Yip." But she said nothing else.

"Beth, math has never been your strong suit," Will said, "but I know you can count. There are eight of us plus two kids."

"Oh, I know. But only seven of you are going. It's my birthday, so Marc's staying with me."

She knew how they were going to react, but Marc didn't. All eyes fell on him.

"Dude." Luke glared at Marc. "Tell me you're not that whipped."

"Whipped?" Marc asked with a single eyebrow arch.

"Yeah," Will agreed.

"Next thing you know, you're going to be skipping baseball games in favor of *The Kardashians*," Danny said, snickering with Nick.

"Beth has no interest in that show. It's never going to be a problem," Marc assured them. "As far as golf, if you had a choice between spending the day with a beautiful woman or seven ugly men, which one of you would play?"

"Ooh," Clayton chanted and fist-bumped Marc, who smiled at him.

Beth shook her head. Marc crooked his finger at her, and she moved to sit on his lap.

"Thanks for your help there, sweetheart." Marc chuckled against her ear, sending a shiver down her spine.

"You have to hold your own in this group," Beth murmured. "And you did."

"Where did you find him?" Nick asked, shaking his head.

"He followed her around like a puppy for a while until she brought him home," Will said, trying again to rile Marc up.

"Yeah, he had to beg for weeks," Danny agreed.

"It was borderline pathetic," Clayton added.

Marc shrugged unapologetically. "Nothing worth having comes easy."

"I got to disagree," Luke said, shaking his head. "Sometimes, it's good even if it's easy." And then he paused and turned to Beth. "But you're not allowed to be easy."

The guys all laughed while Beth shook her head.

"Dude," Clayton said, glancing up from his phone. "You're moving to Colorado?"

Marc snorted. "Or Florida—or I think two days ago it was Texas. No one is changing pitching coaches at this point in the season, no matter what Twitter says."

It was crazy how much speculation about Marc's next job there was buzzing around the sports media. Austin might be doing it on purpose to drum up interest, but Marc kept assuring both her and her brothers he wasn't getting a job until after the playoffs; maybe holiday time in November or December. As always, talk of his career had the guys talking about baseball.

"You want to run with me before dinner?" Beth asked, turning to look at Marc.

He looked over her shoulder, and his brow furrowed. "Do you guys mind watching the kids?"

She knew they didn't, but when she turned around to look, they were all staring at her like she had grown horns in the last few seconds.

"What?" she demanded.

"He can run with you?" Danny asked skeptically.

"Why not?" Beth shook her head. Then surprise turned to glares. She didn't understand what the big deal was.

"Maybe I should stay and watch Mandy and Steve," Marc said, looking as confused as she was. Mandy and Steve were currently on the other side of the room, building LEGO ships. That would keep them entertained for at least another half hour. She sent a look to her brothers, telling them all they better step up.

"No, it's fine. I'll watch 'em," Will said, recovering from whatever the problem was. "I told them I'd take them up to the barn, anyway. Luke'll come with me. Right?" Will threw his bottle cap at his brother when Luke didn't answer.

"Sure," Luke said, glaring at Marc.

Beth didn't understand. She ran every night; it wasn't like any of them ever came with her and now they were feeling left out. And none of the boys had ever had a problem watching the kids before. Even when she'd had to bring other kids with her, they didn't mind. She shook her head and stood up to get changed. She could usually sort through their madness, but this time, she was coming up blank.

AFTER THEY GOT back from their run, Beth took care of dinner while Marc showered. Some of the boys had gotten over whatever their problem was; others hadn't. Marc was as confused as Beth by the boys' reaction to their running together. Her brothers were acting like she'd asked Marc for a quickie before dinner instead of a run. He wondered if that was what they thought they were doing. It had surprised Marc too when she'd asked him to go—she usually liked to run alone—but he hadn't minded going. Especially when she came down in her sports bra and shorts. He'd follow her anywhere like that.

At six-thirty, they were all sitting down to eat. Peas weren't something Marc usually ate, especially not when they were still in the pod, but in the last month of dinners with the Evanses, Marc had learned to eat his veggies. The kids were great about their greens, so he was shocked when the fight ensued at dinner.

"I not eaten them," Mandy said again, pointing to the peas on her plate long after everyone else had finished.

Marc was wiping down the table around Mandy while the rest of the guys were in the kitchen doing the dishes. The Evans rule was a simple one: Beth cooked, and the boys cleaned up every meal with no complaints. Marc had learned that there was nothing Beth hated more than dishes; at her house, he and Steve took care of them.

"They don't have to be your favorite, Mandy, but you need to eat them," Beth said again.

"You mate my life so hart," she replied, glaring at her mother and using a line that Marc had heard from her plenty of times.

"Then you don't get ice cream," Beth said simply.

"Yes, I do," Mandy said with a sassiness that proved she was her mother's daughter.

"No, you don't." Beth always handled Mandy's attitude with a calm, collected response that impressed Marc.

Joey, Luke, and Steve walked into the dining room, each with a bowl of ice cream, and sat down.

"*I want ice cream!*" Mandy screamed. Marc had never seen her pitch a fit like this before, but Beth didn't act like it was anything new.

"Then eat your peas," Beth replied, on the receiving end of Mandy's glare.

Grant walked in a minute later with two bowls in his hand. "Did I hear someone say they wanted ice cream?" he asked, smiling at Mandy.

Marc couldn't believe it. No way should Mandy have ice cream. He looked at Beth, who was taking a deep breath.

"I do!" Mandy smiled, looking proud of herself as Grant set a bowl down in front of her. Marc wondered how much of the tantrum Mandy was having was because she knew one of her uncles would give in.

Beth calmly pushed the bowl back before saying, "Once your peas are gone."

"I no like peas." Mandy's full scowl was back on her face.

"Aww, come on," Grant said as he pushed the bowl back toward the little girl.

Beth's teeth clenched, and then Grant added, "My house, my rules. We don't want the ice cream to melt. She can skip the peas this one time." Mandy rewarded Grant with her sweetest smile, and Grant patted her head. At three, Mandy had already learned how to work her uncle.

Grant didn't get to see the kids much, so it made sense that he'd want to be the fun uncle. All the guys enjoyed being the fun uncle, of course, but this seemed to cross a line. Grant's interference was undermining Beth's parenting, and Marc didn't like it.

"Yeah," Luke said, taking his brother's side, "she's on vacation. Give the girl a break."

Beth looked warily from Grant to Luke to Joey, who was nodding in agreement. Danny walked into the room with his bowl and sat down. Marc would bet that Danny and the others weren't willing to be the bad guys either.

Eating right mattered to Beth. Her kids *asked for* broccoli and spinach pizza with cauliflower crust, for fuck's sake. And Marc had seen Mandy eat peas and like them. This was about not having to listen to Mom when her uncles were around.

Marc wasn't about to let that happen. He'd be the bad guy. He had learned that the kids moved on quickly; if Mandy was mad at him tonight, she'd get over it by tomorrow.

"Amanda," he said, walking toward the little girl. Beth's eyes were on him, and although he was looking only at her daughter, he put his hand on Beth's shoulder. Marc wanted her to know he was on her side, and wanted Mandy to know her mother was right. "I'll put this ice cream in the freezer for when you finish your peas, like *your mom* said."

Mandy turned her scowl on him. She reached up a hand to swipe the peas off the plate, but Marc caught her wrist and held on until she finally looked down at her plate and picked up one of the pea pods. Marc lifted his eyes, daring Grant to fight *him* about it. Grant's eyes narrowed, and his grip tightened on the spoon, but he said nothing, and Marc left the room with the bowl.

He barely had the freezer door shut when Grant walked in.

"Give Marc and me a minute, boys," he said to Will, Nick, and Clayton. Nick and Will headed out to the table with their ice cream.

"What's going on?" Clayton asked, looking from Marc to Grant.

"Out, Clayton," Grant said, but he was glaring at Marc.

"No. What did you do now?" Clayton asked in frustration. Clayton didn't mean any harm in his question, but Marc wanted to ask what he'd done at all.

"I agreed with Beth," Marc said, looking at Clayton before turning to Grant. "Healthy eating habits are important, and Mandy is Beth's daughter. You have no right to interfere."

"And you have no right to get involved in family business," Grant shot back.

In any other situation, Marc might have agreed with him, but not when it was setting a precedent for Mandy that she didn't have to listen to her mother.

"If Beth's involved, I'm involved whether you like it or not."

"Fucking the kid's mother doesn't give you the right—" Grant began.

Marc's head spun. "Don't talk about your sister that way." Marc's tone was low, but deadly serious. Ever since they'd arrived, Marc had gotten the impression that Grant didn't like him, but that was out of line. "Even if Beth and I weren't together, I'd still like Mandy. She's a good kid, but she's not *your* kid."

"She's my niece."

"She's Beth's daughter, and that trumps," Marc snapped at Grant. The two men stepped toward each other.

"And she's your *nothing*," Grant shot back. That was a punch in the gut. Mandy was his... what? Something. Marc didn't know what the word for it would be.

"Whoa—Grant, Marc." Clayton put his hand on his brother's shoulder, both to calm him down and push him back away from Marc. Clayton was bigger than Marc or Grant, but that wouldn't have stopped either of them. Beth walking in with an empty plate, however, did.

"She finished." Beth's smile faded as she walked into the room. "Guys?"

Beth didn't look happy, and Marc took a breath. He turned to the freezer, pulled out Mandy's bowl, reached deep down into himself, and handed it to Grant.

"So go be the good guy. Give her back her ice cream," he said, hoping the bowl could be a peace offering.

Grant's face went white as he stared from the bowl to Marc, then left the room without taking it. Clayton followed him, grabbing the bowl out of Marc's hand.

"Sorry," Marc said. He'd thought letting Grant give her the ice cream would settle things down, not make them worse. "I'm thinking coming this weekend was a bad idea."

"No, I'm glad you're here," she said, shaking her head and then coming up and wrapping her arms around him. "Thank you for taking my side, not letting them bulldoze me."

"You don't need to thank me. I'm always on your side," Marc said and held her close. "You don't even have to ask." He couldn't believe she hadn't figured that out already. Whether it was the media, her father, her brothers, her kids—he was always on her side.

The next hour was tense. Grant left the house, along with Will and Nick, and although Clayton and Danny tried to lighten the mood, Joey and Luke were upset with Marc. Marc didn't think he'd overstepped. More importantly, Beth wasn't angry with him. And surprisingly, neither was Mandy. As soon as she finished her ice cream, she brought Marc her book to read, climbing right into his lap. And by the time the story ended, she was laughing as he tickled her while they debated blue vs. pink, like any other day.

Beth went up to shower, so Marc walked out on the back porch alone. It had started to drizzle about an hour ago, and the smell of wet dirt filled the air. The sky darkened; more rain was coming. After a few minutes, the door opened behind him and he turned, expecting to see Beth.

"I brought you a cold one," Will said, sitting down next to Marc.

"Crossing enemy lines?" Marc asked, but he took the beer.

"Nah, Grant was wrong," Will said, looking out into the fields.

"I know," Marc agreed.

"Yeah, we all do. They're over it. It's hard sometimes." Will sighed. "It's why I told Grant he needed to invite you up this weekend."

"What?" Marc asked, turning to look at Will.

"Pretty soon we'll be replaced in her and the kids' life by a new man. She's going to remarry," Will said simply, but the blood rushed to Marc's head, and he sprang to his feet.

"Whoa." Marc put his hands in the air, warding off Will's statement with the gesture.

"I didn't mean you, moron. Sit down," Will said, shaking his head and handing Marc back the beer he'd pretty much dropped when he jumped up. Marc took it slowly, but didn't sit. "You aren't into marriage, but until now, she'd never let another guy in their lives."

"What?" Marc asked suspiciously. Thunder rolled off in the distance, and his eyes flicked up to the sky. It was going to pour.

"Beth's dated other guys since Bob died, but she picks wimpy losers—men she has no future with," Will said, shaking his head.

Marc raised his eyebrows. "Losers?" He honestly couldn't imagine it. She was too smart for that.

"Yeah, and she thinks she likes them—but she doesn't." Marc could almost laugh at the certainty in Will's statement. "She thinks she wants someone calm and boring, but they can't handle her, and she gets tired of them. She's a lot; she doesn't know when to slow down, and she needs someone to tell her to stop when she's exhausted. She's impulsive and lives the hell out of life, and she needs someone who doesn't stomp that crazy out."

Marc smiled. He couldn't disagree. The one thing Will had left out was fragile, although Beth would kill Marc for even thinking it. But she was, in a way that drew him close, wanting to protect her when she needed it.

Will looked at Marc before he continued. "And she needs someone who can not only be okay with her seven brothers, but knows when it's time to put them in their place. She needs someone more like you, and I think she's finally realized that."

"I've told her how things are with us—she knows."

"Yeah. She's told us," Will agreed—more quickly than Marc would have liked. "She's enjoying you while you're together, but it'll be over by the end of the summer." Marc frowned. "What I meant before was that when things are over with you, she's going to find someone—the right someone this time."

Marc's frown turned into a scowl as he stared out into the rainy evening. He didn't like that idea; the thought of Beth with another man was like another hard punch to the gut. But Will kept talking, ignoring his scowl.

"She's our anchor, and somebody's going to take her away from us."

"I don't think the right guy would do that," Marc said, sitting back down next to Will.

"That's where you're wrong. The right one will. It's half of what will make him right for her," Will answered. "We pull her in a hundred different directions. We all know that. But none of us want to give her up, either."

"Do you know, between texts and calls, her phone rings *constantly* from all of you."

Will shrugged. "What can I say? We're close."

"She loves you, but she also needs a break. Not that she'd ever ask for one," Marc said.

"Exactly, and that's why the right guy will take her away. Not completely, but just enough," Will said. "Can you do us one favor, Marc?"

"What?"

"Don't string them along too much longer. It's not in any of their interests for you to hang around for another six months and then one day show up and say, 'I'm out,'" Will said, observing Marc's reaction.

Marc wanted to be mad, but he couldn't. What Will was asking was fair.

"I'm not going to disappear. I can't give her a permanent commitment, but I also can't walk away," Marc admitted.

Will smirked, but before he could respond, the door behind them opened. Both men turned to see Beth standing there.

"Playing nice?" she asked, pointedly looking at Will.

"Yeah, I was telling Marc he was right about the peas. A peace offering." Will lifted his bottle, and Beth smiled.

"Thank you," she said as she nudged Will with her shoulder.

The sky opened up, and the light rain became a hard pounding. Beth's smile flashed. She got that sparkle in her eyes, the one Marc loved, and her Ugg boots fell with a *thunk* onto the porch. She hopped off the steps into the rain before cocking her head and beckoning them with a single finger.

"Oh, no—no no no," Will said, backing up like she was a venomous snake. "This is *exactly* the kind of crazy I was referring to."

But unlike Will, Marc was helpless to deny the call of the siren, and he found himself in the downpour with a beautiful woman in a soaked shirt and cut-offs, dancing in the rain. Beth swayed and shook to a beat he couldn't hear, and he watched this beautiful creature who continued to amaze him with her ability to enjoy the hell out of life. He smiled even as warmth filled him, in his chest as well as his groin. Damn, she was perfect.

The porch slowly filled with Evanses, including Beth's kids, so they now had an audience. But Marc's attention stayed riveted on the drenched woman next to him.

"Come on, hotshot. Where are your moves?" Beth teased as she twirled and shimmied around him.

His captivation with her left him unable to resist, so he did the Robot to the sound of her cackles. When he looked back to see Beth covering her face with her hands as she laughed, he couldn't stop himself from grabbing her and tossing her over his shoulder, spinning them both. She squirmed, kicked, laughed, and wiggled until Marc felt the little hands of her mini-me grabbing his legs.

"Me turn," Mandy demanded.

Slowly he lowered Beth off his shoulder, but instead of letting her go, he kept her tight to him as he brought Mandy into their wet embrace.

"Are you my dancing in the rain girl?" Beth asked.

"Yes, me got moves," Mandy said, and he released both girls, letting them spin around him again.

"Steve," Beth yelled, and her son came down. "Where's my dancing in the rain man?" she asked when he finally reached them.

Steve simply pointed at Marc. "Although he's not very good."

Marc reached over and gave Steve a noogie, and before Marc knew it, the entire family was dancing in the rain. Danny and Nick threw Will out into the downpour while Clayton snapped a group photo.

"Wall pic," Clayton informed Marc, showing him the photo. He and Beth were in the center, the kids in their arms, all the Evans men around them. And he felt like part of the family.

That made him think about what Will had said.

Marc looked at Beth, a few feet away whispering to Luke. Her blond curls were dripping wet, and she didn't have any makeup on—yet she was breathtakingly beautiful. He imagined her walking out next summer to dance in the rain with someone else. The idea caused something close to pain in his chest.

She turned, as if she could feel his eyes on her, and smiled before heading his way. "Catch me if you can," she whispered, taking off in a sprint across the grass.

"Go; we got the kids," Luke said next to him.

Marc smiled as he chased her through the rain, across the fields and into the barn. She laughed and teased him the entire way. But now they were alone, and he was getting his hands on her. Her wet skin sparkled in the fading light, and she was warm and slick when he reached for her.

Something he couldn't name filled his chest, seeing the desire in her eyes for him alone. He might not be able to offer her a commitment, but he had promised great sex, and that was precisely what he was going to give her. She tossed a blanket on the ground, and he stripped them both down to wet skin.

He should say so many things to her—tell her he cared and didn't want to hurt her—but he couldn't get the words out. So instead, he showed her exactly how much he felt, and hoped that could be enough.

25

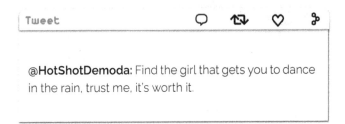

BETH PROPPED HER arms on Marc's chest and looked down into his face. Fear etched his features. Her fingers ran along his cheek.

That was hands down the best sex of her life, and it had been more than her body involved. The second he'd put his hand on her shoulder and told Mandy to eat her peas, she had lost her entire heart to the man. Beth wondered if she'd told him telepathically, because he looked terrified.

"Marc?"

"That's never happened before," he said, turning his eyes her way. "Ever."

She forced a chuckle because her stomach was in her throat. "You mean you've never had mind-blowing sex in a barn?"

He finally cracked a smile.

"I haven't." His face became serious again. "But more importantly, I've never had unprotected sex before, and I'm really hoping you're about to tell me you're on some form of birth control."

"Oh." Her face fell; she hadn't thought of a condom. "I have an IUD."

"Good." He relaxed under her. Now it was her turn to panic.

"But…" Beth swallowed.

"But what?" Marc looked nervous again.

She spun her ring a few times, regrouping. "That won't do anything to prevent STDs," she said. "I haven't slept with anyone in four years, so you don't have to worry. But…?"

He let out his breath.

"Part of the agreement we signed with your father involved a blood test for me. I'm clean," Marc assured her and wrapped his arms around her. "And like I said, I've always used condoms. I'm not sure how that even happened. I have one in my wallet." He pointed to the shorts on the floor and shook his head. "I can only blame the whole 'mind-blowing' part." He smiled again and reached up to brush her hair behind her ear.

She leaned down, resting her head against his shoulder. She loved the intimacy of these moments they had when Marc had his walls down.

"Do you ever think about having more kids?" Marc asked.

"I'd like to have more. I love my big family, and I want that for the kids. Will you?"

"No," Marc said quickly.

"Really?" Beth asked, surprised.

"I'm not father material."

"Marc, that's not true. You're great with Mandy and Steve."

"That's different. I'd resent the sacrifices a parent has to make for their kids. Unlike you—you do it for people who aren't even your kids."

She wasn't sure what he meant.

"How did you do it?" Marc asked, finally tucking his free arm behind his head, looking up at the ceiling.

"Do what?" Beth asked, still not understanding.

"After winning the gold medal, after standing there on the podium with the entire world listening to the National Anthem, how did you walk away?"

Beth didn't answer right away. The question wasn't a straightforward one; really, he was asking how to do it himself.

"I had something I wanted more. It's short-lived, that feeling. Fame and fans are fickle, and boy, did they prove that a few months later, after everything with Corey. But my brothers—they love me. Good or bad; it doesn't matter. I don't need to earn their love. It's unconditional. And that feeling is better."

Marc's hand rubbed along her back, but he said nothing else.

"It was easy for me, but I think it would be a lot harder if something or someone had decided for me." She wished he would say something else, but he just shifted her off his bad shoulder.

"Does it hurt?"

"Not usually." He shook his head. "But it gets stiff sometimes if I overuse it, and I did." She heard the sadness of his laugh.

"What happened that night?" she asked. Marc had never talked about it with her. He stiffened instantly.

"The crash crushed my shoulder. The surgeons rebuilt it, but it's not strong enough to pitch again." He shrugged, but she knew better than to believe his apathy. This was important, and she wanted to learn more.

"Were they your friends, the people in the car with you?" Beth tried again. Marc looked down at her for a minute and then shut his eyes. She didn't expect him to answer.

"Not friends," Marc said finally. He took a deep breath and then added, "One girl was someone I occasionally slept with, and the other two were her friends."

Her heart pinched. It was silly; he'd been with a lot of women. Despite that, the way he talked about this one told her something was different. The accident had killed the two women on the car's passenger side.

"Do you miss her?" Beth asked, and he flinched.

"No," Marc said and opened his weary eyes to look at her. "Beth, I never missed her. It took me three days to even think to ask about them. I—" He cut himself off.

"So why don't you ever talk about the accident?"

Marc shut his eyes again.

"Will you ever get over what happened with Corey and be comfortable in a relationship with someone in the public eye?" he asked instead.

Now it was her turn to flinch. She wanted to say yes because she did that now, with him. But she hated being in the glare of the media. It wasn't comfortable. If anything were to bring up the drama from ten years ago, it would be awful. And now, looking at Marc, the thought that her past could hurt him or what he wanted for his future career was unbearable.

Beth tried to form an answer, but then he opened his eyes.

"You know I hate it that you wear another man's ring," Marc said and glared at her hands.

"Huh?" she asked. She looked down at her fingers fiddling with her ring.

"This," Marc said, spinning the ring on her thumb as she did. "It's Bob's."

"How...?" Beth asked, looking down at it. She rarely even thought of it that way anymore.

"I asked Clayton about it. And I don't like how you spin it so much thinking about him, especially when you're lying here with me." His frown turned into a scowl.

"I wasn't thinking about Bob," Beth said honestly. It had been his voice that echoed in her head when she spun the ring at first, reminding her not to worry so much. But it had stopped being his voice a long time ago.

"Then why do it?" Marc asked.

She shrugged. "It helps me relax."

"What if I asked you to take it off?"

Beth pulled away and sat up.

"I won't," he said finally and leaned up to pull her back.

She settled against him, and his silver chain caught against her cheek. "Is this something special?" she asked, letting her fingers run over the chain and the cross that hung in the middle of his chest.

"The cross was my grandfather's. My grandmother gave it to me when I turned eighteen. She said it would be like my guardian angel. She told me to always wear it, and I would get where I needed to be. My mother believes it's why I lived through the accident. Silly, I know." Marc pulled her on top of him. "But I never take it off. I suppose that's why I'll leave this alone," Marc said as he spun her ring again.

Beth sighed.

"So." Marc's smile became lazy and sexy. "How long do you think we can get away with staying out here?"

"Awhile. I mean, it's not like they don't know why we're out here." Beth chuckled. The barn had been Luke's idea. He'd said it looked like both of them could use a good roll in the hay.

"I don't understand them at all, but I like your brothers." Marc smiled at her and kissed her deeply. "You're going to have to give my shoulder a break this time, though."

"I think I can handle that," Beth murmured against his mouth, realizing they were both using sex to avoid talking about something.

MARC WOKE TO the smell of breakfast. There were two things that could have made his morning better: First, he'd rather be waking up in Beth's bed with her instead of alone in the bottom bunk. Marc hated that after spending hours with her, he'd had to kiss her goodnight at the door to her bedroom. He liked how she fit into the crook of his arm, and how her leg felt when she draped it over his. He loved the feel of her soft, warm skin against him, and the scent of peaches in the air when he shut his eyes.

Second, he didn't like Bob's ring. He didn't have the right to ask her to take it off, he knew, and he'd been an ass about it. The ring hadn't bothered him before his conversation with Will. But now, it kept reminding him she'd been someone else's. And Marc didn't like the idea of Beth being with anyone else.

But his mind circled back to how happy Beth looked in that picture with Bob. She deserved that kind of happiness. Marc made her happy, didn't he?

Last night had made things more complicated. Sex with Beth had always been great, but yesterday had taken it to another level. It was more than the lack of a latex barrier—although having felt what it was like to be inside her, to feel her warm flesh surrounding him, he knew it was going to be damn hard to go back.

No, it wasn't the condom issue. Suddenly sex had become more than physical for him. He had tried to show her how much he cared, and it had become emotional—something sex had never been for him before. When he'd slid into her, he'd felt it in his gut. Every fiber of his body was screaming. *Finally.*

That had forced him to look at the future, at how she would handle him moving back into the spotlight with a job like the one he might get at NESN. Snapping a question at her like that had been the wrong approach. But he didn't want to talk about that fucking accident. His brain had been yelling at him to ask her opinion about NESN, and it came out wrong. Then he'd opened his eyes and seen her playing with Bob's ring. And he snapped.

He shook his head. Things were getting incredibly involved, and he wasn't up for 'involved.'

However, he was up for breakfast and then some fun, and thanks to the best agent in the world, he had everything planned perfectly for Beth's birthday. He grabbed his jeans off the floor and headed down toward the voices he heard coming from the kitchen.

"LUKE, YOU CAN'T," Beth said as she flipped the bacon. Luke wanted to be in Alaska, but it wasn't an option. And this was the third time they were having this discussion. He was trying to annoy her. It was the downside of him working for the national branch of Helping Hands. She was his boss, and he loved to give her crap.

"But it's *Alaska*," Luke moaned.

"Can you please not burn the pancakes?"

Luke grabbed the spatula and flipped them onto the plate.

"Can't one of the others do the Jersey thing?" he asked as he poured more batter onto the griddle.

It was a fair request, and if any of the other guys had the training, she would have let them. But they didn't.

"I'm sorry, but I will not keep hashing this out with you. Think of it this way: You get to spend some quality time with Will."

"Does that mean I'm not allowed to live with you?" Luke joked.

Luke was almost as crappy as Danny was with women. Unlike Will, who preferred a steady girlfriend, Luke had bed buddies. And Beth didn't do bed buddies at her house.

"Ha-ha," Beth said, putting the bacon on the plate with the sausage as Luke flipped the last pancake off the griddle. "Let me put it this way, Luke: I'm asking, not telling. Please?"

He smiled softly. "You know I will."

"Thanks."

Beth turned to carry the plate to the table, but Marc stood in the doorway, frowning.

"Morning," she said, walking toward him, and he kissed her lightly.

"You're making Luke move home?" Marc asked, looking from her to Luke. He didn't seem to like the idea, and she wondered if Marc realized Luke was only joking about moving in with her.

"She's not *making* me; I'm just giving her garbage." Luke shrugged. "I'll call everyone for breakfast."

Marc's gaze followed Luke out of the room. She didn't think Marc had any problem with Luke, but something had upset him.

"You okay?"

"Yeah." He shook his head like he was trying to rid himself of some thought. "Did a package come for me?"

"As a matter of fact, yes. It's on the back porch," she said.

"Perfect," he said and headed out of the room before she could ask him what he'd had shipped here.

MARC BENT DOWN over the box, looking inside. But he didn't see the picnic lunch or the cupcakes; instead, it was Beth's face as she spoke to her brother. She'd turned those emerald-green eyes on Luke and asked him to come home. Marc hadn't heard the entire conversation, but he'd heard enough to know that Beth needed Luke. In the end, Beth didn't tell him what to do, but she had asked him to do something for her. Give up something he wanted for her.

And Luke had agreed.

It didn't bother him that Luke was coming home. It wasn't even the fact that Beth wanted him near that bothered him. The thought that chilled him right to the bone was Beth turning to him and asking him to give up something. To stay in Jersey with her. If he got the job with NESN and she asked him not to take it, he wasn't sure what he'd do—and that fact terrified him.

His father's words echoed through his brain. And maybe his dad was right. Good sex had fogged his mind, and now he was thinking about giving up his whole life. He needed to remember to keep Beth separate from his career, and his life.

26

@MSNnews: Phillies fire Stokes, making room for a new coach. Was the @HotShotDemoda trip to PA coincidence?

@EdwardDCampbell: It's with a great sense of purpose that I announce my resignation from @SecState. Good luck to Jonathan Liam, my deputy, who will be the acting Secretary.

@HotShotDemoda: It's my girl's birthday so let's all show her the love!

BETH, MARC, AND the kids had just walked back into the house from their perfectly planned picnic by the lake on Grant's property when the phone rang. One would think a phone call from her parents on her birthday would have been a birthday wish, but it was her father, so naturally, it was about him. The presence of her, Marc, and her children was required for the official announcement that he had been selected for VP on the Republican ticket. It was scheduled for July 4—tomorrow. Her father didn't care that she was away; only that she drop everything and make the trip to Virginia.

It bothered Marc and her brothers more than it upset her. It outraged them—not only had her parents forgotten her birthday, but they'd ruined her plans. Instead of dwelling on it, Beth insisted that they all have the planned bonfire and enjoy the rest of the day before the four of them had to leave in the early morning.

After four-plus hours of driving the next day, Marc held the door for Beth as she got out of his car, then took Mandy out of his arms.

"We don't have to go home with them, right?" Steve asked, keeping a death grip on Marc's hand as they headed toward the stage.

"No way. We're going to watch the fireworks on the beach from my deck," Marc reminded him. "It might not be as much fun as watching your uncles set them off, but it's still pretty cool." Both kids had hated to leave Grant's before the guys' firework show, but Marc was trying hard to make it up to them.

"Oh yeah." Steve smiled. "And we can have pizza and swim, right?"

Marc nodded. "We'll even ignore bedtime for once," he said, and Steve's grip loosened some.

"Awesome." Steve perked up.

Marc's free arm came around Beth's waist, steering her toward the steps where a group of people waited.

"Steve!" called one of her sister's twins.

Steve's eyes shot up to Marc instead of Beth. "Can I go?"

Marc didn't even check with her before he answered. "Don't wander off," he said, letting go of Steve's hand. "Or get dirty."

Marc had come a long way from the guy who'd fixed her dishwasher two months ago. She remembered the overwhelmed look on his face just from walking into a house with so many kids. Now, she trusted him with both Steve and Mandy completely. He might not think he was 'father material,' but he would make a great dad one day.

She blinked at the pinch that caused. The idea of Marc holding a baby warmed her chest, but it also squeezed her heart. Because as much as she might wish it could be their baby, Marc would be leaving as soon as the fall came, and his new job offer with it. At least that was months away.

"You're late," Paul barked, interrupting her thoughts as they approached him. Paul's eyes drifted down her outfit, and she felt Marc's fingers tighten at her hip. She wore a red shirtdress with a collared V-neck, belted at the waist, and simple red pumps.

"It was a long drive," Marc said.

"Perhaps an early start would have been better," Paul said, looking at Beth again.

It wouldn't have bothered her if he had been looking at her face as opposed to her dress. The dress should have been fine. It wasn't too short or low-cut.

"We had a late night," Marc stated with the kind of smirk that left little doubt about what he was implying. Beth bit her cheek, trying not to laugh at the look on Paul's face. She didn't mind giving him the wrong idea, but the only thing they'd done last night was make s'mores around the campfire.

"Elizabeth," her father bellowed. Beth set Mandy down, adjusted the girl's pretty red-white-and-blue ruffled dress, and took her hand as she walked toward him. "Try your best to stick to this." Her father handed her a piece of paper.

Beth read the list and gritted her teeth. Marc looked over her shoulder.

"Notice it's only *my* name in the memo line because I'm always the problem," Beth sighed. Marc took the paper—a list of talking points for problematic speakers—folded it, and put it inside his suit jacket.

"Please keep that handy for her," the former secretary told him. "And Paul has a packet listing the things you'll be attending for the next month. Get that from him and make sure you review it; it'll tell you our stances so you don't go off-script. It also has information about appropriate attire." Her father frowned at her dress. "A suit would have been better."

"Ed," Marc interrupted curtly, "we need to talk."

Beth looked at Marc, shocked. That was the first time he had spoken to her father like he was a person. Marc never called him anything but 'Secretary,' and he always used a polite, formal tone. She didn't know where this change had come from.

Her father nodded, and Marc turned to her. "Wait here," he said, and lightly kissed her lips before turning away. The way he looked at both her father and Paul, Beth felt like the kiss had branded her. She shivered, liking being claimed by Marc.

The two men walked a short distance away from the group and then settled into a discussion. Neither looked happy, but they continued until finally Marc crossed his arms stubbornly over his chest and shook his head. Beth's father looked over at her, narrowed his eyes, then turned back to Marc. Marc shrugged and said something else. Her father sighed, and then headed straight for Beth.

"Look over the packet and get back to Paul about which of the events you'll attend. And if the kids would prefer not to come—well, I suppose that as their mother, that's your choice."

Her mouth fell open. Her choice?

"Is that a problem?" he asked.

She shook her head, and her father turned and headed directly for his chief of staff. It looked like he was about to rip Paul a new one. She knew the face well. What had Paul done? He rarely got yelled at.

"What did you say to him?" Beth asked as Marc returned to her side and lifted Mandy into his arms.

"I told him I loved your dress," he said.

"Liar." Beth laughed.

"Seriously, I love your dress. You look beautiful. And I told him you and I would attend those events together. I thought he should know."

MARC HAD ALSO told Ed to back the fuck off because he wasn't going to just stand there while Ed and his staff picked on Beth or the kids. Nor was Beth going to be getting any more demanding phone calls. Ed could ask nicely, and if they were available, they would come. If not, well, tough shit. Otherwise, they wouldn't be attending any events. He wasn't telling Beth that, though. She was a wimp about her father. But that was fine. Marc didn't mind standing between them when he needed to. Beth had been tense for hours, in a way that he hadn't seen in weeks. The media was worrying her, and Marc didn't want her upset. Beth was a beautiful, capable woman, and Marc would make damn sure she believed that.

"Let's find Steve and figure out where they want us to be," Marc said, and wrapped his arm around Beth's waist. She sighed contentedly and leaned against him.

He smiled, then his phone buzzed in his pocket. He pulled it out and glanced at the screen to see Austin's number flashing.

He frowned. Austin knew where he was. Why was he calling?

"Everything okay?" Beth asked.

Marc sent her a reassuring smile. "Austin probably wants to remind me to take a picture and send it to him to tweet." He was unwilling to upset her, even as his stomach tightened. "Give me one second."

"Sure," she said. She took Mandy and headed toward the stage. Marc's eyes tracked the red dress the entire way. Even though he hated watching her walk away, he had to admit it was a pretty nice view.

"Yeah?" he said into the phone as he watched Beth's legs. She was up on her toes so the heels of her shoes didn't sink into the grass, and *damn* did it make her legs look good—a hint of the upside-down heart on each calf.

"I am officially your new favorite person," Austin said excitedly.

"I doubt that." But he managed a grin that he was sure Austin could hear in his voice. Beth bent down slightly to put Mandy on her feet. The red hem crept up to mid-thigh, and his grin became a smile just as Mandy turned back to him, waving him over. Marc nodded and stuck a finger in the air. Mandy stomped her foot and frowned. Marc laughed.

"What's funny?" Austin asked.

"Mandy," Marc said with a chuckle.

"All right, fine, Beth and the kids get top billing—but I have good news," Austin assured him.

Marc's eyes hadn't left the girls, and now Steve had joined them. Ed turned, frowned, and said something to Beth, who sighed. She re-tucked Steve's shirt into his pants and ran her hands over his forehead, fixing his hair.

"What?" Marc asked indifferently, his focus on the family across the grass. If Ed said anything else to Beth, Marc was going to have to call Austin back. Mandy pointed over to Marc again, and Marc smiled.

"I just got off the phone with NESN. You got it. They want you to start mid-August and finish the season with the Red Sox," Austin said.

Marc froze. The smile burned off his face instantly.

"In… in Boston?" He heard the accusation in his own voice, and he didn't understand it.

"You would travel with the team if you're announcing for their games." Austin's tone implied it shouldn't need to be explained.

"Fuck," Marc cursed, for the first time in two months—and it was at news that should have thrilled him. Why the hell wasn't he happy?

27

Tweet   💬   🔁   ♡   ⌁

@EdwardDCampbell: So honored to join the @VoteLorettaM team as her VP. We are excited to move the country forward and finally break the glass ceiling by sending a woman to the Oval Office.

@CelebPeopleMag: Marabeth taking a break from the campaign trail to hit a Metros game—how much do we love these two?

THE NEXT MONTH went by too fast for Marc. Suddenly it was August, and he wasn't ready for it. He and Beth were in the city; they had attended the Metros game early in the day and were meeting Austin and Sid for dinner. The guys walked into the private room, where the women were talking and laughing together. Both men stopped in their tracks.

"Damn, we are the luckiest guys around," Austin said softly.

And weren't they? Marc looked at the beautiful women standing on the other side of the room. Both were incredible.

Tonight Beth had straightened her hair so it fell in soft waves, which fit perfectly with the face that screamed *'cover girl.'* He kept telling himself she wasn't his, yet as he stood there looking at her, he couldn't remember exactly why. He couldn't think of anything else he could want.

"The stunner in yellow is all mine, and I'm not sharing," Austin mumbled. Marc would usually have commented jokingly about wanting Sid too, but standing next to Beth, she held no appeal.

"That's fine. I only want the girl in green," Marc said, looking at Beth in her emerald dress. And boy, did he want her. It didn't matter that he'd had her plenty of times in the last week. She got his blood burning with one look from across the room.

The week they had shared was one of the best of his life, in so many ways. Her sister took the kids—hers and Beth's—to Cape Cod. That had given Beth a chance for some R&R, which was much needed since she had all five kids most of the time.

Marc didn't know how much rest Beth got, but they had plenty of relaxation. He'd spent the last six days waking up with Beth in his arms and holding her as he went to sleep. They laughed together and talked. He loved spending every day with her.

Although they had attended almost constant campaign events in the last month, they'd only gone to two local events the previous week. Their absence didn't please her father, particularly since neither his other daughter nor any of his grandkids were available. But he didn't press—mostly because the one time he tried, Marc had reminded Ed that he wasn't putting up with his shit.

The only thing that had put a damper on his week was the new job. Since Marc hadn't been willing to make the trip to Boston, or take time away from Beth, to sign the papers, Austin had brought them with him tonight. While the girls laughed and chatted, he and Austin had gone to the bar, signed his agreement for NESN, and taken the publicity shots that would be going up tomorrow. The whole thing had taken about five minutes. It wasn't a bad gig; just for the last month and a half of the season so the move to Boston would be temporary. The problem was that he hadn't told Beth—still.

She hated life in the spotlight—how could he tell her he was moving back into it? And probably without her?

"This from the man who didn't think he could stand being with the same woman for a whole two months," Austin said, chuckling slightly. "You realize your agreement's been over for a while, right, Marc?"

But the deal had stopped mattering to him long before he'd suggested getting rid of the end date. He'd been taking things one day at a time, enjoying himself.

"I—" He didn't know what he planned to say, so he just stopped.

"Experience has taught me that you don't tire of the right woman, no matter how long it's been," Austin said, and slapped Marc on the back.

Marc frowned. He wasn't in this for the long haul. Austin didn't know that Marc hadn't told Beth about the move or the job.

Everything was about to change.

He'd been clear that if he got a job somewhere else, he and Beth were done, so they were in for a long talk. One that he didn't want to have.

"Yeah," Marc mumbled sadly and went to take Beth her drink.

"YOU OKAY?" BETH asked, setting her hand on Marc's thigh. He'd been quiet all through dinner. Something was going on in his head.

"I'm fine," he said, and set his arm on the back of her chair, rubbing her shoulder.

"Getting jitters?" Austin asked, and Marc tensed.

"Jitters?" Beth asked, looking at Marc.

Marc's lips were in a tight grimace. Something was off.

"How many times do I need to say it? I'm fine," Marc said gruffly.

"Maybe we'd believe you if you hadn't fallen off the face off the earth for the last two months," Sydney teased as she lifted her wine glass.

Marc rolled his eyes.

"You used to spend two or three nights a week at Poison, you know, and now we haven't seen you since June." Her smile disappeared as she took the swallow of her wine.

"Okay, okay." He put his hand up. "I promise we'll come by more often."

"That's not going to be likely, considering your schedule," Austin said.

Marc shot him a nasty glare that Beth didn't understand. Austin's eyes moved from her to Marc again, then he frowned.

"I *said* we'll come by," Marc snapped at Austin.

His stress was becoming clearer every day, but the cause remained unknown. Beth wished he would talk to her. She was trying to understand his need for space, knowing he wasn't used to relationships; she didn't want to overwhelm him. But she was feeling jaded. Beth didn't plan on ruining their last night alone together, but tomorrow they were going to have to talk. Tonight, however, she could do the next best thing and get his mind off it.

The kids wouldn't be back home from Massachusetts until tomorrow, so she and Marc had planned to stay in his apartment in the city tonight. A plan formed in her mind. The question was, could she pull it off?

She knew Marc loved the women who flocked around the ballplayers because they always had a compliment coming his way so that by the end of the night, he felt like the king of the world. Usually, she liked to keep Marc's ego in check, but tonight she would try a different approach.

After they said goodnight, Beth excused herself to the bathroom. She told Marc to wait for her in the bar. She watched as he headed that way, and once Austin and Sydney had left, Beth prepared to pick herself up a baseball player.

"You're Marc Demoda, aren't you?" Beth said, looking starry-eyed as she settled herself on the stool next to Marc and slowly crossed her legs, rubbing her shin lightly against his calf.

"Beth?" Marc asked, confused.

"No, I'm Tiffany." She extended her hand as she tried to give him a sultry look. "I'm a big fan. Huge." She gave him a sheepish smile and cocked her head slightly to the side.

"Are you now?" Marc's eyes twinkled.

"I've always wanted to meet you," Beth said, letting her finger trail lightly over his arm making S shapes. "In the... flesh."

Marc leaned against the back of his stool, looking bemused. "Why is that?" He would not help her out at all.

"Ever since you did that 'Sexiest Man Alive' spread in *People*, I've had a crush on you." Beth wet her lips with the tip of her tongue and Marc's eyes dropped to her mouth. "You're the star of all my favorite fantasies." She nibbled on her bottom lip.

"Well, sweetheart, why don't you tell me about some of them?" he said, drawing the words. "I like a good fantasy."

Beth smiled seductively and lifted her hand, hooking her finger in a gesture that told him to lean in closer. When he did, she whispered a few ideas in his ear and felt a rush of satisfaction at the choked sound that came out of his throat.

"Listen—Tiffany, is it?" Marc asked. His eyes suddenly became dark, and Beth nodded. His hand came up and rubbed her leg. "I have an apartment a couple of blocks from here. Want a nightcap?"

"Are we really getting a drink, or did you have something else in mind?" Beth asked.

Marc laughed wholeheartedly. "How about both?"

"Okay," Beth said, and let Marc help her off the stool.

Beth waited until they were out on the street to say anything else. She kept up the persona for the entire two-block walk to his apartment, telling him how great he was—everything from his unmatchable pitching ability to his stunning looks to his remarkable intelligence to how amazing his butt looked in his Metros uniform. At first she wanted to roll her eyes, but Marc lapped it up, so she had fun with it.

"You know, Tiffany—that jersey you were talking about? I have it upstairs," Marc said, trapping her against the wall with his arms as they waited for the elevator.

His breath danced on her cheek, and she leaned closer, taking a small nibble on his earlobe. She loved his quick intake of breath.

"The one you were wearing when you won the World Series?" Beth asked, then pulled back as another couple entered the lobby.

Marc quickly positioned her so that she was standing in front of him. She smiled over her shoulder as the hard bulge pressed into the small of her back, and he met her gaze with eyes that said, *'Look what you did.'* Marc kept her close, hiding the evidence as they got into the elevator, and he moved to lean against the back wall, spreading his legs and settling her in between them.

The couple looked carefully at her, then Marc, and whispered something quietly to each other. Then they got off the elevator, leaving them alone again.

"They *so* knew who you were," Beth said, looking up at Marc like he was the most fantastic thing on the planet.

"Happens all the time."

"That's because you're the best pitcher New York ever had," Beth said, and his eyes twinkled as he smiled.

"I never get tired of hearing that," he said, pulling her out of the elevator to his apartment door.

"Want me to repeat it?" she asked as he kicked the door shut behind them.

"I can think of better things you could do with that mouth of yours," he said and kissed her as he lifted her off her feet. She wrapped her legs around his waist as he moved down the hallway to his bedroom.

He set her down on the floor and went into his closet, returning quickly with a white and green shirt in his hand. The big '18' on the back of his jersey stood out as he handed it to her.

"I'll get us the drink I promised. Leave the heels on, Tiffany." His eyes flashed as he looked at her black spike heels.

But the jersey bothered her. When she'd told him she wanted to wear it while making love to him, she hadn't expected the damn thing to be right at hand. And suddenly she wondered how many other women had asked him the same thing.

He turned to leave.

"Ah, Marc?" He turned back, hearing the difference in her voice. If she wanted to stop the game, he would.

Beth knew his past. Did she want details? She cleared her throat. "Hurry back, hotshot."

And he did. Marc returned with two beers, then stopped short, nearly dropping them. She'd left the jersey unbuttoned but covering her chest, even as she pulled the sides apart by putting her hands on her hips to show off her black lace thong.

His pupils dilated, and his lips parted. "I always wondered what my jersey would look like on a woman," he choked, trying to recover. "Better than I imagined."

Beth smiled.

He dropped the beers on the dresser and moved to her with determination. He slowed once he had her in his arms, teasing and touching her until she finally couldn't stand it and began begging him.

"You know you're the best, Marc—please, give me what I want," Beth said. He'd made this into a game. If she wanted him, she had to tell him how great he was.

"Really? The best, huh?" He smiled down at her.

"Yes," she said, and then he finally thrust into her, finding the deep angle she craved. The knot built inside her as he moved fast, hard-driving her closer to release. Then he stopped.

"*No!*" she cried, and he laughed.

"Tell me again," Marc teased, holding himself perfectly still. His back was wet with sweat, and he was fighting against his own need to continue the game.

"You're amazing," she panted. "So great, wonderful—you know that, Marc. I need you, please, take me hard," she said, moving her hips and making him grit his teeth.

"Damn right." He rolled, bringing her with him, so she was now on top. He grabbed her hips, guiding her into a slow rhythm—*too* slow, but he wouldn't let go of her.

"Tell me more," he demanded, forcing her to hold perfectly still as he flashed his dimples at her. She looked down into his eyes, stormy with desire, and saw everything she'd ever wanted. How could she not love this man?

"I love you, Marc."

But it was too serious this time. She forgot the playful tone she'd been using, because she was no longer playing the role of Tiffany.

Quickly he rolled again, putting himself back on top, and drove into her with a new, faster rhythm—one that her body wanted so badly. She didn't have time to worry about her slip of the tongue, because her senses swirled. He filled her with a fire that made everything else irrelevant as the world around her shimmered. She shut her eyes, but the shimmering still sparked behind her lids as her hips moved in time with his. He shuddered, and her name flew off his lips with a deep guttural sound, then she gave herself up and finally shattered in an explosion of light. His weight crashed down on top of her, and they both panted for air.

He found his control before she did. He rolled over, pulling her along with him, his jersey floating over them. She rested her head on his chest, listening to the pounding of his heart against her ear.

"We're *definitely* doing that again," Marc mumbled.

"Huh?" Beth asked.

"I loved that game. We're doing it again one day, if I don't have the jersey bronzed first." Marc chuckled, though his breathing hadn't yet returned to normal.

She smiled.

"Was Tiffany that good for you?" she asked teasingly.

"No, not good," he joked, but his arm tightened around her. She pulled away to sit up, and he smiled. "Probably average."

Beth pretended to glare. "Oh, I'm average now, am I?"

His smile faltered, and his reply had no teasing tone anymore. "No. You're the best. You're the best thing that's happened to me for a long time, Beth."

The lump that formed in Beth's throat surprised her, and his arms came around and pulled her close against his chest.

28

BETH OPENED HER eyes, feeling the warmth of Marc tucked around her. All night, he'd held her close, as if he couldn't bear to let her go. Even now, as his long dark eyelashes barely fluttered in his deep sleep, he kept her firmly against his side, her head resting on his shoulder. She let her fingers trace over his pecs and into the ridges of muscle on his stomach that, even as he relaxed in sleep, stood tight.

He hadn't seemed to notice during their little sex game that she had admitted she was in love with him. She'd been careful to keep her feelings to herself so far, and she had worried he was going to panic. But he'd acted as if nothing had happened.

She knew Marc cared about her, and lately there had been moments where she could believe he loved her. She could see it in his eyes, feel it in his touch. He didn't say the words, but for the last few weeks, he hadn't once reminded her this was temporary. Last week, he had even started leaving his baseball glove at her house instead of taking it home.

Her phone buzzed again on the night stand. That was probably what had woken her. She attempted to reach for it.

"Where are you going?" Marc asked, not opening his eyes.

"My phone's going crazy," she said, and he released her waist to let her grab it. She glanced over to see his eyes barely open.

"Kids?"

"Brothers," she said and smirked. "You look like you stepped in dog poop or something."

"Those guys need rules about texting. They fire off messages at one or five in the morning. You're not a twenty-four-hour helpline," he complained, but tossed an arm over his face as she slid her finger to unlock the twenty-five new messages of the group text. "What's the emergency this time?"

She scrolled up to the first few messages, which were screenshots of something on Twitter. She almost rolled her eyes until she saw the photo, then the smile fell off her face. Marc stood holding up a white polo shirt featuring the NESN logo, the restaurant where they'd eaten last night in the background. The caption said 'Big announcement,' but her stomach bottomed out all the same.

Her world stopped as she stared at her phone. More screenshots of posts from other sites confirmed what was clear.

A new job?

A new city?

An apartment?

Marc hadn't mentioned any of it.

"Sweetheart?" Marc said and reached over, but she flinched away.

"There's a picture of you signing a contract." Marc's eyes widened. "Last night, while you and Austin went to the bar for drinks, you signed a contract." He sucked in a breath. "You rented an apartment." His hands fisted, and he swallowed hard. "You're moving to Boston." He glanced away from her out the window and ran his hand through his hair.

His reaction was the only confirmation she needed, and a lump formed in her throat.

He'd told her their relationship would be over if he got a job in another city. But she had expected him to talk to her about it. Honestly, she had hoped he would tell her before he accepted a job, and that Marc might change his mind about breaking up. The idea of distance didn't bother her. She thought their relationship was strong enough to survive separation. But apparently he didn't think she was important enough to mention *any of it* to her.

How could she have been so utterly stupid? The ball of lead settled firmly in her stomach.

"I'm looking for any professional baseball job I can get. You knew that—that was the whole reason we started this." His initial panic had faded, and now his tone had a clipped accusation to it.

"I know what you wanted, and if you'd *told* me about this, I'd be thrilled for you. You didn't, though," she mumbled.

"Fuck that." He slammed his fist against the mattress as he cursed. "Why should I have to?"

And didn't that say it all.

"You don't *have* to. The problem lies in the fact that you didn't *want* to." Her voice was flat, but she grabbed Marc's jersey, the only thing close, and pulled it on before she stood up.

"Why does it have to be a problem?" he asked as she collected her shoes and dress from the floor. "Wait a second, come back here. Where are you going?" He pushed back the sheet and followed her as she headed into the bathroom. "I was going to tell you today."

"You planned to tell me after you announced it to the rest of the world? That's reassuring," Beth said sarcastically, but her heart wasn't in it so the words didn't have the punch she wanted. Her eyes stung, but she refused to fall apart in front of him.

"I don't need to ask for your permission. You don't get to decide what job I take, Beth."

She didn't know where that had come from. "What? I never expected to have a say in what you decided, Marc." She'd *hoped*, but never expected it. "But it's not unreasonable to think that you would tell me before you announced it on Twitter. We might not be a lot of things, but I thought we respected each other. I thought we were friends."

Marc opened his mouth and then shut it again. Beth grabbed her bag from his bathroom and stormed into the master bedroom. Besides the bed and a dresser, there was nothing in this massive room. It was empty—kind of like their relationship.

They didn't have love, they didn't have trust, and apparently, they didn't even have a friendship. She'd thought she was different from his other girls, but now she knew she wasn't. She had just lasted longer.

She needed to leave. She threw on her clothes and had the Uber app open on her phone by the time he came into the room wearing gym shorts.

"It doesn't matter, Marc. It's whatever." She swallowed the lie and prayed her voice wouldn't crack. It would take ten minutes for her ride to arrive, but she clicked confirm before turning to him. "I get it. I'm not that important to you."

The temper flared in his eyes, and his mouth twisted into the familiar *'you're full of shit'* frown. "That's ridiculous. What have I been doing with you for the last few months if you're not important to me?"

"You were looking to change public opinion of you. You did a great job of that—"

She couldn't believe he had the audacity to roll his eyes before he interrupted her.

"If that was all this was, you'd have been fired after a week," Marc snapped. She stared at him, not understanding. "We aren't *in* the media, Beth. I pay people to keep us *out* of it."

"What?" Except for her father's events, they hadn't been spotted in public in weeks. But she hadn't realized he was actively trying to keep the press away.

Marc shook his head. "That's not important."

"I think it's vital, given that our entire relationship was an agreement to be seen in the media," she said.

"That's such crap, Beth. It became more than that silly agreement before we even started sleeping together." His voice was soft again.

"Ha," Beth scoffed as he threw the lie she had believed for so long back at her. It felt like a slap in the face.

He looked shocked. "How can you think that's not true?"

"Name the last two women you slept with before me." She raised her eyebrows at him, but he said nothing. "Should I make it easier? Okay: Name two women you slept with in the year before you met me."

"That's different," Marc said, but now he wasn't looking at her again. "You're different."

"Why?" she demanded, then immediately wished she hadn't asked. He wasn't about to declare his love for her, and she knew it.

"I don't know."

"Right." She turned away and shut her eyes. Did he realize he was crushing her?

Marc sighed, and she turned back to look at him. He tossed his hands in the air. "You're fun, and you make things exciting. Just because I'm moving to Boston doesn't change any of that."

Beth's eyes welled, and she furiously blinked back tears as she looked around the room at the emptiness. The man didn't even want to be too comfortable *in his own house* because he might get attached.

"This is what I was going to tell you today. Moving to Boston doesn't mean I don't still want to see you…"

She heard his whole brief speech. Marc had thought it over for weeks, decided, and still didn't think she was important enough to talk to her about it. That cut the breath right out of her.

"Beth, are you listening to me? We can make this work."

"No." Her voice was so soft she wasn't sure he heard. They couldn't make this work. And she couldn't keep kidding herself. She wanted it all, and he wasn't going to give it to her. She deserved more than that. She shouldn't have let this go on this long. He didn't want a relationship with her, and an 'agreement' couldn't work anymore.

"No?" he asked, shocked.

"No. We can't," she said with the punch that had been missing until this moment.

"Why the hell not?"

"There are lots of reasons, but it all boils down to the fact that I love you, and you think I'm fun. I want forever, and you want sex when we're in the same city. I deserve more than you're offering. I need to move on to someone who can give me a future."

He stared blankly, so she finished it.

"Goodbye, Marc. Good luck in Boston. I hope it's what you've been looking for." Her voice didn't break. She took a step back, looked at him one last time, then turned and left him.

29

THE FRONT DOOR closed behind her. His handling of that exchange had been utterly shitty, but he hadn't been ready for it. Not to mention that Austin posting it on Twitter—before he'd had a chance to talk to her—sucked. In Marc's mind, telling Austin he could post that tweet tomorrow meant after Marc gave him the okay, not at *seven fucking a.m.* What the fuck was that? He wanted to call Austin, but first, he had to deal with the fact that Beth had left. The idea that she was walking out of his life made his entire being rebel.

By the time he opened the door, the elevator was already closing, and just like that, she was gone. She said she deserved more; he had known that all along. Still, he couldn't give it to her, and until today, she'd been happy to take what he could give. He wasn't sure what had suddenly changed.

He should have told her about Boston. He'd wanted to talk to her about it ever since he got the offer. And he *had* planned on talking to her last night, but that sex game they'd played made everything complicated.

When she'd told him that she loved him, she wasn't playing that Tiffany character anymore. How was he supposed to tell the woman he was leaving after *that*? So he'd done what any man would do in his situation: He ignored it.

He had known that telling her about Boston would change everything. It was why he couldn't bring himself to do it. He needed some more time to come up with a plan to convince her that she didn't need more than he could give her. He'd done it before.

Marc's mood was in the toilet by the next night. She wouldn't answer his calls or see him. And sitting in the bar with Austin wasn't helping, because she *was* talking to him.

"I'm sorry you did this to yourself," Austin said, but Marc didn't hear any genuine sympathy in his friend's voice. "She asked me to write up a statement about you two parting on good terms, and to convince you to make it a joint statement since I represent you both."

"Fuck that." Marc slammed his beer on the table. "This is what started all the issues. If you hadn't posted that tweet about NESN, I wouldn't be here. Not everyone needs to know all this shit. Whose business is it but hers and mine what the status of our relationship is?"

"Who *are* you?" Austin scoffed.

"What?"

"You're the man who had me call in your location for years. The guy who gave the paparazzi all the money shots, did any interviews, and kept up with social media at all costs. You made yourself a big deal. Now people want to hear about you."

"I'm not going to talk about Beth. That's private. And I want you to tell her you recommend she doesn't either."

"She wants it released by Sunday morning, with or without your agreement. She's a client, and a friend. Don't make me do this without your input, Marc, because I will."

Marc knew Austin would. He wasn't happy with Marc. Austin and Sid were both *#you should have told her*. Her brothers wouldn't return any of his calls either—not that he expected them to.

"What's her big fucking hurry?" Marc demanded.

Austin looked at him wearily. "Sunday night she has to be at a big-ticket fundraiser, with lots of media. The mayor of New York is going to be there, and the governor. She's sitting with them."

"I'm in Chicago on Sunday for the game; she could say I was working."

"Even with the noon game, you could fly back and be there by eight when everyone sits down for dinner. You two have been almost inseparable for the past few months. If Beth hadn't broken up with you yesterday, wouldn't you fly back?" Austin asked.

"Of course I'd be there for her," Marc snapped.

"And everyone knows that, so your presence is going to be missed. If she doesn't issue a statement, it'll drive the media crazy guessing," Austin explained as if he were talking to a three-year-old.

"Who gives a flying fuck what the media says?"

"*She* does, Marc," Austin said, his eyebrows raised and his jaw clenched. "She wants as little media backlash from this as possible. She hates the attention. You've done your best to shield her for the last two months, but the reality is you're not there anymore. And your decision to suddenly up and move has everyone speculating."

This was part of his concern about this job. Throwing himself back into the spotlight would turn their relationship into more fodder for speculation. He'd been two-stepping with the media for months. He answered very few questions, and made sure Austin kept them at bay by feeding them pictures that didn't intrude and never putting them in a situation where there could be speculation. Marc had also made it clear that Beth's house and the surrounding area were off-limits, or any relationship between him and the rags would end. He'd even paid a security team—which she didn't know about—to keep the rags away from her property. It kept Beth and the kids slightly out of the center stage that the first few weeks of their relationship had pushed on them. But now that he'd be gone all the time, he wasn't going to be the buffer he had been.

Austin continued, "She has lots of things coming up in the next few months that she needs to attend, and even have an escort for. She's trying to be proactive, and I can't say I didn't recommend that." Austin sighed.

"Wait." Marc was only half paying attention, but he hadn't missed that she was going to be taking *dates* to events; from the sound of it, she was starting Sunday. "She's dating?"

"Marc, you're not listening to me." Austin sighed again.

"Yes I am. Yesterday Beth told me she loved me, and now you're telling me she's going out with another guy? There's something fucking wrong with that." He shook his head.

He didn't want her dating someone else. He had no interest in dating another girl. If she loved him, how could she want to date someone else?

"It's not a *date*. She needs an *escort*." Austin rolled his eyes. "Jealous?"

Unquestionably.

"It's shitty." Marc took a long pull from his beer. He remembered what Will had told him about her finding the right guy quickly, and his hand tightened on the bottle. He'd kill 'the right guy' if she did find him.

"You are not being reasonable," Austin said through clenched teeth, and Marc wondered if maybe he'd made that last threat aloud. "She's a camera-shy politician's daughter in the middle of the presidential campaign, and all you're doing is making it harder for her."

"Who's she taking Sunday?" Marc demanded.

Austin glance at the ceiling as if praying for patience before he finally said, "I won't play informant, Marc."

He wanted to kill him. He needed to reach across the table and strangle Austin until he told Marc whom she was going to get dressed up for and whom she would spend the night dancing and laughing alongside.

Austin reminded him, "You didn't think she was important enough to talk to about a life-changing decision. You didn't want any permanent ties. So congrats—you don't have to deal with her life anymore, dumbass.

"Look, I know you care about her. If you both issue a statement saying you broke up and remain friends, it won't be a big deal. There's no story there—as long as you don't *make* one by starting shit. And maybe figure out what you want because I don't think you have any idea."

Marc wanted to yell that he knew what he wanted. He wanted everything back the way it had been when he'd had Beth and her kids in his life. Back when he was happy. Happier than he'd been in years—including when he had played for the Metros.

But that wouldn't happen because he was going to Boston, and the idea of moving lost its appeal. Knowing all this might have changed his decision about going in the first place, so he should have talked to Beth about it. He didn't want her to matter that much, but the truth of it was that she did.

So why hadn't he told her?

He hadn't wanted to hurt her. And now he had.

But he wanted things in life, and she couldn't live in the spotlight, so regardless of anything else, they never could have worked. He should have been able to give up his life of fame for her. But he couldn't. She deserved more than he could give her. Austin was right: If he genuinely cared, he needed to figure out how to move on—because right now he didn't have any idea.

"Issue the statement, then. Sunday morning, whatever she wants. I have no comment other than what she wants me to say, and I won't draw any attention to myself." Marc got up.

"Marc—the security," Austin said, his expression apologetic.

Marc looked at him questioningly.

"I let it pass when you two were together. Protecting your girlfriend without her knowledge is one thing, but now—having her followed, keeping people outside her house... It's stalking," he said, frowning.

Marc gave him a nasty look. "Are you kidding?"

He didn't want to pull security. They were keeping the press away; they were protecting Beth and the kids.

"I know you never ask for updates, you never care what she and the kids are doing, but paying people to follow your ex-girlfriend without her knowledge is textbook stalking," Austin repeated.

He was right.

Marc knocked his knuckles against the table. "Call Ed Campbell and get him to put someone on her. I'll talk to him if I need to. Pull my guys tonight," he said, and walked away.

30

> **Tweet**   💬   🔁   ♡   ⑃
>
> **@NYStarPost**: Turns out it was an old flame @TheCoreyMatthews that broke up Campbell and @HotShotDemoda—and we've got the pictures to prove it.
>
> **@CelebPeopleMag**: How could she?!? Campbell caught cheating on @HotShotDemoda with his former teammate @TheCoreyMatthews
>
> **@USWeekly**: Not just @TheCoreyMatthews! See the photos of Elizabeth Campbell and her many boy toys
>
> **@NYStarPost**: She fooled so many—a look back at Elizabeth Campbell's sordid past

THE PHONE RANG on Sunday morning before the sun was even up. It was too early, and her brothers had all been there way too late.

"Tell me Corey isn't at your house," her father demanded as soon as she said hello.

"What time is it?" Beth said, sitting up, trying to see her clock.

"Is. Corey. There," he demanded, again accenting each word.

"Yes."

"I should have listened to Marc. He said security couldn't wait until Monday. Paul and I are on a flight to Jersey. I've called Austin, and he'll be—"

"What are you talking about?" Beth asked, knowing something terrible had happened. "I talked to him last night, and he said he was issuing a statement from Marc and me this morning."

"Do you live under a rock? You've once again blown up on social media."

Beth's heart stopped. "What?" she said, feeling a little sick. Her mind was jumping to conclusions that she hoped were wrong. They hadn't issued a statement, but she and Marc hadn't been seen together in days. Corey was staying here. Corey and Marc were known for never getting along.

"I like the Post's tweet: 'Matthews replaces Demoda again, this time off the field,' with a picture of you and Corey supposedly taken last night. It's blurry because it was shot through your back windows, but it's clearly you and Corey. Tons of articles claiming he's been living at your house. Rumors you two have been secretly dating for years, that Steve and Mandy are his. A few pictures of your last sexcapade."

This couldn't be happening.

"We've talked it over. Since you and Marc are taking your time to announce you've broken up, we can use that. Marc will fly in tonight for dinner, and you two will play the happy couple—"

"No," Beth said sternly, and probably a little too loud. She wasn't playing 'happy couples' with Marc anymore. Her heart couldn't handle that. She heard stirring from the guest rooms, and Corey and Clayton appeared at her bedroom door.

"Paul thinks Marc will be willing, so I don't see a problem—"

"*I'm* not willing," she said sternly. Corey reached for the phone, and Beth shook her head. The two men both eyed her carefully, probably wondering who was on the phone.

"Elizabeth, be reasonable. Why can't you go to dinner with the man?"

"Because I won't." She was on her feet; her father had no right to ask her to do this. She had told him exactly what happened with Marc. Her eyes stung, and she blinked furiously. Anything to do with Marc was still raw. "Dad—I just… can't."

Corey yanked the phone out of her hand. "Ed," he said.

Beth stared blankly across the room, letting the truth sink in. She'd become the infamous daughter of Ed Campbell again. She ground her teeth. She'd have to see those damn pictures everywhere. And now they were going after her kids? Her hands came up to rub her eyes, but she didn't feel like crying anymore. She was angry.

How *dare* a photographer take a photo from inside her house? What had made them suddenly think that was okay? And why did people want to read and buy this stuff?

She shook her head.

How did these magazines allow these unauthorized photos to be published, whether on their websites or in print? Beth glared. The last time, the story the media had run with was 'sex tape,' not 'unconsented photos'—more sensational if they pretended she had been a willing participant. And her father had never let her say a word to correct anything.

"Clayton, go let Austin in and tell him we'll be down in a few minutes. Beth and I have to talk," Corey said after hanging up with her father.

Clayton nodded and got up, leaving Beth and Corey alone in the room.

Corey took a deep breath and ran his hand through his blond hair. "This is going to throw our past back into the headlines."

She nodded, assuming her father would demand silence

again. Her mind flicked to what Marc would think about that, and the thought of him caused a pang in her chest.

"There won't be much point in hiding our friendship anymore," Beth said with a sigh.

"Sorry," Corey said sympathetically. "I probably shouldn't have stayed here." Beth had been telling him that for a few days.

"Anyway, I thought *you* were the one who didn't want anyone to know we were friends," Beth said.

"What? No." Corey shook his head. She looked up at him in confusion. "Beth," Corey said, drawing out her name like he was in pain, "I never cared about it. I was trying to protect you. It was the only way I could. I had to leave you alone, even when it killed me, because it was better for you. And once you and Bob were married and you started having people call you Beth, people didn't know who you were. It's always been better for *you*."

She had always thought Corey had moved away from her because of the way the media presented her. Beth had always been certain that the reason Corey wanted to keep her a secret was because he was embarrassed by her. Her father was embarrassed. That was why she had assumed Marc would be too.

"It was never fair, the way I got a pat on the back and a wink at interviews while you got called a slut and accused of spiraling out of control. But I didn't know how to fix any of it." Corey paused uncomfortably, and Beth thought he was about to say something else, but he didn't.

Beth blinked, and it was like a light had come on in a dark room. "It was unfair to both of us. And we were too young to handle it. We shouldn't have had to."

"We should have talked about this a long time ago. Things could have been different." Corey hugged her tightly, then sighed. "Now we have a mess to clean up. Marc's been helping me with the media—"

"He what?" She pulled back, staring up at him.

"He taught me the difference between being a politician in the media and being a superstar. I don't need to be on good terms with them; *they* need to be on good terms with *me*." He pulled away from Beth and stood thinking for a minute before he laid out his plan. "You and I need to come clean about our friendship. Tonight I'll take you to dinner, and we'll tell everyone we're friends. No one will believe us, but that doesn't matter. Marc will be back in Boston tomorrow, and I have an off day. I'll fly up and make sure he and I have a very public, very friendly lunch. He'll even get me a ticket for the game Monday night, and we'll go out for drinks afterward."

"Why?" Beth asked.

"The rumor now is that I stole you from him. I'm giving them a different story. In this one, he's going to be my friend." From the look on Corey's face, that idea didn't sit well.

"Will he even do that?" she asked.

Corey's jaw tightened. "Judging from the sheer number of missed calls and ignored messages on my phone, I'd say he's pretty eager to see me."

"Cor—" She didn't want to have the *'you may not kill Marc'* conversation again. She'd done that several times now with all the guys over the past few days. Beth understood that they were mad—and, though they wouldn't admit it, hurt by him too. But she didn't want them going over and yelling. She had to move on; reliving it over and over would suck.

"You didn't want me involved, but now I am," he said. "Get dressed." Then he left.

But their plan went out the window. By nine o'clock that morning, every website boasted pictures of her—not only with Corey, but with Paul, Austin, all her brothers, and numerous other men, some of whom she hardly knew. Although none of the pictures by themselves were all that bad, putting them all together in a group did the job. The headlines all read *'The Secretary's Daughter and Her Many Boy Toys.'*

By that afternoon, her values, parenting, and morals were all fair game in the Democrats' campaign stump speeches. They even speculated whether she had the right to be on the board of Helping Hands. Questions about her 'relapsing' into drugs floated all over social media. And Twitter was blowing up.

She had once more become a media frenzy. It was her worst nightmare all over again.

"Elizabeth." Her father paced in the family room while she sat on the sofa, staring at the wall. Half her brothers, her dad's people, and Austin all stood around waiting for direction on what to do now.

It had been a hell of a few days for Beth, and her father was about to tell her to hide out at Grant's farm, far away from the media. She knew what was coming—and she wasn't doing it. She'd spent ten years biting her tongue, so worried about causing him another mess that she hadn't wanted to do anything that might rock the boat.

"I'm not going to Grant's," she said.

Her father blinked as if she hadn't spoken English. But before she could add more, the front door opened. Beth's head whipped around to see who her dad's security would have possibly let in.

"Senator McGomry?" Beth stood there, in shock, looking at the presidential candidate—who should have been too busy to stop by New Jersey—standing in her cream pantsuit in the middle of the living room.

"I've told you before, you can call me Loretta." The older woman smiled at her. "I got a phone call"—her rich brown eyes shot over to Austin—"telling me there was a story I needed to come hear."

"Loretta," Beth's father began, "I have this handled. I told you I'd take care of it so we don't get any backlash."

Loretta's lips tightened into a grimace, and she crossed her arms. "Since you and I don't see eye to eye on most women's issues, and I've come to learn family values actually mean very little to you, I'm going to talk to your daughter myself." Senator McGomry swung her fierce, intelligent eyes to Beth again.

Beth had met the senator a few times, but that didn't make her feel any less intimidated. Loretta was tall and striking with her dark hair and umber skin. But it was her commanding, capable presence that stood out. The woman wasn't a career politician. She was a businesswoman, one of the first female CEOs in big tech. She had pivoted into politics with a focus on affordable daycare, safety at all schools, family medical leave—topics that weren't usually part of the conservative platform. At every campaign event Beth had seen her, she was well-liked and came across as warm and caring. The media, however, used words like 'ice queen,' 'abrasive,' even 'nasty.'

"If anyone knows about the double standard in the media, it's me," Loretta said with a smirk. "I had to bring *Campbell* on the ticket to make me seem more likable."

A few people around the room covered their barks of laughter with a cough.

"But from what I've heard," she continued, "you could be the poster girl for media double standards."

Beth opened her mouth to say she didn't need to be a poster girl for anything, but she stopped. She glanced at her father—the 'family man' who let his daughter constantly be thrown to the wolves—then to Corey, who was high-fived and slapped on the back for the exact same things she was attacked over. *And even Marc,* she thought; he was currently getting huge ratings and had gained thousands of followers in the last week because social media made him the victim in a breakup *he* had caused.

"Being able to have a voice is only a good thing if you choose to use it. I didn't get into politics to become president. I did it to fix things—like the double standards women face," Loretta said. "But if we don't stand up and demand to be heard, we can't make things change. Hiding does no one any good."

Loretta's brown eyes met Beth's. "I'm willing to give you a platform to show the world how the media spins a story, how they blend truth and lies until they're all gray. I believe it's something we as a society need to be more aware of in general—but in the end, it's up to you."

Ed scoffed. "I'm not going to let her—"

"*Enough!*"

Everyone fell stone silent.

She had shocked them, she knew. But Beth continued, "Dad, I have let you control everything for the past ten years, because I was afraid. But I'm done. I've done it your way, and now it's my turn. So start listening to what *I* want, because sometimes it has to be about me."

The presidential contender glanced down at her phone as it beeped. Then her eyes shot to Austin with a smirk. "It's good you want to talk—because after what was just tweeted, people will be begging to speak with you."

31

@HotShotDemoda: I want to make three points very clear (thread): I've been quiet about my breakup because it's not anyone else's business, but since the world sees fit to attack a woman who doesn't deserve it, I'm forced to speak. My relationship with Beth ended because I moved to Boston. There was no cheating by either of us. (1/3) Beth made it clear to me that she and Corey were friends before we ever went on a date. The only reason the rest of the world didn't know that, is because of the attacks she has endured. (2/3) I care deeply about this wonderful woman, and any media outlet or handle that doesn't show the utmost respect to her and her family will be unfollowed and blocked, and I will maintain no relationship with the source moving forward. (3/3)

@LorettaMcGomry: As a country, we need to look closely at the double standard we let the media get away with. Part of my platform is giving women a voice and ending that hypocrisy. I'm lucky enough to know Elizabeth Campbell, who has spent a decade living with a sensationalized story that let most off the hook while her name was dragged through the mud.

MARC THREW THE *People* magazine on the table with a grunt. The untold story of Elizabeth Campbell Evans, with a ten-page spread of photos and an interview. She talked about her kids, Helping Hands, her father, and her life in between being America's golden girl and today.

She'd spent the last month giving newspaper interviews and appearing on morning talk shows, national news shows, local shows, late-night talk shows, podcasts—she did everything. And almost everything was fair game. She talked about her political views, what it had been like to win Olympic gold at eighteen, her fall from grace, how she'd felt when her husband died. She discussed raising her kids alone, her close relationship with her late husband's seven brothers, her charity, her friendship with Corey—she opened up about it all.

The only thing no one ever mentioned was Marc. His tweet was the most anyone said about their relationship.

"It's a good article, isn't it?" Austin said from the door. "She's done a sensational job. The Democratic conventions started Monday, and they have yet to bring up her name."

Beth had done a fabulous job of making herself vulnerable, likable, and human. She admitted she'd made mistakes, but who didn't? And once the country got a good view of the real Beth, they loved her.

"Did you come all the way here just to show me this?" He didn't know what Austin wanted. Marc was in his white polo and navy blazer, although he still had an hour before he had to move to the other side of the suite and start calling Boston's game against the Phillies. It sucked being in Philly—he was so close to home, yet unable to go back to his house in Ambra. His apartment in Boston was nice enough—fully furnished, so he didn't have to deal with anything—but he missed Ambra.

Although it wasn't his house he wanted there.

"I thought you'd be happy to see it. You were worried about her." Austin grabbed the magazine and flipped to the pictures.

There was one of Beth and Austin with a few different people from Helping Hands, including her brother Luke, who, Marc knew, worked for a branch of the organization. Another showed Beth with her two kids and a photo of Bob propped on her knee. There was one of her on Corey's back, mimicking a picture from their Olympic days. Marc's favorite was Beth sitting on Danny and Clayton's shoulders with her other brothers around them. The caption said, *'Our anchor in calm seas and rough waters.'*

The truth was, he had been furious on Beth's behalf when she was being dragged through the mud because the Democrats wanted to get a jump in the polls. There wasn't much truth to any of what was being said, and he knew what it must have done to her.

And that was only made worse because he thought about her constantly. Not because she was in the news, but because everything reminded him of her. He missed the smell of peaches on his pillows; he missed her nagging about taking his shoes off when he walked into the house; he missed the way she curled up next to him on the couch and talked her way through *Sports Center*. He missed the way she made him feel. He missed *her*.

He sighed. "Thanks, but I don't live under a rock."

Austin frowned.

"I don't have much time. If you have a point, get to it."

"Two points," Austin said. "First, as your agent—"

"I've been good," Marc said defensively. At first he'd gone out for drinks with the guys when he was traveling with the team, but he hadn't done that in weeks. And there hadn't been a woman who had even sparked enough interest to make him want to talk to her. He showed up early to work, and was doing a fantastic job on-air.

"You've been a saint." Austin frowned, as if he disapproved. "I want to talk about job offers. Have you looked at any of them?"

"I will," Marc promised. He needed to drum up some enthusiasm to read through the offers. But he had no more interest in them than he had in his current job—which would be over in three days since, much to the displeasure of everyone at the station, he hadn't taken the contract extension. The whole idea of baseball pissed him off. He needed to get over that.

Austin sighed.

"I *will*."

But Austin didn't look convinced.

"Was that it?"

"No. As your friend…" Austin's expression softened. "You are *miserable*, dude. Sid and I are worried about you. When you're not working, you're becoming a hermit."

"I'm fine," Marc lied. Miserable was closer to the truth. "I'm just not used to the long days and jet lag anymore."

"You miss Beth."

"No shit." Marc sighed as he flopped his head back, messing up the hair that his stylist had just finished. But Beth deserved forever, and he wasn't someone who could give it to her. So he had to suffer to give her what she needed.

"Then do something about it!" Austin exclaimed in frustration.

"I don't do forever, and that's what she wants," Marc said. He got up, walked toward the window, and looked down to the grass field below. Then he did a double take. Beth and

Steve and two of her brothers stood out in the grass, talking to some Phillies players.

"That's the other reason I'm here. McGomry canceled. She's stuck in Florida—the weather's bad and her plane is grounded—so Beth's throwing out the first pitch for her."

"What?" Marc demanded, spinning back around.

"Steve knows you're here. He's been watching the Boston games since you moved. He was hoping you would come down and say hi."

Marc was out the door before Austin even finished speaking. If Austin was up here, that meant Beth was okay with Steve seeing him, and Marc didn't care about anything else. He didn't slow down until his feet hit the grass and Steve turned his way.

"Marc!" Steve called. Beth turned, and her big green eyes met his for a brief moment before she turned back to her brothers.

But that was okay. Marc bent down and wrapped Steve in a bear hug, and he felt himself smile for the first time in forever. Steve talked a mile a minute, but Marc had to swallow the lump in his throat before he could respond.

"If your mom says it's okay, want to see the locker room?" he asked.

Steve nodded before running the ten feet to Beth and yanking on the red-and-white-striped Phillies jersey she wore.

Every part of him wanted to cross the grass and talk to her, to pull her into his arms and hold her tight, never letting go.

"You going to go talk to her?" Austin asked, coming up behind him.

God, he wished he could, but it wasn't fair. He wouldn't hurt her more. "She wants nothing to do with me. And you told me to move on."

"You're not moving on, and you need her back." Austin frowned. "Marc, you—"

But Marc cut him off. "Don't," he said.

Then Steve came back, and Marc took his hand and led him down the steps.

32

BETH WATCHED AS Marc and Steve headed down the steps into the dugout. Seeing Marc, being so close, was a special kind of torture. Especially since Steve was over the moon about getting to see him again. The kids missed Marc almost as much as Beth did. Although the story in the media was now painting her in a better light and she was doing well—and, to be honest, she'd had fun doing some of the many interviews in the last month—nothing about what she wanted changed.

Nor had anything changed for Marc.

He was great on air. The buzz was that he was one of the best new voices in baseball. She was bittersweetly happy for him.

Beth had known Marc would be here today when Senator McGomry called and asked her to do her a favor, but she couldn't say no to the woman who had become her champion for the last few weeks. So here she was, throwing out the first pitch to start the game, but desperately wishing she could run away as fast as she could because it hurt so fiercely.

She'd been with the kids at Grant's farm, spending the weekend with him and Nick, who was on another seven-day leave from the Navy. Both guys had said they'd come out to the game with her, and although she was glad not to be alone, the two of them together was a constant one-upping contest. She had to tell two thirty-year-old men that they couldn't see who could spit farthest, and it was getting old.

"I'm not sure that's the best idea," Grant said, nodding at Marc and Steve.

Beth's head whipped around, and her eyes narrowed. Grant was the only one of her brothers who was happy that she and Marc had broken up.

"What do you mean? Steve's thrilled."

Grant shook his head. "The bastard is trying to worm his way into your bed again, and he's using Steve to do it."

"Are you kidding me?" she asked. Watching Marc hug her son, even a stranger would have seen the unfeigned affection.

"I can't believe how blind you are," Grant mumbled.

Beth's eyes widened. She might be upset by everything that had happened, but Grant was way off-base.

"*I'm* not the blind one. You've been nothing but cold to Marc. I get it: He's not your big brother, and it's hard for you to trust anyone who's not family. But Bob died. I've been letting your attitude slide because I assumed you'd come around like everyone else did, but I'm done with it, Grant." The next words hurt to say, but she pushed them out. "Marc and I are over, but that doesn't mean I'm going to be patient when you don't get on board with what I want in the future. And today, I want my son to be happy." She glared at him, and he glanced away.

"THAT'S MY GIRL," Marc murmured an hour later as Beth tossed a solid pitch toward home plate.

"What?" Austin asked, looking up from his phone. "Oh yeah. I wasn't worried. She's got a pretty good arm, and she told me she'd been watching you give Steve pointers. I think it would have been worse if it was McGomry."

"Yeah, there's not much Beth can't do," he agreed. "Man, I love that woman." Marc smiled as he watched Beth wave before heading back into the Phillies' dugout.

"What?" Austin asked, pleasantly surprised.

Marc's heart faltered as he realized what he'd said. He—loved. That woman. He—

Holy shit.

He *loved* her.

What Marc wanted, what he needed—it was always her. He'd thought he would resent her for taking baseball away from him, but he had ended up resenting the game because it had taken *her* away. He was such a fuckup.

"Marc?" Austin waited for him to say something.

"Austin, I love her. I'm completely and totally in love with Beth and her two kids. They're everything I need."

"I know, dumbass." Austin sighed.

"Why the hell didn't *I* know?" Marc said, thrown slightly off-kilter by the realization.

Austin shrugged. "I'm guessing you couldn't see the forest through all the trees. But…"

"What?" Marc said desperately.

"Well, Sid and I have been wondering what you were going to do when you finally figured it out."

"I'm gonna tell her," Marc said, as if it was obvious—but he wasn't sure how. He couldn't do it over text or on the phone. Steve had said they were heading out as soon as Beth pitched, so even if he didn't have to be on the air, he wouldn't be able to catch her before they headed back to Grant's farm. And Marc doubted he'd be welcome showing up there.

Austin snickered. "Best of luck with that." He slapped Marc on the back, and a frigid chill raced through him at the idea she might have already moved on.

"What does that mean?"

"Elizabeth Campbell Evans has an army around her, and in case you forgot, you pissed them *all* off. Before you get to the girl, you have to get through her boys," Austin said.

The game was a blur. Everyone said he called it well, but he remembered none of it. All he could think about was Beth. How the fuck was he getting her back?

Finally back at his house in Jersey, Marc should have felt better— but he didn't. He leaned against the stone mantle of his fireplace looking at the reminder of why he was about to make an ass of himself. They all stood wrapped together in the photo—Beth, Steve, Mandy, and Marc, soaking wet from the rain. He wanted to spend a lifetime dancing in the summer showers with them.

It was almost seven thirty; almost time. Marc was worried about his plan, but he'd spent four days trying to get anyone near Beth to talk to him, and no one would. Although Sid and Austin were happy that he had finally figured out what he wanted, neither would get in the middle of the mess he'd made. He couldn't blame them.

He couldn't even get Corey, who had gone out on a limb for him professionally, to return any of his calls. So he'd been feeling desperate when he'd sent that text message.

Marc had given the seven guys two days' notice to get to his house, and had threatened them with something that none of them would ignore. But they would all come in with guns blazing, he knew. He hadn't changed the code to open the gate, and nothing had ever stopped any of the men from barging into his house before, so he wasn't surprised when the front door slammed open at twenty-five after seven.

He grabbed a bottle from the bucket of beers he'd set out on his coffee table, then stood in front of the fireplace, braced for their wrath and praying that one of them might listen.

Corey led the pack.

"What the hell is wrong with you?" Corey demanded harshly. The six faces behind him didn't look too friendly either, but the fact they stopped just inside the room to give him a chance to explain was a positive sign.

"I got beer," Marc said and pointed with his bottle to the table.

"Not interested," sneered Danny, who never turned down a beer.

"You wanted to talk, we came," Luke said. "Now tell us what you have to say." Luke cracked his knuckles.

"Quickly. I don't have much patience, and I'm trained to kill without leaving evidence," Nick said, his face not carrying a flicker of emotion.

That calmness should have been reassuring compared to the heat radiating off the rest of them, but it wasn't. Nick was the one Marc knew the least about, and his threat seemed sincere. And now that the men were in the room, spilling his guts was a lot harder.

"Why don't we sit, so I can explain what I need," Marc said. But no one made a move to do so.

"What could you possibly need?" Corey demanded. "Your life is back on track. I put in a good word with the Metros, and I know they offered you the assistant job for next season since Simpson is retiring. You got your job with the Metros, everything you wanted."

Marc opened his mouth to tell Corey that he had *nothing* he wanted, but before he could speak, his house vibrated as the front door slammed open again, and Clayton's voice boomed into the air.

"Where the hell is he? I'm not wasting any time with pleasantries before I kill the son of a bitch. I've been benched for two games, might lose my starting position, I spent six hours on a flight across the country, I'm tired, hungry, and angry." Clayton stormed into the room. He had grown in two months, bulked up for his football season.

From the looks on the faces of the seven other men in the room, they were as surprised to see Clayton here as Marc was.

"Clay." Will's voice sounded like he was about to lay into him.

"Oh, fuck off. I don't care if I wasn't asked to be here. Beth is as important to me as any of you, whether or not Marc realizes it." Clayton shot Marc a look full of disdain. Of all Beth's brothers, he and Clayton always gotten along the best.

"Clayton, the only reason I didn't ask you to come is that I didn't want you to have to choose between football and Beth," Marc explained.

"If you had *any* idea how important she is to me, you would know there's no choice. Fuck football," Clayton snapped. "So get on with this."

"Can we please sit?" Marc asked again, then moved to a chair and sat himself down.

"You've got one minute to tell us what we have to do so you don't release more sex photos." Danny glared. His easy-going, fun-loving nature was gone as he stood in front of Marc—and Marc was feeling hopeless.

"Damn it, Danny, I don't have any photos. I never did. I just needed to get you all here. I've been trying to get her to talk to me, and she won't." Marc ran his hand through his hair and let every bit of his desperation flood his voice. "I fucked up. I know that now, and I fucked up even more for taking so long to figure it out. But please—I love her, and I need your help. I..." He sighed and kicked the table with his foot. "I just *need her.*"

At first, no one moved. His heart sank and he let his head fall into his hands. Then Grant stepped up from the back of the group, grabbed a beer from the bucket, and sat down. Marc looked at Grant, and saw sympathy there instead of anger. Grant was the last person Marc had thought would believe him, but it seemed he did.

"You look like horse shit," Grant said. He nodded to his other brothers. No one else moved. "She told me I never gave Marc a chance, and she was right. I was too blind to see what was in front of me."

Still no one moved.

Grant waved a hand at Marc. "He's hurting. I saw heartbreak in the mirror every day for two years after my wife left; I know what it looks like. We came to listen, so sit. Listen. Give the man a chance. This shouldn't be about what we want." Grant's tone didn't leave any room for argument, and slowly they moved forward, grabbed their beers, and sat down—except Nick, who paced in front of the fireplace.

Marc regarded them all warily.

"This is your chance. Hurt her again, and I'll have you stampeded by horses," Grant said seriously.

Marc nodded in response before looking at everyone else.

"You know this was a shitty way to get our help," Luke said. He was sitting down, but he still looked mad.

Clayton's mouth twitched at the corners, and some of the anger faded from his eyes. "You know what Beth would say about that, don't you?"

Danny chuckled.

"You can't choose someone's method of reaching out," Will said, and he almost smiled too. "I believe that's what she told us the first time we were pissed off at Marc for messing with her." A few of the men nodded. "Is this going to become a habit?"

"I sincerely hope not. You'll help me?" Marc asked, unwilling to let the hope bubble up yet.

"What do you want us to do, Demoda?" Corey asked warily. "We're not forcing her to ignore you."

"I want your help to see her, so I can tell her how I feel. After I talk to her, if she wants me gone, I'll never bother her again," Marc promised. And if that happened—if he told her everything and she still sent him away—he didn't know what he would do.

"What exactly do you plan to say?" Grant asked, sitting back and crossing his ankle over his knee.

"First, I'm going to explain why I'm such a fuckup and apologize. Then I'm going to tell her I love her and hope she'll forgive me. I'm going to ask her to marry me," Marc said, looking around at the men to see how they would respond.

"Marc," Corey said hesitantly, "life on the road can be hard when you have a family back home. They need someone who can be around more than three months of the year."

Over the years, he had watched too many guys trying to balance the demands of baseball and a family not to know how hard it could be.

"Corey, I'm not sure what I'm going to do next season. Honestly, I have more job offers than I know what to do with, but I can't see anything past needing Beth back."

Corey's face softened into a smile.

"Finally got your priorities in order, huh, Demoda?" he said, almost sadly.

A couple of guys chuckled, but Grant's voice interrupted them.

"If you travel next year, are you going to fuck around on her?"

Everything in Marc went cold as the room went silent, and he turned his stare on Grant.

"Willing women are everywhere; it would be pretty easy to forget about her and bring someone back to your hotel room," Grant continued.

Marc reminded himself that Grant was only looking out for his sister, which Marc should appreciate, not resent. "I don't cheat—ever. I've seen over and over what it does to someone when their husband can't stay faithful. I know the temptations of being a rich, famous athlete—better than you do. I've had fifteen years of getting my rocks off with random women, and I'm done with that. There's only one I want. Two weeks of an empty bed on the road so I can have Beth next to me when I'm home is an easy trade-off."

The men all looked at Grant, who was watching Marc. Finally Grant said, "Okay." He smiled. "I trust you. If you're what she wants, then I'm on your team."

Marc smiled back before turning to look at the other guys, and Will answered his unasked question.

"The rest of us realized we could trust you after you danced in the rain. Grant was the only holdout. Just don't make us regret it *again*."

"Never," Marc promised honestly.

"Okay, I have a plan." Corey sighed. "But she's going to chew my head off if you fuck this up."

Marc relaxed for the first time in weeks. He looked from one man to the next. There wasn't another group of guys in the world, not even a baseball team, that Marc wanted to be a part of more than this group in his living room. He'd found where he belonged. Finally.

33

"HE'S LATE." BETH slammed her purse down on the table
as she sat. Corey had asked her to be his date tonight for the
end-of-season party the Metros' owner threw every year. The
team invited all current and past players, so Marc would be
there. Despite that, she had agreed to go—she owed Corey
for all the events he'd accompanied her to in the last month.
"I don't want to make a scene, and coming into a party late
always makes a scene."

"Maybe you should wear a different dress," Luke said, not
looking up from his phone.

"What's wrong with this one?" Beth demanded.

"Philips is an old man; you might give him a heart attack.
If the owner dies, Corey won't get a new contract."

Beth looked down; the emerald satin dress didn't look so
revealing at first glance. But the dress plunged to the small of

her back, and with every step her favorite black heels and her entire right leg were on full display.

"Think I should change?"

"I figure you're going for the 'eat your heart out' look," Luke said, shrugging. Then he looked up. "You haven't been this nervous about a media appearance in months."

"I'm not nervous." The press didn't scare her anymore. They would always tell whatever story they wanted, but standing up and speaking out helped get the truth across, and she believed she could do that now. She wanted to say Loretta helped, but it had started before she offered her support. Slowly, over the last six months, she'd developed confidence she never had. And she wouldn't pretend Marc hadn't helped with that. "When will it get easier to see him?"

"It'll get easier after tonight," Luke promised.

But Beth didn't believe that.

"Ms. Evans." The man popped his head in the door, and his eyes lingered down to her legs. "They opened the gate for your date, and he said he's running late. He's asked you to please meet him outside." She had almost gotten used to the Secret Service presence in her life over the last few months. Since Beth had become such a public figure, her father insisted on Secret Service protection until after the election.

"Yeah, yeah." She sighed. "He might as well honk the horn."

"Give him heck. A gentleman always picks a lady up at her door." Luke smiled.

"Corey's never been a gentleman, but I don't want to be too late."

"If you want to stay in the city, I'll be here all night," he reminded her again.

329

She couldn't imagine wanting to spend any more time than necessary at this party. She rolled her eyes and headed for the car. The wind picked up as soon as she walked off the porch, and she wrapped her arms around herself, eyeing the limo warily.

"Beth!" Luke called from the door, and she turned back to see him waving her purse.

Beth grabbed it while her dress whipped and swirled around her legs. She spun back and walked to the car door, which the suit opened for her. Another agent was already sitting in the front seat next to the driver. She didn't see Corey, but she climbed in, ready to give him hell.

"I swear to God, Cor, you better have—" But the words died on her lips when she saw the man sitting across from her. She sat there, shocked, as the door shut.

As much as she hated to admit it, the sight of Marc made her heart swell even as her chest ached and her stomach flipped. She couldn't speak past the lump in her throat.

"You take my breath away, do you know that? I think you are the most beautiful woman I've ever laid eyes on," he said. His eyes bored into her, lapping up every inch. Marc's foot brushed against hers, and the heat radiated up to her stomach. She crossed her legs, looked out the window, and the car lurched forward. There was no escape from him.

"If that dress was supposed to make me miserable," Marc said, continuing to fill the silence, "it worked." His eyes raked over her.

She'd known she was going to see him tonight—maybe across the room, or in passing, she'd thought. She hadn't planned on sitting in a limo with him. It hurt as much as it had the day she walked out of his apartment. She pulled deep from her reserves and looked at the man blankly.

"Where's Corey?" she asked, her heart about to explode from the pressure.

MARC SIGHED. THE surprise flashed across Beth's face, and then something else was there for a moment before the shutters crashed down and every discernable emotion disappeared. He hated it, but it wasn't a surprise. With the trust gone, he had expected her to shut down.

"I wanted a chance to talk to you, and you're hard to reach. Corey'll meet us there."

If things went the way he wanted them to, he hoped Beth would skip the party and head to his house. But he had a lot of work ahead of him to get there.

"What did you want to say?" Her voice was laced with pleasant coolness. Then her eyes suddenly widened in shock. "Wait." She threw her hand into the air before he could say anything. "We're riding in a limo."

If that was what broke through her composure, then he was grateful Corey had decided it was the best way to see her. The idea hadn't thrilled him at first, of course, but when Corey had asked if Beth was worth it, Marc knew she was.

MARC'S MOUTH TWITCHED. "Yes, we are."

It sounded stupid and obvious, but Marc didn't ride in cars. "No, I mean, *you're* riding in a limo."

"Yes," Marc agreed.

"But you don't."

"I needed to see you," he said simply, but she knew it wasn't simple. He wouldn't have gotten into the car if it wasn't necessary, and she felt the first glimmer of hope.

"You're not worried?" Beth asked, looking at the driver behind his head, and Marc reached up and closed the divider.

"About a lot of things, but at the moment the car isn't on my radar," Marc said.

Beth's heart stuttered.

He moved to sit next to her but made no other move to touch her. "Beth, I want to talk to you about my parents."

"Your *parents*?" The glimmer of hope vanished.

"I'm going to start there because I don't know how else to," he said. Then he reached for her hand, pulling it into his. His hand was warm and soft, and it felt so right wrapped around hers. "My dad was a minor league pitcher when he met my mom. My mother ended up pregnant. My father felt responsible so he gave up baseball, they married, and he took a job at an appliance repair shop his father's friend owned. My mom dropped out of school to raise me. They both gave up their lives and started this new life because they *had* to. Neither has ever said they wished I wasn't born, but they resent each other, and in a lot of ways, I think they resent me."

She couldn't imagine that being true. "Marc, I'm sure—" But he cut her off, looking so sad it broke her heart.

"They love me, they're proud of me, but honestly, if they could go back, they would change history. I grew up in a house built with lost dreams, and I thought that's what family meant, an unwanted responsibility. I didn't want that. I was going to be different. I would make sure I could make all my own decisions with no regrets."

He was explaining why he hadn't told her about Boston. Understandable or not, it still hurt. And she didn't want to hear about it, because it wasn't changing anything. The problems went deeper than him not telling her. She pulled her hands back, but Marc held on tight.

"Please don't give up on me, Beth." Marc's voice broke, and he cleared his throat. Their eyes met. He needed to do this, even if it changed nothing.

"Go on," she said hesitantly.

"Last year, I answered my phone, and a girl I'd slept with told me she was having my baby. I'd been stressing for weeks after we hooked up because the condom had broken. I had given her my number and told her to call. But even still getting that call I felt like I was drowning. I didn't love her—hell, I hardly knew her." Marc paused. She squeezed his hand and nodded encouragement. "I didn't want a baby. But she was having one, and I was responsible. I took her out one night after a game. I invited her and some friends to a party with some guys from the team. She wanted to leave, and I felt like I should at least make sure she got home. The guy who was driving was high as a kite."

"This was the night of the accident," Beth said, and Marc nodded.

"The baby that would have been my child died that night along with their mother, and all I felt was relief and anger that I had sacrificed my career."

"People deal with things differently. I'm sure a part of you had to connect how the woman was like your mother, and you were your father."

"Yes—and how, with a small twist of fate, my father could have been the one not caring that I'd never been born. Because if my mom had died while she was pregnant, he *wouldn't* have cared. I'd spent a lifetime hearing how he and I were the same; that we didn't have it in us to love. Reacting to the accident the same way he would have was all the proof I needed. I was just as shitty as he was.

"I should have talked to someone," Marc continued, looking at the floor of the limo. "But instead, my solution was to drink too much, stay out all night at clubs or parties, and sleep with any woman willing to fuck me."

"But…?" Beth said and reached up to rub the tears off his cheeks.

"But you made me want to be better because I wanted to be someone you could respect," Marc said. "I met your family, and the more time I spent with you, I saw that family doesn't have to mean resentment even if you sacrifice for them. Because you don't do it out of responsibility. You do it out of love. My family was an embarrassment, and I didn't want you to meet them because they aren't like yours."

"Marc, I—"

"No, listen: Every time I saw them, my father would tell me that being with you was stupid, and if I got a job in another city, I'd have to give it up for you. He kept saying I was thinking with the wrong head, that I could get good sex anywhere, that he and I weren't built to love."

Beth's mouth dropped open.

"Yeah, my dad's a real ass. And until recently, I thought I was like that too. I thought I was selfish and couldn't love anyone." Marc sighed, but he continued before she could say anything. "Then, Boston. It stunned me when they offered me the job. I wanted to talk to you about it."

"But you didn't," Beth said, the accusation heavy in her voice. She glanced down.

"No, be mad, Beth, but don't pretend you don't care." Beth looked up, and her expression hardened, but his didn't change. "I didn't tell you because if you had asked me not to take the job, I wouldn't have. And that terrified me. So I waited until I had signed the contracts so I couldn't back out—but I still couldn't get the words out. Because I knew it would change things, and I didn't want that. Honest to God, Beth, I wasn't ready to let you go." He looked up at her again desperately, then continued. "I should have realized then: The problem wasn't only that I didn't want to tell you, but that I didn't want the job."

"You didn't want the job?" That threw Beth for a loop. "Marc, you'd been waiting for *months* for something like that."

"I know. I should have wanted it. But my priorities had already shifted."

"Shifted?"

"I wasn't doing interviews that cut into my time with you. I canceled appointments to go to Steve's games. I canceled twice on NESN simply because I wanted to be home so you could run, and I wouldn't miss reading Mandy her bedtime story. I wasn't trying, but the less interested I became, the more they wanted me."

Beth swallowed. "Marc, I didn't know we were—"

He cut her off. "No, I was choosing you, at every step, before I realized it was a choice. But I didn't realize I was doing it. Then, after a week of traveling with the team, I resented the hell out of it. Everything I wanted was back in Jersey. I blamed the job for the fact that everything was a mess."

"It was only a matter of time, Marc. If you hadn't gone to Boston, something else would have happened."

"I think you're wrong. I'm not quick, but I would have figured it out eventually. Instead, I took the job, and I missed you more than I ever missed the game."

"More than baseball?" The hope she'd been fighting since she had gotten into the car spread slowly through her system, and she couldn't stop it.

"No contest," he said, and reached his hand up to rub along her cheek. "It took me too long to realize I had repeated my father's mistakes exactly. I gave up what I loved for something I thought I wanted. Because Beth, I'm completely in love with you."

"You were… you what?" Beth stumbled over the words as her heart skipped a beat.

"Beth, when I met you five months ago, my entire world changed, and everything became better. Two months ago, I didn't know how to tell you that you were different. But I know now.

"I could have told you that you give me a reason to smile; that you challenge me to stay on my toes. You reach into my gut and stir desires I've never felt before. I should have told you that you're different, because my days are better when you're in them and even the simplest things are fun because you're there.

"But mostly, I should have said I love you, and I can't imagine my life without you in it. I know what to say now, but the problem is I'm not sure if it's too late."

"It's not," Beth said as a tear slipped out and rolled down her cheek. Everything she'd ever wanted to hear had just come out of his mouth. "It's not too late." Marc wiped the tear away with the pad of his thumb.

"Are you sure?"

"I love you, Marc—but I want a life partner. I need you to talk to me from now on, or we won't ever work."

"That won't be a problem. I have a few job offers sitting at home, and I can't decide what I want. I was hoping we could talk them over, figure out what we want."

Just like that, Beth threw herself into his arms and kissed him.

Marc pulled back before she wanted him to. "I have something for you," he said, and settled her back on her seat.

"What?" Beth said, looking up into his eyes in confusion.

Marc handed her a little black box. Her heart sped up as she moved to open it. The lid creaked, revealing a ring sitting in black velvet. It wasn't the kind of ring she had expected, and her eyes flew up to Marc's.

"I'm hoping this might be a solution for that gold band on your thumb." She eyed him warily. "Don't get upset—just listen. When I told you I didn't like you wearing another man's ring, you told me it wasn't about him."

"Yes," she said, looking at the ring sitting in the box. It was a band too, but instead of the pure gold, this one had three colors of metal woven together, lacing through one another.

"I figured it out. You spin the ring when you're trying not to worry. It's reminding you that things work out," Marc said, wrapping his arm around her and pulling her close. "I still don't like you wearing another man's ring, even if it is Bob's wedding band. But this." He pointed to the ring in the box. "This we can both like because it's a piece of your past and your future."

"What do you mean?"

"First I want you to know, Luke helped me pull this off, and I ran it by all your brothers and Corey first, but this is all on me," Marc said quickly. "If you get upset, I accept full responsibility."

"Okay," Beth said apprehensively. She looked at the ring again. The three metals were twined together, but each was still a thin individual band, one in white gold, one in yellow gold, and one in rose gold. They snaked around each other, blending to form one thick band instead of three separate ones.

"I had this ring custom-made, and I wanted it to be truly meaningful. So the rose gold is from your promise ring from Corey, and the yellow gold was your wedding ring from Bob. Both of those men are part of you, and I don't want to take that away. Instead, I want to add to it."

Her heart stuttered. "And the white gold?" she asked.

Marc looked like he thought she might hurl the box at him, though she had no intention of doing that.

"That's for your connection with me," he said quietly. "I had the jeweler use my cross, because if you're wearing it, I'm exactly where I need to be."

She pulled the gold band off her thumb and put the other one in its place.

"Thank you for understanding," Beth said, and she leaned over to kiss him.

"You're not mad?" Marc asked, twisting the new ring on her thumb a few times.

"No. This feels right."

"Good." Marc smiled for a minute, then he looked slightly nervous again. He took a deep breath and let it out before continuing. "I know I said I missed you and the kids, and all I've wanted was things to go back to the way things were, but that's not exactly true. Hanging out at your house every night and then going home alone isn't working for me."

"I swear, if you tell me you want to bring other women home at night, I might kill you." Beth crossed her arms in front of her chest. He threw his head back and laughed, suddenly he didn't look nervous anymore.

"Beth, that is the last thing I was thinking." His tone became serious again, but his eyes were laughing. "I want it to be my hand that lifts your veil when you say I do. I want it to be my hand in yours while we raise two of the most amazing kids on the planet, and my hands that hold our future children." He pulled away and got down on one knee on the floor of the limo.

"Elizabeth Campbell Evans, will you marry me?"

Marc flicked the second ring box open with his thumb to reveal a giant emerald surrounded by two diamonds set in a thin white-gold band.

She stared. He wanted her and her kids and even some of their own. Marc wanted forever. She couldn't find her voice.

"Beth, sweetheart, it would be nice if you answer me before I have a heart attack here."

She couldn't imagine how he could have any doubt.

"Yes, yes, sorry, yes," she said, and her eyes filled with tears as she flung herself again at the man she loved.

He kissed her with a passion that she felt to her soul before finally pulling back. Marc took the ring out of the box and slipped it onto her finger.

"I looked at the diamonds, but then I saw this one, and it was you. It sparkles like your eyes," he said, and then lifted her hand where the ring now sat and kissed it. "How set are you on going to this party?"

"Why?" she asked.

"I thought maybe we could head to my place."

"Hoping to get lucky, hotshot?"

"I don't think I could get any luckier than I already am, Beth." Marc wrapped his arm around her, keeping her close as he pushed the intercom button to the front of the car. "Hey, Joe, change of plans. Take us home."

Epilogue

WHAT A DIFFERENCE A YEAR MAKES. Marc's fiancée—two words that, a year ago, he never would have thought he'd ever string together—was curled up in the crook of his arm while his future stepson sat on his other side. Instead of feeling stressed or resentful about the responsibility he was taking on, he was excited. He would never be forced to give up what he wanted for his wife or kids because now what he wanted most was his family. And if he ever got back into the MLB as a coach, Beth and the kids would be there alongside him.

He and Beth had looked over the announcing jobs, the coaching jobs, and the offer from ESPN, and together they'd figured out what would work best for them. She was okay with him taking whichever he wanted, even if it meant long hours and traveling without them. For now, he had taken a job as the head coach of a local high school baseball team. That way, he could be involved with the sport he loved, but he would be home with his family instead of waking up in a different city every few days and talking to them on the phone. And he'd be around to coach Steve's baseball team, too—something both he and Steve wanted.

Marc's soon-to-be stepdaughter was sitting on Corey Matthews' lap. Twelve months ago, who would have thought Corey would be sitting in Marc's house? Corey had signed a four-year contract with the Metros, and was sitting pretty in the rotation's top spot. Although he was disappointed that Marc had turned down the coaching job with the Metros, Marc promised to work with Corey when his pitching got all fucked up again. So the Metros signed a retainer with Marc to consult when the team's pitchers needed extra help.

The four other men crowded around the room watching Thursday night football were his soon-to-be brothers-in-law, Will, Luke, Joey, and Grant. In the last month, he and Grant had strengthened their relationship. Grant now respected and encouraged Marc's role in Beth's and the kids' lives. His relationship with the rest of the men had picked up where it had left off, and they'd welcomed Marc into the family. He enjoyed having brothers—even if they did all want a piece of Beth's time—but he had set serious ground rules.

Clayton, Danny, and Nick weren't coming home until tomorrow, and even then, Nick and Clayton had to take an early flight back out west Sunday morning. They would pull Beth in seven different directions while they were here, and she would love it. Next week, though, he would have her all to himself. And he intended to make the most of every minute.

Marc's father and mother had taken the news of his engagement better than Marc had thought they would. Marc's mother was relieved that he had finally come to his senses about what was important, and his father, after a shouting match, begrudgingly agreed that Marc wasn't making the same mistake he had. Marc doubted his father would ever truly understand his decision, though. His sister, most surprisingly, was almost as smitten with Beth as he was. Although the girls had a working relationship because of Helping Hands in the past, they were quickly becoming close friends and Glory spent lots of time around Marc's house. Beth even invited Glory over to all of their beer nights, at which point Marc thought he might throttle his beautiful little fiancée. He might like her brothers, but there was no way he was going to have them sniffing around his little sister. He knew the boys too well for that.

"You look happy," Beth said, looking at him.

"I'll be even happier in two days," Marc said, giving the woman he loved a squeeze.

If it had been up to Marc, he would have married Beth the day after asking her. But she wanted her entire family there, and with her father's campaign schedule, Marc settled for the weekend after the election. The month of waiting seemed like an eternity, which was ironic for a man who had never thought he wanted to be married.

Now, he wanted his family all together and all under his roof, where they belonged. They had moved most of Beth's and the kids' stuff to his house. The kids each had their own rooms, which he painted for them himself with their 'help.' He even turned his bar room into a playroom for them.

His once showpiece family room now was a place where kids spilled juice, knocked over lamps, and jumped on the sofas. Beth hung pictures of the kids, him, and the guys, and coloring pictures and tests hung on his fridge. Half of the time, his house looked like a natural disaster zone, messy and cluttered—and he loved it. It was lived in and full of joy. At the age of thirty-four, he finally had a real home.

"You know, dude, you have a crap TV; why don't you put a bigger one up there?" Luke asked, pointing his beer at the television bolted above the mantle on the stone fireplace.

Here they go again.

"Clayton and I have been telling him that for months," Will agreed.

"Danny told me it's 'cause he's cheap," Joey threw out, making the rest of them chuckle.

"Exactly. He even made me bring the beer tonight," Corey teased, although everyone knew damn well it was Corey's turn. Plus Marc had plenty in the fridge if Corey didn't.

"It's not money. A bigger TV would look dumb," Beth said from beside him. That was the real issue: A bigger television wouldn't fit.

"Not cheap, but definitely whipped." Grant smirked into his bottle.

"Get used to it. You're becoming an Evans in a few days," Will reminded him.

But even as the guys continued to give him shit, Marc couldn't dispute that he was entirely under Beth's spell.

Mandy climbed off Corey and moved over toward Marc, pulling herself into his lap without asking. This was a little girl who knew how to get what she wanted—and boy, would she drive both him and Beth crazy when she hit the teen years. He couldn't wait.

In a few days, he would finally have everything he never knew he'd always wanted. That thought made him smile again as Mandy rested her head against him, and he pulled both Steve and Beth against his chest.

Finally.

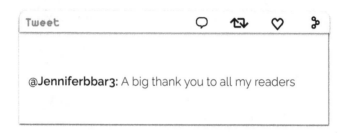

@**Jenniferbbar3:** A big thank you to all my readers

Dear Reader,

First, let me just say a massive THANK YOU! Thank you for reading More Than the Game. Thank you for supporting me. It's only because readers exist writers get to live out their dreams.

I've had these characters in my head and played around with them for years. Their story has morphed and changed as time went on and finally became something I (and my mother and sister-in-law) fell in love with. The process was long and frustrating at times, but I will miss Marc and Beth, so they will both come back in all the Evans books.

I hope you loved them as much as I did. I loved Marc's utter stupidity about what was going on. And Beth's ability to keep it together because I definitely don't have that. These two finding their happily ever after was so much fun.

347

If you want more of Beth and Marc, head to my website for Bonus Epilogue, Jennibara.com/bonus-epilogues and if you just love the Evanses, check out my website for Pre-order for More Than Fine coming in December.

Finally, yes that is my actual twitter handle and I'd love you to connect with me there or on Facebook or Instagram.

Remember: Live in your world, fall in love in mine.

Jenni
www.jennibara.com

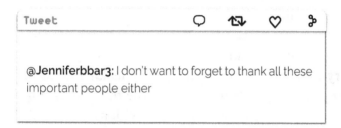

Tweet

@**Jenniferbbar3:** I don't want to forget to thank all these important people either

A big thank you to my wonderful husband, who has the patience to deal with me living in another world half the time. You can laugh when I zone out thinking about a scene in the middle of our conversation and love me even with all the voices in my head. All of me loves you! To my kids who have to hear, "Hold on a second, mom is writing."—it takes a lot for you all to deal with my writing, but you all are awesome about it.

Thank you to my parents, who support me in all I do all the time. I couldn't get through life without you guys. Being able to count on you both all the time for help or support, or encouragement, is the best gift. Thank you for being examples I can stride to be with my kids and being the best grandparents ever.

Katie, I don't even know where to start. Thank you for finding me and reaching out. This would never have happened if you didn't. Thank you for being my first rounds of edits on everything and then being willing to read it again and again!

Thank you for listening to me say I can't do this and convincing me every time I can! You're the best.

Amanda, Craig, Carly, and all my other beta readers, your feedback is priceless. Thank you!

Amy, thanks for reminding me the water was off—plus all the other reading and editing you have done for me. I'll thank Will next time.

Elayne, thank you for all your countless edits and your patience with me asking questions and helping me make sure everything was spot on. Thank you for making me laugh with your emails and side notes. You made the process fun. And thank you for going back and forth with me about 'the ring' and 'the shirt.' Plus, for dealing with all the baseball terms. BOSox is a thing I promise.

Kari, your cover is incredible, and your patience with me asking for changes was unending. I sing your praises to everyone.

Moe, thank you for your ability to make me look fabulous. And for all your opinions while listening to me talk books all the time even though you hate it. I love you, my sister!

Thank you, Erica, Natalie, and Patti, for telling me I don't stink at this and encouraging me to do something with it. And big thank you to the rest of my friends and family who have helped me with encouragement and feedback. Even the stuff I didn't go with, like 'girl on the left.' I love you all and am so thankful for your support.

About the Author

Jenni Bara lives in New Jersey, working as a paralegal in family law, writing real-life unhappily ever-afters every day. In turn, she spends her free time with anything that keeps her laughing, including life with four kids, or five, if you count her husband.
She is just starting her career as a romance author writing books with an outstanding balance of life, love, and laughter.

CPSIA information can be obtained
at www.ICGtesting.com
Printed in the USA
BVHW071048270821
615078BV00002BA/12